King Coal

King Coal

Upton Sinclair

ÆGYPAN PRESS

Upton Sinclair lived from 1878 until 1968.

King Coal
A publication of
ÆGYPAN PRESS

www.aegypan.com

To
MARY CRAIG KIMBROUGH

To whose persistence in the perilous task of tearing her husband's manuscript to pieces, the reader is indebted for the absence of most of the faults from this book.

Introduction

Upton Sinclair is one of the not too many writers who have consecrated their lives to the agitation for social justice, and who have also enrolled their art in the service of a set purpose. A great and non-temporizing enthusiast, he never flinched from making sacrifices. Now and then he attained great material successes as a writer, but invariably he invested and lost his earnings in enterprises by which he had hoped to ward off injustice and to further human happiness. Though disappointed time after time, he never lost faith nor courage to start again.

As a convinced socialist and eager advocate of unpopular doctrines, as an exposer of social conditions that would otherwise be screened away from the public eye, the most influential journals of his country were as a rule arraigned against him. Though always a poor man, though never willing to grant to publishers the concessions essential for many editions and general popularity, he was maliciously represented to be a carpet knight of radicalism and a socialist millionaire. He has several times been obliged to change his publisher, which goes to prove that he is no seeker of material gain.

Upton Sinclair is one of the writers of the present time most deserving of a sympathetic interest. He shows his patriotism as an American, not by joining in hymns to the very conditional kind of liberty peculiar to the United States, but by agitating for infusing it with the elixir of real liberty, the liberty of humanity. He does not limit himself to a dispassionate and entertaining description of things as they are. But in his appeals to the honor and good-fellowship of his compatriots, he opens their eyes to the appalling conditions under which wage-earning slaves are living by the hundreds of thousands. His object is to better these unnatural conditions, to obtain for the very poorest a glimpse of light and happiness, to make even them realize the sensation of cozy well-being and the comfort of knowing that justice is to be found also for them.

King Coal

This time Upton Sinclair has absorbed himself in the study of the miner's life in the lonesome pits of the Rocky Mountains, and his sensitive and enthusiastic mind has brought to the world an American parallel to *Germinal*, Emile Zola's technical masterpiece.

The conditions described in the two books are, however, essentially different. While Zola's working-men are all natives of France, one meets in Sinclair's book a motley variety of European emigrants, speaking a Babel of languages and therefore debarred from forming some sort of association to protect themselves against being exploited by the anonymous limited Company. Notwithstanding this natural bar against united action on the part of the wage-earning slaves, the Company feels far from at ease and jealously guards its interests against any attempt of organizing the men.

A young American of the upper class, with great sympathy for the downtrodden and an honest desire to get a first-hand knowledge of their conditions in order to help them, decides to take employment in a mine under a fictitious name and dressed like a working-man. His unusual way of trying to obtain work arouses suspicion. He is believed to be a professional strike-leader sent out to organize the miners against their exploiters, and he is not only refused work, but thrashed mercilessly. When finally he succeeds in getting inside, he discovers with growing indignation the shameless and inhuman way in which those who unearth the black coal are being exploited.

These are the fundamental ideas of the book, but they give but a faint notion of the author's poetic attitude. Most beautifully is this shown in Hal's relation to a young Irish girl, Red Mary. She is poor, and her daily life harsh and joyless, but nevertheless her wonderful grace is one of the outstanding features of the book. The first impression of Mary is that of a Celtic Madonna with a tender heart for little children. She develops into a Valkyrie of the working-class, always ready to fight for the worker's right.

The last chapters of the book give a description of the miners' revolt against the Company. They insist upon their right to choose a deputy to control the weighing-in of the coal, and upon having the mines sprinkled regularly to prevent explosion. They will also be free to buy their food and utensils wherever they like, even in shops not belonging to the Company.

In a postscript Sinclair explains the fundamental facts on which his work of art has been built up. Even without the postscript one could not help feeling convinced that the social conditions he describes are true to life. The main point is that Sinclair has not allowed himself to become inspired by hackneyed phrases that bondage and injustice and the other evils and crimes of Kingdoms have been banished from Republics, but that he is earnestly pointing to the honeycombed ground on which the greatest modern money-power has been built. The fundament of this power is not granite, but mines. It lives and breathes in the light, because it has thousands of unfortunates toiling in the darkness. It lives and has its being in proud liberty because thousands are slaving for it, whose thralldom is the price of this liberty.

This is the impression given to the reader of this exciting novel.

— Georg Brandes

BOOK ONE
THE DOMAIN OF KING COAL
SECTION I.

*T*he town of Pedro stood on the edge of the mountain country; a straggling assemblage of stores and saloons from which a number of branch railroads ran up into the canyons, feeding the coal-camps. Through the week it slept peacefully; but on Saturday nights, when the miners came trooping down, and the ranchmen came in on horseback and in automobiles, it wakened to a seething life.

At the railroad station, one day late in June, a young man alighted from a train. He was about twenty-one years of age, with sensitive features, and brown hair having a tendency to waviness. He wore a frayed and faded suit of clothes, purchased in a quarter of his home city where the Hebrew merchants stand on the sidewalks to offer their wares; also a soiled blue shirt without a tie, and a pair of heavy boots which had seen much service. Strapped on his back was a change of clothing and a blanket, and in his pockets a comb, a toothbrush, and a small pocket mirror.

Sitting in the smoking-car of the train, the young man had listened to the talk of the coal-camps, seeking to correct his accent. When he got off the train he proceeded down the track and washed his hands with cinders, and lightly powdered some over his face. After studying the effect of this in his mirror, he strolled down the main street of Pedro, and, selecting a little tobacco-shop, went in. In as surly a voice as he could muster, he inquired of the proprietress, "Can you tell me how to get to the Pine Creek mine?"

The woman looked at him with no suspicion in her glance. She gave the desired information, and he took a trolley and got off at the foot of the Pine Creek canyon, up which he had a thirteen-mile trudge. It was a sunshiny day, with the sky crystal clear, and the mountain air invigorating. The young man seemed to be happy, and as he strode on his way, he sang a song with many verses:

"Old King Coal was a merry old soul,
     And a merry old soul was he;
He made him a college all full of knowledge —
     Hurrah for you and me!

"Oh, Liza-Ann, come out with me,
     The moon is a-shinin' in the monkey-puzzle tree;
Oh, Liza-Ann, I have began
     To sing you the song of Harrigan!

"He keeps them a-roll, this merry old soul —
     The wheels of industree;
A-roll and a-roll, for his pipe and his bowl
     And his college facultee!

"Oh, Mary-Jane, come out in the lane,
     The moon is a-shinin' in the old pecan;
Oh, Mary-Jane, don't you hear me a-sayin'
     I'll sing you the song of Harrigan!

"So hurrah for King Coal, and his fat pay-roll,
     And his wheels of industree!
Hurrah for his pipe, and hurrah for his bowl —
     And hurrah for you and me!

"Oh, Liza-Ann, come out with me,
     The moon is a-shinin' —"

And so on and on — as long as the moon was a-shinin' on a college campus. It was a mixture of happy nonsense and that questioning with which modern youth has begun to trouble its elders. As a marching tune, the song was a trifle swift for the grades of a mountain canyon; Warner could stop and shout to the canyon-walls, and listen to their answer, and then march on again. He had youth in his heart, and love and curiosity; also he had some change in his trousers' pocket, and a ten dollar bill, for extreme emergencies, sewed up in his belt. If a photographer for Peter Harrigan's General Fuel Company could have got a snap-shot of him that morning, it might have served as a "portrait of a coal-miner" in any "prosperity" publication.

But the climb was a stiff one, and before the end the traveler became aware of the weight of his boots, and sang no more. Just as the sun was sinking up the canyon, he came upon his destination — a gate across the road, with a sign upon it:

PINE CREEK COAL CO.
PRIVATE PROPERTY
TRESPASSING FORBIDDEN

Hal approached the gate, which was of iron bars, and padlocked. After standing for a moment to get ready his surly voice, he kicked upon the gate and a man came out of a shack inside.

"What do you want?" said he.

"I want to get in. I'm looking for a job."

"Where do you come from?"

"From Pedro."

"Where you been working?"

"I never worked in a mine before."

"Where did you work?"

"In a grocery-store."

"What grocery-store?"

"Peterson & Co., in Western City."

The guard came closer to the gate and studied him through the bars.

"Hey, Bill!" he called, and another man came out from the cabin. "Here's a guy says he worked in a grocery, and he's lookin' for a job."

"Where's your papers?" demanded Bill.

Everyone had told Hal that labor was scarce in the mines, and that the companies were ravenous for men; he had supposed that a working-man would only have to knock, and it would be opened unto him. "They didn't give me no papers," he said, and added, hastily, "I got drunk and they fired me." He felt quite sure that getting drunk would not bar one from a coal camp.

But the two made no move to open the gate. The second man studied him deliberately from top to toe, and Hal was uneasily aware of possible sources of suspicion. "I'm all right," he declared. "Let me in, and I'll show you."

Still the two made no move. They looked at each other, and then Bill answered, "We don't need no hands."

"But," exclaimed Hal, "I saw a sign down the canyon —"

"That's an old sign," said Bill.

"But I walked all the way up here!"

"You'll find it easier walkin' back."

"But — it's night!"

"Scared of the dark, kid?" inquired Bill, facetiously.

"Oh, say!" replied Hal. "Give a fellow a chance! Ain't there some way I can pay for my keep — or at least for a bunk tonight?"

"There's nothin' for you," said Bill, and turned and went into the cabin.

The other man waited and watched, with a decidedly hostile look. Hal strove to plead with him, but thrice he repeated, "Down the canyon with you." So at last Hal gave up, and moved down the road a piece and sat down to reflect.

It really seemed an absurdly illogical proceeding, to post a notice, "Hands Wanted," in conspicuous places on the roadside, causing a man to climb thirteen miles up a mountain canyon, only to be turned off without explanation. Hal was convinced that there must be jobs inside the stockade, and that if only he could get at the bosses he could persuade them. He got up and walked down the road a quarter of a mile, to where the railroad-track crossed it, winding up the canyon. A train of "empties" was passing, bound into the camp, the cars rattling and bumping as the engine toiled up the grade. This suggested a solution of the difficulty.

It was already growing dark. Crouching slightly, Hal approached the cars, and when he was in the shadows, made a leap and swung onto one of them. It took but a second to clamber in, and he lay flat and waited, his heart thumping.

Before a minute had passed he heard a shout, and looking over, he saw the Cerberus of the gate running down a path to the track, his companion, Bill, just behind him. "Hey! come out of there!" they yelled; and Bill leaped, and caught the car in which Hal was riding.

The latter saw that the game was up, and sprang to the ground on the other side of the track and started out of the camp. Bill followed him, and as the train passed, the other man ran down the track to join him. Hal was walking rapidly, without a word; but the Cerberus of the gate had many words, most of them unprintable, and he seized Hal by the collar, and shoving him violently, planted a kick upon that portion of his anatomy which nature has constructed for the reception of kicks. Hal recovered his balance, and, as the man was still pursuing him, he turned and aimed a blow, striking him on the chest and making him reel.

Hal's big brother had seen to it that he knew how to use his fists; he now squared off, prepared to receive the second of his assailants. But in coal-camps matters are not settled in that primitive way, it appeared. The man halted, and the muzzle of a revolver came suddenly under Hal's nose. "Stick 'em up!" said the man.

This was a slang which Hal had never heard, but the meaning was inescapable; he "stuck 'em up." At the same moment his first assailant rushed at him, and dealt him a blow over the eye which sent him sprawling backward upon the stones.

SECTION 2.

*W*hen Hal came to himself again he was in darkness, and was conscious of agony from head to toe. He was lying on a stone floor, and he rolled over, but soon rolled back again, because there was no part of his back which was not sore. Later on, when he was able to study himself, he counted over a score of marks of the heavy boots of his assailants.

He lay for an hour or two, making up his mind that he was in a lock-up, because he could see the starlight through iron bars. He could hear somebody snoring, and he called half a dozen times, in a louder and louder voice, until at last, hearing a growl, he inquired, "Can you give me a drink of water?"

"I'll give you hell if you wake me up again," said the voice; after which Hal lay in silence until morning.

A couple of hours after daylight, a man entered his cell. "Get up," said he, and added a prod with his foot. Hal had thought he could not do it, but he got up.

"No funny business now," said his jailer, and grasping him by the sleeve of his coat, marched him out of the cell and down a little corridor into a sort of office, where sat a red-faced personage with a silver shield upon the lapel of his coat. Hal's two assailants of the night before stood nearby.

"Well, kid?" said the personage in the chair. "Had a little time to think it over?" "Yes," said Hal, briefly.

"What's the charge?" inquired the personage, of the two watchmen.

"Trespassing and resisting arrest."

"How much money you got, young fellow?" was, the next question. Hal hesitated.

"Speak up there!" said the man.

"Two dollars and sixty-seven cents," said Hal — "as well as I can remember."

"Go on!" said the other. "What you givin' us?" And then, to the two watchmen, "Search him."

"Take off your coat and pants," said Bill, promptly, "and your boots."

"Oh, I say!" protested Hal.

"Take 'em off!" said the man, and clenched his fists. Hal took 'em off, and they proceeded to go through the pockets, producing a purse with the amount stated, also a cheap watch, a strong pocketknife, the tooth-brush, comb and mirror, and two white handkerchiefs, which they looked at contemptuously and tossed to the spittle-drenched floor.

They unrolled the pack, and threw the clean clothing about. Then, opening the pocket-knife, they proceeded to pry about the soles and heels of the boots, and to cut open the lining of the clothing. So they found the ten dollars in the belt, which they tossed onto the table with the other belongings. Then the personage with the shield announced, "I fine you twelve dollars and sixty-seven cents, and your watch and knife." He added, with a grin, "You can keep your snot-rags."

"Now see here!" said Hal, angrily. "This is pretty raw!"

"You get your duds on, young fellow, and get out of here as quick as you can, or you'll go in your shirt-tail."

But Hal was angry enough to have been willing to go in his skin. "You tell me who you are, and your authority for this procedure?"

"I'm marshal of the camp," said the man.

"You mean you're an employee of the General Fuel Company? And you propose to rob me —"

"Put him out, Bill," said the marshal. And Hal saw Bill's fists clench.

"All right," he said, swallowing his indignation. "Wait till I get my clothes on." And he proceeded to dress as quickly as possible; he rolled up his blanket and spare clothing, and started for the door.

"Remember," said the marshal, "straight down the canyon with you, and if you show your face round here again, you'll get a bullet through you."

So Hal went out into the sunshine, with a guard on each side of him as an escort. He was on the same mountain road, but in the midst of the company-village. In the distance he saw the great building of the breaker, and heard the incessant roar of machinery and falling coal. He marched past a double lane of company houses and shanties, where slattern women in doorways and dirty children digging in the dust of the roadside paused and grinned at him — for he limped as he walked, and it was evident enough what had happened to him.

Hal had come with love and curiosity. The love was greatly diminished — evidently this was not the force which kept the wheels of industry a-roll. But the curiosity was greater than ever. What was there so carefully hidden inside this coal-camp stockade?

Hal turned and looked at Bill, who had showed signs of humor the day before. "See here," said he, "you fellows have got my money, and you've blacked my eye and kicked me blue, so you ought to be satisfied. Before I go, tell me about it, won't you?"

"Tell you what?" growled Bill.

"Why did I get this?"

"Because you're too gay, kid. Didn't you know you had no business trying to sneak in here?"

"Yes," said Hal; "but that's not what I mean. Why didn't you let me in at first?"

"If you wanted a job in a mine," demanded the man, "why didn't you go at it in the regular way?"

"I didn't know the regular way."

"That's just it. And we wasn't takin' chances with you. You didn't look straight."

"But what did you think I was? What are you afraid of?"

"Go on!" said the man. "You can't work me!"

Hal walked a few steps in silence, pondering how to break through. "I see you're suspicious of me," he said. "I'll tell you the truth, if you'll let me." Then, as the other did not forbid him, "I'm a college boy, and I wanted to see life and shift for myself a while. I thought it would be a lark to come here."

"Well," said Bill, "this ain't no foot-ball field. It's a coal-mine."

Hal saw that his story had been accepted. "Tell me straight," he said, "what did you think I was?"

"Well, I don't mind telling," growled Bill. "There's union agitators trying to organize these here camps, and we ain't taking no chances with 'em. This company gets its men through agencies, and if you'd went and satisfied them, you'd 'a been passed in the regular way. Or if you'd went to the office down in Pedro and got a pass, you'd 'a been all right. But when a guy turns up at the gate, and looks like a dude and talks like a college perfessor, he don't get by, see?"

"I see," said Hal. And then, "If you'll give me the price of a breakfast out of my money, I'll be obliged."

"Breakfast is over," said Bill. "You sit round till the pinyons gets ripe." He laughed; but then, mellowed by his own joke, he took a quarter from his pocket and passed it to Hal. He opened the padlock on the gate and saw him out with a grin; and so ended Hal's first turn on the wheels of industry.

SECTION 3.

*H*al Warner started to drag himself down the road, but was unable to make it. He got as far as a brooklet that came down the mountainside, from which he might drink without fear of typhoid; there he lay the whole day, fasting. Towards evening a thunderstorm came up, and he crawled under the shelter of a rock, which was no shelter at all. His single blanket was soon soaked through, and he passed a night almost as miserable as the previous one. He could not sleep, but he could think, and he thought about what had happened to him. "Bill" had said that a coal mine was not a foot-ball field, but it seemed to Hal that the net impress of the two was very much the same. He congratulated himself that his profession was not that of a union organizer.

At dawn he dragged himself up, and continued his journey, weak from cold and unaccustomed lack of food. In the course of the day he reached a power-station near the foot of the canyon. He did not have the price of a meal, and was afraid to beg; but in one of the group of buildings by the roadside was a store, and he entered and inquired concerning prunes, which were twenty-five cents a pound. The price was high, but so was the altitude, and as Hal found in the course of time, they explained the one by the other — not explaining, however, why the altitude of the price was always greater than the altitude of the store. Over the counter he saw a sign: "We buy scrip at ten percent discount." He had heard rumors of a state law forbidding payment of wages in "scrip"; but he asked no questions, and carried off his very light pound of prunes, and sat down by the roadside and munched them.

Just beyond the power-house, down on the railroad track, stood a little cabin with a garden behind it. He made his way there, and found a one-legged old watchman. He asked permission to spend the night on the floor of the cabin; and seeing the old fellow look at his black eye, he explained, "I tried to get a job at the mine, and they thought I was a union organizer."

"Well," said the man, "I don't want no union organizers round here."

"But I'm not one," pleaded Hal.

"How do I know what you are? Maybe you're a company spy."

"All I want is a dry place to sleep," said Hal. "Surely it won't be any harm for you to give me that."

"I'm not so sure," the other answered. "However, you can spread your blanket in the corner. But don't you talk no union business to me."

Hal had no desire to talk. He rolled himself in his blanket and slept like a man untroubled by either love or curiosity. In the morning the old fellow gave him a slice of corn bread and some young onions out of his garden, which had a more delicious taste than any breakfast that had ever been served him. When Hal thanked his host in parting, the latter remarked: "All right, young fellow, there's one thing you can do to pay me, and that is, say nothing about it. When a man has grey hair on his head and only one leg, he might as well be drowned in the creek as lose his job."

Hal promised, and went his way. His bruises pained him less, and he was able to walk. There were ranch-houses in sight — it was like coming back suddenly to America!

SECTION 4.

*H*al had now before him a week's adventures as a hobo: a genuine hobo, with no ten dollar bill inside his belt to take the reality out of his experiences. He took stock of his worldly goods and wondered if he still looked like a dude. He recalled that he had a smile which had fascinated the ladies; would it work in combination with a black eye? Having no other means of support, he tried it on susceptible looking housewives, and found it so successful that he was tempted to doubt the wisdom of honest labor. He sang the Harrigan song no more, but instead the words of a hobo-song he had once heard:

"Oh, what's the use of workin' when there's women in the land?"

The second day he made the acquaintance of two other gentlemen of the road, who sat by the railroad-track toasting some bacon over a fire. They welcomed him, and after they had heard his story, adopted him into the fraternity and instructed him in its ways of life. Pretty soon he made the acquaintance of one who had been a miner, and was able to give him the information he needed before climbing another canyon.

"Dutch Mike" was the name this person bore, for reasons he did not explain. He was a black-eyed and dangerous-looking rascal, and when the subject of mines and mining was broached, he opened up the flood-gates of an amazing reservoir of profanity. He was through with that game — Hal or any other God-damned fool might have his job for the asking. It was only because there were so many natural-born God-damned fools in the world that the game could be kept going. "Dutch Mike" went on to relate dreadful tales of mine-life, and to summon before him the ghosts of one pit-boss after another, consigning them to the fires of eternal perdition.

"I wanted to work while I was young," said he, "but now I'm cured, an' fer good." The world had come to seem to him a place especially constructed for the purpose of making him work, and every faculty he possessed was devoted to foiling this plot. Sitting by a campfire near the stream which ran down the valley, Hal had a merry time pointing out to "Dutch Mike" how he worked harder at dodging work than other men worked at working. The hobo did not seem to mind that, however — it was a matter of principle with him, and he was willing to make sacrifices for his convictions. Even when they had sent him to the work-house, he had refused to work; he had been shut in a dungeon, and had nearly died on a diet of bread and water, rather than work. If everybody would do the same, he said, they would soon "bust things."

Hal took a fancy to this spontaneous revolutionist, and traveled with him for a couple of days, in the course of which he pumped him as to details of the life of a miner. Most of the companies used regular employment agencies, as the guard had mentioned; but the trouble was, these agencies got something from your pay for a long time — the bosses were "in cahoots" with them. When Hal wondered if this were not against the law, "Cut it out, Bo!" said his companion. "When you've had a job for a while, you'll know that the law in a coal-camp is what your boss tells you." The hobo went on to register his conviction that when one man has the giving of jobs, and other men have to scramble for them, the law would never have much to say in the deal. Hal judged this a profound observation, and wished that it might be communicated to the professor of political economy at Harrigan.

On the second night of his acquaintance with "Dutch Mike," their "jungle" was raided by a constable with half a dozen deputies; for a determined effort was being made just then to drive vagrants from the neighborhood — or to get them to work in the mines. Hal's friend, who slept with one eye open, made a break in the darkness, and Hal followed him, getting under the guard of the raiders by a foot-ball trick. They left their food and blankets behind them, but "Dutch Mike" made light of this, and lifted a chicken from a roost to keep them cheerful through the night hours, and stole a change of underclothing off a clothes-line the next day. Hal ate the chicken, and wore the underclothing, thus beginning his career in crime.

Parting from "Dutch Mike," he went back to Pedro. The hobo had told him that saloon-keepers nearly always had friends in the coal-camps, and could help a fellow to a job. So Hal began enquiring, and the second one replied, Yes, he would give him a letter to a man at North Valley, and if he got the job, the friend would deduct a dollar a month from his pay. Hal agreed, and set out upon another tramp up another canyon, upon the strength of a sandwich "bummed" from a ranch-house at the entrance to the valley. At another stockaded gate of the General Fuel Company he presented his letter, addressed to a person named O'Callahan, who turned out also to be a saloon-keeper.

The guard did not even open the letter, but passed Hal in at sight of it, and he sought out his man and applied for work. The man said he would help him, but would have to deduct a dollar a month for himself, as well as a dollar for his friend in Pedro. Hal kicked at this, and they bartered back and forth; finally, when Hal turned away and threatened to appeal directly to the "super," the saloon-keeper compromised on a dollar and a half.

"You know mine-work?" he asked.

"Brought up at it," said Hal, made wise, now, in the ways of the world.

"Where did you work?"

Hal named several mines, concerning which he had learned something from the hoboes. He was going by the name of "Joe Smith," which he judged likely to be found on the payroll of any mine. He had more than a week's growth of beard to disguise him, and had picked up some profanity as well.

The saloon-keeper took him to interview Mr. Alec Stone, pit-boss in Number Two mine, who inquired promptly: "You know anything about mules?"

"I worked in a stable," said Hal, "I know about horses."

"Well, mules is different," said the man. "One of my stable-men got the colic the other day, and I don't know if he'll ever be any good again."

"Give me a chance," said Hal. "I'll manage them."

The boss looked him over. "You look like a bright chap," said he. "I'll pay you forty-five a month, and if you make good I'll make it fifty."

"All right, sir. When do I start in?"

"You can't start too quick to suit me. Where's your duds?"

"This is all I've got," said Hal, pointing to the bundle of stolen underwear in his hand.

"Well, chuck it there in the corner," said the man; then suddenly he stopped, and looked at Hal, frowning. "You belong to any union?"

"Lord, no!"

"Did you *ever* belong to any union?"

"No, sir. Never."

The man's gaze seemed to imply that Hal was lying, and that his secret soul was about to be read. "You have to swear to that, you know, before you can work here."

"All right," said Hal, "I'm willing."

"I'll see you about it tomorrow," said the other. "I ain't got the paper with me. By the way, what's your religion?"

"Seventh Day Adventist."

"Holy Christ! What's that?"

"It don't hurt," said Hal. "I ain't supposed to work on Saturdays, but I do."

"Well, don't you go preachin' it round here. We got our own preacher — you chip in fifty cents a month for him out of your wages. Come ahead now, and I'll take you down." And so it was that Hal got his start in life.

SECTION 5.

*T*he mule is notoriously a profane and godless creature; a blind alley of Nature, so to speak, a mistake of which she is ashamed, and which she does not permit to reproduce itself. The thirty mules under Hal's charge had been brought up in an environment calculated to foster the worst tendencies of their natures. He soon made the discovery that the "colic" of his predecessor had been caused by a mule's hind foot in the stomach; and he realized that he must not let his mind wander for an instant, if he were to avoid this dangerous disease.

These mules lived their lives in the darkness of the earth's interior; only when they fell sick were they taken up to see the sunlight and to roll about in green pastures. There was one of them called "Dago Charlie," who had learned to chew tobacco, and to rummage in the pockets of the miners and their "buddies." Not knowing how to spit out the juice, he would make himself ill, and then he would swear off from indulgence. But the drivers and the pit-boys knew his failing, and would tempt "Dago Charlie" until he fell from grace. Hal soon discovered this moral tragedy, and carried the pain of it in his soul as he went about his all-day drudgery.

He went down the shaft with the first cage, which was very early in the morning. He fed and watered his charges, and helped to harness them. Then, when the last four hoofs had clattered away, he cleaned out the stalls, and mended harness, and obeyed the orders of any person older than himself who happened to be about.

Next to the mules, his torment was the "trapper-boys," and other youngsters with whom he came into contact. He was a newcomer, and so they hazed him; moreover, he had an inferior job — there seemed to their minds to be something humiliating and comic about the task of tending mules. These urchins came from a score of nations of Southern Europe and Asia; there were flat-faced Tartars and swarthy Greeks and shrewd-eyed little Japanese. They spoke a compromise language, consisting mainly of English curse words and obscenities; the filthiness which their minds had spawned was incredible to one born and raised in the sunlight. They alleged obscenities of their mothers and their grandmothers; also of the Virgin Mary, the one mythological character they had heard of. Poor little creatures of the dark, their souls grimed and smutted even more quickly and irrevocably than their faces!

Hal had been advised by his boss to inquire for board at "Reminitsky's." He came up in the last car, at twilight, and was directed to a dimly lighted building of corrugated iron, where upon inquiry he was met by a stout Russian, who told him he could be taken care of for twenty-seven dollars a month, this including a cot in a room with eight other single men. After deducting a dollar and a half a month for his saloon-keepers, fifty cents for the company clergyman and a dollar for the company doctor, fifty cents a month for wash-house privileges and fifty cents for a sick and accident benefit fund, he had fourteen dollars a month with which to clothe himself, to found a family, to provide himself with beer and tobacco, and to patronize the libraries and colleges endowed by the philanthropic owners of coal mines.

Supper was nearly over at Reminitsky's when he arrived; the floor looked like the scene of a cannibal picnic, and what food was left was cold. It was always to be this way with him, he found, and he had to make the best of it. The dining room of this boarding-house, owned and managed by the G.F.C., brought to his mind the state prison, which he had once visited — with its rows of men sitting in silence, eating starch and grease out of tin-plates. The plates here were of crockery half an inch thick, but the starch and grease never failed; the formula of Reminitsky's cook seemed to be, When in doubt add grease, and boil it in. Even ravenous as Hal was after his long tramp and his labor below ground, he could hardly swallow this food. On Sundays, the only time he ate by daylight, the flies swarmed over everything, and he remembered having heard a physician say that an enlightened man should be more afraid of a fly than of a Bengal tiger. The boarding-house provided him with a cot and a supply of vermin, but with no blanket, which was a necessity in the mountain regions. So after supper he had to seek out his boss, and arrange to get credit at the company-store. They were willing to give a certain amount of credit, he found, as this would enable the camp-marshal to keep him from straying. There was no law to hold a man for debt — but Hal knew by this time how much a camp-marshal cared for law.

SECTION 6.

*F*or three days Hal toiled in the bowels of the mine, and ate and pursued vermin at Reminitsky's. Then came a blessed Sunday, and he had a couple of free hours to see the sunlight and to get a look at the North Valley camp. It was a village straggling along more than a mile of the mountain canyon. In the center were the great breaker-buildings, the shaft-house, and the power-house with its tall chimneys; nearby were the company-store and a couple of saloons. There were several board-ing-houses like Reminitsky's, and long rows of board cabins containing from two to four rooms each, some of them occupied by several families. A little way up a slope stood a school-house, and another small one-room building which served as a church; the clergyman belonging to the General Fuel Company denomination. He was given the use of the building, by way of start over the saloons, which had to pay a heavy rental to the company; it seemed a proof of the innate perversity of human nature that even in spite of this advantage, heaven was losing out in the struggle against hell in the coal-camp.

As one walked through this village, the first impression was of desolation. The mountains towered, barren and lonely, scarred with the wounds of geologic ages. In these canyons the sun set early in the afternoon, the snow came early in the fall; everywhere Nature's hand seemed against man, and man had succumbed to her power. Inside the camps one felt a still more cruel desolation — that of sordidness and animalism. There were a few pitiful attempts at vegetable-gardens, but the cinders and smoke killed everything, and the prevailing color was of grime. The landscape was strewn with ash-heaps, old wire and tomato-cans, and smudged and smutty children playing.

There was a part of the camp called "shanty-town," where, amid miniature mountains of slag, some of the lowest of the newly-arrived foreigners had been permitted to build themselves shacks out of old boards, tin, and sheets of tar-paper. These homes were beneath the dignity of chicken-houses, yet in some of them a dozen people were crowded, men and women sleeping on old rags and blankets on a cinder floor. Here the babies swarmed like maggots. They wore for the most part a single ragged smock, and their bare buttocks were shamelessly upturned to the heavens. It was so the children of the cave-men must have played, thought Hal; and waves of repulsion swept over him. He had come with love and curiosity, but both motives failed here. How could a man of sensitive nerves, aware of the refinements and graces of life, learn to love these people, who were an affront to his every sense — a stench to his nostrils, a jabbering to his ear, a procession of deformities to his eye? What had civilization done for them? What could it do? After all, what were they fit for, but the dirty work they were penned up to do? So spoke the haughty race-consciousness of the Anglo-Saxon, contemplating these Mediterranean hordes, the very shape of whose heads was objectionable.

But Hal stuck it out; and little by little new vision came to him. First of all, it was the fascination of the mines. They were old mines — veritable cities tunneled out beneath the mountains, the main passages running for miles. One day Hal stole off from his job, and took a trip with a "rope-rider," and got through his physical senses a realization of the vastness and strangeness and loneliness of this labyrinth of night. In Number Two mine the vein ran up at a slope of perhaps five degrees; in part of it the empty cars were hauled in long trains by an endless rope, but coming back loaded, they came of their own gravity. This involved much work for the "spraggers," or boys who did the braking; it sometimes meant run-away cars, and fresh perils added to the everyday perils of coal-mining.

The vein varied from four to five feet in thickness; a cruelty of nature which made it necessary that the men at the "working face" — the place where new coal was being cut — should learn to shorten their stature. After Hal had squatted for a while and watched them at their tasks, he understood why they walked with head and shoulders bent over and arms hanging down, so that, seeing them coming out of the shaft in the gloaming, one thought of a file of baboons. The method of getting out the coal was to "undercut" it with a pick, and then blow it loose with a charge of powder. This meant that the miner had to lie on his side while working, and accounted for other physical peculiarities.

Thus, as always, when one understood the lives of men, one came to pity instead of despising. Here was a separate race of creatures, subterranean, gnomes, pent up by society for purposes of its own. Outside in the sunshine-flooded canyon, long lines of cars rolled down with their freight of soft-coal; coal which would go to the ends of the earth, to places the miner never heard of, turning the wheels of industry whose products the miner would never see. It would make precious silks for fine ladies, it would cut precious jewels for their adornment; it would carry long trains of softly upholstered cars across deserts and over mountains; it would drive palatial steamships out of wintry tempests into gleaming tropic seas. And the fine ladies in their precious silks and jewels would eat and sleep and laugh and lie at ease — and would know no more of the stunted creatures of the dark than the stunted creatures knew of them. Hal reflected upon this, and subdued his Anglo-Saxon pride, finding forgiveness for what was repulsive in these people — their barbarous, jabbering speech, their vermin-ridden homes, their bare-bottomed babies.

SECTION 7.

*I*t chanced before many days that Hal got a holiday, relieving the monotony of his labors as stableman: an accidental holiday, not provided for in his bargain with the pit-boss. Something went wrong with the ventilating-course in Number Two, and he began to notice a headache, and heard the men grumbling that their lamps were burning low. Then, as matters began to get serious, orders came to get the mules to the surface.

Which meant an amusing adventure. The delight of Hal's pets at seeing the sunlight was irresistibly comic. They could not be kept from lying down and rolling on their backs in the cinder-strewn street; and when they were corralled in a distant part of the camp where actual grass grew, they abandoned themselves to rapture like a horde of school children at a picnic.

So Hal had a few free hours; and being still young and not cured of idle curiosities, he climbed the canyon wall to see the mountains. As he was sliding down again, toward evening, a vivid spot of color was painted into his picture of mine-life; he found himself in somebody's back yard, and being observed by somebody's daughter, who was taking in the family wash. It was a splendid figure of a lass, tall and vigorous, with the sort of hair that in polite circles is called auburn, and that flaming color in the cheeks which is Nature's recompense to people who live where it rains all the time. She was the first beautiful sight Hal had seen since he had come up the canyon, and it was only natural that he should be interested. It seemed to him that, so long as the girl stared, he had a right to stare back. It did not occur to him that he too was a pleasing sight — that the mountain air had given color to his cheeks and a shine to his gay brown eyes, while the mountain winds had blown his wavy brown hair.

"Hello," said she, at last, in a warm voice, unmistakably Irish.

"Hello yourself," said Hal, in the accepted dialect; then he added, with more elegance, "Pardon me for trespassing on your wash."

Her grey eyes opened wider. "Go on!" she said.

"I'd rather stay," said Hal. "It's a beautiful sunset."

"I'll move, so ye can see it better." She carried her armful of clothes over and dropped them into the basket.

"No," said Hal, "it's not so fine now. The colors have faded."

She turned and gazed at him again. "Go on wid ye! I been teased about my hair since before I could talk."

"'Tis envy," said Hal, dropping into her way of speech; and he came a few steps nearer, so that he could inspect the hair more closely. It lay above her brow in undulations which were agreeable to the decorative instinct, and a tight heavy braid of it fell over her shoulders and swung to her waist-line. He observed the shoulders, which were sturdy, obviously accustomed to hard labor; not conforming to accepted romantic standards of femininity, yet having an athletic grace of their own. They were covered with a faded blue calico dress, unfortunately not entirely clean; also, the young man noticed, there was a rent in one shoulder through which a patch of skin was visible. The girl's eyes, which had been following his, became defiant; she tossed a piece of her washing over the shoulder, where it stayed through the balance of the interview.

"Who are ye?" she demanded, suddenly.

"My name's Joe Smith. I'm a stableman in Number Two."

"And what were ye doin' up there, if a body might ask?" She lifted her grey eyes to the bare mountainside, down which he had come sliding in a shower of loose stones and dirt.

"I've been surveying my empire," said he.

"Your what?"

"My empire. The land belongs to the company, but the landscape belongs to him who cares for it."

She tossed her head a little. "Where did ye learn to talk like ye do?"

"In another life," said he — "before I became a stableman. Not in entire forgetfulness, but trailing clouds of glory did I come."

For a moment she wrestled with this. Then a smile broke upon her face. "Sure, 'tis like a poetry-book! Say some more!"

"*O, singe fort, so suess und fein!*" quoted Hal — and saw her look puzzled.

"Aren't you American?" she inquired; and he laughed. To speak a foreign language in North Valley was not a mark of culture!

"I've been listening to the crowd at Reminitsky's," he said, apologetically.

"Oh! You eat there?"

"I go there three times a day. I can't say I eat very much. Could you live on greasy beans?"

"Sure," laughed the girl, "the good old pertaties is good enough for me."

"I should have said you lived on rose leaves!" he observed.

"Go on wid ye! 'Tis the blarney-stone ye been kissin'!"

"'Tis no stone I'd be wastin' my kisses on."

"Ye're gettin' bold, Mister Smith. I'll not listen to ye." And she turned away, and began industriously taking her clothes from the line. But Hal did not want to be dismissed. He came a step closer.

"Coming down the mountainside," he said, "I found something wonderful. It's bare and grim up there, but I came on a sheltered corner where the sun shone, and there was a wild rose. Only one! I thought to myself, 'So roses grow, even in the loneliest parts of the world!'"

"Sure, 'tis a poetry-book again!" she cried. "Why didn't ye bring the rose?"

"There is a poetry-book that tells us to 'leave the wild-rose on its stalk.' It will go on blooming there; but if one were to pluck it, it would wither in a few hours."

He had meant nothing more by this than to keep the conversation going. But her answer turned the tide of their acquaintance.

"Ye can never be sure, lad. Perhaps tonight a storm may come and blow it to pieces. Perhaps if ye'd pulled it and been happy, 'twould 'a been what the rose was for."

Whatever of unconscious patronage there had been in the poet's attitude was lost now in the eternal mystery. Whether the girl knew it — or cared — she had won the woman's first victory. She had caught the man's mind and pinned it with curiosity. What did this wild rose of the mining camps mean?

The wild rose, apparently unconscious that she had said anything epoch-making, was busy with the wash; and meantime Hal Warner studied her features and pondered her words. From a lady of sophistication they would have meant only one thing, an invitation; but in this girl's clear grey eyes was nothing of wantonness, only pain. But what was this pain in the face and words of one so young, so eager and alive? Was it the melancholy of her race, the thing one got in old folk-songs? Or was it a new and special kind of melancholy, engendered in mining-camps in the far West of America?

The girl's countenance was as intriguing as her words. Her grey eyes were set under sharply defined dark brows, which did not match her hair. Her lips also were sharply defined, and straight, almost without curves, so that it seemed as if her mouth had been painted in carmine upon her face. These features gave her, when she stared at you, an aspect vivid and startling, bold, with a touch of defiance. But when she smiled, the red lips would curve into gentler lines, and the grey eyes would become wistful, and seemingly darker in color. Winsome indeed, but not simple, was this Irish lass!

SECTION 8.

*H*al asked the name of his new acquaintance, and she told him it was Mary Burke. "Ye've not been here long, I take it," she said, "or ye'd have heard of 'Red Mary.' 'Tis along of this hair."

"I've not been here long," he answered, "but I shall hope to stay now — along of this hair! May I come to see you some time, Miss Burke?"

She did not reply, but glanced at the house where she lived. It was an unpainted, three room cabin, more dilapidated than the average, with bare dirt and cinders about it, and what had once been a picket-fence, now falling apart and being used for stove-wood. The windows were cracked and broken, and upon the roof were signs of leaks that had been crudely patched.

"May I come?" he made haste to ask again — so that he would not seem to look too critically at her home.

"Perhaps ye may," said the girl, as she picked up the clothes basket. He stepped forward, offering to carry it, but she did not give it up. Holding it tight, and looking him defiantly in the face, she said, "Ye may come, but ye'll not find it a happy place to visit, Mr. Smith. Ye'll hear soon enough from the neighbors."

"I don't think I know any of your neighbors," said he.

There was sympathy in his voice; but her look was no less defiant. "Ye'll hear about it, Mr. Smith; but ye'll hear also that I hold me head up. And 'tis not so easy to do that in North Valley."

"You don't like the place?" he asked; and he was amazed by the effect of this question, which was merely polite. It was as if a storm cloud had swept over the girl's face. "I hate it! 'Tis a place of fear and devils!"

He hesitated a moment; then, "Will you tell me what you mean by that when I come?"

But "Red Mary" was winsome again. "When ye come, Mr. Smith, I'll not be entertaining ye with troubles. I'll put on me company manner, and we'll go out for a nice walk, if ye please."

All the way as he walked back to Reminitsky's to supper, Hal thought about this girl; not merely her pleasantness to the eye, so unexpected in this place of desolation, but her personality, which baffled him — the pain that seemed always just beneath the surface of her thoughts, the fierce pride which flashed out at the slightest suggestion of sympathy, the way she had of brightening when he spoke the language of metaphor, however trite. How had she come to know about poetry-books? He wanted to know more about this miracle of Nature — this wild rose blooming on a bare mountainside!

SECTION 9.

*T*here was one of Mary Burke's remarks upon which Hal soon got light — her statement that North Valley was a place of fear. He listened to the tales of these underworld men, until it came so that he shuddered with dread each time that he went down in the cage.

There was a wire-haired and almond eyed Korean, named Cho, a "rope-rider" in Hal's part of the mine. He was one of those who had charge of the long trains of cars, called "trips," which were hauled through the main passage-ways; the name "rope-rider" came from the fact that he sat on the heavy iron ring to which the rope was attached. He invited Hal to a seat with him, and Hal accepted, at peril of his job as well as of his limbs. Cho had picked up what he fondly thought was

English, and now and then one could understand a word. He pointed upon the ground, and shouted above the rattle of the cars: "Big dust!" Hal saw that the ground was covered with six inches of coal-dust, while on the old disused walls one could write his name in it. "Much blow-up!" said the rope-rider; and when the last empty cars had been shunted off into the working-rooms, and he was waiting to make up a return "trip," he labored with gestures to explain what he meant. "Load cars. Bang! Bust like hell!"

Hal knew that the mountain air in this region was famous for its dryness; he learned now that the quality which meant life to invalids from every part of the world meant death to those who toiled to keep the invalids warm. Driven through the mines by great fans, this air took out every particle of moisture, and left coal dust so thick and dry that there were fatal explosions from the mere friction of loading-shovels. So it happened that these mines were killing several times as many men as other mines throughout the country.

Was there no remedy for this, Hal asked, talking with one of his mule-drivers, Tim Rafferty, the evening after his ride with Cho. There was a remedy, said Tim — the law required sprinkling the mines with "adobe-dust"; and once in Tim's life, he remembered this law's being obeyed. There had come some "big fellows" inspecting things, and previous to their visit there had been an elaborate campaign of sprinkling. But that had been several years ago, and now the apparatus was stored away, nobody knew where, and one heard nothing about sprinkling.

It was the same with precautions against gas. The North Valley mines were especially "gassy," it appeared. In these old rambling passages one smelt a stink as of all the rotten eggs in all the barn-yards of the world; and this sulfuretted hydrogen was the least dangerous of the gases against which a miner had to contend. There was the dreaded "choke-damp," which was odorless, and heavier than air. Striking into soft, greasy coal, one would open a pocket of this gas, a deposit laid up for countless ages, awaiting its predestined victim. A man might sink to sleep as he lay at work, and if his "buddy," or helper, happened to be out of sight, and to delay a minute too long, it would be all over with the man. And there was the still more dreaded "firedamp," which might wreck a whole mine, and kill scores and even hundreds of men.

Against these dangers there was a "fire-boss," whose duty was to go through the mine, testing for gas, and making sure that the ventilating-course was in order, and the fans working properly. The "fire-boss" was supposed to make his rounds in the early morning, and the law specified that no one should go to work till he had certified that all was safe. But what if the "fire-boss" overslept himself, or happened to be drunk? It was too much to expect thousands of dollars to be lost for such a reason. So sometimes one saw men ordered to their work, and sent down grumbling and cursing. Before many hours some of them would be prostrated with headache, and begging to be taken out; and perhaps the superintendent would not let them out, because if a few came, the rest would get scared and want to come also.

Once, only last year, there had been an accident of that sort. A young mule-driver, a Croatian, told Hal about it while they sat munching the contents of their dinner-pails. The first cage-load of men had gone down into the mine, sullenly protesting; and soon afterwards someone had taken down a naked light, and there had been an explosion which had sounded like the blowing up of the inside of the world. Eight men had been killed, the force of the explosion being so great that some of the bodies had been wedged between the shaft wall and the cage, and it had been necessary to cut them to pieces to get them out. It was them Japs that were to blame, vowed Hal's informant. They hadn't ought to turn them loose in coal mines, for the devil himself couldn't keep a Jap from sneaking off to get a smoke.

So Hal understood how North Valley was a place of fear. What tales the old chambers of these mines could have told, if they had had voices! Hal watched the throngs pouring in to their labors, and reflected that according to the statisticians of the government eight or nine of every thousand of them were destined to die violent deaths before a year was out, and some thirty more would be badly injured. And they knew this, they knew it better than all the statisticians of the government; yet they went to their tasks! Reflecting upon this, Hal was full of wonder. What was the force that kept men at such a task? Was it a sense of duty? Did they understand that society had to have coal and that someone had to do the "dirty work" of providing it? Did they have a vision of a future, great and wonderful, which was to grow out of their ill-requited toil? Or were they simply fools or cowards, submitting blindly, because they had not the wit nor the will to do otherwise? Curiosity held him, he wanted to understand the inner souls of these silent and patient armies which through the ages have surrendered their lives to other men's control.

SECTION 10.

*H*al was coming to know these people; to see them no longer as a mass, to be despised or pitied in bulk, but as individuals, with individual temperaments and problems, exactly like people in the world of the sunlight. Mary Burke and Tim Rafferty, Cho the Korean and Madvik the Croatian — one by one these individualities etched themselves into the foreground of Hal's picture, making it a thing of life, moving him to sympathy and fellowship. Some of these people, to be sure, were stunted and dulled to a sordid ugliness of soul and body — but on the other hand, some of them were young, and had the light of hope in their hearts, and the spark of rebellion.

There was "Andy," a boy of Greek parentage; Androkulos was his right name — but it was too much to expect anyone to get that straight in a coal-camp. Hal noticed him at the store, and was struck by his beautiful features, and the mournful look in his big black eyes. They got to talking, and Andy made the discovery that Hal had not spent all his time in coal-camps, but had seen the great world. It was pitiful, the excitement that came into his voice; he was yearning for life, with its joys and adventures — and it was his destiny to sit ten hours a day by the side of a chute, with the rattle of coal in his ears and the dust of coal in his nostrils, picking out slate with his fingers. He was one of many scores of "breaker-boys."

"Why don't you go away?" asked Hal.

"Christ! How I get away? Got mother, two sisters."

"And your father?" So Hal made the discovery that Andy's father had been one of those men whose bodies had had to be cut to pieces to get them out of the shaft. Now the son was chained to the father's place, until his time too should come!

"Don't want to be miner!" cried the boy. "Don't want to get *kil-lid!*"

He began to ask, timidly, what Hal thought he could do if he were to run away from his family and try his luck in the world outside. Hal, striving to remember where he had seen olive-skinned Greeks with big black eyes in this beautiful land of the free, could hold out no better prospect than a shoe-shining parlor, or the wiping out of washbowls in a hotel-lavatory, handing over the tips to a fat padrone.

Andy had been to school, and had learned to read English, and the teacher had loaned him books and magazines with wonderful pictures in them; now he wanted more than pictures, he wanted the things which they portrayed. So Hal came face to face with one of the difficulties of mine-operators. They gathered a population of humble serfs, selected from twenty or thirty races of hereditary bondsmen; but owing to the absurd American custom of having public-schools, the children of this population learned to speak English, and even to read it. So they became too good for their lot in life; and then a wandering agitator would get in, and all of a sudden there would be hell. Therefore in every coal-camp had to be another kind of "fire-boss," whose duty it was to guard against another kind of explosions — not of carbon monoxide, but of the human soul.

The immediate duties of this office in North Valley devolved upon Jeff Cotton, the camp-marshal. He was not at all what one would have expected from a person of his trade — lean and rather distinguished-looking, a man who in evening clothes might have passed for a diplomat. But his mouth would become ugly when he was displeased, and he carried a gun with six notches upon it; also he wore a deputy-sheriff's badge, to give him immunity for other notches he might wish to add. When Jeff Cotton came near, any man who was explosive went off to be explosive by himself. So there was "order" in North Valley, and it was only on Saturday and Sunday nights, when the drunks had to be suppressed, or on Monday mornings when they had to be haled forth and kicked to their work, that one realized upon what basis this "order" rested.

Besides Jeff Cotton, and his assistant, "Bud" Adams, who wore badges, and were known, there were other assistants who wore no badges, and were not supposed to be known. Coming up in the cage one evening, Hal made some remark to the Croatian mule-driver, Madvik, about the high price of company-store merchandise, and was surprised to get a sharp kick on the ankle. Afterwards, as they were on their way to supper, Madvik gave him the reason. "Red-faced feller, Gus. Look out for him — company spotter."

"Is that so?" said Hal, with interest. "How do you know?"

"I know. Everybody know."

"He don't look like he had much sense," said Hal — who had got his idea of detectives from Sherlock Holmes.

"No take much sense. Go pit-boss, say, 'Joe feller talk too much. Say store rob him.' Any damn fool do that. Hey?"

"To be sure," admitted Hal. "And the company pays him for it?"

"Pit-boss pay him. Maybe give him drink, maybe two bits. Then pit-boss come to you: 'You shoot your mouth off too much, feller. Git the hell out of here!' See?"

Hal saw.

"So you go down canyon. Then maybe you go 'nother mine. Boss say, 'Where you work?' You say 'North Valley.' He say, 'What your name?' You say, 'Joe Smith.' He say, 'Wait.' He go in, look at paper; he come out, say, 'No job!' You say, 'Why not?' He say, 'Shoot off your mouth too much, feller. Git the hell out of here!' See?"

"You mean a black-list," said Hal.

"Sure, black-list. Maybe telephone, find out all about you. You do anything bad, like talk union" — Madvik had dropped his voice and whispered the word "union" — "they send your picture — don't get job nowhere in state. How you like that?"

SECTION II.

*B*efore long Hal had a chance to see this system of espionage at work, and he began to understand something of the force which kept these silent and patient armies at their tasks. On a Sunday morning he was strolling with his mule-driver friend Tim Rafferty, a kindly lad with a pair of dreamy blue eyes in his coal-smutted face. They came to Tim's home, and he invited Hal to come in and meet his family. The father was a bowed and toil-worn man, but with tremendous strength in his solid frame, the product of many generations of labor in coal-mines. He was known as "Old Rafferty," despite the fact that he was well under fifty. He had been a pit-boy at the age of nine, and he showed Hal a faded leather album with pictures of his ancestors in the "oul' country" — men with sad, deeply lined faces, sitting very stiff and solemn to have their presentments made permanent for posterity.

The mother of the family was a gaunt, grey-haired woman, with no teeth, but with a warm heart. Hal took to her, because her home was clean; he sat on the family doorstep, amid a crowd of little Rafferties with newly-washed Sunday faces, and fascinated them with tales of adventures cribbed from Clark Russell and Captain Mayne Reid. As a reward he was invited to stay for dinner, and had a clean knife and fork, and a clean plate of steaming hot potatoes, with two slices of salt pork on the side. It was so wonderful that he forthwith inquired if he might forsake his company boarding-house and come and board with them.

Mrs. Rafferty opened wide her eyes. "Sure," exclaimed she, "do you think you'd be let?"

"Why not?" asked Hal.

"Sure, 'twould be a bad example for the others."

"Do you mean I *have* to board at Reminitsky's?"

"There be six company boardin'-houses," said the woman.

"And what would they do if I came to you?"

"First you'd get a hint, and then you'd go down the canyon, and maybe us after ye."

"But there's lots of people have boarders in shanty-town," objected Hal.

"Oh! Them wops! Nobody counts them — they live any way they happen to fall. But you started at Reminitsky's, and 'twould not be healthy for them that took ye away."

"I see," laughed Hal. "There seem to be a lot of unhealthy things hereabouts."

"Sure there be! They sent down Nick Ammons because his wife bought milk down the canyon. They had a sick baby, and it's not much you get in this thin stuff at the store. They put chalk in it, I think; any way, you can see somethin' white in the bottom."

"So you have to trade at the store, too!"

"I thought ye said ye'd worked in coal-mines," put in Old Rafferty, who had been a silent listener.

"So I have," said Hal. "But it wasn't quite that bad."

"Sure," said Mrs. Rafferty, "I'd like to know where 'twas then — in this country. Me and me old man spent weary years a-huntin'."

Thus far the conversation had proceeded naturally; but suddenly it was as if a shadow passed over it — a shadow of fear. Hal saw Old Rafferty look at his wife, and frown and make signs to her. After all, what did they know about this handsome young stranger, who talked so glibly, and had been in so many parts of the world?

"'Tis not complainin' we'd be," said the old man.

And his wife made haste to add, "If they let peddlers and the like of them come in, 'twould be no end to it, I suppose. We find they treat us here as well as anywhere."

"'Tis no joke, the life of workin' men, wherever ye try it," added the other; and when young Tim started to express an opinion, they shut him up with such evident anxiety that Hal's heart ached for them, and he made haste to change the subject.

SECTION 12.

On the evening of the same Sunday Hal went to pay his promised call upon Mary Burke. She opened the front door of the cabin to let him in, and even by the dim rays of the little kerosene lamp, there came to him an impression of cheerfulness. "Hello," she said — just as she had said it when he had slid down the mountain into the family wash. He followed her into the room, and saw that the impression he had got of cheerfulness came from Mary herself. How bright and fresh she looked! The old blue calico, which had not been entirely clean, was newly laundered now, and on the shoulder where the rent had been was a neat patch of unfaded blue.

There being only three rooms in Mary's home, two of these necessarily bedrooms, she entertained her company in the kitchen. The room was bare, Hal saw — there was not even so much as a clock by way of ornament. The only charm the girl had been able to give to it, in preparation for company, was that of cleanness. The board floor had been newly sanded and scrubbed; the kitchen table also had been scrubbed, and the kettle on the stove, and the cracked teapot and bowls on the shelf. Mary's little brother and sister were in the room: Jennie, a dark-eyed, dark-haired little girl, frail, with a sad, rather frightened face; and Tommie, a round headed youngster, like a thousand other round headed and freckle-faced boys. Both of them were now sitting very straight in their chairs, staring at the visitor with a certain resentment, he thought. He suspected that they had been included in the general scrubbing. Inasmuch as it had been uncertain just when the visitor would come, they must have been required to do this every night, and he could imagine family disturbances, with arguments possibly not altogether complimentary to Mary's new "feller."

There seemed to be a certain uneasiness in the place.

Mary did not invite her company to a seat, but stood irresolute; and after Hal had ventured a couple of friendly remarks to the children, she said, abruptly, "Shall we be takin' that walk that we spoke of, Mr. Smith?"

"Delighted!" said Hal; and while she pinned on her hat before the broken mirror on the shelf, he smiled at the children and quoted two lines from his Harrigan song —

"Oh, Mary-Jane, come out in the lane,
The moon is a-shinin' in the old pecan!"

Tommie and Jennie were too shy to answer, but Mary exclaimed, "'Tis in a tin-can ye see it shinin' here!"

They went out. In the soft summer night it was pleasant to stroll under the moon — especially when they had come to the remoter parts of the village, where there were not so many weary people on doorsteps and children playing noisily. There were other young couples walking here, under the same moon; the hardest day's toil could not so sap their energies that they did not feel the spell of this soft summer night.

Hal, being tired, was content to stroll and enjoy the stillness; but Mary Burke sought information about the mysterious young man she was with. "Ye've not worked long in coal-mines, Mr. Smith?" she remarked.

Hal was a trifle disconcerted. "How did you find that out?"

"Ye don't look it — ye don't talk it. Ye're not like anybody or anything around here. I don't know how to say it, but ye make me think more of the poetry-books."

Flattered as Hal was by this naïve confession, he did not want to talk of the mystery of himself. He took refuge in a question about the "poetry-books." "I've read some," said the girl; "more than ye'd have thought, perhaps." This with a flash of her defiance.

He asked more questions, and learned that she, like the Greek boy, "Andy," had come under the influence of that disturbing American institution, the public-school; she had learned to read, and the pretty young teacher had helped her, lending her books and magazines. Thus she had been given a key to a treasure-house, a magic carpet on which to travel over the world. These similes Mary herself used — for the Arabian Nights had been one of the books that were loaned to her. On rainy days she would hide behind the sofa, reading at a spot where the light crept in — so that she might be safe from small brothers and sisters!

Joe Smith had read these same books, it appeared; and this seemed remarkable to Mary, for books cost money and were hard to get. She explained how she had searched the camp for new magic carpets, finding a "poetry-book" by Longfellow, and a book of American history, and a story called *David Copperfield,* and last and strangest of all, another story called *Pride and Prejudice.* A curious freak of fortune — the prim and sentimentally quivering Jane Austen in a coal-camp in a far Western wilderness! An adventure for Jane, as well as for Mary!

What had Mary made of it, Hal wondered. Had she reveled, shop-girl fashion, in scenes of pallid ease? He learned that what she had made of it was despair. This world outside, with its freedom and cleanness, its people living gracious and worth-while lives, was not for her; she was chained to a scrub-pail in a coal-camp. Things had got so much worse since the death of her mother, she said. Her voice had become dull and hard — Hal thought that he had never heard a young voice express such hopelessness.

"You've never been anywhere but here?" he asked.

"I been in two other camps," she said — "first the Gordon, and then East Run. But they're all alike."

"But you've been down to the towns?"

"Only for a day, once or twice a year. Once I was in Sheridan, and in a church I heard a lady sing."

She stopped for a moment, lost in this memory. Then suddenly her voice changed — and he could imagine in the darkness that she had tossed her head defiantly. "I'll not be entertainin' company with my troubles! Ye know how tiresome that is when ye hear it from somebody else — like my next-door neighbor, Mrs. Zamboni. D' ye know her?"

"No," said Hal.

"The poor old lady has troubles enough, God knows. Her man's not much good — he's troubled with the drink; and she's got eleven childer, and that's too many for one woman. Don't ye think so?"

She asked this with a naïveté which made Hal laugh. "Yes," he said, "I do."

"Well, I think people'd help her more if she'd not complain so! And half of it in the Slavish language, that a body can't understand!" So Mary began to tell funny things about Mrs. Zamboni and her other polyglot neighbors, imitating their murdering of the Irish dialect. Hal thought her humor was naïve and delightful, and he led her on to more cheerful gossip during the remainder of their walk.

SECTION 13.

*B*ut then, as they were on their way home, tragedy fell upon them. Hearing a step behind them, Mary turned and looked; then catching Hal by the arm, she drew him into the shadows at the side, whispering to him to be silent. The bent figure of a man went past them, lurching from side to side.

When he had turned and gone into the house, Mary said, "It's my father. He's ugly when he's like that." And Hal could hear her quick breathing in the darkness.

So that was Mary's trouble — the difficulty in her home life to which she had referred at their first meeting! Hal understood many things in a flash — why her home was bare of ornament, and why she did not invite her company to sit down. He stood silent, not knowing what to say. Before he could find the word, Mary burst out, "Oh, how I hate O'Callahan, that sells the stuff to my father! His home with plenty to eat in it, and his wife dressin' in silk and goin' down to mass every Sunday, and thinkin' herself too good for a common miner's daughter! Sometimes I think I'd like to kill them both."

"That wouldn't help much," Hal ventured.

"No, I know — there'd only be some other one in his place. Ye got to do more than that, to change things here. Ye got to get after them that make money out of O'Callahan."

So Mary's mind was groping for causes! Hal had thought her excitement was due to humiliation, or to fear of a scene of violence when she reached home; but she was thinking of the deeper aspects of this terrible drink problem. There was still enough unconscious snobbery in Hal Warner for him to be surprised at this phenomenon in a common miner's daughter; and so, as at their first meeting, his pity was turned to intellectual interest.

"They'll stop the drink business altogether some day," he said. He had not known that he was a Prohibitionist; he had become one suddenly!

"Well," she answered, "they'd best stop it soon, if they don't want to he too late. 'Tis a sight to make your heart sick to see the young lads comin' home staggerin', too drunk even to fight."

Hal had not had time to see much of this aspect of North Valley. "They sell to boys?" he asked.

"Sure, who's to care? A boy's money's as good as a man's."

"But I should think the company —"

"The company lets the saloon-buildin' — that's all the company cares."

"But they must care something about the efficiency of their hands!"

"Sure, there's plenty more where they come from. When ye can't work, they fire ye, and that's all there is to it."

"And is it so easy to get skilled men?"

"It don't take much skill to get out coal. The skill is in keepin' your bones whole — and if you can stand breakin' 'em, the company can stand it."

They had come to the little cabin. Mary stood for a moment in silence. "I'm talkin' bitter again!" she exclaimed suddenly. "And I promised ye me company manner! But things keep happening to set me off." And she turned abruptly and ran into the house. Hal stood for a moment wondering if she would return; then, deciding that she had meant that as good night, he went slowly up the street.

He fought against a mood of real depression, the first he had known since his coming to North Valley. He had managed so far to keep a certain degree of aloofness, that he might see this industrial world without prejudice. But tonight his pity for Mary had involved him more deeply. To be sure, he might be able to help her, to find her work in some less crushing environment; but his mind went on to the question – how many girls might there be in mining-camps, young and eager, hungering for life, but crushed by poverty, and by the burden of the drink problem?

A man walked past Hal, greeting him in the semi-darkness with a nod and a motion of the hand. It was the Reverend Spragg, the gentleman who was officially commissioned to combat the demon rum in North Valley.

Hal had been to the little white church the Sunday before, and heard the Reverend Spragg preach a doctrinal sermon, in which the blood of the lamb was liberally sprinkled, and the congregation heard where and how they were to receive compensation for the distresses they endured in this vale of tears.

What a mockery it seemed! Once, indubitably, people had believed such doctrines; they had been willing to go to the stake for them. But now nobody went to the stake for them – on the contrary, the company compelled every worker to contribute out of his scanty earnings towards the preaching of them. How could the most ignorant of zealots confront such an arrangement without suspicion of his own piety? Somewhere at the head of the great dividend-paying machine that was called the General Fuel Company must be some devilish intelligence that had worked it all out, that had given the orders to its ecclesiastical staff: "We want the present – we leave you the future! We want the bodies – we leave you the souls! Teach them what you will about heaven – so long as you let us plunder them on earth!"

In accordance with this devil's program, the Reverend Spragg might denounce the demon rum, but he said nothing about dividends based on the renting of rum-shops, nor about local politicians maintained by company contributions, plus the profits of wholesale liquor. He said nothing about the conclusions of modern hygiene, concerning over-work as a cause of the craving for alcohol; the phrase "industrial drinking," it seemed, was not known in General Fuel Company theology! In fact, when you listened to such a sermon, you would never have guessed that the hearers of it had physical bodies at all; certainly you would never have guessed that the preacher had a body, which was nourished by food produced by the overworked and under-nourished wage-slaves whom he taught!

SECTION 14.

*F*or the most part the victims of this system were cowed and spoke of their wrongs only in whispers; but there was one place in the camp, Hal found, where they could not keep silence, where their sense of outrage battled with their fear. This place was the solar plexus of the mine-organism, the center of its nervous energies; to change the simile, it was the judgment-seat, where the miner had sentence passed upon him — sentence either to plenty, or to starvation and despair.

This place was the "tipple," where the coal that came out of the mine was weighed and recorded. Every digger, as he came from the cage, made for this spot. There was a bulletin-board, and on it his number, and the record of the weights of the cars he had sent out that day. And every man, no matter how ignorant, had learned enough English to read those figures.

Hal had gradually come to realize that here was the place of drama. Most of the men would look, and then, without a sound or glance about, would slouch off with drooping shoulders. Others would mumble to themselves — or, what amounted to the same thing, would mumble to one another in barbarous dialects. But about one in five could speak English; and scarcely an evening passed that some man did not break loose, shaking his fist at the sky, or at the weigh-boss — behind the latter's back. He might gather a knot of fellow-grumblers about him; it was to be noted that the camp-marshal had the habit of being on hand at this hour.

It was on one of these occasions that Hal first noticed Mike Sikoria, a grizzle-haired old Slovak, who had spent twenty years in the mines of these regions. All the bitterness of all the wrongs of all these years welled up in Old Mike, as he shouted his score aloud: "Nineteen, twenty-two, twenty-four, twenty! Is that my weight, Mister? You want me to believe that's my weight?"

"That's your weight," said the weigh-boss, coldly.

"Well, by Judas, your scale is off, Mister! Look at them cars — them cars is big! You measure them cars, Mister — seven feet long, three and a half feet high, four feet wide. And you tell me them don't go but twenty?"

"You don't load them right," said the boss.

"Don't load them right?" echoed the old miner; he became suddenly plaintive, as if more hurt than angered by such an insinuation. "You know all the years I work, and you tell me I don't know a load? When I load a car, I load him like a miner, I don't load him like a Jap, that don't know about a mine! I put it up — I chunk it up like a stack of hay. I load him square — like that." With gestures the old fellow was illustrating what he meant. "See there! There's a ton on the top, and a ton and a half on the bottom — and you tell me I get only nineteen, twenty!"

"That's your weight," said the boss, implacably.

"But, Mister, your scale is wrong! I tell you I used to get my weight. I used to get forty-five, forty-six on them cars. Here's my buddy — ask him if it ain't so. What is it, Bo?"

"Um m m-mum," said Bo, who was a Negro — though one could hardly be sure of this for the coal-dust on him.

"I can't make a living no more!" exclaimed the old Slovak, his voice trembling and his wizened dark eyes full of pleading. "What you think I make? For fifteen days, fifty cents! I pay board, and so help me God, Mister — and I stand right here — I swear for God I make fifty cents. I dig the coal and I ain't got no weight, I ain't got nothing! Your scale is wrong!"

"Get out!" said the weigh-boss, turning away.

"But, Mister!" cried Old Mike, following behind him, and pouring his whole soul into his words. "What is this life, Mister? You work like a burro, and you don't get nothing for it! You burn your own powder — half a dollar a day powder — what you think of that? Crosscut — and you get nothing! Take the skip and a pillar, and you get nothing! Brush — and you get nothing! Here, by Judas, a poor man, going and working his body to the last point, and blood is run out! You starve me to death, I say! I have got to have something to eat, haven't I?"

And suddenly the boss whirled upon him. "Get the hell out of here!" he shouted. "If you don't like it, get your time and quit. Shut your face, or I'll shut it for you."

The old man quailed and fell silent. He stood for a moment more, biting his whiskered lips nervously; then his shoulders sank together, and he turned and slunk off, followed by his Negro helper.

SECTION 15.

Old Mike boarded at Reminitsky's, and after supper was over, Hal
sought him out. He was easy to know, and proved an interesting
acquaintance. With the help of his eloquence Hal wandered through a
score of camps in the district. The old fellow had a temper that he could
not manage, and so he was always on the move; but all places were alike,
he said — there was always some trick by which a miner was cheated of
his earnings. A miner was a little business man, a contractor who took
a certain job, with its expenses and its chance of profit or loss. A "place"
was assigned to him by the boss — and he undertook to get out the coal
from it, being paid at the rate of fifty-five cents a ton for each ton of
clean coal. In some "places" a man could earn good money, and in
others he would work for weeks, and not be able to keep up with his
store-account.

It all depended upon the amount of rock and slate that was found
with the coal. If the vein was low, the man had one or two feet of rock
to take off the ceiling, and this had to be loaded on separate cars and
taken away. This work was called "brushing," and for it the miner
received no pay. Or perhaps it was necessary to cut through a new
passage, and clean out the rock; or perhaps to "grade the bottom," and
lay the ties and rails over which the cars were brought in to be loaded;
or perhaps the vein ran into a "fault," a broken place where there was
rock instead of coal — and this rock must be hewed away before the
miner could get at the coal. All such work was called "dead-work," and
it was the cause of unceasing war. In the old days the company had paid
extra for it; now, since they had got the upper hand of the men, they
were refusing to pay. And so it was important to the miner to have a
"place" assigned him where there was not so much of this dead work.
And the "place" a man got depended upon the boss; so here, at the very
outset, was endless opportunity for favoritism and graft, for quarreling,
or "keeping in" with the boss. What chance did a man stand who was
poor and old and ugly, and could not speak English good? inquired old
Mike, with bitterness. The boss stole his cars and gave them to other
people; he took the weight off the cars, and gave them to fellows who

boarded with him, or treated him to drinks, or otherwise curried favor with him.

"I work five days in the Southeastern," said Mike, and when I work them five days, so help me God, brother, if I don't get up out of this chair, fifteen cents I was still in the hole yet. Fourteen inches of rock! And the Mr. Bishop — that is the superintendent — I says, 'Do you pay something for that rock?' 'Huh?' says he. 'Well,' I says, 'if you don't pay nothing for the rock, I don't go ahead with it. I ain't got no place to put that rock.' 'Get the hell out of here,' says he, and when I started to fight he pull gun on me. And then I go to Cedar Mountain, and the super give me work there, and he says, 'You go Number Four,' and he says, 'Rail is in Number Three, and the ties.' And he says, 'I pay you for it when you put it in.' So I take it away and I put it in, and I work till twelve o'clock. Carried the three pair of rails and the ties, and I pulled all the spikes — "

"Pulled the spikes?" asked Hal.

"Got no good spikes. Got to use old spikes, what you pull out of them old ties. So then I says, 'What is my half day, what you promise me?' Says he, 'You ain't dug no coal yet!' 'But, mister,' says I, 'you promise me pay to pull them spikes and put in them ties!' Says he, 'Company pay nothin' for dead work — you know that,' says he, and that is all the satisfaction I get."

"And you didn't get your half day's pay?"

"Sure I get nothin'. Boss do just as he please in coal mine."

SECTION 16.

*T*here was another way, Old Mike explained, in which the miner was at the mercy of others; this was the matter of stealing cars. Each miner had brass checks with his number on them, and when he sent up a loaded car, he hung one of these checks on a hook inside. In the course of the long journey to the tipple, someone would change the check, and the car was gone. In some mines, the number was put on the car with chalk; and how easy it was for someone to rub it out and change it! It appeared to Hal that it would have been a simple matter to put a number padlock on the car, instead of a check; but such an equipment would have cost the company one or two hundred dollars, he was told, and so the stealing went on year after year.

"You think it's the bosses steal these cars?" asked Hal.

"Sometimes bosses, sometimes bosses' friend — sometimes company himself steal them from miners." In North Valley it was the company, the old Slovak insisted. It was no use sending up more than six cars in one day, be declared; you could never get credit for more than six. Nor was it worth while loading more than a ton on a car; they did not really weigh the cars, the boss just ran them quickly over the scales, and had orders not to go above a certain average. Mike told of an Italian who had loaded a car for a test, so high that he could barely pass it under the roof of the entry, and went up on the tipple and saw it weighed himself, and it was sixty-five hundred pounds. They gave him thirty-five hundred, and when he started to fight, they arrested him. Mike had not seen him arrested, but when he had come out of the mine, the man was gone, and nobody ever saw him again. After that they put a door onto the weigh-room, so that no one could see the scales.

The more Hal listened to the men and reflected upon these things, the more he came to see that the miner was a contractor who had no opportunity to determine the size of the contract before he took it on, nor afterwards to determine how much work he had done. More than that, he was obliged to use supplies, over the price and measurements of which he had no control. He used powder, and would find himself docked at the end of the month for a certain quantity, and if the quantity was wrong, he would have no redress. He was charged a certain sum for "black-smithing" — the keeping of his tools in order; and he would find a dollar or two deducted from his account each month, even though he had not been near the blacksmith shop.

Let any business-man in the world consider the proposition, thought Hal, and say if he would take a contract upon such terms! Would a man undertake to build a dam, for example, with no chance to measure the ground in advance, nor any way of determining how many cubic yards of concrete he had to put in? Would a grocer sell to a customer who proposed to come into the store and do his own weighing — and meantime locking the grocer outside? Merely to put such questions was to show the preposterousness of the thing; yet in this district were fifteen thousand men working on precisely such terms.

Under the state law, the miner had a right to demand a check-weigh-man to protect his interest at the scales, paying this check-weighman's wages out of his own earnings. Whenever there was any public criticism about conditions in the coal-mines, this law would be triumphantly cited by the operators; and one had to have actual experience in order to realize what a bitter mockery this was to the miner.

In the dining room Hal sat next to a fair-haired Swedish giant named Johannson, who loaded timbers ten hours a day. This fellow was one who indulged in the luxury of speaking his mind, because he had youth and huge muscles, and no family to tie him down. He was what is called a "blanket-stiff," wandering from mine to harvest-field and from harvest-field to lumber-camp. Someone broached the subject of check-weighmen to him, and the whole table heard his scornful laugh. Let any man ask for a check-weighman!

"You mean they would fire him?" asked Hal.

"Maybe!" was the answer. "Maybe they make him fire himself."

"How do you mean?"

"They make his life one damn misery till he go."

So it was with check-weighman — as with scrip, and with company stores, and with all the provisions of the law to protect the miner against accidents. You might demand your legal rights, but if you did, it was a matter of the boss's temper. He might make your life one damn misery till you went of your own accord. Or you might get a string of curses and an order, "Down the canyon!" — and likely as not the toe of a boot in your trouser-seat, or the muzzle of a revolver under your nose.

SECTION 17.

Such conditions made the coal-district a place of despair. Yet there were men who managed to get along somehow, and to raise families and keep decent homes. If one had the luck to escape accident, if he did not marry too young, or did not have too many children; if he could manage to escape the temptations of liquor, to which overwork and monotony drove so many; if, above all, he could keep on the right side of his boss — why then he might have a home, and even a little money on deposit with the company.

Such a one was Jerry Minetti, who became one of Hal's best friends. He was a Milanese, and his name was Gerolamo, which had become Jerry in the "melting-pot." He was about twenty-five years of age, and what is unusual with the Italians, was of good stature. Their meeting took place — as did most of Hal's social experiences — on a Sunday. Jerry had just had a sleep and a wash, and had put on a pair of new blue overalls, so that he presented a cheering aspect in the sunlight. He walked with his head up and his shoulders square, and one could see that he had few cares in the world.

But what caught Hal's attention was not so much Jerry as what followed at Jerry's heels; a perfect reproduction of him, quarter-size, also with a newly-washed face and a pair of new blue overalls. He too had his head up, and his shoulders square, and he was an irresistible object, throwing out his heels and trying his best to keep step. Since the longest strides he could take left him behind, he would break into a run, and getting close under his father's heels, would begin keeping step once more.

Hal was going in the same direction, and it affected him like the music of a military band; he too wanted to throw his head up and square his shoulders and keep step. And then other people, seeing the grin on his face, would turn and watch, and grin also. But Jerry walked on gravely, unaware of this circus in the rear.

They went into a house; and Hal, having nothing to do but enjoy life, stood waiting for them to come out. They returned in the same procession, only now the man had a sack of something on his shoulder, while the little chap had a smaller load poised in imitation. So Hal grinned again, and when they were opposite him, he said, "Hello."

"Hello," said Jerry, and stopped. Then, seeing Hal's grin, he grinned back; and Hal looked at the little chap and grinned, and the little chap grinned back. Jerry, seeing what Hal was grinning at, grinned more than ever; so there stood all three in the middle of the road, grinning at one another for no apparent reason.

"Gee, but that's a great kid!" said Hal.

"Gee, you bet!" said Jerry; and he set down his sack. If someone desired to admire the kid, he was willing to stop any length of time.

"Yours?" asked Hal.

"You bet!" said Jerry, again.

"Hello, Buster!" said Hal.

"Hello yourself!" said the kid. One could see in a moment that he had been in the "melting-pot."

"What's your name?" asked Hal.

"Jerry," was the reply.

"And what's his name?" Hal nodded towards the man —

"Big Jerry."

"Got anymore like you at home?"

"One more," said Big Jerry. "Baby."

"He ain't like me," said Little Jerry. "He's little."

"And you're big?" said Hal.

"He can't walk!"

"Neither can you walk!" laughed Hal, and caught him up and slung him onto his shoulder. "Come on, we'll ride!"

So Big Jerry took up his sack again, and they started off; only this time it was Hal who fell behind and kept step, squaring his shoulders and flinging out his heels. Little Jerry caught onto the joke, and giggled and kicked his sturdy legs with delight. Big Jerry would look round, not knowing what the joke was, but enjoying it just the same.

They came to the three-room cabin which was Both Jerrys' home; and Mrs. Jerry came to the door, a black-eyed Sicilian girl, who did not look old enough to have even one baby. They had another bout of grinning, at the end of which Big Jerry said, "You come in?"

"Sure," said Hal.

"You stay supper," added the other. "Got spaghetti."

"Gee!" said Hal. "All right, let me stay, and pay for it."

"Hell, no!" said Jerry. "You no pay!"

"No! No pay!" cried Mrs. Jerry, shaking her pretty head energetically.

"All right," said Hal, quickly, seeing that he might hurt their feelings. "I'll stay if you're sure you have enough."

"Sure, plenty!" said Jerry. "Hey, Rosa?"

"Sure, plenty!" said Mrs. Jerry.

"Then I'll stay," said Hal. "You like spaghetti, Kid?"

"Jesus!" cried Little Jerry.

Hal looked about him at this Dago home. It was a tome in keeping with its pretty occupant. There were lace curtains in the windows, even shinier and whiter than at the Rafferties; there was an incredibly bright-colored rug on the floor, and bright colored pictures of Mount Vesuvius and of Garibaldi on the walls. Also there was a cabinet with many interesting treasures to look at — a bit of coral and a conch-shell, a shark's tooth and an Indian arrow-head, and a stuffed linnet with a glass cover over him. A while back Hal would not have thought of such things as especially stimulating to the imagination; but that was before he had begun to spend five-sixths of his waking hours in the bowels of the earth.

He ate supper, a real Dago supper; the spaghetti proved to be real Dago spaghetti, smoking hot, with tomato sauce and a rich flavor of meat-juice. And all through the meal Hal smacked his lips and grinned at Little Jerry, who smacked his lips and grinned back. It was all so different from feeding at Reminitsky's pig-trough, that Hal thought he had never had such a good supper in his life before. As for Mr. and Mrs. Jerry, they were so proud of their wonderful kid, who could swear in English as good as a real American, that they were in the seventh heaven.

When the meal was over, Hal leaned back and exclaimed, just as he had at the Rafferties', "Lord, how I wish I could board here!"

He saw his host look at his wife. "All right," said he. "You come here. I board you. Hey, Rosa?"

"Sure," said Rosa.

Hal looked at them, astonished. "You're sure they'll let you?" he asked.

"Let me? Who stop me?"

"I don't know. Maybe Reminitsky. You might get into trouble."

Jerry grinned. "I no fraid," said he. "Got friends here. Carmino my cousin. You know Carmino?"

"No," said Hal.

"Pit-boss in Number One. He stand by me. Old Reminitsky go hang! You come here, I give you bunk in that room, give you good grub. What you pay Reminitsky?"

"Twenty-seven a month."

"All right, you pay me twenty-seven, you get everything good. Can't get much stuff here, but Rosa good cook, she fix it."

Hal's new friend — besides being a favorite of the boss — was a "shot-firer"; it was his duty to go about the mine at night, setting off the charges of powder which the miners had got ready by day. This was dangerous work, calling for a skilled man, and it paid pretty well; so Jerry got on in the world and was not afraid to speak his mind, within certain limits. He ignored the possibility that Hal might be a company spy, and astonished him by rebellious talk of the different kinds of graft in North Valley, and at other places he had worked since coming to America as a boy. Minetti was a Socialist, Hal learned; he took an Italian Socialist paper, and the clerk at the post office knew what sort of paper it was, and would "josh" him about it. What was more remarkable, Mrs. Minetti was a Socialist also; that meant a great deal to a man, as Jerry explained, because she was not under the domination of a priest.

SECTION 18.

*H*al made the move at once, sacrificing part of a month's board, which Reminitsky would charge against his account with the company. But he was willing to pay for the privilege of a clean home and clean food. To his amusement he found that in the eyes of his Irish friends he was losing caste by going to live with the Minettis. There were most rigid social lines in North Valley, it appeared. The Americans and English and Scotch looked down upon the Welsh and Irish; the Welsh and Irish looked down upon the Dagoes and Frenchies; the Dagoes and Frenchies looked down upon Polacks and Hunkies, these in turn upon Greeks, Bulgarians and "Montynegroes," and so on through a score of races of Eastern Europe, Lithuanians, Slovaks, and Croatians, Armenians, Romanians, Rumelians, Ruthenians — ending up with Greasers, niggers, and last and lowest, Japs.

It was when Hal went to pay another call upon the Raffertys that he made this discovery. Mary Burke happened to be there, and when she caught sight of him, her grey eyes beamed with mischief. "How do ye do, Mr. Minetti?" she cried.

"How do ye do, Miss Rosetti?" he countered.

"You lika da spagett?"

"You no lika da spagett?"

"I told ye once," laughed the girl — "the good old pertaties is good enough for me!"

"And you remember," said he, "what I answered?"

Yes, she remembered! Her cheeks took on the color of the rose-leaves he had specified as her probable diet.

And then the Rafferty children, who had got to know Hal well, joined in the teasing. "Mister Minetti! Lika da spagetti!" Hal, when he had grasped the situation, was tempted to retaliate by reminding them that he had offered to board with the Irish, and been turned down; but he feared that the elder Rafferty might not appreciate this joke, so instead he pretended to have supposed all along that the Raffertys were Italians. He addressed the elder Rafferty gravely, pronouncing the name with the accent on the second syllable — "Signer Rafferti"; and this so amused the old man that he chuckled over it at intervals for an hour. His heart warmed to this lively young fellow; he forgot some of his suspicions, and after the youngsters had been sent away to bed, he talked more or less frankly about his life as a coal-miner.

"Old Rafferty" had once been on the way to high station. He had been made tipple-boss at the San José mine, but had given up his job because he had thought that his religion did not permit him to do what he was ordered to do. It had been a crude proposition of keeping the men's score at a certain level, no matter how much coal they might send up; and when Rafferty had quit rather than obey such orders, he had had to leave the mine altogether; for of course everybody knew why he had quit, and his mere presence had the effect of keeping discontent alive.

"You think there are no honest companies at all?" Hal asked.

The old man answered, "There be some, but 'tis not so easy as ye might think to be honest. They have to meet each other's prices, and when one short-weights, the others have to. 'Tis a way of cuttin' wages without the men findin' it out; and there be people that do not like to fall behind with their profits." Hal found himself thinking of old Peter Harrigan, who controlled the General Fuel Company, and had made the remark: "I am a great clamorer for dividends!"

"The trouble with the miner," continued Old Rafferty, "is that he has no one to speak for him. He stands alone —"

During this discourse, Hal had glanced at "Red Mary," and noticed that she sat with her arms on the table, her sturdy shoulders bowed in a fashion which told of a hard day's toil. But here she broke into the conversation; her voice came suddenly, alive with scorn: "The trouble with the miner is that he's a *slave!*"

"Ah, now —" put in the old man, protestingly.

"He has the whole world against him, and he hasn't got the sense to get together — to form a union, and stand by it!"

There fell a sudden silence in the Rafferty home. Even Hal was startled — for this was the first time during his stay in the camp that he had heard the dread word "union" spoken above a whisper.

"I know!" said Mary, her grey eyes full of defiance. "Ye'll not have the word spoken! But some will speak it in spite of ye!"

"'Tis all very well," said the old man. "When ye're young, and a woman too —"

"A woman! Is it only the women that can have courage?"

"Sure," said he, with a wry smile, "'tis the women that have the tongues, and that can't be stopped from usin' them. Even the boss must know that."

"Maybe so," replied Mary. "And maybe 'tis the women have the most to suffer in a coal-camp; and maybe the boss knows that." The girl's cheeks were red.

"Mebbe so," said Rafferty; and after that there was silence, while he sat puffing his pipe. It was evident that he did not care to go on, that he did not want union speeches made in his home. After a while Mrs. Rafferty made a timid effort to change the course of the talk, by asking after Mary's sister, who had not been well; and after they had discussed remedies for the ailments of children, Mary rose, saying, "I'll be goin' along."

Hal rose also. "I'll walk with you, if I may," he said.

"Sure," said she; and it seemed that the cheerfulness of the Rafferty family was restored by the sight of a bit of gallantry.

SECTION 19.

*T*hey strolled down the street, and Hal remarked, "That's the first word I've heard here about a union."

Mary looked about her nervously. "Hush!" she whispered.

"But I thought you said you were talking about it!"

She answered, "'Tis one thing, talkin' in a friend's house, and another outside. What's the good of throwin' away your job?"

He lowered his voice. "Would you seriously like to have a union here?"

"Seriously?" said she. "Didn't ye see Mr. Rafferty — what a coward he is? That's the way they are! No, 'twas just a burst of my temper. I'm a bit crazy tonight — something happened to set me off."

He thought she was going on, but apparently she changed her mind. Finally he asked, "What happened?"

"Oh, 'twould do no good to talk," she answered; and they walked a bit farther in silence.

"Tell me about it, won't you?" he said; and the kindness in his tone made its impression.

"'Tis not much ye know of a coal-camp, Joe Smith," she said. "Can't ye imagine what it's like — bein' a woman in a place like this? And a woman they think good-lookin'!"

"Oh, so it's that!" said he, and was silent again. "Someone's been troubling you?" he ventured after a while.

"Sure! Someone's always troublin' us women! Always! Never a day but we hear it. Winks and nudges — everywhere ye turn."

"Who is it?"

"The bosses, the clerks — anybody that has a chance to wear a stiff collar, and thinks he can offer money to a girl. It begins before she's out of short skirts, and there's never any peace afterwards."

"And you can't make them understand?"

"I've made them understand me a bit; now they go after my old man."

"What?"

"Sure! D'ye suppose they'd not try that? Him that's so crazy for liquor, and can never get enough of it!"

"And your father? —" But Hal stopped. She would not want that question asked!

She had seen his hesitation, however. "He was a decent man once," she declared. "'Tis the life here, that turns a man into a coward. 'Tis everything ye need, everywhere ye turn — ye have to ask favors from some boss. The room ye work in, the dead work they pile on ye; or maybe 'tis more credit ye need at the store, or maybe the doctor to come when ye're sick. Just now 'tis our roof that leaks — so bad we can't find a dry place to sleep when it rains."

"I see," said Hal. "Who owns the house?"

"Sure, there's none but company houses here."

"Who's supposed to fix it?"

"Mr. Kosegi, the house-agent. But we gave him up long ago — if he does anything, he raises the rent. Today my father went to Mr. Cotton. He's supposed to look out for the health of the place, and it seems hardly healthy to keep people wet in their beds."

"And what did Cotton say?" asked Hal, when she stopped again.

"Well, don't ye know Jeff Cotton — can't ye guess what he'd say? 'That's a fine girl ye got, Burke! Why don't ye make her listen to reason?' And then he laughed, and told me old father he'd better learn to take a hint. 'Twas bad for an old man to sleep in the rain — he might get carried off by pneumonia."

Hal could no longer keep back the question, "What did your father do?"

"I'd not have ye think hard of my old father," she said, quickly. "He used to be a fightin' man, in the days before O'Callahan had his way with him. But now he knows what a camp-marshal can do to a miner!"

SECTION 20.

Mary Burke had said that the company could stand breaking the bones of its men; and not long after Number Two started up again, Hal had a chance to note the truth of this assertion.

A miner's life depended upon the proper timbering of the room where he worked. The company undertook to furnish the timbers, but when the miner needed them, he would find none at hand, and would have to make the mile-long trip to the surface. He would select timbers of the proper length, and would mark them — the understanding being that they were to be delivered to his room by some of the laborers. But then someone else would carry them off — here was more graft and favoritism, and the miner might lose a day or two of work, while meantime his account was piling up at the store, and his children might have no shoes to go to school. Sometimes he would give up waiting for timbers, and go on taking out coal; so there would be a fall of rock — and the coroner's jury would bring in a verdict of "negligence," and the coal-operators would talk solemnly about the impossibility of teaching caution to miners. Not so very long ago Hal had read an interview which the president of the General Fuel Company had given to a newspaper, in which he set forth the idea that the more experience a miner had the more dangerous it was to employ him, because he thought he knew it all, and would not heed the wise regulations which the company laid down for his safety!

In Number Two mine there were some places being operated by the "room and pillar" method; the coal being taken out as from a series of rooms, the portion corresponding to the walls of the rooms being left to uphold the roof. These walls are the "pillars"; and when the end of the vein is reached, the miner begins to work backwards, "pulling the pillars," and letting the roof collapse behind him. This is a dangerous task; as he works, the man has to listen to the drumming sounds of the rock above his head, and has to judge just when to make his escape. Sometimes he is too anxious to save a tool; or sometimes the collapse comes without warning. In that case the victim is seldom dug out; for it must be admitted that a man buried under a mountain is as well buried as a company could be expected to arrange it.

In Number Two mine a man was caught in this way. He stumbled as he ran, and the lower half of his body was pinned fast; the doctor had to come and pump opiates into him, while the rescue crew was digging him loose. The first Hal knew of the accident was when he saw the body stretched out on a plank, with a couple of old sacks to cover it. He noticed that nobody stopped for a second glance. Going up from work, he asked his friend Madvik, the mule driver, who answered, "Lit'uanian feller — got mash." And that was all. Nobody knew him, and nobody cared about him.

It happened that Mike Sikoria had been working nearby, and was one of those who helped to get the victim out. Mike's Negro "buddy" had been in too great haste to get some of the rock out of the way, and had got his hand crushed, and would not be able to work for a month or so. Mike told Hal about it, in his broken English. It was a terrible thing to see a man trapped like that, gasping, his eyes almost popping out of his head. Fortunately he was a young fellow, and had no family.

Hal asked what they would do with the body; the answer was they would bury him in the morning. The company had a piece of ground up the canyon.

"But won't they have an inquest?" he inquired.

"Inques'?" repeated the other. "What's he?"

"Doesn't the coroner see the body?"

The old Slovak shrugged his bowed shoulders; if there was a coroner in this part of the world, he had never heard of it; and he had worked in a good many mines, and seen a good many men put under the ground. "Put him in a box and dig a hole," was the way he described the procedure.

"And doesn't the priest come?"

"Priest too far away."

Afterwards Hal made inquiry among the English-speaking men, and learned that the coroner did sometimes come to the camp. He would empanel a jury consisting of Jeff Cotton, the marshal, and Predovich, the Galician Jew who worked in the company store, and a clerk or two from the company's office, and a couple of Mexican laborers who had no idea what it was all about. This jury would view the corpse, and ask a couple of men what had happened, and then bring in a verdict: "We find that the deceased met his death from a fall of rock caused by his own fault." (In one case they had added the picturesque detail: "No relatives, and damned few friends!")

For this service the coroner got a fee, and the company got an official verdict, which would be final in case some foreign consul should threaten a damage suit. So well did they have matters in hand that nobody in North Valley had ever got anything for death or injury; in fact, as Hal found later, there had not been a damage suit filed against any coal-operator in that county for twenty-three years!

This particular, accident was of consequence to Hal, because it got him a chance to see the real work of mining. Old Mike was without a helper, and made the proposition that Hal should take the job. It was better than a stableman's, for it paid two dollars a day.

"But will the boss let me change?" asked Hal.

"You give him ten dollar, he change you," said Mike.

"Sorry," said Hal, "I haven't got ten dollars."

"You give him ten dollar credit," said the other.

And Hal laughed. "They take scrip for graft, do they?"

"Sure they take him," said Mike.

"Suppose I treat my mules bad?" continued the other. "So I can make him change me for nothing!"

"He change you to hell!" replied Mike. "You get him cross, he put us in bad room, cost us ten dollar a week. No, sir — you give him drink, say fine feller, make him feel good. You talk American — give him jolly!"

SECTION 21.

*H*al was glad of this opportunity to get better acquainted with his pit-boss. Alec Stone was six feet high, and built in proportion, with arms like hams — soft with fat, yet possessed of enormous strength. He had learned his manner of handling men on a sugar-plantation in Louisiana — a fact which, when Hal heard it, explained much. Like a stage-manager who does not heed the real names of his actors, but calls them by their character-names, Stone had the habit of addressing his men by their nationalities: "You, Polack, get that rock into the car! Hey, Jap, bring them tools over here! Shut your mouth, now, Dago, and get to work, or I'll kick the breeches off you, sure as you're alive!"

Hal had witnessed one occasion when there was a dispute as to whose duty it was to move timbers. There was a great two-handled cross-cut saw lying on the ground, and Stone seized it and began to wave it, like a mighty broadsword, in the face of a little Bohemian miner. "Load them timbers, Hunkie, or I'll carve you into bits!" And as the terrified man shrunk back, he followed, until his victim was flat against a wall, the weapon swinging to and fro under his nose after the fashion of "The Pit and the Pendulum." "Carve you into pieces, Hunkie! Carve you into stew-meat!" When at last the boss stepped back, the little Bohemian leaped to load the timbers.

The curious part about it to Hal was that Stone seemed to be reasonably good-natured about such proceedings. Hardly one time in a thousand did he carry out his bloodthirsty threats, and like as not he would laugh when he had finished his tirade, and the object of it would grin in turn — but without slackening his frightened efforts. After the broad-sword waving episode, seeing that Hal had been watching, the boss remarked, "That's the way you have to manage them wops." Hal took this remark as a tribute to his American blood, and was duly flattered.

He sought out the boss that evening, and found him with his feet upon the railing of his home. "Mr. Stone," said he, "I've something I'd like to ask you."

"Fire away, kid," said the other.

"Won't you come up to the saloon and have a drink?"

"Want to get something out of me, hey? You can't work me, kid!" But nevertheless he slung down his feet from the railing, and knocked the ashes out of his pipe and strolled up the street with Hal.

"Mr. Stone," said Hal, "I want to make a change."

"What's that? Got a grouch on them mules?"

"No, sir, but I got a better job in sight. Mike Sikoria's buddy is laid up, and I'd like to take his place, if you're willing."

"Why, that's a nigger's place, kid. Ain't you scared to take a nigger's place?"

"Why, sir?"

"Don't you know about hoodoos?"

"What I want," said Hal, "is the nigger's pay."

"No," said the boss, abruptly, "you stick by them mules. I got a good stableman, and I don't want to spoil him. You stick, and by and by I'll give you a raise. You go into them pits, the first thing you know you'll get a fall of rock on your head, and the nigger's pay won't be no good to you."

They came to the saloon and entered. Hal noted that a silence fell within, and everyone nodded and watched. It was pleasant to be seen going out with one's boss.

O'Callahan, the proprietor, came forward with his best society smile and joined them, and at Hal's invitation they ordered whiskies. "No, you stick to your job," continued the pit-boss. "You stay by it, and when you've learned to manage mules, I'll make a boss out of you, and let you manage men."

Some of the bystanders tittered. The pit-boss poured down his whiskey, and set the glass on the bar. "That's no joke," said he, in a tone that everyone could hear. "I learned that long ago about niggers. They'd say to me, 'For God's sake, don't talk to our niggers like that. Some night you'll have your house set afire.' But I said, 'Pet a nigger, and you've got a spoiled nigger.' I'd say, 'Nigger, don't you give me any of your imp, or I'll kick the breeches off you.' And they knew I was a gentleman, and they stepped lively."

"Have another drink," said Hal.

The pit-boss drank, and becoming more sociable, told nigger stories. On the sugar-plantations there was a rush season, when the rule was twenty hours' work a day; when some of the niggers tried to shirk it, they would arrest them for swearing or crap-shooting, and work them as convicts, without pay. The pit-boss told how one "buck" had been brought before the justice of the peace, and the charge read, "being cross-eyed"; for which offence he had been sentenced to sixty days' hard labor. This anecdote was enjoyed by the men in the saloon — whose race-feelings seemed to be stronger than their class-feelings.

When the pair went out again, it was late, and the boss was cordial.

"Mr. Stone," began Hal, "I don't want to bother you, but I'd like first rate to get more pay. If you could see your way to let me have that buddy's job, I'd be more than glad to divide with you."

"Divide with me?" said Stone. "How d'ye mean?" Hal waited with some apprehension — for if Mike had not assured him so positively, he would have expected a swing from the pit-boss's mighty arm.

"It's worth about fifteen a month more to me. I haven't any cash, but if you'd be willing to charge off ten dollars from my store-account, it would be well worth my while."

They walked for a short way in silence. "Well, I'll tell you," said the boss, at last; "that old Slovak is a kicker — one of these fellows that thinks he could run the mine if he had a chance. And if you get to listenin' to him, and think you can come to me and grumble, by God —"

"That's all right, sir," put in Hal, quickly. "I'll manage that for you — I'll shut him up. If you'd like me to, I'll see what fellows he talks with, and if any of them are trying to make trouble, I'll tip you off."

"Now that's the talk," said the boss, promptly. "You do that, and I'll keep my eye on you and give you a chance. Not that I'm afraid of the old fellow — I told him last time that if I heard from him again, I'd kick the breeches off him. But when you got half a thousand of this foreign scum, some of them Anarchists, and some of them Bulgars and Montynegroes that's been fightin' each other at home —"

"I understand," said Hal. "You have to watch 'em."

"That's it," said the pit-boss. "And by the way, when you tell the store-clerk about that fifteen dollars, just say you lost it at poker."

"I said ten dollars," put in Hal, quickly.

"Yes, I know," responded the other. "But *I* said fifteen!"

SECTION 22.

*H*al told himself with satisfaction that he was now to do the real work of coal-mining. His imagination had been occupied with it for a long time; but as so often happens in the life of man, the first contact with reality killed the results of many years' imagining. It killed all imagining, in fact; Hal found that his entire stock of energy, both mental and physical, was consumed in enduring torment. If anyone had told him the horror of attempting to work in a room five feet high, he would not have believed it. It was like some of the dreadful devices of torture which one saw in European castles, the "iron maiden" and the "spiked collar." Hal's back burned as if hot irons were being run up and down it; every separate joint and muscle cried aloud. It seemed as if he could never learn the lesson of the jagged ceiling above his head — he bumped it and continued to bump it, until his scalp was a mass of cuts and bruises, and his head ached till he was nearly blind, and he would have to throw himself flat on the ground.

Then old Mike Sikoria would grin. "I know. Like green mule! Some day get tough!"

Hal recalled the great thick calluses on the flanks of his former charges, where the harness rubbed against them. "Yes, I'm a 'green mule,' all right!"

It was amazing how many ways there were to bruise and tear one's fingers, loading lumps of coal into a car. He put on a pair of gloves, but these wore through in a day. And then the gas, and the smoke of powder, stifling one; and the terrible burning of the eyes, from the dust and the feeble light. There was no way to rub these burning eyes, because everything about one was equally dusty. Could anybody have imagined the torment of that — any of those ladies who rode in softly upholstered parlor-cars, or reclined upon the decks of steam-ships in gleaming tropic seas?

Old Mike was good to his new "buddy." Mike's spine was bent and his hands were hardened by forty years of this sort of toil, so he could do the work of two men, and entertain his friend with comments into the bargain. The old fellow had the habit of talking all the time, like a child; he would talk to his helper, to himself, to his tools. He would call these tools by obscene and terrifying names — but with entire friendliness and good humor. "Get in there, you son-of-a-gun!" he would say to his pick. "Come along here, you wop!" he would say to his car. "In with you, now, you old buster!" he would say to a lump of coal. And he would lecture Hal on the details of mining. He would tell stories of successful days, or of terrible mishaps. Above all he would tell about rascality — cursing the "G.F.C.," its foremen and superintendents, its officials, directors and stock-holders, and the world which permitted such a criminal institution to exist.

Noon-time would come, and Hal would lie upon his back, too worn to eat. Old Mike would sit munching; his abundant whiskers came to a point on his chin, and as his jaws moved, he looked for all the world like an aged billy goat. He was a kind-hearted and anxious old billy goat, and sought to tempt his buddy with a bit of cheese or a swig of cold coffee. He believed in eating — no man could keep up steam if he did not stoke the furnace. Failing in this, he would try to divert Hal's mind, telling stories of mining-life in America and Russia. He was most proud to have an "American feller" for a buddy, and tried to make the work as easy as possible, for fear lest Hal might quit.

Hal did not quit; but he would drag himself out towards night, so exhausted that he would fall asleep in the cage. He would fall asleep at supper, and go in and sink down on his cot and sleep like a log. And oh, the torture of being routed out before daybreak! Having to shake the sleep out of his head, and move his creaking joints, and become aware of the burning in his eyes, and the blisters and sores on his hands!

It was a week before he had a moment that was not pain; and he never got fully used to the labor. It was impossible for anyone to work so hard and keep his mental alertness, his eagerness and sensitiveness; it was impossible to work so hard and be an adventurer — to be anything, in fact, but a machine. Hal had heard that phrase of contempt, "the inertia of the masses," and had wondered about it. He no longer wondered, he knew. Could a man be brave enough to protest to a pit-boss when his body was numb with weariness? Could he think out a definite conclusion as to his rights and wrongs, and back his conclusion with effective action, when his mental faculties were paralyzed by such weariness of body?

Hal had come here, as one goes upon the deck of a ship in mid-ocean, to see the storm. In this ocean of social misery, of ignorance and despair, one saw upturned, tortured faces, writhing limbs and clutching hands; in one's ears was a storm of lamentation, upon one's cheek a spray of blood and tears. Hal found himself so deep in this ocean that he could no longer find consolation in the thought that he could escape whenever he wanted to: that he could say to himself, It is sad, it is terrible — but thank God, I can get out of it when I choose! I can go back into the warm and well-lighted saloon and tell the other passengers how picturesque it is, what an interesting experience they are missing!

SECTION 23.

*D*uring these days of torment, Hal did not go to see "Red Mary"; but then, one evening, the Minettis' baby having been sick, she came in to ask about it, bringing what she called "a bit of a custard" in a bowl.

Hal was suspicious enough of the ways of men, especially of business-men; but when it came to women he was without insight — it did not occur to him as singular that an Irish girl with many troubles at home should come out to nurse a Dago woman's baby. He did not reflect that there were plenty of sick Irish babies in the camp, to whom Mary might have taken her "bit of a custard." And when he saw the surprise of Rosa, who had never met Mary before, he took it to be the touching gratitude of the poor!

There are, in truth, many kinds of women, with many arts, and no man has time to learn them all. Hal had observed the shop-girl type, who dress themselves with many frills, and cast side-long glances, and indulge in fits of giggles to attract the attention of the male; he was familiar with the society-girl type, who achieve the same end with more subtle and alluring means. But could there be a type who hold little Dago babies in their laps, and call them pretty Irish names, and feed them custard out of a spoon? Hal had never heard of that kind, and he thought that "Red Mary" made a charming picture — a Celtic Madonna with a Sicilian infant in her arms.

He noticed that she was wearing the same faded blue calico-dress with a patch on the shoulder. Man though he was, he realized that dress is an important consideration in the lives of women. He was tempted to suspect that this blue calico might be the only dress that Mary owned; but seeing it newly laundered every time, he concluded that she must have at least one other. At any rate, here she was, crisp and fresh-looking; and with the new shining costume, she had put on the long promised "company manner": high spirits and badinage, precisely like any belle of the world of luxury, who powders and bedecks herself for a ball. She had been grim and complaining in former meetings with this interesting young man; she had frightened him away, apparently; perhaps she could win him back by womanliness and good humor.

She rallied him upon his battered scalp and his creaking back, telling him he looked ten years older — which he was fully prepared to believe. Also she had fun with him for working under a Slovak — another loss of caste, it appeared! This was a joke the Minettis could share in — especially Little Jerry, who liked jokes. He told Mary how Joe Smith had had to pay fifteen dollars for his new job, besides several drinks at O'Callahan's. Also he told how Mike Sikoria had called Joe his "green mule." Little Jerry complained about the turn of events, for in the old days Joe had taught him a lot of fine new games — and now he was sore, and would not play them. Also, in the old days he had sung a lot of jolly songs, full of the most fascinating rhymes. There was a song about a "monkey puzzle tree!" Had Mary ever seen that kind of tree? Little

Jerry never got tired of trying to imagine what it might look like.

The Dago urchin stood and watched gravely while Mary fed the custard to the baby; and when two or three spoonfuls were held out to him, he opened his mouth wide, and afterwards licked his lips. Gee, that was good stuff!

When the last taste was gone, he stood gazing at Mary's shining coronet. "Say," said he, "was your hair always like that?"

Hal and Mary burst into laughter, while Rosa cried "Hush!" She was never sure what this youngster would say next.

"Sure, did ye think I painted it?" asked Mary.

"I didn't know," said Little Jerry. "It looks so nice and new." And he turned to Hal. "Ain't it?"

"You bet," said Hal, and added, "Go on and tell her about it. Girls like compliments."

"Compliments?" echoed Little Jerry. "What's that?"

"Why," said Hal, "that's when you say that her hair is like the sunrise, and her eyes are like twilight, or that she's a wild rose on a mountainside."

"Oh," said the Dago urchin, somewhat doubtfully. "Anyhow," he added, "she make nice custard!"

SECTION 24.

*T*he time came for Mary to take her departure, and Hal got up, wincing with pain, to escort her home. She regarded him gravely, having not realized before how seriously he was suffering. As they walked along she asked, "Why do ye do such work, when ye don't have to?"

"But I *do* have to! I have to earn a living!"

"Ye don't have to earn it that way! A bright young fellow like you — an American!"

"Well," said Hal, "I thought it would be interesting to see coal mining."

"Now ye've seen it," said the girl — "now quit!"

"But it won't do me any harm to go on for a while!"

"Won't it? How can ye know? When any day they may carry you out on a plank!"

Her "company manner" was gone; her voice was full of bitterness, as

it always was when she spoke of North Valley. "I know what I'm tellin'
ye, Joe Smith. Didn't I lose two brothers in it — as fine lads as ye'd find
anywhere in the world! And many another lad I've seen go in laughin',
and come out a corpse — or what is worse, for workin' people, a cripple.
Sometimes I'd like to go and stand at the pit-mouth in the mornin' and
cry to them, 'Go back, go back! Go down the canyon this day! Starve,
if ye have to, beg if ye have to, only find some other work but coal-
minin'!'"

Her voice had risen to a passion of protest; when she went on a new
note came into it — a note of personal terror. "It's worse now — since
you came, Joe! To see ye settin' out on the life of a miner — you, that
are young and strong and different. Oh, go away, Joe, go away while ye
can!"

He was astonished at her intensity. "Don't worry about me, Mary,"
he said. "Nothing will happen to me. I'll go away after a while."

The path was irregular, and he had been holding her arm as they
walked. He felt her trembling, and went on again, quickly, "It's not I
that should go away, Mary. It's yourself. You hate the place — it's terrible
for you to have to live here. Have you never thought of going away?"

She did not answer at once, and when she did the excitement was
gone from her voice; it was flat and dull with despair. "'Tis no use to
think of me. There's nothin' I can do — there's nothin' any girl can do
when she's poor. I've tried — but 'tis like bein' up against a stone wall.
I can't even save the money to get on a train with! I've tried it — I been
savin' for two years — and how much d'ye think I got, Joe? Seven dollars!
Seven dollars in two years! No — ye can't save money in a place where
there's so many things that wring the heart. Ye may hate them for being
cowards — but ye must help when ye see a man killed, and his family
turned out without a roof to cover them in the winter-time!"

"You're too tender-hearted, Mary."

"No, 'tis not that! Should I go off and leave me own brother and
sister, that need me?"

"But you could earn money and send it to them."

"I earn a little here — I do cleanin' and nursin' for some that need
me."

"But outside — couldn't you earn more?"

"I could get a job in a restaurant for seven or eight a week, but I'd
have to spend more, and what I sent home would not go so far, with
me away. Or I could get a job in some other woman's home, and work
fourteen hours a day for it. But, Joe, 'tis not more drudgery I want, 'tis
somethin' fair to look upon — somethin' of my own!" She flung out
her arms suddenly like one being stifled. "Oh, I want somethin' that's

fair and clean!"

Again he felt her trembling. Again the path was rough, and having an impulse of sympathy, he put his arm about her. In the world of leisure, one might indulge in such considerateness, and he assumed it would not he different with a miner's daughter. But then, when she was close to him, he felt, rather than heard, a sob.

"Mary!" he whispered; and they stopped. Almost without realizing it, he put his other arm about her, and in a moment more he felt her warm breath on his cheek, and she was trembling and shaking in his embrace. "Joe! Joe!" she whispered. *"You* take me away!"

She was a rose in a mining-camp, and Hal was deeply moved. The primrose path of dalliance stretched fair before him, here in the soft summer night, with a moon overhead which bore the same message as it bore in the Italian gardens of the leisure-class. But not many minutes passed before a cold fear began to steal over Hal. There was a girl at home, waiting for him; and also there was the resolve which had been growing in him since his coming to this place — a resolve to find some way of compensation to the poor, to repay them for the freedom and culture he had taken; not to prey upon them, upon any individual among them. There were the Jeff Cottons for that!

"Mary," he pleaded, "we mustn't do this."

"Why not?"

"Because — I'm not free. There is someone else."

He felt her start, but she did not draw away.

"Where?" she asked, in a low voice.

"At home, waiting for me."

"And why didn't ye tell me?"

"I don't know."

Hal realized in a moment that the girl had ground of complaint against him. According to the simple code of her world, he had gone some distance with her; he had been seen to walk out with her, he had been accounted her "fellow." He had led her to talk to him of herself — he had insisted upon having her confidences. And these people who were poor did not have subtleties, there was no room in their lives for intellectual curiosities, for Platonic friendships or philanderings. "Forgive me, Mary!" he said.

She made no answer; but a sob escaped her, and she drew back from his arms — slowly. He struggled with an impulse to clasp her again. She was beautiful, warm with life — and so much in need of happiness!

But he held himself in check, and for a minute or two they stood apart. Then he asked, humbly, "We can still be friends, Mary, can't we? You must know — I'm so *sorry!"*

But she could not endure being pitied. "'Tis nothin'," she said. "Only I thought I was going to get away! That's what ye mean to me."

SECTION 25.

*H*al had promised Alec Stone to keep a look-out for trouble-makers; and one evening the boss stopped him on the street, and asked him if he had anything to report. Hal took the occasion to indulge his sense of humor.

"There's no harm in Mike Sikoria," said he. "He likes to shoot off his head, but if he's got somebody to listen, that's all he wants. He's just old and grouchy. But there's another fellow that I think would bear watching."

"Who's that?" asked the boss.

"I don't know his last name. They call him Gus and he's a 'cager.' Fellow with a red face."

"I know," said Stone – "Gus Durking."

"Well, he tried his best to get me to talk about unions. He keeps bringing it up, and I think he's some kind of trouble-maker."

"I see," said the boss. "I'll get after him."

"You won't say I told you," said Hal, anxiously.

"Oh, no – sure not." And Hal caught the trace of a smile on the pit-boss's face.

He went away, smiling in his turn. The "red-faced feller. Gus," was the person Madvik had named as being a "spotter" for the company!

There were ins and outs to this matter of "spotting," and sometimes it was not easy to know what to think. One Sunday morning Hal went for a walk up the canyon, and on the way he met a young chap who got to talking with him, and after a while brought up the question of working-conditions in North Valley. He had only been there a week, he said, but everybody he had met seemed to be grumbling about short weight. He himself had a job as an "outside man," so it made no difference to him, but he was interested, and wondered what Hal had found.

Straightway came the question, was this really a workingman, or had Alec Stone set someone to spying upon his spy. This was an intelligent fellow, an American – which in itself was suspicious, for most of the new men the company got in were from "somewhere East of Suez."

Hal decided to spar for a while. He did not know, he said, that conditions were any worse here than elsewhere. You heard complaints, no matter what sort of job you took.

Yes, said the stranger, but matters seemed to be especially bad in the coal-camps. Probably it was because they were so remote, and the companies owned everything in sight.

"Where have you been?" asked Hal, thinking that this might trap him.

But the other answered straight; he had evidently worked in half a dozen of the camps. In Mateo he had paid a dollar a month for wash-house privileges, and there had never been any water after the first three men had washed. There had been a common wash-tub for all the men, an unthinkably filthy arrangement. At Pine Creek — Hal found the very naming of the place made his heart stand still — at Pine Creek he had boarded with his boss, but the roof of the building leaked, and everything he owned was ruined; the boss would do nothing — yet when the boarder moved, he lost his job. At East Ridge, this man and a couple of other fellows had rented a two room cabin and started to board themselves, in spite of the fact that they had to pay a dollar-fifty a sack for potatoes and eleven cents a pound for sugar at the company store. They had continued until they made the discovery that the water supply had run short, and that the water for which they were paying the company a dollar a month was being pumped from the bottom of the mine, where the filth of mules and men was plentiful!

Hal forced himself to remain non-committal; he shook his head and said it was too bad, but the workers always got it in the neck, and he didn't see what they could do about it. So they strolled back to the camp, the stranger evidently baffled, and Hal, for his part, feeling like the reader of a detective story at the end of the first chapter. Was this young man the murderer, or was he the hero? One would have to read on in the book to find out!

SECTION 26.

*H*al kept his eye upon his new acquaintance, and perceived that he was talking with others. Before long the man tackled Old Mike; and

Mike of course could not refuse an invitation to grumble, though it came from the devil himself. Hal decided that something must be done about it.

He consulted his friend Jerry, who, being a radical, might have some touch-stone by which to test the stranger. Jerry sought him out at noon-time, and came back and reported that he was as much in the dark as Hal. Either the man was an agitator, seeking to "start something," or else he was a detective sent in by the company. There was only one way to find out — which was for someone to talk freely with him, and see what happened to that person!

After some hesitation, Hal decided that he would be the victim. It reawakened his love of adventure, which digging in a coal-mine had subdued in him. The mysterious stranger was a new sort of miner, digging into the souls of men; Hal would countermine him, and perhaps blow him up. He could afford the experiment better than some others — better, for example, than little Mrs. David, who had already taken the stranger into her home, and revealed to him the fact that her husband had been a member of the most revolutionary of all miners' organizations, the South Wales Federation.

So next Sunday Hal invited the stranger for another walk. The man showed reluctance — until Hal said that he wanted to talk to him. As they walked up the canyon, Hal began, "I've been thinking about what you said of conditions in these camps, and I've concluded it would be a good thing if we had a little shaking up here in North Valley."

"Is that so?" said the other.

"When I first came here, I used to think the men were grouchy. But now I've had a chance to see for myself, and I don't believe anybody gets a square deal. For one thing, nobody gets full weight in these mines — at least not unless he's some favorite of the boss. I'm sure of it, for I've tried all sorts of experiments with my partner. We've loaded a car extra light, and got eighteen hundredweight, and then we've loaded one high and solid, so that we'd know it had twice as much in it — but all we ever got was twenty-two and twenty-three. There's just no way you can get over that — though everybody knows those big cars can be made to hold two or three tons."

"Yes, I suppose they might," said the other.

"And if you get the smallest piece of rock in, you get a 'double-O,' sure as fate; and sometimes they say you got rock in when you didn't. There's no law to make them prove it."

"No, I suppose not."

"What it comes to is simply this — they make you think they are paying fifty-five a ton, but they've secretly cut you down to thirty-five.

And yesterday at the company-store I paid a dollar and a half for a pair of blue overalls that I'd priced in Pedro for sixty cents."

"Well," said the other, "the company has to haul them up here, you know!"

So, gradually, Hal made the discovery that the tables were turned — the mysterious personage was now occupied in holding *him* at arm's length! For some reason, Hal's sudden interest in industrial justice had failed to make an impression.

So his career as a detective came to an inglorious end. "Say, man!" he exclaimed "What's your game, anyhow?"

"Game?" said the other, quietly. "How do you mean?"

"I mean, what are you here for?"

"I'm here for two dollars a day — the same as you, I guess."

Hal began to laugh. "You and I are like a couple of submarines, trying to find each other under water. I think we'd better come to the surface to do our fighting."

The other considered the simile, and seemed to like it. "You come first," said he. But he did not smile. His quiet blue eyes were fixed on Hal with deadly seriousness.

"All right," said Hal; "my story isn't very thrilling. I'm not an escaped convict, I'm not a company spy, as you may be thinking. Nor am I a 'natural born' coal-miner. I happen to have a brother and some friends at home who think they know about the coal-industry, and it got on my nerves, and I came to see for myself. That's all, except that I've found things interesting, and want to stay on a while, so I hope you aren't a 'dick'!"

The other walked in silence, weighing Hal's words. "That's not exactly what you'd call a usual story," he remarked, at last.

"I know," replied Hal. "The best I can say for it is that it's true."

"Well," said the stranger, "I'll take a chance on it. I have to trust somebody, if I'm ever to get anywhere. I picked you out because I liked your face." He gave Hal another searching look as he walked. "Your smile isn't that of a cheat. But you're young — so let me remind you of the importance of secrecy in this place."

"I'll keep mum," said Hal; and the stranger opened a flap inside his shirt, and drew out a letter which certified him to be Thomas Olson, an organizer for the United Mine-Workers, the great national union of the coal-miners!

SECTION 27.

*H*al was so startled by this discovery that he stopped in his tracks and gazed at the man. He had heard a lot about "trouble-makers" in the camps, but so far the only kind he had seen were those hired by the company to make trouble for the men. But now, here was a union organizer! Jerry had suggested the possibility, but Hal had not thought of it seriously; an organizer was a mythological creature, whispered about by the miners, cursed by the company and its servants, and by Hal's friends at home. An incendiary, a fire-brand, a loudmouthed, irresponsible person, stirring up blind and dangerous passions! Having heard such things all his life, Hal's first impulse was of distrust. He felt like the one-legged old switchman who had given him a place to sleep, after his beating at Pine Creek, and who had said, "Don't you talk no union business to me!"

Seeing Hal's emotion, the organizer gave an uneasy laugh. "While you're hoping I'm not a 'dick,' I trust you understand I'm hoping *you're* not one."

Hal's answer was to the point. "I was taken for an organizer once," he said, and his hands sought the seat of his ancient bruises.

The other laughed. "You got off with a beating? You were lucky. Down in Alabama, not so long ago, they tarred and feathered one of us."

Dismay came upon Hal's face; but after a moment he too began to laugh. "I was just thinking about my brother and his friends — what they'd have said if I'd come home from Pine Creek in a coat of tar and feathers!"

"Possibly," ventured the other, "they'd have said you got what you deserved."

"Yes, that seems to be their attitude. That's the rule they apply to all the world — if anything goes wrong with you, it must he your own fault. It's a land of equal opportunity."

"And you'll notice," said the organizer, "that the more privileges people have had, the more boldly they talk that way."

Hal began to feel a sense of comradeship with this stranger, who was able to understand one's family troubles! It had been a long time since Hal had talked with anyone from the outside world, and he found it a relief to his mind. He remembered how, after he had got his beating, he had lain out in the rain and congratulated himself that he was not what the guards had taken him for. Now he was curious about the psychology of an organizer. A man must have strong convictions to follow that occupation!

He made the remark, and the other answered, "You can have my pay anytime you'll do my work. But let me tell you, too, it isn't being beaten and kicked out of camp that bothers one most; it isn't the camp-marshal and the spy and the blacklist. Your worst troubles are inside the heads of the fellows you're trying to help! Have you ever thought what it would mean to try to explain things to men who speak twenty different languages?"

"Yes, of course," said Hal. "I wonder how you ever get a start."

"Well, you look for an interpreter — and maybe he's a company spy. Or maybe the first man you try to convert reports you to the boss. For, of course, some of the men are cowards, and some of them are crooks; they'll sell out the next fellow for a better 'place' — maybe for a glass of beer."

"That must have a tendency to weaken your convictions," said Hal.

"No," said the other, in a matter of fact tone. "It's hard, but one can't blame the poor devils. They're ignorant — kept so deliberately. The bosses bring them here, and have a regular system to keep them from getting together. And of course these European peoples have their old prejudices — national prejudices, religious prejudices, that keep them apart. You see two fellows, one you think is exactly as miserable as the other — but you find him despising the other, because back home he was the other's superior. So they play into the bosses' hands."

SECTION 28.

*T*hey had come to a remote place in the canyon, and found themselves seats on a flat rock, where they could talk in comfort.

"Put yourself in their place," said the organizer. "They're in a strange country, and one person tells them one thing, and another tells them something else. The masters and their agents say: 'Don't trust the union agitators. They're a lot of grafters, they live easy and don't have to work. They take your money and call you out on strike, and you lose your jobs and your home; they sell you out, maybe, and go on to some other place to repeat the same trick.' And the workers think maybe that's true;

they haven't the wit to see that if the union leaders are corrupt, it must be because the bosses are buying them. So you see, they're completely bedeviled; they don't know which way to turn."

The man was speaking quietly, but there was a little glow of excitement in his face. "The company is forever repeating that these people are satisfied — that it's we who are stirring them up. But are they satisfied? You've been here long enough to know!"

"There's no need to discuss that," Hal answered. "Of course they're not satisfied! They've seemed to me like a lot of children crying in the dark — not knowing what's the matter with them, or who's to blame, or where to turn for help."

Hal found himself losing his distrust of this man. He did not correspond in any way to Hal's imaginary picture of a union organizer; he was a blue-eyed, clean-looking young American, and instead of being wild and loud-mouthed, he seemed rather wistful. He had indignation, of course, but it did not take the form of ranting or florid eloquence; and this repression was making its appeal to Hal, who, in spite of his democratic impulses, had the habits of thought of a class which shrinks from noisiness and overemphasis.

Also Hal was interested in his attitude towards the weaknesses of working-people. The "inertia" of the poor, which caused so many people to despair for them — their cowardice and instability — these were things about which Hal had heard all his life. "You can't help them," people would say. "They're dirty and lazy, they drink and shirk, they betray each other. They've always been like that." The idea would be summed up in a formula: "You can't change human nature!" Even Mary Burke, herself one of the working-class, spoke of the workers in this angry and scornful way. But Olson had faith in their manhood, and went ahead to awaken and teach them.

To his mind the path was clear and straight. "They must be taught the lesson of solidarity. As individuals, they're helpless in the power of the great corporations; but if they stand together, if they sell their labor as a unit — then they really count for something." He paused, and looked at the other inquiringly. "How do you feel about unions?"

Hal answered, "They're one of the things I want to find out about. You hear this and that — there's so much prejudice on each side. I want to help the under dog, but I want to be sure of the right way."

"What other way is there?" And Olson paused. "To appeal to the tender hearts of the owners?"

"Not exactly; but mightn't one appeal to the world in general — to public opinion? I was brought up an American, and learned to believe in my country. I can't think but there's some way to get justice. Maybe if the men were to go into politics —"

"Politics?" cried Olson. "My God! How long have you been in this place?"

"Only a couple of months."

"Well, stay till November, and see what they do with the ballot-boxes in these camps!"

"I can imagine, of course —"

"No, you can't. Anymore than you could imagine the graft and the misery!"

"But if the men should take to voting together —"

"How *can* they take to voting together — when anyone who mentions the idea goes down the canyon? Why, you can't even get naturalization papers, unless you're a company man; they won't register you, unless the boss gives you an okay How are you going to make a start, unless you have a union?"

It sounded reasonable, Hal had to admit; but he thought of the stories he had heard about "walking delegates," all the dreadful consequences of "union domination." He had not meant to go in for unionism!

Olson was continuing. "We've had laws passed, a whole raft of laws about coal-mining — the eight-hour law, the anti-scrip law, the company-store law, the mine-sprinkling law, the check-weighman law. What difference has it made in North Valley that there are such laws on the statute-books? Would you ever even know about them?"

"Ah, now!" said Hal. "If you put it that way — if your movement is to have the law enforced — I'm with you!"

"But how will you get the law enforced, except by a union? No individual man can do it — it's 'down the canyon' with him if he mentions the law. In Western City our union people go to the state officials, but they never do anything — and why? They know we haven't got the men behind us! It's the same with the politicians as it is with the bosses — the union is the thing that counts!"

Hal found this an entirely new argument. "People don't realize that idea — that men have to be organized to get their *legal* rights."

And the other threw up his hands with a comical gesture. "My God! If you want to make a list of the things that people don't realize about us miners!"

SECTION 29.

Olson was eager to win Hal, and went on to tell all the secrets of his work. He sought men who believed in unions, and were willing to take the risk of trying to convert others. In each place he visited he would get a group together, and would arrange some way to communicate with them after he left, smuggling in propaganda literature for distribution. So there would be the nucleus of an organization. In a year or two they would have such a nucleus in every camp, and then they would be ready to come into the open, calling meetings in the towns, and in places in the canyons to which the miners would flock. So the flame of revolt would leap up; men would join the movement faster than the companies could get rid of them, and they would make a demand for their rights, backed with the threat of a strike throughout the entire district.

"You understand," added Olson, "we have a legal right to organize — even though the bosses disapprove. You need not stand back on that score."

"Yes," said Hal; "but it occurs to me that as a matter of tactics, it would be better here in North Valley if you chose some issue there's less controversy about; if, for instance, you'd concentrate on getting a check-weighman."

The other smiled. "We'd have to have a union to back the demand; so what's the difference?"

"Well," argued Hal, "there are prejudices to be reckoned with. Some people don't like the idea of a union — they think it means tyranny and violence —"

The organizer laughed. "You aren't convinced but that it does yourself, are you! Well, all I can tell you is, if you want to tackle the job of getting a check-weighman in North Valley, I'll not stand in your way!"

Here was an idea — a real idea! Life had grown dull for Hal since he had become a buddy, working in a place five feet high. This would promise livelier times!

But was it a thing he wanted to do? So far he had been an observer of conditions in this coal-camp. He had convinced himself that conditions were cruel, and he had pretty well convinced himself that the cruelty was needless and deliberate. But when it came to a question of an action to be taken — then he hesitated, and old prejudices and fears made themselves heard. He had been told that labor was "turbulent" and "lazy," that it had to be "ruled with a strong hand"; now, was he willing to weaken the strong hand, to ally himself with those who "fomented labor troubles?"

But this would not be the same thing, he told himself. This suggestion of Olson's was different from trade unionism, which might be a demoralizing force, leading the workers from one demand to another, until they were seeking to "dominate industry." This would be merely an appeal to the law, a test of that honesty and fair dealing to which the company everywhere laid claim. If, as the bosses proclaimed, the workers were fully protected by the check-weighman law; if, as all the world was made to believe, the reason there was no check-weighman was simply because the men did not ask for one — why, then there would be no harm done. If on the other hand a demand for a right that was not merely a legal right, but a moral right as well — if that were taken by the bosses as an act of rebellion against the company — well, Hal would understand a little more about the "turbulence" of labor! If, as Old Mike and Johannson and the rest maintained, the bosses would "make your life one damn misery" till you left — then he would be ready to make a few damn miseries for the bosses in return!

"It would be an adventure," said Hal, suddenly.

And the other laughed. "It would that!"

"You're thinking I'll have another Pine Creek experience," Hal added. "Well, maybe so — but I have to try things out for myself. You see, I've got a brother at home, and when I think about going in for revolution, I have imaginary arguments with him. I want to be able to say 'I didn't swallow anybody's theories; I tried it for myself, and this is what happened.'"

"Well," replied the organizer, "that's all right. But while you're seeking education for yourself and your brother, don't forget that I've already got my education. I *know* what happens to men who ask for a check-weighman, and I can't afford to sacrifice myself proving it again."

"I never asked you to," laughed Hal. "If I won't join your movement, I can't expect you to join mine! But if I can find a few men who are willing to take the risk of making a demand for a check-weighman — that won't hurt your work, will it?"

"Sure not!" said the other. "Just the opposite — it'll give me an object lesson to point to. There are men here who don't even know they've a legal right to a check-weighman. There are others who know they don't get their weights, but aren't sure its the company that's cheating them. If the bosses should refuse to let anyone inspect the weights, if they should go further and fire the men who ask it — well, there'll be plenty of recruits for my union local!"

"All right," said Hal. "I'm not setting out to recruit your union local, but if the company wants to recruit it, that's the company's affair!" And on this bargain the two shook hands.

BOOK TWO
THE SERFS OF KING COAL
SECTION I.

*H*al was now started upon a new career, more full of excitements than that of stableman or buddy, with perils greater than those of falling rock or the hind feet of mules in the stomach. The inertia which overwork produces had not had time to become a disease with him; youth was on his side, with its zest for more and yet more experience. He found it thrilling to be a conspirator, to carry about with him secrets as dark and mysterious as the passages of the mine in which he worked.

But Jerry Minetti, the first person he told of Tom Olson's purpose in North Valley, was older in such thrills. The carefree look which Jerry was accustomed to wear vanished abruptly, and fear came into his eyes. "I know it come some day," he exclaimed — "trouble for me and Rosa!"

"How do you mean?"

"We get into it — get in sure. I say Rosa, 'Call yourself Socialist — what good that do? No help any. No use to vote here — they don't count no Socialist vote, only for joke!' I say, 'Got to have union. Got to strike!' But Rosa say, 'Wait little bit. Save little bit money, let children grow up. Then we help, no care if we no got any home.'"

"But we're not going to start a union now!" objected Hal. "I have another plan for the present."

Jerry, however, was not to be put at ease. "No can wait!" he declared. "Men no stand it! I say, 'It come some day quick — like blow-up in mine! Somebody start fight, everybody fight.'" And Jerry looked at Rosa, who sat with her black eyes fixed anxiously upon her husband. "We get into it," he said; and Hal saw their eyes turn to the room where Little Jerry and the baby were sleeping.

Hal said nothing — he was beginning to understand the meaning of rebellion to such people. He watched with curiosity and pity the struggle that went on; a struggle as old as the soul of man — between the voice of self-interest, of comfort and prudence, and the call of duty, of the ideal. No trumpet sounded for this conflict, only the still small voice within.

After a while Jerry asked what it was Hal and Olson had planned; and Hal explained that he wanted to make a test of the company's attitude toward the check-weighman law. Hal thought it a fine scheme; what did Jerry think?

Jerry smiled sadly. "Yes, fine scheme for young feller — no got family!"

"That's all right," said Hal, "I'll take the job — I'll be the check-weighman."

"Got to have committee," said Jerry — "committee go see boss."

"All right, but we'll get young fellows for that too — men who have no families. Some of the fellows who live in the chicken-coops in shanty-town. They won't care what happens to them."

But Jerry would not share Hal's smile. "No got sense 'nough, them fellers. Take sense to stick together." He explained that they would need a group of men to stand back of the committee; such a group would have to be organized, to hold meetings in secret — it would be practically the same thing as a union, would be so regarded by the bosses and their spotters. And no organization of any sort was permitted in the camps. There had been some Serbians who had wanted to belong to a fraternal order back in their home country, but even that had been forbidden. If you wanted to insure your life or your health, the company would attend to it — and get the profit from it. For that matter, you could not even buy a post office money-order, to send funds back to the old country; the post office clerk, who was at the same time a clerk in the company-store, would sell you some sort of a store-draft.

So Hal was facing the very difficulties about which Olson had warned him. The first of them was Jerry's fear. Yet Hal knew that Jerry was no "coward"; if any man had a contempt for Jerry's attitude, it was because he had never been in Jerry's place!

"All I'll ask of you now is advice," said Hal. "Give me the names of some young fellows who are trustworthy, and I'll get their help without anybody suspecting you."

"You my boarder!" was Jerry's reply to this.

So again Hal was "up against it." "You mean that would get you into trouble?"

"Sure! They know we talk. They know I talk Socialism, anyhow. They fire me sure!"

"But how about your cousin, the pit-boss in Number One?"

"He no help. May be get fired himself. Say damn fool — board check-weighman!"

"All right," said Hal. "Then I'll move away now, before it's too late. You can say I was a trouble-maker, and you turned me off."

The Minettis sat gazing at each other — a mournful pair. They hated to lose their boarder, who was such good company, and paid them such good money. As for Hal, he felt nearly as bad, for he liked Jerry and his girl-wife, and Little Jerry — even the black-eyed baby, who made so much noise and interrupted conversation!

"No!" said Jerry. "I no run, away! I do my share!"

"That's all right," replied Hal. "You do your share — but not just yet. You stay on in the camp and help Olson after I'm fired. We don't want the best men put out at once."

So, after further argument, it was decided, and Hal saw little Rosa sink back in her chair and draw a deep breath of relief. The time for martyrdom was put off; her little three-roomed cabin, her furniture and her shining pans and her pretty white lace curtains, might be hers for a few weeks longer!

SECTION 2.

*H*al went back to Reminitsky's boarding-house; a heavy sacrifice, but not without its compensations, because it gave him more chance to talk with the men.

He and Jerry made up a list of those who could be trusted with the secret: the list beginning with the name of Mike Sikoria. To be put on a committee, and sent to interview a boss, would appeal to Old Mike as the purpose for which he had been put upon earth! But they would not tell him about it until the last minute, for fear lest in his excitement he might shout out the announcement the next time he lost one of his cars.

There was a young Bulgarian miner named Wresmak who worked near Hal. The road into this man's room ran up an incline, and he had hardly been able to push his "empties" up the grade. While he was sweating and straining at the task, Alec Stone had come along, and having a giant's contempt for physical weakness, began to cuff him. The man raised his arm — whether in offence or to ward off the blow, no one could be sure; but Stone fell upon him and kicked him all the way down the passage, pouring out upon him furious curses. Now the man was in another room, where he had taken out over forty car-loads of rock, and been allowed only three dollars for it. No one who watched his face when the pit-boss passed would doubt that this man would be ready to take his chances in a movement of protest.

Then there was a man whom Jerry knew, who had just come out of the hospital, after contact with the butt-end of the camp-marshal's revolver. This was a Pole, who unfortunately did not know a word of English; but Olson, the organizer, had got into touch with another Pole, who spoke a little English, and would pass the word on to his fellow-countryman. Also there was a young Italian, Rovetta, whom Jerry knew and whose loyalty he could vouch for.

There was another person Hal thought of — Mary Burke. He had been deliberately avoiding her of late; it seemed the one safe thing to do — although it seemed also a cruel thing, and left his mind ill at ease. He went over and over what had happened. How had the trouble got started? It is a man's duty in such cases to take the blame upon himself; but a man does not like to take blame upon himself, and he tries to make it as light as possible. Should Hal say that it was because he had been too officious that night in helping Mary where the path was rough? She had not actually needed such help, she was quite as capable on her feet as he! But he had really gone farther than that — he had had a definite sentimental impulse; and he had been a cad — he should have known all along that all this girl's discontent, all the longing of her starved soul, would become centered upon him, who was so "different," who had had opportunity, who made her think of the "poetry-books!"

But here suddenly seemed a solution of the difficulty; here was a new interest for Mary, a safe channel in which her emotions could run. A woman could not serve on a miners' committee, but she would be a good adviser, and her sharp tongue would be a weapon to drive others into line. Being aflame with this enterprise, Hal became impersonal, man-fashion — and so fell into another sentimental trap! He did not stop to think that Mary's interest in the check-weighman movement might be conditioned in part by a desire to see more of him; still less did it occur to him that he might be glad for a pretext to see Mary.

No, he was picturing her in a new role, an activity more inspiriting than cooking and nursing. His "poetry-book" imagination took fire; he gave her a hope and a purpose, a pathway with a goal at the end. Had there not been women leaders in every great proletarian movement?

He went to call on her, and met her at the door of her cabin. "'Tis a cheerin' sight to see ye, Joe Smith!" she said. And she looked him in the eye and smiled.

"The same to you, Mary Burke!" he answered.

She was game, he saw; she was going to be a "good sport." But he noticed that she was paler than when he had seen her last. Could it be that these gorgeous Irish complexions ever faded? He thought that she was thinner too; the old blue calico seemed less tight upon her.

Hal plunged into his theme. "Mary, I had a vision of you today!"

"Of me, lad? What's that?"

He laughed. "I saw you with a glory in your face, and your hair shining like a crown of gold. You were mounted on a snow-white horse, and wore a robe of white, soft and lustrous — like Joan of Arc, or a leader in a suffrage parade. You were riding at the head of a host — I've still got the music in my ears, Mary!"

"Go on with ye, lad — what's all this about?"

"Come in and I'll tell you," he said.

So they went into the bare kitchen, and sat in bare wooden chairs — Mary folding her hands in her lap like a child who has been promised a fairy-story. "Now hurry," said she. "I want to know about this new dress ye're givin' me. Are ye tired of me old calico?"

He joined in her smile. "This is a dress you will weave for yourself, Mary, out of the finest threads of your own nature — out of courage and devotion and self-sacrifice."

"Sure, 'tis the poetry-book again! But what is it ye're really meanin'?"

He looked about him. "Is anybody here?"

"Nobody."

But instinctively he lowered his voice as he told his story. There was an organizer of the "big union" in the camp, and he was going to rouse the slaves to protest.

The laughter went out of Mary's face. "Oh! It's that!" she said, in a flat tone. The vision of the snow-white horse and the soft and lustrous robe was gone. "Ye can never do anything of that sort here!"

"Why not?"

"'Tis the men in this place. Don't ye remember what I told ye at Mr. Rafferty's? They're cowards!"

"Ah, Mary, it's easy to say that. But it's not so pleasant being turned out of your home —"

"Do ye have to tell me that?" she cried, with sudden passion. "Haven't I seen that?"

"Yes, Mary; but I want to *do* something —"

"Yes, and haven't I wanted to do something? Sure, I've wanted to bite off the noses of the bosses!"

"Well," he laughed, "we'll make that a part of our program." But Mary was not to be lured into cheerfulness; her mood was so full of pain and bewilderment that he had an impulse to reach out and take her hand again. But he checked that; he had come to divert her energies into a safe channel!

"We must waken these men to resistance, Mary!"

"Ye can't do it, Joe — not the English-speakin' men. The Greeks and the Bulgars, maybe — they're fightin' at home, and they might fight here. But the Irish never — never! Them that had any backbone went out long ago. Them that stayed has been made into boot-licks. I know them, every man of them. They grumble, and curse the boss, but then they think of the blacklist, and they go back and cringe at his feet."

"What such men want —"

"'Tis booze they want, and carousin' with the rotten women in the coal-towns, and sittin' up all night winnin' each other's money with a greasy pack of cards! They take their pleasure where they find it, and 'tis nothin' better they want."

"Then, Mary, if that's so, don't you see it's all the more reason for trying to teach them? If not for their own sakes, for the sake of their children! The children, mustn't grow up like that! They are learning English, at least —"

Mary gave a scornful laugh. "Have ye been up to that school?"

He answered no; and she told him there were a hundred and twenty children packed in one room, three in a seat, and solid all round the wall. She went on, with swift anger — the school was supposed to be paid for out of taxes, but as nobody owned any property but the company, it was all in the company's hands. The school-board consisted of Mr. Cartwright, the mine-superintendent, and Jake Predovich, a clerk in the store, and the preacher, the Reverend Spraggs. Old Spraggs would bump his nose on the floor if the "super" told him to.

"Now, now!" said Hal, laughing. "You're down on him because his grandfather was an Orangeman!"

SECTION 3.

Mary Burke had been suckled upon despair, and the poison of it was deep in her blood. Hal began to realize that it would be as hard to give her a hope as to rouse the workers whom she despised. She was brave enough, no doubt, but how could he persuade her to be brave for men who had no courage for themselves?

"Mary," he said, "in your heart you don't really hate these people. You know how they suffer, you pity them for it. You give their children your last cent when they need it —"

"Ah, lad!" she cried, and he saw tears suddenly spring into her eyes. "'Tis because I love them so that I hate them! Sometimes 'tis the bosses I would murder, sometimes 'tis the men. What is it ye're wantin' me to do?"

And then, even before he could answer, she began to run over the list of her acquaintances in the camp. Yes, there was one man Hal ought to talk to; he would be too old to join them, but his advice would be invaluable, and they could be sure he would never betray them. That was old John Edstrom, a Swede from Minnesota, who had worked in this district from the time the mines had first started up. He had been active in the great strike eight years ago, and had been black-listed, his four sons with him. The sons were scattered now to the four parts of the world, but the father had stayed nearby, working as a ranch-hand and railroad laborer, until a couple of years ago, during a rush season, he had got a chance to come back into the mines.

He was old, old, declared Mary — must be sixty. And when Hal remarked that that did not sound so frightfully aged, she answered that one seldom heard of a man being able to work in a coal-mine at that age; in fact, there were not many who managed to live to that age. Edstrom's wife was dying now, and he was having a hard time.

"'Twould not be fair to let such an old gentleman lose his job," said Mary. "But at least he could give ye good advice."

So that evening the two of them went to call on John Edstrom, in a tiny unpainted cabin in "shanty-town," with a bare earth floor, and a half partition of rough boards to hide his dying wife from his callers. The woman's trouble was cancer, and this made calling a trying matter, for there was a fearful odor in the place. For some time it was impossible for Hal to force himself to think about anything else; but finally he overcame this weakness, telling himself that this was a war, and that a man must be ready for the hospital as well as for the parade-ground.

He looked about, and saw that the cracks of Edstrom's cabin were stopped with rags, and the broken windowpanes mended with brown paper. The old man had evidently made an effort to keep the place neat, and Hal noticed a row of books on a shelf. Because it was cold in these mountain regions at night, even in September, the old man had a fire in the little cast-iron stove, and sat huddled by it. There were only a few hairs left on his head, and his scrubby beard was as white as anything could be in a coal-camp. The first impression of his face was of its pallor, and then of the benevolence in the faded dark eyes; also his voice was gentle, like a caress. He rose to greet his visitors, and put out to Hal a trembling hand, which resembled the paw of some animal, horny and misshapen. He made a move to draw up a bench, and apologized for his unskillful house-keeping. It occurred to Hal that a man might be able to work in a coal-mine at sixty, and not be able to work in it at sixty-one.

Hal had requested Mary to say nothing about his purpose, until after he had a chance to judge for himself. So now the girl inquired about Mrs. Edstrom. There was no news, the man answered; she was lying in a stupor, as usual. Dr. Barrett had come again, but all he could do was to give her morphine. No one could do anymore, the doctor declared.

"Sure, he'd not know it if they could!" sniffed Mary.

"He's not such a bad one, when he's sober," said Edstrom, patiently.

"And how often is that?" sniffed Mary again. She added, by way of explanation to Hal, "He's a cousin of the super."

Things were better here than in some places, said Edstrom. At Harvey's Run, where he had worked, a man had got his eye hurt, and had lost it through the doctor's instrument slipping; broken arms and legs had been set wrong, and either the men had to go through life as cripples, or go elsewhere and have the bones re-broken and reset, It was like everything else — the doctor was a part of the company machine, and if you had too much to say about him, it was down the canyon with you. You not only had a dollar a month taken out of your pay, but if you were injured, and he came to attend you, he would charge whatever extra he pleased.

"And you have to pay?" asked Hal.

"They take it off your account," said the old man.

"Sometimes they take it when he's done nothin' at all," added Mary. "They charged Mrs. Zamboni twenty-five dollars for her last baby — and Dr. Barrett never set foot across her door till three hours after the baby was in my arms!"

SECTION 4.

*T*he talk went on. Wishing to draw the old man out, Hal spoke of various troubles of the miners, and at last he suggested that the remedy might be found in a union. Edstrom's dark eyes studied him, and then turned to Mary. "Joe's all right," said the girl, quickly. "You can trust him."

Edstrom made no direct answer to this, but remarked that he had once been in a strike. He was a marked man, now, and could only stay in the camp so long as he attended strictly to his own affairs. The part he had played in the big strike had never been forgotten; the bosses had let him work again, partly because they had needed him at a rush time, and partly because the pit-boss happened to be a personal friend.

"Tell him about the big strike," said Mary. "He's new in this district."

The old man had apparently accepted Mary's word for Hal's good faith, for he began to narrate those terrible events which were a whispered tradition of the camps. There had been a mighty effort of ten thousand slaves for freedom; and it had been crushed with utter ruthlessness. Ever since these mines had been started, the operators had controlled the local powers of government, and now, in the emergency, they had brought in the state militia as well, and used it frankly to drive the strikers back to work. They had seized the leaders and active men, and thrown them into jail without trial or charges; when the jails would hold no more, they kept some two hundred in an open stockade, called a "bull-pen," and finally they loaded them into freight-cars, took them at night out of the state, and dumped them off in the midst of the desert without food or water.

John Edstrom had been one of these men. He told how one of his sons had been beaten and severely injured in jail, and how another had been kept for weeks in a damp cellar, so that he had come out crippled with rheumatism for life. The officers of the state militia had done these things; and when some of the local authorities were moved to protest, the militia had arrested them — even the judges of the civil courts had been forbidden to sit, under threat of imprisonment. "To hell with the constitution!" had been the word of the general in command; his subordinate had made famous the saying, "No habeas corpus; we'll give them post-mortems!"

Tom Olson had impressed Hal with his self-control, but this old man made an even deeper impression upon him. As he listened, he became humble, touched with awe. Incredible as it might seem, when John Edstrom talked about his cruel experiences, it was without bitterness in his voice, and apparently without any in his heart. Here, in the midst of want and desolation, with his family broken and scattered, and the wolf of starvation at his door, he could look back upon the past without hatred of those who had ruined him. Nor was this because he was old and feeble, and had lost the spirit of revolt; it was because he had studied economics, and convinced himself that it was an evil system which blinded men's eyes and poisoned their souls. A better day was coming, he said, when this evil system would be changed, and it would be possible for men to be merciful to one another.

At this point in the conversation, Mary Burke gave voice once more to her corroding despair. How could things ever be changed? The bosses were mean-hearted, and the men were cowards and traitors. That left nobody but God to do the changing — and God had left things as they were for such a long time!

Hal was interested to hear how Edstrom dealt with this attitude. "Mary," he said, "did you ever read about ants in Africa?"

"No," said she.

"They travel in long columns, millions and millions of them. And when they come to a ditch, the front ones fall in, and more and more of them on top, till they fill up the ditch, and the rest cross over. We are ants, Mary."

"No matter how many go in," cried the girl, "none will ever get across. There's no bottom to the ditch!"

He answered: "That's more than any ant can know. Mary. All they know is to go in. They cling to each other's bodies, even in death; they make a bridge, and the rest go over."

"I'll step one side!" she declared, fiercely. "I'll not throw meself away."

"You may step one side," answered the other — "but you'll step back into line again. I know you better than you know yourself, Mary."

There was silence in the little cabin. The winds of an early fall shrilled outside, and life suddenly seemed to Hal a stern and merciless thing. He had thought in his youthful fervor it would be thrilling to be a revolutionist; but to be an ant, one of millions and millions, to perish in a bottomless ditch — that was something a man could hardly bring himself to face! He looked at the bowed figure of this white haired toiler, vague in the feeble lamplight, and found himself thinking of Rembrandt's painting, the Visit of Emmaus: the ill-lighted room in the dirty tavern, and the two ragged men, struck dumb by the glow of light about the forehead of their table-companion. It was not fantastic to imagine a glow of light about the forehead of this soft-voiced old man!

"I never had any hope it would come in my time," the old man was saying gently. "I did use to hope my boys might see it — but now I'm not sure even of that. But in all my life I never doubted that some day the working-people will cross over to the promised land. They'll no longer be slaves, and what they make won't be wasted by idlers. And take it from one who knows, Mary — for a workingman or woman not to have that faith, is to have lost the reason for living."

Hal decided that it would be safe to trust this man, and told him of his check-weighman plan. "We only want your advice," he explained, remembering Mary's warning. "Your sick wife —"

But the old man answered, sadly, "She's almost gone, and I'll soon be following. What little strength I have left might as well be used for the cause."

SECTION 5.

*T*his business of conspiracy was grimly real to men whose living came out of coal; but Hal, even at the most serious moments, continued to find in it the thrill of romance. He had read stories of revolutionists, and of the police who hunted them. That such excitements were to be had in Russia, he knew; but if anyone had told him they could be had in his own free America, within a few hours' journey of his home city and his college-town, he could not have credited the statement.

The evening after his visit to Edstrom, Hal was stopped on the street by his boss. Encountering him suddenly, Hal started, like a pick-pocket who runs into a policeman.

"Hello, kid," said the pit-boss.

"Hello, Mr. Stone," was the reply.

"I want to talk to you," said the boss.

"All right, sir." And then, under his breath, "He's got me!"

"Come up to my house," said Stone; and Hal followed, feeling as if hand-cuffs were already on his wrists.

"Say," said the man, as they walked, "I thought you were going to tell me if you'd heard any talk."

"I haven't heard any, sir."

"Well," continued Stone, "you want to get busy; there's sure to be kickers in every coal-camp." And deep within, Hal drew a sigh of relief. It was a false alarm!

They came to the boss's house, and he took a chair on the piazza and motioned Hal to take another. They sat in semi-darkness, and Stone dropped his voice as he began. "What I want to talk to you about now is something else — this election."

"Election, sir?"

"Didn't you know there was one? The Congressman in this district died, and there's a special election three weeks from next Tuesday."

"I see, sir." And Hal chuckled inwardly. He would get the information which Tom Olson had recommended to him!

"You ain't heard any talk about it?" inquired the pit-boss.

"Nothing at all, sir. I never pay much attention to politics — it ain't in my line."

"Well, that's the way I like to hear a miner talk!" said the pit-boss, with heartiness. "If they all had sense enough to leave politics to the politicians, they'd be a sight better off. What they need is to tend to their own jobs."

"Yes, sir," agreed Hal, meekly — "like I had to tend to them mules, if I didn't want to get the colic."

The boss smiled appreciatively. "You've got more sense than most of 'em. If you'll stand by me, there'll be a chance for you to move up in the world."

"Thank you, Mr. Stone," said Hal. "Give me a chance."

"Well now, here's this election. Every year they send us a bunch of campaign money to handle. A bit of it might come your way."

"I could use it, I reckon," said Hal, brightening visibly. "What is it you want?"

There was a pause, while Stone puffed on his pipe. He went on, in a businesslike manner. "What I want is somebody to feel things out a bit, and let me know the situation. I thought it better not to use the men that generally work for me, but somebody that wouldn't be suspected. Down in Sheridan and Pedro they say the Democrats are making a big stir, and the company's worried. I suppose you know the 'G.F.C.' is Republican."

"I've heard so."

"You might think a congressman don't have much to do with us, way off in Washington; but it has a bad effect to have him campaigning, telling the men the company's abusing them. So I'd like you just to kind o' circulate a bit, and start the men on politics, and see if any of them have been listening to this MacDougall talk. (MacDougall's this here Democrat, you know.) And I want to find out whether they've been sending in literature to this camp, or have any agents here. You see, they claim the right to come in and make speeches, and all that sort of thing. North Valley's an incorporated town, so they've got the law on their side, in a way, and if we shut 'em out, they make a howl in the papers, and it looks bad. So we have to get ahead of them in quiet ways. Fortunately there ain't any hall in the camp for them to meet in, and we've made a local ordinance against meetings on the street. If they try to bring in circulars, something has to happen to them before they get distributed. See?"

"I see," said Hal; he thought of Tom Olson's propaganda literature!

"We'll pass the word out, — it's the Republican the company wants elected; and you be on the lookout and see how they take it in the camp."

"That sounds easy enough," said Hal. "But tell me, Mr. Stone, why do you bother? Do so many of these wops have votes?"

"It ain't the wops so much. We get them naturalized on purpose — they vote our way for a glass of beer. But the English-speaking men, or the foreigners that's been here too long, and got too big for their breeches — they're the ones we got to watch. If they get to talking politics, they don't stop there; the first thing you know, they're listening to union agitators, and wanting to run the camp."

"Oh yes, I see!" said Hal, and wondered if his voice sounded right.

But the pit-boss was concerned with his own troubles. "As I told Si Adams the other day, what I'm looking for is fellows that talk some new lingo — one that nobody will ever understand! But I suppose that would be too easy. There's no way to keep them from learning some English!"

Hal decided to make use of this opportunity to perfect his education. "Surely, Mr. Stone," he remarked, "you don't have to count any votes if you don't want to!"

"Well, I'll tell you," replied Stone; "it's a question of the easiest way to manage things. When I was superintendent over to Happy Gulch, we didn't waste no time on politics. The company was Democratic at that time, and when election night come, we wrote down four hundred votes for the Democratic candidates. But the first thing we knew, a bunch of fellers was taken into town and got to swear they'd voted the Republican ticket in our camp. The Republican papers were full of it, and some fool judge ordered a recount, and we had to get busy over night and mark up a new lot of ballots. It gave us a lot of bother!"

The pit-boss laughed, and Hal joined him discreetly.

"So you see, you have to learn to manage. If there's votes for the wrong candidate in your camp, the fact gets out, and if the returns is too one-sided, there's a lot of grumbling. There's plenty of bosses that don't care, but I learned my lesson that time, and I got my own method

— that is not to let any opposition start. See?"

"Yes, I see."

"Maybe a mine-boss has got no right to meddle in politics — but there's one thing he's got the say about, and that is who works in his mine. It's the easiest thing to weed out — weed out —" Hal never forgot the motion of beefy hands with which Alec Stone illustrated these words. As he went on, the tones of his voice did not seem so good-natured as usual. "The fellows that don't want to vote my way can go somewhere else to do their voting. That's all I got to say on politics!"

There was a brief pause, while Stone puffed on his pipe. Then it may have occurred to him that it was not necessary to go into so much detail in breaking in a political recruit. When he resumed, it was in a good-natured tone of dismissal. "That's what you do, kid. Tomorrow you get a sprained wrist, so you can't work for a few days, and that'll give you a chance to bum round and hear what the men are saying. Meantime, I'll see you get your wages."

"That sounds all right," said Hal; but showing only a small part of his satisfaction!

The pit-boss rose from his chair and knocked the ashes from his pipe. "Mind you — I want the goods. I've got other fellows working, and I'm comparing 'em. For all you know, I may have somebody watching you."

"Yes," said Hal, and grinned cheerfully. "I'll not fail to bear that in mind."

SECTION 6.

*T*he first thing Hal did was to seek out Tom Olson and narrate this experience. The two of them had a merry time over it. "I'm the favorite of a boss now!" laughed Hal.

But the organizer became suddenly serious. "Be careful what you do for that fellow."

"Why?"

"He might use it on you later on. One of the things they try to do if you make any trouble for them, is to prove that you took money from them, or tried to."

"But he won't have any proofs."

"That's my point — don't give him any. If Stone says you've been playing the political game for him, then some fellow might remember that you did ask him about politics. So don't have any marked money on you."

Hal laughed. "Money doesn't stay on me very long these days. But what shall I say if he asks me for a report?"

"You'd better put your job right through, Joe — so that he won't have time to ask for any report."

"All right," was the reply. "But just the same, I'm going to get all the fun there is, being the favorite of a boss!"

And so, early the next morning when Hal went to his work he proceeded to "sprain his wrist." He walked about in pain, to the great concern of Old Mike; and when finally he decided that he would have to lay off, Mike followed him half way to the shaft, giving him advice about hot and cold cloths. Leaving the old Slovak to struggle along as best he could alone, Hal went out to bask in the wonderful sunshine of the upper world, and the still more wonderful sunshine of a boss's favor.

First he went to his room at Reminitsky's, and tied a strip of old shirt about his wrist, and a clean handkerchief on top of that; by this symbol he was entitled to the freedom of the camp and the sympathy of all men, and so he sallied forth.

Strolling towards the tipple of Number One, he encountered a wiry, quick-moving little man, with restless black eyes and a lean, intelligent face. He wore a pair of common miner's "jumpers," but even so, he was not to be taken for a workingman. Everything about him spoke of authority.

"Morning, Mr. Cartwright," said Hal.

"Good morning," replied the superintendent; then, with a glance at Hal's bandage, "You hurt?"

"Yes, sir. Just a bit of sprain, but I thought I'd better lay off."

"Been to the doctor?"

"No, sir. I don't think it's that bad."

"You'd better go. You never know how bad a sprain is."

"Right, sir," said Hal. Then, as the superintendent was passing, "Do you think, Mr. Cartwright, that MacDougall stands any chance of being elected?"

"I don't know," replied the other, surprised. "I hope not. You aren't going to vote for him, are you?"

"Oh, no. I'm a Republican — born that way. But I wondered if you'd heard any MacDougall talk."

"Well, I'm hardly the one that would hear it. You take an interest in politics?"

"Yes, sir — in a way. In fact, that's how I came to get this wrist."

"How's that? In a fight?"

"No, sir; but you see, Mr. Stone wanted me to feel out sentiment in the camp, and he told me I'd better sprain my wrist and lay off."

The "super," after staring at Hal, could not keep from laughing. Then he looked about him. "You want to be careful, talking about such things."

"I thought I could surely trust the superintendent," said Hal, dryly.

The other measured him with his keen eyes; and Hal, who was getting the spirit of political democracy, took the liberty of returning the gaze. "You're a wide-awake young fellow," said Cartwright, at last. "Learn the ropes here, and make yourself useful, and I'll see you're not passed over."

"All right, sir — thank you."

"Maybe you'll be made an election-clerk this time. That's worth three dollars a day, you know."

"Very good, sir." And Hal put on his smile again. "They tell me you're the mayor of North Valley."

"I am."

"And the justice of the peace is a clerk in your store. Well, Mr. Cartwright, if you need a president of the board of health or a dog catcher, I'm your man — as soon, that is, as my wrist gets well."

And so Hal went on his way. Such "joshing" on the part of a "buddy" was of course absurdly presumptuous; the superintendent stood looking after him with a puzzled frown upon his face.

SECTION 7.

*H*al did not look back, but turned into the company-store. "North Valley Trading Company" read the sign over the door; within was a Serbian woman pointing out what she wanted to buy, and two little Lithuanian girls watching the weighing of a pound of sugar. Hal strolled up to the person who was doing the weighing, a middle-aged man with a yellow moustache stained with tobacco-juice. "Morning, Judge."

"Huh!" was the reply from Silas Adams, justice of the peace in the town of North Valley.

"Judge," said Hal, "what do you think about the election?"

"I don't think about it," said the other. "Busy weighin' sugar."

"Anybody round here going to vote for MacDougall?"

"They better not tell me if they are!"

"What?" smiled Hal. "In this free American republic?"

"In this part of the free American republic a man is free to dig coal, but not to vote for a skunk like MacDougall." Then, having tied up the sugar, the "J.P." whittled off a fresh chew from his plug, and turned to Hal. "What'll you have?"

Hal purchased half a pound of dried peaches, so that he might have an excuse to loiter, and be able to keep time with the jaws of the Judge. While the order was being filled, he seated himself upon the counter. "You know," said he, "I used to work in a grocery."

"That so? Where at?"

"Peterson & Co., in American City." Hal had told this so often that he had begun to believe it.

"Pay pretty good up there?"

"Yes, pretty fair." Then, realizing that he had no idea what would constitute good pay in a grocery, Hal added, quickly, "Got a bad wrist here!"

"That so?" said the other.

He did not show much sociability; but Hal persisted, refusing to believe that anyone in a country store would miss an opening to discuss politics, even with a miner's helper. "Tell me," said he, "just what is the matter with MacDougall?"

"The matter with him," said the Judge, "is that the company's against him." He looked hard at the young miner. "You meddlin' in politics?" he growled. But the young miner's gay brown eyes showed only appreciation of the earlier response; so the "J.P." was tempted into specifying the would-be congressman's vices. Thus conversation started; and pretty soon the others in the store joined in — "Bob" Johnson, bookkeeper and post-master, and "Jake" Predovich, the Galician Jew who was a member of the local school-board, and knew the words for staple groceries in fifteen languages.

Hal listened to an exposition of the crimes of the political opposition in Pedro County. Their candidate, MacDougall, had come to the state as a "tin-horn gambler," yet now he was going around making speeches in churches, and talking about the moral sentiment of the community. "And him with a district chairman keeping three families in Pedro!" declared Si Adams.

"Well," ventured Hal, "if what I hear is true, the Republican chairman isn't a plaster saint. They say he was drunk at the convention —"

"Maybe so," said the "J.P." "But we ain't playin' for the prohibition vote; and we ain't playin' for the labor vote — tryin' to stir up the riff-raff in these coal-camps, promisin' 'em high wages an' short hours. Don't he know he can't get it for 'em? But he figgers he'll go off to Washington and leave us here to deal with the mess he's stirred up!"

"Don't you fret," put in Bob Johnson — "he ain't goin' to no Washin'ton."

The other two agreed, and Hal ventured again, "He says you stuff the ballot-boxes."

"What do you suppose his crowd is doin' in the cities? We got to meet 'em some way, ain't we?"

"Oh, I see," said Hal, naïvely. "You stuff them worse!"

"Sometimes we stuff the boxes, and sometimes we stuff the voters." There was an appreciative titter from the others, and the "J.P." was moved to reminiscence. "Two years ago I was election clerk, over to Sheridan, and we found we'd let 'em get ahead of us — they had carried the whole state. 'By God,' said Alf. Raymond, 'we'll show 'em a trick from the coal-counties! And there won't be no recount business either!' So we held back our returns till the rest had come in, and when we seen how many votes we needed, we wrote 'em down. And that settled it."

"That seems a simple method," remarked Hal. "They'll have to get up early to beat Alf."

"You bet you!" said Si, with the complacency of one of the gang. "They call this county the 'Empire of Raymond.'"

"It must be a cinch," said Hal — "being the sheriff, and having the naming of so many deputies as they need in these coal-camps!"

"Yes," agreed the other. "And there's his wholesale liquor business, too. If you want a license in Pedro county, you not only vote for Alf, but you pay your bills on time!"

"Must be a fortune in that!" remarked Hal; and the Judge, the Post-master and the School-commissioner appeared like children listening to a story of a feast. "You bet you!"

"I suppose it takes money to run politics in this county," Hal added.

"Well, Alf don't put none of it up, you can bet! That's the company's job."

This from the Judge; and the School-commissioner added, "De coin in dese camps is beer."

"Oh, I see!" laughed Hal. "The companies buy Alf's beer, and use it to get him votes!"

"Sure thing!" said the Post-master.

At this moment he happened to reach into his pocket for a cigar, and Hal observed a silver shield on the breast of his waistcoat. "That a deputy's badge?" he inquired, and then turned to examine the School-commissioner's costume. "Where's yours?"

"I git mine ven election comes," said Jake, with a grin.

"And yours, Judge?"

"I'm a justice of the peace, young feller," said Silas, with dignity.

Leaning round, and observing a bulge on the right hip of the School-commissioner, Hal put out his hand towards it. Instinctively the other moved his hand to the spot.

Hal turned to the Post-master. "Yours?" he asked.

"Mine's under the counter," grinned Bob.

"And yours, Judge?"

"Mine's in the desk," said the Judge.

Hal drew a breath. "Gee!" said he. "It's like a steel trap!" He managed to keep the laugh on his face, but within he was conscious of other feelings than those of amusement. He was losing that "first fine careless rapture" with which he had set out to run with the hare and the hounds in North Valley!

SECTION 8.

*T*wo days after this beginning of Hal's political career, it was arranged that the workers who were to make a demand for a check-weighman should meet in the home of Mrs. David. When Mike Sikoria came up from the pit that day, Hal took him aside and told him of the gathering. A look of delight came upon the old Slovak's face as he listened; he grabbed his buddy by the shoulders, crying, "You mean it?"

"Sure meant it," said Hal. "You want to be on the committee to go and see the boss?"

"Pluha biedna!" cried Mike — which is something dreadful in his own language. "By Judas, I pack up my old box again!"

Hal felt a guilty pang. Should he let this old man into the thing? "You think you'll have to move out of camp?" he asked.

"Move out of state this time! Move back to old country, maybe!" And Hal realized that he could not stop him now, even if he wanted to. The old fellow was so much excited that he hardly ate any supper, and his buddy was afraid to leave him alone, for fear he might blurt out the news.

It had been agreed that those who attended the meeting should come one by one, and by different routes. Hal was one of the first to arrive, and he saw that the shades of the house had been drawn, and the lamps turned low. He entered by the back door, where "Big Jack" David stood on guard. "Big Jack," who had been a member of the South Wales Federation at home, made sure of Hal's identity, and then passed him in without a word.

Inside was Mike — the first on hand. Mrs. David, a little black-eyed woman with a never-ceasing tongue, was bustling about, putting things in order; she was so nervous that she could not sit still. This couple had come from their birth-place only a year or so ago, and had brought all their wedding presents to their new home — pictures and bric-a-brac and linen. It was the prettiest home Hal had so far been in, and Mrs. David was risking it deliberately, because of her indignation that her husband had had to foreswear his union in order to get work in America.

The young Italian, Rovetta, came, then old John Edstrom. There being not chairs enough in the house, Mrs. David had set some boxes against the wall, covering them with cloth; and Hal noticed that each person took one of these boxes, leaving the chairs for the later comers. Each one as he came in would nod to the others, and then silence would fall again.

When Mary Burke entered, Hal divined from her aspect and manner that she had sunk back into her old mood of pessimism. He felt a momentary resentment. He was so thrilled with this adventure; he wanted everybody else to be thrilled — especially Mary! Like everyone who has not suffered much, he was repelled by a condition of perpetual suffering in another. Of course Mary had good reasons for her black moods — but she herself considered it necessary to apologize for what she called her "complainin'!" She knew that he wanted her to help encourage the others; but here she was, putting herself in a corner and watching this wonderful proceeding, as if she had said: "I'm an ant, and I stay in line — but I'll not pretend I have any hope in it!"

Rosa and Jerry had insisted on coming, in spite of Hal's offer to spare them. After them came the Bulgarian, Wresmak; then the Polacks, Klowoski and Zamierowski. Hal found these difficult names to remember, but the Polacks were not at all sensitive about this; they would grin good-naturedly while he practiced, nor would they mind if he gave it up and called them Tony and Pete. They were humble men, accustomed all their lives to being driven about. Hal looked from one to another of their bowed forms and toil-worn faces, appearing more than ever somber and mournful in the dim light; he wondered if the cruel persecution which had driven them to protest would suffice to hold them in line.

Once a newcomer, having misunderstood the orders, came to the front door and knocked; and Hal noted that everyone started, and some rose to their feet in alarm. Again he recognized the atmosphere of novels of Russian revolutionary life. He had to remind himself that these men and women, gathered here like criminals, were merely planning to ask for a right guaranteed them by the law!

The last to come was an Austrian miner named Huszar, with whom Olson had got into touch. Then, it being time to begin, everybody looked uneasily at everybody else. Few of them had conspired before, and they did not know quite how to set about it. Olson, the one who would naturally have been their leader, had deliberately stayed away. They must run this check-weighman affair for themselves!

"Somebody talk," said Mrs. David at last; and then, as the silence continued, she turned to Hal. "You're going to be the check-weighman. You talk."

"I'm the youngest man here," said Hal, with a smile. "Some older fellow talk."

But nobody else smiled. "Go on!" exclaimed old Mike; and so at last Hal stood up. It was something he was to experience many times in the future; because he was an American, and educated, he was forced into a position of leadership.

"As I understand it, you people want a check-weighman. Now, they tell me the pay for a check-weighman should be three dollars a day, but we've got only seven miners among us, and that's not enough. I will offer to take the job for twenty-five cents a day from each man, which will make a dollar-seventy-five, less than what I'm getting now as a buddy. If we get thirty men to come in, then I'll take ten cents a day from each, and make the full three dollars. Does that seem fair?"

"Sure!" said Mike; and the others added their assent by word or nod.

"All right. Now, there's nobody that works in this mine but knows the men don't get their weight. It would cost the company several hundred dollars a day to give us our weight, and nobody should be so foolish as to imagine they'll do it without a struggle. We've got to make up our minds to stand together."

"Sure, stand together!" cried Mike.

"No get check-weighman!" exclaimed Jerry, pessimistically.

"Not unless we try, Jerry," said Hal.

And Mike thumped his knee. "Sure try! And get him too!"

"Right!" cried "Big Jack." But his little wife was not satisfied with the response of the others. She gave Hal his first lesson in the drilling of these polyglot masses.

"Talk to them. Make them understand you!" And she pointed them out one by one with her finger: "You! You! Wresmak, here, and you, Klowoski, and you, Zam — you other Polish fellow. Want check-weighman. Want to get all weight. Get all our money. Understand?"

"Yes, yes!"

"Get committee, go see super! Want check-weighman. Understand? Got to have check-weighman! No back down, no scare."

"No — no scare!" Klowoski, who understood some English, explained rapidly to Zamierowski; and Zamierowski, whose head was still plastered where Jeff Cotton's revolver had hit it, nodded eagerly in assent. In spite of his bruises, he would stand by the others, and face the boss.

This suggested another question. "Who's going to do the talking to the boss?"

"You do that," said Mrs. David, to Hal.

"But I'm the one that's to be paid. It's not for me to talk."

"No one else can do it right," declared the woman.

"Sure — got to be American feller!" said Mike.

But Hal insisted. If he did the talking, it would look as if the check-weighman had been the source of the movement, and was engaged in making a good paying job for himself.

There was discussion back and forth, until finally John Edstrom spoke up. "Put me on the committee."

"You?" said Hal. "But you'll be thrown out! And what will your wife do?"

"I think my wife is going to die tonight," said Edstrom, simply.

He sat with his lips set tightly, looking straight before him. After a pause he went on: "If it isn't tonight, it will be tomorrow, the doctor says; and after that, nothing will matter. I shall have to go down to Pedro to bury her, and if I have to stay, it will make little difference to me, so I might as well do what I can for the rest of you. I've been a miner all my life, and Mr. Cartwright knows it; that might have some weight with him. Let Joe Smith and Sikoria and myself be the ones to go and see him, and the rest of you wait, and don't give up your jobs unless you have to."

SECTION 9.

*H*aving settled the matter of the committee, Hal told the assembly how Alec Stone had asked him to spy upon the men. He thought they should know about it; the bosses might try to use it against him, as

Olson had warned. "They may tell you I'm a traitor," he said. "You must trust me."

"We trust you!" exclaimed Mike, with fervor; and the others nodded their agreement.

"All right," Hal answered. "You can rest sure of this one thing — if I get onto that tipple, you're going to get your weights!"

"Hear, hear!" cried "Big Jack," in English fashion. And a murmur ran about the room. They did not dare make much noise, but they made clear that that was what they wanted.

Hal sat down, and began to unroll the bandage from his wrist. "I guess I'm through with this," he said, and explained how he had come to wear it.

"What?" cried Old Mike. "You fool me like that?" And he caught the wrist, and when he had made sure there was no sign of swelling upon it, he shook it so that he almost sprained it really, laughing until the tears ran down his cheeks. "You old son-of-a-gun!" he exclaimed. Meantime Klowoski was telling the story to Zamierowski, and Jerry Minetti was explaining it to Wresmak, in the sort of pidgin-English which does duty in the camps. Hal had never seen such real laughter since coming to North Valley.

But conspirators cannot lend themselves long to merriment. They came back to business again. It was agreed that the hour for the committee's visit to the superintendent should be quitting-time on the morrow. And then John Edstrom spoke, suggesting that they should agree upon their course of action in case they were offered violence.

"You think there's much chance of that?" said someone.

"Sure there be!" cried Mike Sikoria. "One time in Cedar Mountain we go see boss, say air-course blocked. What you think he do them fellers? He hit them one lick in nose, he kick them three times in behind, he run them out!"

"Well," said Hal, "if there's going to be anything like that, we must be ready."

"What you do?" demanded Jerry.

It was time for Hal's leadership. "If he hits me one lick in the nose," he declared, "I'll hit him one lick in the nose, that's all."

There was a bit of applause at this. That was the way to talk! Hal tasted the joys of his leadership. But then his fine self-confidence met with a sudden check — a "lick in the nose" of his pride, so to speak. There came a woman's voice from the corner, low and grim: "Yes! And get ye'self killed for all your trouble!"

He looked towards Mary Burke, and saw her vivid face, flushed and frowning. "What do you mean?" he asked. "Would you have us turn and run away?"

"I would that!" said she. "Rather than have ye killed, I would! What'll ye do if he pulls his gun on ye?"

"Would he pull his gun on a committee?"

Old Mike broke in again. "One time in Barela — ain't I told you how I lose my cars? I tell weigh-boss somebody steal my cars, and he pull gun on me, and he say, 'Get the hell off that tipple, you old billy goat, I shoot you full of holes!'"

Among his class-mates at college, Hal had been wont to argue that the proper way to handle a burglar was to call out to him, saying, "Go ahead, old chap, and help yourself; there's nothing here I'm willing to get shot for." What was the value of anything a burglar could steal, in comparison with a man's own life? And surely, one would have thought, this was a good time to apply the plausible theory. But for some reason Hal failed even to remember it. He was going ahead, precisely as if a ton of coal per day was the one thing of consequence in life!

"What shall we do?" he asked. "We don't want to back out."

But even while he asked the question, Hal was realizing that Mary was right. His was the attitude of the leisure-class person, used to having his own way; but Mary, though she had a temper too, was pointing the lesson of self-control. It was the second time tonight that she had injured his pride. But now he forgave her in his admiration; he had always known that Mary had a mind and could help him! His admiration was increased by what John Edstrom was saying — they must do nothing that would injure the cause of the "big union," and so they must resolve to offer no physical resistance, no matter what might be done to them.

There was vehement argument on the other side. "We fight! We fight!" declared Old Mike, and cried out suddenly, as if in anticipation of the pain in his injured nose. "You say me stand that?"

"If you fight back," said Edstrom, "we'll all get the worst of it. The company will say we started the trouble, and put us in the wrong. We've got to make up our mind to rely on moral force."

So, after more discussion, it was agreed; every man would keep his temper — that is, if he could! So they shook hands all round, pledging themselves to stand firm. But, when the meeting was declared adjourned, and they stole out one by one into the night, they were a very sober and anxious lot of conspirators.

SECTION 10.

*H*al slept but little that night. Amid the sounds of the snoring of eight of Reminitsky's other boarders, he lay going over in his mind various things which might happen on the morrow. Some of them were far from pleasant things; he tried to picture himself with a broken nose, or with tar and feathers on him. He recalled his theory as to the handling of burglars. The "G.F.C." was a burglar of gigantic and terrible proportions; surely this was a time to call out, "Help yourself!" But instead of doing it, Hal thought about Edstrom's ants, and wondered at the power which made them stay in line.

When morning came, he went up into the mountains, where a man may wander and renew his moral force. When the sun had descended behind the mountaintops, he descended also, and met Edstrom and Sikoria in front of the company office.

They nodded a greeting, and Edstrom told Hal that his wife had died during the day. There being no undertaker in North Valley, he had arranged for a woman friend to take the body down to Pedro, so that he might be free for the interview with Cartwright. Hal put his hand on the old man's shoulder, but attempted no word of condolence; he saw that Edstrom had faced the trouble and was ready for duty.

"Come ahead," said the old man, and the three went into the office. While a clerk took their message to the inner office, they stood for a couple of minutes, shifting uneasily from one foot to the other, and turning their caps in their hands in the familiar manner of the lowly.

At last Mr. Cartwright appeared in the doorway, his small sparely-built figure eloquent of sharp authority. "Well, what's this?" he inquired.

"If you please," said Edstrom, "we'd like to speak to you. We've decided, sir, that we want to have a check-weighman."

"*What?*" The word came like the snap of a whip.

"We'd like to have a check-weighman, sir."

There was a moment's silence. "Come in here." They filed into the inner office, and he shut the door.

"Now. What's this?"

Edstrom repeated his words again.

"What put that notion into your heads?"

"Nothing, sir; only we thought we'd be better satisfied."

"You think you're not getting your weight?"

"Well, sir, you see — some of the men — we think it would be better if we had the check-weighman. We're willing to pay for him."

"Who's this check-weighman to be?"

"Joe Smith, here."

Hal braced himself to meet the other's stare. "Oh! So it's you!" Then, after a moment, "So that's why you were feeling so gay!"

Hal was not feeling in the least gay at the moment; but he forbore to say so. There was a silence.

"Now, why do you fellows want to throw away your money?" The superintendent started to argue with them, showing the absurdity of the notion that they could gain anything by such a course. The mine had been running for years on its present system, and there had never been any complaint. The idea that a company as big and as responsible as the "G.F.C." would stoop to cheat its workers out of a few tons of coal! And so on, for several minutes.

"Mr. Cartwright," said Edstrom, when the other had finished, "you know I've worked all my life in mines, and most of it in this district. I am telling you something I know when I say there is general dissatisfaction throughout these camps because the men feel they are not getting their weight. You say there has been no public complaint; you understand the reason for this —"

"What is the reason?"

"Well," said Edstrom, gently, "maybe you don't know the reason — but anyway we've decided that we want a check-weighman."

It was evident that the superintendent had been taken by surprise, and was uncertain how to meet the issue. "You can imagine," he said, at last, "the company doesn't relish hearing that its men believe it's cheating them —"

"We don't say the company knows anything about it, Mr. Cartwright. It's possible that some people may be taking advantage of us, without either the company or yourself having anything to do with it. It's for your protection as well as ours that a check-weighman is needed."

"Thank you," said the other, dryly. His tone revealed that he was holding himself in by an effort. "Very well," he added, at last. "That's enough about the matter, if your minds are made up. I'll give you my decision later."

This was a dismissal, and Mike Sikoria turned humbly, and started to the door. But Edstrom was one of the ants that did not readily "step one side"; and Mike took a glance at him, and then stepped back into line in a hurry, as if hoping his delinquency had not been noted.

"If you please, Mr. Cartwright," said Edstrom, "we'd like your decision, so as to have the check-weighman start in the morning."

"What? You're in such a hurry?"

"There's no reason for delay, sir. We've selected our man, and we're ready to pay him."

"Who are the men who are ready to pay him? Just you two"

"I am not at liberty to name the other men, sir."

"Oh! So it's a secret movement!"

"In a way — yes, sir."

"Indeed!" said the superintendent, ominously. "And you don't care what the company thinks about it!"

"It's not that, Mr. Cartwright, but we don't see anything for the company to object to. It's a simple business arrangement —"

"Well, if it seems simple to you, it doesn't to me," snapped the other. And then, getting himself in hand, "Understand me, the company would not have the least objection to the men making sure of their weights, if they really think it's necessary. The company has always been willing to do the right thing. But it's not a matter that can be settled off hand. I will let you know later."

Again they were dismissed, and again Old Mike turned, and Edstrom also. But now another ant sprang into the ditch. "Just when will you be prepared to let the check-weighman begin work, Mr. Cartwright?" asked Hal.

The superintendent gave him a sharp look, and again it could be seen that he made a strong effort to keep his temper. "I'm not prepared to say," he replied. "I will let you know, as soon as convenient to me. That's all now." And as he spoke he opened the door, putting something into the action that was a command.

"Mr. Cartwright," said Hal, "there's no law against our having a check-weighman, is there?"

The look which these words drew from the superintendent showed that he knew full well what the law was. Hal accepted this look as an answer, and continued, "I have been selected by a committee of the men to act as their check-weighman, and this committee has duly notified the company. That makes me a check-weighman, I believe, Mr. Cartwright, and so all I have to do is to assume my duties." Without waiting for the superintendent's answer, he walked to the door, followed by his somewhat shocked companions.

SECTION 11.

*A*t the meeting on the night before it had been agreed to spread the news of the check-weighman movement, for the sake of its propaganda value. So now when the three men came out from the office, there was a crowd waiting to know what had happened; men clamored questions, and each one who got the story would be surrounded by others eager to hear. Hal made his way to the boarding-house, and when he had finished his supper, he set out from place to place in the camp, telling the men about the check-weighman plan and explaining that it was a legal right they were demanding. All this while Old Mike stayed on one side of him, and Edstrom on the other; for Tom Olson had insisted strenuously that Hal should not be left alone for a moment. Evidently the bosses had given the same order; for when Hal came out from Reminitsky's, there was "Jake" Predovich, the store-clerk, on the fringe of the crowd, and he followed wherever Hal went, doubtless making note of everyone he spoke to.

They consulted as to where they were to spend the night. Old Mike was nervous, taking the activities of the spy to mean that they were to be thugged in the darkness. He told horrible stories of that sort of thing. What could be an easier way for the company to settle the matter? They would fix up some story; the world outside would believe they had been killed in a drunken row, perhaps over some woman. This last suggestion especially troubled Hal; he thought of the people at home. No, he must not sleep in the village! And on the other hand he could not go down the canyon, for if he once passed the gate, he might not be allowed to repass it.

An idea occurred to him. Why not go *up* the canyon? There was no stockade at the upper end of the village — nothing but wilderness and rocks, without even a road.

"But where we sleep?" demanded Old Mike, aghast.

"Outdoors," said Hal.

"*Pluha biedna!* And get the night air into my bones?"

"You think you keep the day air in your bones when you sleep inside?" laughed Hal.

"Why don't I, when I shut them windows tight, and cover up my bones?"

"Well, risk the night air once," said Hal. "It's better than having somebody let it into you with a knife."

"But that fellow Predovich — he follow us up canyon too!"

"Yes, but he's only one man, and we don't have to fear him. If he went back for others, he'd never be able to find us in the darkness."

Edstrom, whose notions of anatomy were not so crude as Mike's, gave his support to this suggestion; so they got their blankets and stumbled up the canyon in the still, star-lit night. For a while they heard the spy behind them, but finally his footsteps died away, and after they had moved on for some distance, they believed they were safe till daylight. Hal had slept out many a night as a hunter, but it was a new adventure to sleep out as the game!

At dawn they rose, and shook the dew from their blankets, and wiped it from their eyes. Hal was young, and saw the glory of the morning, while poor Mike Sikoria groaned and grumbled over his stiff and aged joints. He thought he had ruined himself forever, but he took courage at Edstrom's mention of coffee, and they hurried down to breakfast at their boarding-house.

Now came a critical time, when Hal had to be left by himself. Edstrom was obliged to go down to see to his wife's funeral; and it was obvious that if Mike Sikoria were to lay off work, he would be providing the boss with an excuse for firing him. The law which provided for a check-weighman had failed to provide for a check-weighman's body-guard!

Hal had announced his program in that flash of defiance in Cartwright's office. As soon as work started up, he went to the tipple. "Mr. Peters," he said, to the tipple-boss, "I've come to act as check-weighman."

The tipple-boss was a man with a big black moustache, which made him look like the pictures of Nietzsche. He stared at Hal, frankly dumbfounded. "What the devil?" said he.

"Some of the men have chosen me check-weighman," explained Hal, in a businesslike manner. "When their cars come up, I'll see to their weights."

"You keep off this tipple, young fellow!" said Peters. His manner was equally businesslike.

So the would-be check-weighman came out and sat on the steps to wait. The tipple was a fairly public place, and he judged he was as safe there as anywhere. Some of the men grinned and winked at him as they went about their work; several found a chance to whisper words of encouragement. And all morning he sat, like a protestant at the palace-gates of a mandarin in China, It was tedious work, but he believed that he would be able to stand it longer than the company.

SECTION 12.

*I*n the middle of the morning a man came up to him — "Bud" Adams, a younger brother of the "J.P.," and Jeff Cotton's assistant. Bud was stocky, red-faced, and reputed to be handy with his fists. So Hal rose up warily when he saw him.

"Hey, you," said Bud. "There's a telegram at the office for you."

"For me?"

"Your name's Joe Smith, ain't it?"

"Yes."

"Well, that's what it says."

Hal considered for a moment. There was no one to be telegraphing Joe Smith. It was only a ruse to get him away.

"What's in the telegram?" he asked.

"How do I know?" said Bud.

"Where is it from?"

"I dunno that."

"Well," said Hal, "you might bring it to me here."

The other's eyes flew open. This was not a revolt, it was a revolution! "Who the hell's messenger boy do you think I am?" he demanded.

"Don't the company deliver telegrams?" countered Hal, politely. And Bud stood struggling with his human impulses, while Hal watched him cautiously. But apparently those who had sent the messenger had given him precise instructions; for he controlled his wrath, and turned and strode away.

Hal continued his vigil. He had his lunch with him; and was prepared to eat alone — understanding the risk that a man would be running who showed sympathy with him. He was surprised, therefore, when Johannson, the giant Swede, came and sat down by his side. There also came a young Mexican laborer, and a Greek miner. The revolution was spreading!

Hal felt sure the company would not let this go on. And sure enough, towards the middle of the afternoon, the tipple-boss came out and beckoned to him. "Come here, you!" And Hal went in.

The "weigh-room" was a fairly open place; but at one side was a door into an office. "This way," said the man.

But Hal stopped where he was.

"This is where the check-weighman belongs, Mr. Peters."

"But I want to talk to you."

"I can hear you, sir." Hal was in sight of the men, and he knew that was his only protection.

The tipple-boss went back into the office; and a minute later Hal saw what had been intended. The door opened and Alec Stone came out.

He stood for a moment looking at his political henchman. Then he came up. "Kid," he said, in a low voice, "you're overdoing this. I didn't intend you to go so far."

"This is not what you intended, Mr. Stone," answered Hal.

The pit-boss came closer yet. "What you looking for, kid? What you expect to get out of this?"

Hal's gaze was unwavering. "Experience," he replied.

"You're feeling smart, sonny. But you'd better stop and realize what you're up against. You ain't going to get away with it, you know; get that through your head — you ain't going to get away with it. You'd better come in and have a talk with me."

There was a silence.

"Don't you know how it'll be, Smith? These little fires start up — but we put 'em out. We know how to do it, we've got the machinery. It'll all be forgotten in a week or two, and then where'll you be at? Can't you see?"

As Hal still made no reply, the other's voice dropped lower. "I understand your position. Just give me a nod, and it'll be all right. You tell the men that you've watched the weights, and that they're all right. They'll be satisfied, and you and me can fix it up later."

"Mr. Stone," said Hal, with intense gravity, "am I correct in the impression that you are offering me a bribe?"

In a flash, the man's self-control vanished. He thrust his huge fist within an inch of Hal's nose, and uttered a foul oath. But Hal did not remove his nose from the danger-zone, and over the fist a pair of angry brown eyes gazed at the pit-boss. "Mr. Stone, you had better realize this situation. I am in dead earnest about this matter, and I don't think it will be safe for you to offer me violence."

For a moment or two the man continued to glare at Hal; but it appeared that he, like Bud Adams, had been given instructions. He turned abruptly and strode back into the office.

Hal stood for a bit, until he had made sure of his composure. After which he strolled over towards the scales. A difficulty had occurred to him for the first time — that he did not know anything about the working of coal-scales.

But he was given no time to learn. The tipple-boss reappeared. "Get out of here, fellow!" said he.

"But you invited me in," remarked Hal, mildly.

"Well, now I invite you out again."

And so the protestant resumed his vigil at the mandarin's palace-gates.

SECTION 13.

*W*hen the quitting-whistle blew, Mike Sikoria came quickly to join Hal and hear what had happened. Mike was exultant, for several new men had come up to him and offered to join the check-weighman movement. The old fellow was not sure whether this was owing to his own eloquence as a propagandist, or to the fine young American buddy he had; but in either case he was equally proud. He gave Hal a note which had been slipped into his hand, and which Hal recognized as coming from Tom Olson. The organizer reported that everyone in the camp was talking check-weighman, and so from a propaganda standpoint they could count their move a success, no matter what the bosses might do. He added that Hal should have a number of men stay with him that night, so as to have witnesses if the company tried to "pull off anything." "And be careful of the new men," he added; "one or two of them are sure to be spies."

Hal and Mike discussed their program for the second night. Neither of them were keen for sleeping out again — the old Slovak because of his bones, and Hal because he saw there were now several spies following them about. At Reminitsky's, he spoke to some of those who had offered their support, and asked them if they would be willing to spend the night with him in Edstrom's cabin. Not one shrank from this test of sincerity; they all got their blankets, and repaired to the place, where Hal lighted the lamp and held an impromptu check-weighman meeting — and incidentally entertained himself with a spy-hunt!

One of the newcomers was a Pole named Wojecicowski; this, on top of Zamierowski, caused Hal to give up all effort to call the Poles by their names. "Woji" was an earnest little man, with a pathetic, tired face. He explained his presence by the statement that he was sick of being robbed; he would pay his share for a check-weighman, and if they fired him, all right, he would move on, and to hell with them. After which declaration he rolled up in a blanket and went to snoring on the floor of the cabin. That did not seem to be exactly the conduct of a spy.

Another was an Italian, named Farenzena; a dark-browed and sinis-ter-looking fellow, who might have served as a villain in any melodrama. He sat against the wall and talked in guttural tones, and Hal regarded him with deep suspicion. It was not easy to understand his English, but finally Hal managed to make out the story he was telling — that he was in love with a "fanciulla," and that the "fanciulla" was playing with him. He had about made up his mind that she was a coquette, and not worth bothering with, so he did not care any curses if they sent him down the canyon. "Don't fight for fanciulla, fight for check-weighman!" he con-cluded, with a growl.

Another volunteer was a Greek laborer, a talkative young chap who had sat with Hal at lunch-time, and had given his name as Apostolikas. He entered into fluent conversation with Hal, explaining how much interested he was in the check-weighman plan; he wanted to know just what they were going to do, what chance of success they thought they had, who had started the movement and who was in it. Hal's replies took the form of little sermons on working-class solidarity. Each time the man would start to "pump" him, Hal would explain the importance of the present issue to the miners, how they must stand by one another and make sacrifices for the good of all. After he had talked abstract theories for half an hour, Apostolikas gave up and moved on to Mike Sikoria, who, having been given a wink by Hal, talked about "scabs," and the dreadful things that honest workingmen would do to them. When finally the Greek grew tired again, and lay down on the floor, Hal moved over to Old Mike and whispered that the first name of Apos-tolikas must be Judas!

SECTION 14.

Old Mike went to sleep quickly; but Hal had not worked for several days, and had exciting thoughts to keep him awake. He had been lying quiet for a couple of hours, when he became aware that someone was moving in the room. There was a lamp burning dimly, and through half-closed eyes he made out one of the men lifting himself to a sitting position. At first he could not be sure which one it was, but finally he recognized the Greek.

Hal lay motionless, and after a minute or so he stole another look and saw the man crouching and listening, his hands still on the floor. Through half opened eye-lids Hal continued to steal glimpses, while the other rose and tiptoed towards him, stepping carefully over the sleeping forms.

Hal did his best to simulate the breathing of sleep: no easy matter, with the man stooping over him, and a knife-thrust as one of the possibilities of the situation. He took the chance, however; and after what seemed an age, he felt the man's fingers lightly touch his side. They moved down to his coat-pocket.

"Going to search me!" thought Hal; and waited, expecting the hand to travel to other pockets. But after what seemed an interminable period, he realized that Apostolikas had risen again, and was stepping back to his place. In a minute more he had lain down, and all was still in the cabin.

Hal's hand moved to the pocket, and his fingers slid inside. They touched something, which he recognized instantly as a roll of bills.

"I see!" thought he. "A frame-up!" And he laughed to himself, his mind going back to early boyhood — to a dilapidated trunk in the attic of his home, containing story-books that his father had owned. He could see them now, with their worn brown covers and crude pictures: *The Luck and Pluck Series*, by Horatio Alger; *Live or Die, Rough and Ready*, etc. How he had thrilled over the story of the country-boy who comes to the city, and meets the villain who robs his employer's cash-drawer and drops the key of it into the hero's pocket! Evidently someone connected with the General Fuel Company had read Horatio Alger!

Hal realized that he could not be too quick about getting those bills out of his pocket. He thought of returning them to "Judas," but decided that he would save them for Edstrom, who was likely to need money before long. He gave the Greek half an hour to go to sleep, then with his pocket-knife he gently picked out a hole in the cinders of the floor and buried the money as best he could. After which he wormed his way to another place, and lay thinking.

SECTION 15.

*W*ould they wait until morning, or would they come soon? He was inclined to the latter guess, so he was only slightly startled when, an hour or two later, he heard the knob of the cabin door turned. A moment later came a crash and the door was burst open, with the shoulder of a heavy man behind it.

The room was in confusion in a second. Men sprang to their feet, crying out; others sat up bewildered, still half asleep. The room was bright from an electric torch in the hands of one of the invaders. "There's the fellow!" cried a voice, which Hal instantly recognized as belonging to Jeff Cotton, the camp-marshal. "Stick 'em up, there! You, Joe Smith!" Hal did not wait to see the glint of the marshal's revolver.

There followed a silence. As this drama was being staged for the benefit of the other men, it was necessary to give them time to get thoroughly awake, and to get their eyes used to the light. Meantime Hal stood, his hands in the air. Behind the torch he could make out the faces of the marshal, Bud Adams, Alec Stone, Jake Predovich, and two or three others.

"Now, men," said Cotton, at last, "you are some of the fellows that want a check-weighman. And this is the man you chose. Is that right?"

There was no answer.

"I'm going to show you the kind of fellow he is. He came to Mr. Stone here and offered to sell you out."

"It's a lie, men," said Hal, quietly.

"He took some money from Mr. Stone to sell you out!" insisted the marshal.

"It's a lie," said Hal, again.

"He's got that money now!" cried the other.

And Hal cried, in turn, "They are trying to frame something on me, boys! Don't let them fool you!"

"Shut up," commanded the marshal; then, to the men, "I'll show you. I think he's got that money on him now. Jake, search him."

The store-clerk advanced.

"Watch out, boys!" exclaimed Hal. "They will put something in my pockets." And then to Old Mike, who had started angrily forward, "It's all right, Mike! Let them alone!"

"Jake, take off your coat," ordered Cotton. "Roll up your sleeves. Show your hands."

It was for all the world like the performance of a prestidigitator. The little Jew took off his coat and rolled up his sleeves above his elbows. He exhibited his hands to the audience, turning them this way and that; then, keeping them out in front of him, he came slowly towards Hal, like a hypnotist about to put him to sleep.

"Watch him!" said Cotton. "He's got that money on him, I know."

"Look sharp!" cried Hal. "If it isn't there, they'll put it there."

"Keep your hands up, young fellow," commanded the marshal. "Keep back from him there!" This last to Mike Sikoria and the other spectators, who were pressing nearer, peering over one another's shoulders.

It was all very serious at the time, but afterwards, when Hal recalled the scene, he laughed over the grotesque figure of Predovich searching his pockets while keeping as far away from him as possible, so that everyone might know that the money had actually come out of Hal's pocket. The searcher put his hands first in the inside pockets, then in the pockets of Hal's shirt. Time was needed to build up this climax!

"Turn around," commanded Cotton; and Hal turned, and the Jew went through his trouser-pockets. He took out in turn Hal's watch, his comb and mirror, his handkerchief; after examining them and holding them up, he dropped them onto the floor. There was a breathless hush when he came to Hal's purse, and proceeded to open it. Thanks to the greed of the company, there was nothing in the purse but some small change. Predovich closed it and dropped it to the floor.

"Wait now! He's not through!" cried the master of ceremonies. "He's got that money somewhere, boys! Did you look in his side-pockets, Jake?"

"Not yet," said Jake.

"Look sharp!" cried the marshal; and everyone craned forward eagerly, while Predovich stooped down on one knee, and put his hand into one coat pocket and then into the other.

He took his hand out again, and the look of dismay upon his face was so obvious that Hal could hardly keep from laughing. "It ain't dere!" he declared.

"What?" cried Cotton, and they stared at each other. "By God, he's got rid of it!"

"There's no money on me, boys!" proclaimed Hal. "It's a job they are trying to put over on us."

"He's hid it!" shouted the marshal. "Find it, Jake!"

Then Predovich began to search again, swiftly, and with less circumstance. He was not thinking so much about the spectators now, as about all that good money gone for nothing! He made Hal take off his coat, and ripped open the lining; he unbuttoned the trousers and felt inside; he thrust his fingers down inside Hal's shoes.

But there was no money, and the searchers were at a standstill. "He took twenty-five dollars from Mr. Stone to sell you out!" declared the marshal. "He's managed to get rid of it somehow."

"Boys," cried Hal, "they sent a spy in here, and told him to put money on me." He was looking at Apostolikas as he spoke; he saw the man start and shrink back.

"That's him! He's a scab!" cried Old Mike. "He's got the money on him, I bet!" And he made a move towards the Greek.

So the camp-marshal realized suddenly that it was time to ring down the curtain on this drama. "That's enough of this foolishness," he declared. "Bring that fellow along here!" And in a flash a couple of the party had seized Hal's wrists, and a third had grabbed him by the collar of his shirt. Before the miners had time to realize what was happening, they had rushed their prisoner out of the cabin.

The quarter of an hour which followed was an uncomfortable one for the would-be check-weighman. Outside, in the darkness, the camp-marshal was free to give vent to his rage, and so was Alec Stone. They poured out curses upon him, and kicked him and cuffed him as they went along. One of the men who held his wrists twisted his arm, until he cried out with pain; then they cursed him harder, and bade him hold his mouth. Down the dark and silent street they went swiftly, and into the camp-marshal's office, and upstairs to the room which served as the North Valley jail. Hal was glad enough when they left him here, slamming the iron door behind them.

SECTION 16.

*I*t had been a crude and stupid plot, yet Hal realized that it was adapted to the intelligence of the men for whom it was intended. But for the accident that he had stayed awake, they would have found the money on him, and next morning the whole camp would have heard that he had sold out. Of course his immediate friends, the members of the committee, would not have believed it; but the mass of the workers would have believed it, and so the purpose of Tom Olson's visit to North Valley would have been balked. Throughout the experiences which were to come to him, Hal retained his vivid impression of that adventure; it served to him as a symbol of many things. Just as the bosses had tried to bedevil him, to destroy his influence with his followers, so later on he saw them trying to bedevil the labor-movement, to confuse the intelligence of the whole country.

Now Hal was in jail. He went to the window and tried the bars – but found that they had been made for such trials. Then he groped his way about in the darkness, examining his prison, which proved to be a steel cage built inside the walls of an ordinary room. In one corner was a bench, and in another corner another bench, somewhat broader, with a mattress upon it. Hal had read a little about jails — enough to cause him to avoid this mattress. He sat upon the bare bench, and began to think.

It is a fact that there is a peculiar psychology incidental to being in jail; just as there is a peculiar psychology incidental to straining your back and breaking your hands loading coal-cars in a five foot vein; and another, and quite different psychology, produced by living at ease off the labors of coal-miners. In a jail, you have first of all the sense of being an animal; the animal side of your being is emphasized, the animal passions of hatred and fear are called into prominence, and if you are to escape being dominated by them, it can only be by intense and concentrated effort of the mind. So, if you are a thinking man, you do a great deal of thinking in a jail; the days are long, and the nights still longer — you have time for all the thoughts you can have.

The bench was hard, and seemed to grow harder. There was no position in which it could be made to grow soft. Hal got up and paced about, then he lay down for a while, then got up and walked again; and all the while he thought, and all the while the jail-psychology was being impressed upon his mind.

First, he thought about his immediate problem. What were they going to do to him? The obvious thing would be to put him out of camp, and so be done with him; but would they rest content with that, in their irritation at the trick he had played? Hal had heard vaguely of that native American institution, the "third degree," but had never had occasion to think of it as a possibility in his own life. What a difference it made, to think of it in that way!

Hal had told Tom Olson that he would not pledge himself to organize a union, but that he would pledge himself to get a check-weighman; and Olson had laughed, and seemed quite content — apparently assuming that it would come to the same thing. And now, it rather seemed that Olson had known what he was talking about. For Hal found his thoughts no longer troubled with fears of labor union domination and walking delegate tyranny; on the contrary, he became suddenly willing for the people of North Valley to have a union, and to be as tyrannical as they knew how! And in this change, though Hal had no idea of it, he was repeating an experience common among reformers; many of whom begin as mild and benevolent advocates of some obvious bit of justice, and under the operation of the jail-psychology are made into blazing and determined revolutionists. "Eternal spirit of the chainless mind," says Byron. "Greatest in dungeons Liberty thou art!"

The poet goes on to add that "When thy sons to fetters are confined —" then "Freedom's fame finds wings on every wind." And just as it was in Chillon, so it seemed to be in North Valley. Dawn came, and Hal stood at the window of his cell, and heard the whistle blow and saw the workers going to their tasks, the toil-bent, pallid faced creatures of the underworld, like a file of baboons in the half-light. He waved his hand to them, and they stopped and stared, and then waved back; he realized that every one of those men must be thinking about his imprisonment, and the reason for it — and so the jail-psychology was being communicated to them. If any of them cherished distrust of unions, or doubt of the need of organization in North Valley — that distrust and that doubt were being dissipated!

— There was only one thing discouraging about the matter, as Hal thought it over. Why should the bosses have left him here in plain sight, when they might so easily have put him into an automobile, and whisked him down to Pedro before daylight? Was it a sign of the contempt they felt for their slaves? Did they count upon the sight of the prisoner in the window to produce fear instead of resentment? And might it not be that they understood their workers better than the would-be check-weighman? He recalled Mary Burke's pessimism about them, and anxiety gnawed at his soul; and — such is the operation of the jail-psychology — he fought against this anxiety. He hated the company for its cynicism, he clenched his hands and set his teeth, desiring to teach the bosses a lesson, to prove to them that their workers were not slaves, but men!

SECTION 17.

*T*oward the middle of the morning, Hal heard footsteps in the corridor outside, and a man whom he did not know opened the barred door and set down a pitcher of water and a tin plate with a hunk of bread on it. When he started to leave, Hal spoke: "Just a minute, please."

The other frowned at him.

"Can you give me any idea how long I am to stay in here?"

"I cannot," said the man.

"If I'm to be locked up," said Hal, "I've certainly a right to know what is the charge against me."

"Go to blazes!" said the other, and slammed the door and went down the corridor.

Hal went to the window again, and passed the time watching the people who went by. Groups of ragged children gathered, looking up at him, grinning and making signs — until someone appeared below and ordered them away.

As time passed, Hal became hungry. The taste of bread, eaten alone, becomes speedily monotonous, and the taste of water does not relieve it; nevertheless, Hal munched the bread, and drank the water, and wished for more.

The day dragged by; and late in the afternoon the keeper came again, with another hunk of bread and another pitcher of water. "Listen a moment," said Hal, as the man was turning away.

"I got nothin' to say to you," said the other.

"I have something to say to you," pleaded Hal. "I have read in a book — I forget where, but it was written by some doctor — that white bread does not contain the elements necessary to the sustaining of the human body."

"Go on!" growled the jailer. "What yer givin' us?"

"I mean," explained Hal, "a diet of bread and water is not what I'd choose to live on."

"What would yer choose?"

The tone suggested that the question was a rhetorical one; but Hal took it in good faith. "If I could have some beefsteak and mashed potatoes —"

The door of the cell closed with a slam whose echoes drowned out the rest of that imaginary menu. And so once more Hal sat on the hard bench, and munched his hunk of bread, and thought jail-thoughts.

When the quitting-whistle blew, he stood at the window, and saw the groups of his friends once again, and got their covert signals of encouragement. Then darkness fell, and another long vigil began.

It was late; Hal had no means of telling how late, save that all the lights in the camps were out. He made up his mind that he was in for the night, and had settled himself on the floor with his arm for a pillow, and had dozed off to sleep, when suddenly there came a scraping sound against the bars of his window. He sat up with a start, and heard another sound, unmistakably the rustling of paper. He sprang to the window, where by the faint light of the stars he could make out something dangling. He caught at it; it seemed to be an ordinary notebook, such as stenographers use, tied on the end of a pole.

Hal looked out, but could see no one. He caught hold of the pole and jerked it, as a signal; and then he heard a whisper which he recognized instantly as Rovetta's. "Hello! Listen. Write your name hundred times in book. I come back. Understand?"

The command was a sufficiently puzzling one, but Hal realized that this was no time for explanations. He answered, "Yes," and broke the string and took the notebook. There was a pencil attached, with a piece of cloth wrapped round the point to protect it.

The pole was withdrawn, and Hal sat on the bench, and began to write, three or four times on a page, "Joe Smith — Joe Smith — Joe Smith." It is not hard to write "Joe Smith," even in darkness, and so, while his hand moved, Hal's mind was busy with this mystery. It was fairly to be assumed that his committee did not want his autograph to distribute for a souvenir; they must want it for some vital purpose, to meet some new move of the bosses. The answer to this riddle was not slow in coming: having failed in their effort to find money on him, the bosses had framed up a letter, which they were exhibiting as having been written by the would-be check-weigh-man. His friends wanted his signature to disprove the authenticity of the letter.

Hal wrote a free and rapid hand, with a generous flourish; he felt sure it would be different from Alec Stone's idea of a working-boy's scrawl. His pencil flew on and on — "Joe Smith — Joe Smith —" page after page, until he was sure that he had written a signature for every miner in the camp, and was beginning on the buddies. Then, hearing a whistle outside, he stopped and sprang to the window.

"Throw it!" whispered a voice; and Hal threw it. He saw a form vanish up the street, after which all was quiet again. He listened for a while, to see if he had roused his jailer; then he lay down on the bench — and thought more jail-thoughts!

SECTION 18.

Morning came, and the mine-whistle blew, and Hal stood at the window again. This time he noticed that some of the miners on their way to work had little strips of paper in their hands, which strips they waved conspicuously for him to see. Old Mike Sikoria came along, having a whole bunch of strips in his hands, which he was distributing to all who would take them. Doubtless he had been warned to proceed secretly, but the excitement of the occasion had been too much for him;

he capered about like a young spring lamb, and waved the strips at Hal in plain sight of all the world.

Such indiscreet behavior met the return it invited. As Hal watched, he saw a stocky figure come striding round the corner, confronting the startled old Slovak. It was Bud Adams, the mine-guard, and his hard fists were clenched, and his whole body gathered for a blow. Mike saw him, and was as if suddenly struck with paralysis; his toil-bent shoulders sunk together, and his hands fell to his sides — his fingers opening, and his precious strips of paper fluttering to the ground. Mike stared at Bud like a fascinated rabbit, making no move to protect himself.

Hal clutched the bars, with an impulse to leap to his friend's defense. But the expected blow did not fall; the mine-guard contented himself with glaring ferociously, and giving an order to the old man. Mike stooped and picked up the papers — the process taking him some time, as he was unable or unwilling to take his eyes off the mine-guard's. When he got them all in his hands, there came another order, and he gave them up to Bud. After which he fell back a step, and the other followed, his fists still clenched, and a blow seeming about to leap from him every moment. Mike receded another step, and then another — so the two of them backed out of sight around the corner. Men who had been witnesses of this little drama turned and slunk off, and Hal was given no clue as to its outcome.

A couple of hours afterwards, Hal's jailer came up, this time without any bread and water. He opened the door and commanded the prisoner to "come along." Hal went downstairs, and entered Jeff Cotton's office.

The camp-marshal sat at his desk with a cigar between his teeth. He was writing, and he went on writing until the jailer had gone out and closed the door. Then he turned his revolving chair and crossed his legs, leaning back and looking at the young miner in his dirty blue overalls, his hair tousled and his face pale from his period of confinement. The camp-marshal's aristocratic face wore a smile. "Well, young fellow," said he, "you've been having a lot of fun in this camp."

"Pretty fair, thank you," answered Hal.

"Beat us out all along the line, hey?" Then, after a pause, "Now, tell me, what do you think you're going to get out of it?"

"That's what Alec Stone asked me," replied Hal. "I don't think it would do much good to explain. I doubt if you believe in altruism anymore than Stone does."

The camp-marshal took his cigar from his mouth, and flicked off the ashes. His face became serious, and there was a silence, while he studied Hal. "You a union organizer?" he asked, at last.

"No," said Hal.

"You're an educated man; you're no laborer, that I know. Who's paying you?"

"There you are! You don't believe in altruism."

The other blew a ring of smoke across the room. "Just want to put the company in the hole, hey? Some kind of agitator?"

"I am a miner who wants to be a check-weighman."

"Socialist?"

"That depends upon developments here."

"Well," said the marshal, "you're an intelligent chap, that I can see. So I'll lay my hand on the table and you can study it. You're not going to serve as check-weighman in North Valley, nor any other place that the 'G.F.C.' has anything to do with. Nor are you going to have the satisfaction of putting the company in a hole. We're not even going to beat you up and make a martyr of you. I was tempted to do that the other night, but I changed my mind."

"You might change the bruises on my arm," suggested Hal, in a pleasant voice.

"We're going to offer you the choice of two things," continued the marshal, without heeding this mild sarcasm. "Either you will sign a paper admitting that you took the twenty-five dollars from Alec Stone, in which case we will fire you and call it square; or else we will prove that you took it, in which case we will send you to the pen for five or ten years. Do you get that?"

Now when Hal had applied for the job of check-weighman, he had been expecting to be thrown out of the camp, and had intended to go, counting his education complete. But here, as he sat and gazed into the marshal's menacing eyes, he decided suddenly that he did not want to leave North Valley. He wanted to stay and take the measure of this gigantic "burglar," the General Fuel Company.

"That's a serious threat, Mr. Cotton," he remarked. "Do you often do things like that?"

"We do them when we have to," was the reply.

"Well, it's a novel proposition. Tell me more about it. What will the charge be?"

"I'm not sure about that — we'll put it up to our lawyers. Maybe they'll call it conspiracy, maybe blackmail. They'll make it whatever carries a long enough sentence."

"And before I enter my plea, would you mind letting me see the letter I'm supposed to have written."

"Oh, you've heard about the letter, have you?" said the camp-marshal, lifting his eyebrows in mild surprise. He took from his desk a sheet of paper and handed it to Hal, who read:

"Dere mister Stone, You don't need worry about the check-wayman. Pay me twenty five dollars, and I will fix it right. Yours try, Joe Smith."

Having taken in the words of the letter, Hal examined the paper, and perceived that his enemies had taken the trouble, not merely to forge a letter in his name, but to have it photographed, to have a cut made of the photograph, and to have it printed. Beyond doubt they had distributed it broadcast in the camp. And all this in a few hours! It was as Olson had said — a regular system to keep the men bedeviled.

SECTION 19.

*H*al took a minute or so to ponder the situation. "Mr. Cotton," he said, at last. "I know how to spell better than that. Also my handwriting is a bit more fluent."

There was a trace of a smile about the marshal's cruel lips. "I know," he replied. "I've not failed to compare them."

"You have a good secret-service department!" said Hal.

"Before you get through, young fellow, you'll discover that our legal department is equally efficient."

"Well," said Hal, "they'll need to be; for I don't see how you can get round the fact that I'm a check-weighman, chosen according to the law, and with a group of the men behind me."

"If that's what you're counting on," retorted Cotton, "you may as well forget it. You've got no group anymore."

"Oh! You've got rid of them?"

"We've got rid of the ring-leaders."

"Of whom?"

"That old billy goat, Sikoria, for one."

"You've shipped him?"

"We have."

"I saw the beginning of that. Where have you sent him?"

"That," smiled the marshal, "is a job for *your* secret-service department!"

"And who else?"

"John Edstrom has gone down to bury his wife. It's not the first time that dough-faced old preacher has made trouble for us, but it'll be the last. You'll find him in Pedro — probably in the poor-house."

"No," responded Hal, quickly — and there came just a touch of elation in his voice — "he won't have to go to the poor-house at once. You see, I've just sent twenty-five dollars to him."

The camp-marshal frowned. "Really!" Then, after a pause, "You *did* have that money on you! I thought that lousy Greek had got away with it!"

"No. Your knave was honest. But so was I. I knew Edstrom had been getting short weight for years, so he was the one person with any right to the money."

This story was untrue, of course; the money was still buried in Edstrom's cabin. But Hal meant for the old miner to have it in the end, and meantime he wanted to throw Cotton off the track.

"A clever trick, young man!" said the marshal. "But you'll repent it before you're through. It only makes me more determined to put you where you can't do us any harm."

"You mean in the pen? You understand, of course, it will mean a jury trial. You can get a jury to do what you want?"

"They tell me you've been taking an interest in politics in Pedro County. Haven't you looked into our jury-system?"

"No, I haven't got that far."

The marshal began blowing rings of smoke again.

"Well, there are some three hundred men on our jury-list, and we know them all. You'll find yourself facing a box with Jake Predovich as foreman, three company-clerks, two of Alf Raymond's saloon-keepers, a ranchman with a mortgage held by the company-bank, and five Mexicans who have no idea what it's all about, but would stick a knife into your back for a drink of whiskey. The District Attorney is a politician who favors the miners in his speeches, and favors us in his acts; while Judge Denton, of the district court, is the law partner of Vagleman, our chief-counsel. Do you get all that?"

"Yes," said Hal. "I've heard of the 'Empire of Raymond'; I'm interested to see the machinery. You're quite open about it!"

"Well," replied the marshal, "I want you to know what you're up against. We didn't start this fight, and we're perfectly willing to end it without trouble. All we ask is that you make amends for the mischief you've done us."

"By 'making amends,' you mean I'm to disgrace myself — to tell the men I'm a traitor?"

"Precisely," said the marshal.

"I think I'll have a seat while I consider the matter," said Hal; and he took a chair, and stretched out his legs, and made himself elaborately comfortable. "That bench upstairs is frightfully hard," said he, and smiled mockingly upon the camp-marshal.

SECTION 20.

*W*hen this conversation was continued, it was upon a new and unexpected line. "Cotton," remarked the prisoner, "I perceive that you are a man of education. It occurs to me that once upon a time you must have been what the world calls a gentleman."

The blood started into the camp-marshal's face. "You go to hell!" said he.

"I did not intend to ask questions," continued Hal. "I can well understand that you mightn't care to answer them. My point is that, being an ex-gentleman, you may appreciate certain aspects of this case which would be beyond the understanding of a nigger-driver like Stone, or an efficiency expert like Cartwright. One gentleman can recognize another, even in a miner's costume. Isn't that so?"

Hal paused for an answer, and the marshal gave him a wary look. "I suppose so," he said.

"Well, to begin with, one gentleman does not smoke without inviting another to join him."

The man gave another look. Hal thought he was going to consign him to Hades once more; but instead he took a cigar from his vest-pocket and held it out.

"No, thank you," said Hal, quietly. "I do not smoke. But I like to be invited."

There was a pause, while the two men measured each other.

"Now, Cotton," began the prisoner, "you pictured the scene at my trial. Let me carry on the story for you. You have your case all framed up, your hand-picked jury in the box, and your hand-picked judge on the bench, your hand-picked prosecuting-attorney putting through the job; you are ready to send your victim to prison, for an example to the rest of your employees. But suppose that, at the climax of the proceedings, you should make the discovery that your victim is a person who cannot be sent to prison?"

"Cannot be sent to prison?" repeated the other. His tone was thoughtful. "You'll have to explain."

"Surely not to a man of your intelligence! Don't you know, Cotton, there are people who cannot be sent to prison?"

The camp-marshal smoked his cigar for a bit. "There are some in this county," said he. "But I thought I knew them all."

"Well," said Hal, "has it never occurred to you that there might be some in this *state?*"

There followed a long silence. The two men were gazing into each other's eyes; and the more they gazed, the more plainly Hal read uncertainty in the face of the marshal.

"Think how embarrassing it would be!" he continued. "You have your drama all staged – as you did the night before last – only on a larger stage, before a more important audience; and at the *dénouement* you find that, instead of vindicating yourself before the workers in North Valley, you have convicted yourself before the public of the state. You have shown the whole community that you are law-breakers; worse than that – you have shown that you are jack-asses!"

This time the camp-marshal gazed so long that his cigar went out. And meantime Hal was lounging in his chair, smiling at him strangely. It was as if a transformation was taking place before the marshal's eyes; the miner's "jumpers" fell away from Hal's figure, and there was a suit of evening-clothes in their place!

"Who the devil are you?" cried the man.

"Well now!" laughed Hal. "You boast of the efficiency of your secret service department! Put them at work upon this problem. A young man, age twenty-one, height five feet ten inches, weight one hundred and fifty-two pounds, eyes brown, hair chestnut and rather wavy, manner genial, a favorite with the ladies – at least that's what the society notes say – missing since early in June, supposed to be hunting mountain-goats in Mexico. As you know, Cotton, there's only one city in the state that has any 'society,' and in that city there are only twenty-five or thirty families that count. For a secret service department like that of the 'G.F.C.', that is really too easy."

Again there was a silence, until Hal broke it. "Your distress is a tribute to your insight. The company is lucky in the fact that one of its camp-marshals happens to be an ex-gentleman."

Again the other flushed. "Well, by God!" he said, half to himself; and then, making a last effort to hold his bluff – "You're kidding me!"

"'Kidding,' as you call it, is one of the favorite occupations of society, Cotton. A good part of our intercourse consists of it – at least among the younger set."

Suddenly the marshal rose. "Say," he demanded, "would you mind going back upstairs for a few minutes?"

Hal could not restrain his laughter at this. "I should mind it very much," he said. "I have been on a bread and water diet for thirty-six hours, and I should like very much to get out and have a breath of fresh air."

"But," said the other, lamely, "I've got to send you up there."

"That's another matter," replied Hal. "If you send me, I'll go, but it's your look-out. You've kept me here without legal authority, with no charge against me, and without giving me an opportunity to see counsel. Unless I'm very much mistaken, you are liable criminally for that, and the company is liable civilly. That is your own affair, of course. I only want to make clear my position — when you ask me would I *mind* stepping upstairs, I, answer that I would mind very much indeed."

The camp-marshal stood for a bit, chewing nervously on his extinct cigar. Then he went to the door. "Hey, Gus!" he called. Hal's jailer appeared, and Cotton whispered to him, and he went away again. "I'm telling him to get you some food, and you can sit and eat it here. Will that suit you better?"

"It depends," said Hal, making the most of the situation. "Are you inviting me as your prisoner, or as your guest?"

"Oh, come off!" said the other.

"But I have to know my legal status. It will be of importance to my lawyers."

"Be my guest," said the camp-marshal.

"But when a guest has eaten, he is free to go out, if he wishes to!"

"I will let you know about that before you get through."

"Well, be quick. I'm a rapid eater."

"You'll promise you won't go away before that?"

"If I do," was Hal's laughing reply, "it will be only to my place of business. You can look for me at the tipple, Cotton!"

SECTION 21.

*T*he marshal went out, and a few moments later the jailer came back, with a meal which presented a surprising contrast to the ones he had previously served. There was a tray containing cold ham, a couple of soft boiled eggs, some potato salad, and a cup of coffee with rolls and butter.

"Well, well!" said Hal, condescendingly. "That's even nicer than beefsteak and mashed potatoes!" He sat and watched, not offering to help, while the other made room for the tray on the table in front of him. Then the man stalked out, and Hal began to eat.

Before he had finished, the camp-marshal returned. He seated himself in his revolving chair, and appeared to be meditative. Between bites, Hal would look up and smile at him.

"Cotton," said he, "you know there is no more certain test of breeding than table-manners. You will observe that I have not tucked my napkin in my neck, as Alec Stone would have done."

"I'm getting you," replied the marshal.

Hal set his knife and fork side by side on his plate. "Your man has overlooked the finger-bowl," he remarked. "However, don't bother. You might ring for him now, and let him take the tray."

The camp-marshal used his voice for a bell, and the jailer came. "Unfortunately," said Hal, "when your people were searching me, night before last, they dropped my purse, so I have no tip for the waiter."

The "waiter" glared at Hal as if he would like to bite him; but the camp-marshal grinned. "Clear out, Gus, and shut the door," said he.

Then Hal stretched his legs and made himself comfortable again. "I must say I like being your guest better than being your prisoner!"

There was a pause.

"I've been talking it over with Mr. Cartwright," began the marshal. "I've got no way of telling how much of this is bluff that you've been giving me, but it's evident enough that you're no miner. You may be some newfangled kind of agitator, but I'm damned if I ever saw an agitator that had tea-party manners. I suppose you've been brought up to money; but if that's so, why you want to do this kind of thing is more than I can imagine."

"Tell me, Cotton," said Hal, "did you never hear of *ennui?*"

"Yes," replied the other, "but aren't you rather young to be troubled with that complaint?"

"Suppose I've seen others suffering from it, and wanted to try a different way of living from theirs?"

"If you're what you say, you ought to be still in college."

"I go back for my senior year this fall."

"What college?"

"You doubt me still, I see!" said Hal, and smiled. Then, unexpectedly, with a spirit which only moonlit campuses and privilege could beget, he chanted:

"Old King Coal was a merry old soul,
    And a merry old soul was he;

He made him a college, all full of knowledge —
   Hurrah for you and me!"

"What college is that?" asked the marshal. And Hal sang again:

"Oh, Liza-Ann, come out with me,
   The moon is a-shinin' in the monkey-puzzle tree!
   Oh, Liza-Ann, I have began
   To sing you the song of Harrigan!"

"Well, well!" commented the marshal, when the concert was over. "Are there many more like you at Harrigan?"
   "A little group — enough to leaven the lump."
   "And this is your idea of a vacation?"
   "No, it isn't a vacation; it's a summer-course in practical sociology."
   "Oh, I see!" said the marshal; and he smiled in spite of himself.
   "All last year we let the professors of political economy hand out their theories to us. But somehow the theories didn't seem to correspond with the facts. I said to myself, 'I've got to check them up.' You know the phrases, perhaps — individualism, *laissez faire*, freedom of contract, the right of every man to work for whom he pleases. And here you see how the theories work out — a camp-marshal with a cruel smile on his face and a gun on his hip, breaking the laws faster than a governor can sign them."
   The camp-marshal decided suddenly that he had had enough of this "tea-party." He rose to his feet to cut matters short. "If you don't mind, young man," said he, "we'll get down to business!"

SECTION 22.

*H*e took a turn about the room, then he came and stopped in front of Hal. He stood with his hands thrust into his pockets, with a certain jaunty grace that was out of keeping with his occupation. He was a handsome devil, Hal thought — in spite of his dangerous mouth, and the marks of dissipation on him.
   "Young man," he began, with another effort at geniality. "I don't know who you are, but you're wide awake; you've got your nerve with

you, and I admire you. So I'm willing to call the thing off, and let you go back and finish that course at college."

Hal had been studying the other's careful smile. "Cotton," he said, at last, "let me get the proposition clear. I don't have to say I took that money?"

"No, we'll let you off from that."

"And you won't send me to the pen?"

"No. I never meant to do that, of course. I was only trying to bluff you. All I ask is that you clear out, and give our people a chance to forget."

"But what's there in that for me, Cotton? If I had wanted to run away, I could have done it anytime during the last eight or ten weeks."

"Yes, of course, but now it's different. Now it's a matter of my consideration."

"Cut out the consideration!" exclaimed Hal. "You want to get rid of me, and you'd like to do it without trouble. But you can't — so forget it."

The other was staring, puzzled. "You mean you expect to stay here?"

"I mean just that."

"Young man, I've had enough of this! I've got no more time to play. I don't care who you are, I don't care about your threats. I'm the marshal of this camp, and I have the job of keeping order in it. I say you're going to get out!"

"But, Cotton," said Hal, "this is an incorporated town! I have a right to walk on the streets — exactly as much right as you."

"I'm not going to waste time arguing. I'm going to put you into an automobile and take you down to Pedro!"

"And suppose I go to the District Attorney and demand that he prosecute you?"

"He'll laugh at you."

"And suppose I go to the Governor of the state?"

"He'll laugh still louder."

"All right, Cotton; maybe you know what you're doing; but I wonder — I wonder just how sure you feel. Has it never occurred to you that your superiors might not care to have you take these high-handed steps?"

"My superiors? Who do you mean?"

"There's one man in the state you must respect — even though you despise the District Attorney and the Governor. That is Peter Harrigan."

"Peter Harrigan?" echoed the other; and then he burst into a laugh. "Well, you *are* a merry lad!"

Hal continued to study him, unmoved. "I wonder if you're sure! He'll stand for everything you've done."

"He will!" said the other.

"For the way you treat the workers? He knows you are giving short weights."

"Oh hell!" said the other. "Where do you suppose he got the money for your college?"

There was a pause; at last the marshal asked, defiantly, "Have you got what you want?"

"Yes," replied Hal. "Of course, I thought it all along, but it's hard to convince other people. Old Peter's not like most of these Western wolves, you know; he's a pious high-church man."

The marshal smiled grimly. "So long as there are sheep," said he, "there'll be wolves in sheep's clothing."

"I see," said Hal. "And you leave them to feed on the lambs!"

"If any lamb is silly enough to be fooled by that old worn-out skin," remarked the marshal, "it deserves to be eaten."

Hal was studying the cynical face in front of him. "Cotton," he said, "the shepherds are asleep; but the watchdogs are barking. Haven't you heard them?"

"I hadn't noticed."

"They are barking, barking! They are going to wake the shepherds! They are going to save the sheep!"

"Religion don't interest me," said the other, looking bored; "your kind anymore than Old Peter's."

And suddenly Hal rose to his feet. "Cotton," said he, "my place is with the flock! I'm going back to my job at the tipple!" And he started towards the door.

SECTION 23.

Jeff Cotton sprang forward. "Stop!" he cried.

But Hal did not stop.

"See here, young man!" cried the marshal. "Don't carry this joke too far!" And he sprang to the door, just ahead of his prisoner. His hand moved toward his hip.

"Draw your gun, Cotton," said Hal; and, as the marshal obeyed, "Now I will stop. If I obey you in future, it will be at the point of your revolver."

The marshal's mouth was dangerous-looking. "You may find that in this country there's not so much between the drawing of a gun and the firing of it!"

"I've explained my attitude," replied Hal. "What are your orders?"

"Come back and sit in this chair."

So Hal sat, and the marshal went to his desk, and took up the telephone. "Number seven," he said, and waited a moment. "That you, Tom? Bring the car right away."

He hung up the receiver, and there followed a silence; finally Hal inquired, "I'm going to Pedro?"

There was no reply.

"I see I've got on your nerves," said Hal. "But I don't suppose it's occurred to you that you deprived me of my money last night. Also, I've an account with the company, some money coming to me for my work? What about that?"

The marshal took up the receiver and gave another number. "Hello, Simpson. This is Cotton. Will you figure out the time of Joe Smith, buddy in Number Two, and send over the cash. Get his account at the store; and be quick, we're waiting for it. He's going out in a hurry." Again he hung up the receiver.

"Tell me," said Hal, "did you take that trouble for Mike Sikoria?"

There was silence.

"Let me suggest that when you get my time, you give me part of it in scrip. I want it for a souvenir."

Still there was silence.

"You know," persisted the prisoner, tormentingly, "there's a law against paying wages in scrip."

The marshal was goaded to speech. "We don't pay in scrip."

"But you do, man! You know you do!"

"We give it when they ask their money ahead."

"The law requires you to pay them twice a month, and you don't do it. You pay them once a month, and meantime, if they need money, you give them this imitation money!"

"Well, if it satisfies them, where's your kick?"

"If it doesn't satisfy them, you put them on the train and ship them out?"

The marshal sat in silence, tapping impatiently with his fingers on the desk.

"Cotton," Hal began, again, "I'm out for education, and there's something I'd like you to explain to me — a problem in human psychology. When a man puts through a deal like this, what does he tell himself about it?"

"Young man," said the marshal, "if you'll pardon me, you are getting to be a bore."

"Oh, but we've got an automobile ride before us! Surely we can't sit in silence all the way!" After a moment he added, in a coaxing tone, "I really want to learn, you know. You might be able to win me over."

"No!" said Cotton, promptly. "I'll not go in for anything like that!"

"But why not?"

"Because, I'm no match for you in long-windedness. I've heard you agitators before, you're all alike: you think the world is run by talk — but it isn't."

Hal had come to realize that he was not getting anywhere in his duel with the camp-marshal. He had made every effort to get somewhere; he had argued, threatened, bluffed, he had even sung songs for the marshal! But the marshal was going to ship him out, that was all there was to it.

Hal had gone on with the quarrel, simply because he had to wait for the automobile, and because he had endured indignities and had to vent his anger and disappointment. But now he stopped quarreling suddenly. His attention was caught by the marshal's words, "You think the world is run by talk!" Those were the words Hal's brother always used! And also, the marshal had said, "You agitators!" For years it had been one of the taunts Hal had heard from his brother, "You will turn into one of these agitators!" Hal had answered, with boyish obstinacy, "I don't care if I do!" And now, here the marshal was calling him an agitator, seriously, without an apology, without the license of blood relationship. He repeated the words, "That's what gets me about you agitators — you come in here trying to stir these people up —"

So that was the way Hal seemed to the "G.F.C.!" He had come here intending to be a spectator, to stand on the deck of the steamer and look down into the ocean of social misery. He had considered every step so carefully before he took it! He had merely tried to be a check-weighman, nothing more! He had told Tom Olson he would not go in for unionism; he had had a distrust of union organizers, of agitators of all sorts — blind, irresponsible persons who went about stirring up dangerous passions. He had come to admire Tom Olson — but that had only partly removed his prejudices; Olson was only one agitator, not the whole lot of them!

But all his consideration for the company had counted for nothing; likewise all his efforts to convince the marshal that he was a leisure-class person. In spite of all Hal's "tea-party manners," the marshal had said, "You agitators!" What was he judging by, Hal wondered. Had he, Hal Warner, come to look like one of these blind, irresponsible persons? It was time that he took stock of himself!

Had two months of "dirty work" in the bowels of the earth changed him so? The idea was bound to be disconcerting to one who had been a favorite of the ladies! Did he talk like it? — he who had been "kissing the Blarney-stone!" The marshal had said he was "long-winded!" Well, to be sure, he had talked a lot; but what could the man expect — having shut him up in jail for two nights and a day, with only his grievances to brood over! Was that the way real agitators were made — being shut up with grievances to brood over?

Hal recalled his broodings in the jail. He had been embittered; he had not cared whether North Valley was dominated by labor unions. But that had all been a mood, the same as his answer to his brother; that was jail psychology, a part of his summer course in practical sociology. He had put it aside; but apparently it had made a deeper impression upon him than he had realized. It had changed his physical aspect! It had made him look and talk like an agitator! It had made him "irresponsible," "blind!"

Yes, that was it! All this dirt, ignorance, disease, this knavery and oppression, this maiming of men in body and soul in the coal-camps of America — all this did not exist — it was the hallucination of an "irresponsible" brain! There was the evidence of Hal's brother and the camp-marshal to prove it; there was the evidence of the whole world to prove it! The camp-marshal and his brother and the whole world could not be "blind!" And if you talked to them about these conditions, they shrugged their shoulders, they called you a "dreamer," a "crank," they said you were "off your trolley"; or else they became angry and bitter, they called you names; they said, "You agitators!"

SECTION 24.

The camp-marshal of North Valley had been "agitated" to such an extent that he could not stay in his chair. All the harassments of his troubled career had come pouring into his mind. He had begun pacing the floor, and was talking away, regardless of whether Hal listened or not.

"A campful of lousy wops! They can't understand any civilized language, they've only one idea in the world — to shirk every lick of work they can, to fill up their cars with slate and rock and blame it on some other fellow, and go off to fill themselves with booze. They won't work fair, they won't fight fair — they fight with a knife in the back! And you agitators with your sympathy for them — why the hell do they come to this country, unless they like it better than their own?"

Hal had heard this question before; but they had to wait for the automobile — and being sure that he was an agitator now, he would make all the trouble he could! "The reason is obvious enough," he said. "Isn't it true that the 'G.F.C.' employs agents abroad to tell them of the wonderful pay they get in America?"

"Well, they get it, don't they? Three times what they ever got at home!"

"Yes, but it doesn't do them any good. There's another fact which the 'G.F.C.' doesn't mention — that the cost of living is even higher than the wages. Then, too, they're led to think of America as a land of liberty; they come, hoping for a better chance for themselves and their children; but they find a camp-marshal who's off in his geography — who thinks the Rocky Mountains are somewhere in Russia!"

"I know that line of talk!" exclaimed the other. "I learned to wave the starry flag when I was a kid. But I tell you, you've got to get coal mined, and it isn't the same thing as running a Fourth of July celebration. Some church people make a law they shan't work on Sunday — and what comes of that? They have thirty-six hours to get soused in, and so they can't work on Monday!"

"Surely there's a remedy, Cotton! Suppose the company refused to rent buildings to saloon-keepers?"

"Good God! You think we haven't tried it? They go down to Pedro for the stuff, and bring back all they can carry — inside them and out. And if we stop that — then our hands move to some other camps, where they can spend their money as they please. No, young man, when you have such cattle, you have to drive them! And it takes a strong hand to do it — a man like Peter Harrigan. If there's to be any coal, if industry's to go on, if there's to be any progress —"

"We have that in our song!" laughed Hal, breaking into the camp-marshal's discourse —

"He keeps them a-roll, that merry old soul —
     The wheels of industree;
  A-roll and a-roll, for his pipe and his bowl
     And his college facultee!"

"Yes," growled the marshal. "It's easy enough for you smart young chaps to make verses, while you're living at ease on the old man's bounty. But that don't answer any argument. Are you college boys ready to take over his job? Or these Democrat politicians that come in here, talking fool-talk about liberty, making labor laws for these wops —"

"I begin to understand," said Hal. "You object to the politicians who pass the laws, you doubt their motives — and so you refuse to obey. But why didn't you tell me sooner you were an anarchist?"

"Anarchist?" cried the marshal. "*Me* an anarchist?"

"That's what an anarchist is, isn't it?"

"Good God! If that isn't the limit! You come here, stirring up the men — a union agitator, or whatever you are — and you know that the first idea of these people, when they do break loose, is to put dynamite in the shafts and set fire to the buildings!"

"Do they do that?" There was surprise in Hal's tone.

"Haven't you read what they did in the last big strike? That dough-faced old preacher, John Edstrom, could tell you. He was one of the bunch."

"No," said Hal, "you're mistaken. Edstrom has a different philosophy. But others did, I've no doubt. And since I've been here, I can understand their point of view entirely. When they set fire to the buildings, it was because they thought you and Alec Stone might be inside."

The marshal did not smile.

"They want to destroy the properties," continued Hal, "because that's the only way they can think of to punish the tyranny and greed of the owners. But, Cotton, suppose someone were to put a new idea into their heads; suppose someone were to say to them, 'Don't destroy the properties — *take them!*'"

The other stared. "Take them! So that's your idea of morality!"

"It would be more moral than the method by which Peter got them in the beginning."

"What method is that?" demanded the marshal, with some appearance of indignation. "He paid the market-price for them, didn't he?"

"He paid the market-price for politicians. Up in Western City I happen to know a lady who was a school-commissioner when he was buying school-lands from the state — lands that were known to contain coal. He was paying three dollars an acre, and everybody knew they were worth three thousand."

"Well," said Cotton, "if you don't buy the politicians, you wake up some fine morning and find that somebody else has bought them. If you have property, you have to protect it."

"Cotton," said Hal, "you sell Old Peter your time — but surely you might keep part of your brains! Enough to look at your monthly pay-check and realize that you too are a wage-slave, not much better than the miners you despise."

The other smiled. "My check might be bigger, I admit; but I've figured over it, and I think I have an easier time than you agitators. I'm top-dog, and I expect to stay on top."

"Well, Cotton, on that view of life, I don't wonder you get drunk now and then. A dog-fight, with no faith or humanity anywhere! Don't think I'm sneering at you — I'm talking out of my heart to you. I'm not so young, nor such a fool, that I haven't had the dog-fight aspect of things brought to my attention. But there's something in a fellow that insists he isn't all dog; he has at least a possibility of something better. Take these poor under-dogs sweating inside the mountain, risking their lives every hour of the day and night to provide you and me with coal to keep us warm — to 'keep the wheels of industry a-roll' —"

SECTION 25.

*T*hese were the last words Hal spoke. They were obvious enough words, yet when he looked back upon the coincidence, it seemed to him a singular one. For while he was sitting there chatting, it happened that the poor under-dogs inside the mountain were in the midst of one of those experiences which make the romance and terror of coal-mining. One of the boys who were employed underground, in violation of the child labor law, was in the act of bungling his task. He was a "spragger," whose duty it was to thrust a stick into the wheel of a loaded car to hold it; and he was a little chap, and the car was in motion when he made the attempt. It knocked him against the wall — and so there was a load of coal rolling down grade, pursued too late by half a dozen men. Gathering momentum, it whirled round a curve and flew from the track, crashing into timbers and knocking them loose. With the timbers came a shower of coal-dust, accumulated for decades in these old workings; and at the same time came an electric light wire, which, as it touched the car, produced a spark.

And so it was that Hal, chatting with the marshal, suddenly felt, rather than heard, a deafening roar; he felt the air about him turn into a living thing which struck him a mighty blow, hurling him flat upon the floor. The windows of the room crashed inward upon him in a shower of glass, and the plaster of the ceiling came down on his head in another shower.

When he raised himself, half stunned, he saw the marshal, also on the floor; these two conversationalists stared at each other with horrified eyes. Even as they crouched, there came a crash above their heads, and half the ceiling of the room came toward them, with a great piece of timber sticking through. All about them were other crashes, as if the end of the world had come.

They struggled to their feet, and rushing to the door, flung it open, just as a jagged piece of timber shattered the side-walk in front of them. They sprang back again, "Into the cellar!" cried the marshal, leading the way to the back-stairs.

But before they had started down these stairs, they realized that the crashing had ceased. "What is it?" gasped Hal, as they stood.

"Mine-explosion," said the other; and after a few seconds they ran to the door again.

The first thing they saw was a vast pillar of dust and smoke, rising into the sky above them. It spread before their dazed eyes, until it made night of everything about them. There was still a rain of lighter debris pattering down over the village; as they stared, and got their wits about them, remembering how things had looked before this, they realized that the shaft-house of Number One had disappeared.

"Blown up, by God!" cried the marshal; and the two ran out into the street, and looking up, saw that a portion of the wrecked building had fallen through the roof of the jail above their heads.

The rain of debris had now ceased, but there were clouds of dust which covered the two men black; the clouds grew worse, until they could hardly see their way at all. And with the darkness there fell silence, which, after the sound of the explosion and the crashing of debris, seemed the silence of death.

For a few moments Hal stood dazed. He saw a stream of men and boys pouring from the breaker; while from every street there appeared a stream of women; women old, women young – leaving their cooking on the stove, their babies in the crib, with their older children screaming at their skirts, they gathered in swarms about the pit-mouth, which was like the steaming crater of a volcano.

Cartwright, the superintendent, appeared, running toward the fan-house. Cotton joined him, and Hal followed. The fan-house was a wreck, the giant fan lying on the ground a hundred feet away, its blades smashed. Hal was too inexperienced in mine-matters to get the full significance of this; but he saw the marshal and the superintendent stare blankly at each other, and heard the former's exclamation, "That does for us!" Cartwright said not a word; but his thin lips were pressed together, and there was fear in his eyes.

Back to the smoking pit-mouth the two men hurried, with Hal
following. Here were a hundred, two hundred women crowded, clamoring questions all at once. They swarmed about the marshal, the superintendent, the other bosses — even about Hal, crying hysterically in
Polish and Bohemian and Greek. When Hal shook his head, indicating
that he did not understand them, they moaned in anguish, or shrieked
aloud. Some continued to stare into the smoking pit-mouth; others
covered the sight from their eyes, or sank down upon their knees,
sobbing, praying with uplifted hands.

Little by little Hal began to realize the full horror of a mine-disaster.
It was not noise and smoke and darkness, nor frantic, wailing women;
it was not anything above ground, but what was below in the smoking
black pit! It was men! Men whom Hal knew, whom he had worked with
and joked with, whose smiles he had shared; whose daily life he had
come to know! Scores, possibly hundreds of them, they were down here
under his feet — some dead, others injured, maimed. What would they
do? What would those on the surface do for them? Hal tried to get to
Cotton, to ask him questions; but the camp-marshal was surrounded,
besieged. He was pushing the women back, exclaiming, "Go away! Go
home!"

What? Go home? they cried. When their men were in the mine? They
crowded about him closer, imploring, shrieking.

"Get out!" he kept exclaiming. "There's nothing you can do! There's
nothing anybody can do yet! Go home! Go home!" He had to beat them
back by force, to keep them from pushing one another into the pit-
mouth.

Everywhere Hal looked were women in attitudes of grief: standing
rigid, staring ahead of them as if in a trance; sitting down, rocking to
and fro; on their knees with faces uplifted in prayer; clutching their
terrified children about their skirts. He saw an Austrian woman, a
pitiful, pale young thing with a ragged grey shawl about her head,
stretching out her hands and crying: "Mein Mann! Mein Mann!"
Presently she covered her face, and her voice died into a wail of despair:
"O, mein Mann! O, mein Mann!" She turned away, staggering about
like some creature that has received a death wound. Hal's eyes followed
her; her cry, repeated over and over incessantly, became the leitmotif of
this symphony of horror.

He had read about mine-disasters in his morning newspaper; but here
a mine-disaster became a thing of human flesh and blood. The unen-
durable part of it was the utter impotence of himself and of all the
world. This impotence became clearer to him each moment — from the

exclamations of Cotton and of the men he questioned. It was mon-
strous, incredible — but it was so! They must send for a new fan, they
must wait for it to be brought in, they must set it up and get it into
operation; they must wait for hours after that while smoke and gas were
cleared out of the main passages of the mine; and until this had been
done, there was nothing they could do — absolutely nothing! The men
inside the mine would stay. Those who had not been killed outright
would make their way into the remoter chambers, and barricade themselves against the deadly "after damp." They would wait, without food
or water, with air of doubtful quality — they would wait and wait, until
the rescue-crew could get to them!

SECTION 26.

*A*t moments in the midst of this confusion, Hal found himself trying
to recall who had worked in Number One, among the people he knew.
He himself had been employed in Number Two, so he had naturally
come to know more men in that mine. But he had known some from
the other mine — Old Rafferty for one, and Mary Burke's father for
another, and at least one of the members of his check-weighman group
— Zamierowski. Hal saw in a sudden vision the face of this patient little
man, who smiled so good-naturedly while Americans were trying to say
his name. And Old Rafferty, with all his little Rafferties, and his piteous
efforts to keep the favor of his employers! And poor Patrick Burke,
whom Hal had never seen sober; doubtless he was sober now, if he was
still alive!

Then in the crowd Hal encountered Jerry Minetti, and learned that
another man who had been down was Farenzena, the Italian whose
"fanciulla" had played with him; and yet another was Judas Apostolikas
— having taken his thirty pieces of silver with him into the deathtrap!

People were making up lists, just as Hal was doing, by asking questions of others. These lists were subject to revision — sometimes under
dramatic circumstances. You saw a woman weeping, with her apron to
her eyes; suddenly she would look up, give a piercing cry, and fling her
arms about the neck of some man. As for Hal, he felt as if he were
encountering a ghost when suddenly he recognized Patrick Burke,
standing in the midst of a group of people. He went over and heard the

old man's story — how there was a Dago fellow who had stolen his timbers, and he had come up to the surface for more; so his life had been saved, while the timber-thief was down there still — a judgment of Providence upon mine-miscreants!

Presently Hal asked if Burke had been to tell his family. He had run home, he said, but there was nobody there. So Hal began pushing his way through the throngs, looking for Mary, or her sister Jennie, or her brother Tommie. He persisted in this search, although it occurred to him to wonder whether the family of a hopeless drunkard would appreciate the interposition of Providence in his behalf.

He encountered Olson, who had had a narrow escape, being employed as a surface-man near the hoist. All this was an old story to the organizer, who had worked in mines since he was eight years old, and had seen many kinds of disaster. He began to explain things to Hal, in a matter of fact way. The law required a certain number of openings to every mine, also an escape-way with ladders by which men could come out; but it cost good money to dig holes in the ground.

At this time the immediate cause of the explosion was unknown, but they could tell it was a "dust explosion" by the clouds of coke-dust, and no one who had been into the mine and seen its dry condition would doubt what they would find when they went down and traced out the "force" and its effects. They were supposed to do regular sprinkling, but in such matters the bosses used their own judgment.

Hal was only half listening to these explanations. The thing was too raw and too horrible to him. What difference did it make whose fault it was? The accident had happened, and the question was now how to meet the emergency! Underneath Olson's sentences he heard the cry of men and boys being asphyxiated in dark dungeons — he heard the wailing of women, like a surf beating on a distant shore, or the faint, persistent accompaniment of muted strings: "O, mein Mann! O, mein Mann!"

They came upon Jeff Cotton again. With half a dozen men to help him, he was pushing back the crowd from the pit-mouth, and stretching barbed wired to hold them back. He was none too gentle about it, Hal thought; but doubtless women are provoking when they are hysterical. He was answering their frenzied questions, "Yes, yes! We're getting a new fan. We're doing everything we can, I tell you. We'll get them out. Go home and wait."

But of course no one would go home. How could a woman sit in her house, or go about her ordinary tasks of cooking or washing, while her man might be suffering asphyxiation under the ground? The least she could do was to stand at the pit-mouth — as near to him as she could get! Some of them stood motionless, hour after hour, while others wandered through the village streets, asking the same people, over and over again, if they had seen their loved ones. Several had turned up, like Patrick Burke; there seemed always a chance for one more.

SECTION 27.

*I*n the course of the afternoon Hal came upon Mary Burke on the street. She had long ago found her father, and seen him off to O'Callahan's to celebrate the favors of Providence. Now Mary was concerned with a graver matter. Number Two Mine was in danger! The explosion in Number One had been so violent that the gearing of the fan of the other mine, nearly a mile up the canyon, had been thrown out of order. So the fan had stopped; and when someone had gone to Alec Stone, asking that he bring out the men, Stone had refused. "What do ye think he said?" cried Mary. "What do ye think? 'Damn the men! Save the mules!'"

Hal had all but lost sight of the fact that there was a second mine in the village, in which hundreds of men and boys were still at work. "Wouldn't they know about the explosion?" he asked.

"They might have heard the noise," said Mary. "But they'd not know what it was; and the bosses won't tell them till they've got out the mules."

For all that he had seen in North Valley, Hal could hardly credit that story. "How do you know it, Mary?"

"Young Rovetta just told me. He was there, and heard it with his own ears."

He was staring at her. "Let's go and make sure," he said, and they started up the main street of the village. On the way they were joined by others — for already the news of this fresh trouble had begun to spread. Jeff Cotton went past them in an automobile, and Mary exclaimed, "I told ye so! When ye see him goin', ye know there's dirty work to be done!"

They came to the shaft-house of Number Two, and found a swarm of people, almost a riot. Women and children were shrieking and gesticulating, threatening to break into the office and use the mine-telephone to warn the men themselves. And here was the camp-marshal driving them back. Hal and Mary arrived in time to see Mrs. David, whose husband was at work in Number Two, shaking her fist in the marshal's face and screaming at him like a wildcat. He drew his revolver upon her; and at this Hal started forward. A blind fury seized him — he would have thrown himself upon the marshal.

But Mary Burke stopped him, flinging her arms about him, and pinning him by main force. "No, no!" she cried. "Stay back, man! D'ye want to get killed?"

He was amazed at her strength. He was amazed also at the vehemence of her emotion. She was calling him a crazy fool, and names even more harsh. "Have ye no more sense than a woman? Running into the mouth of a revolver like that!"

The crisis passed in a moment, for Mrs. David fell back, and then the marshal put up his weapon. But Mary continued scolding Hal, trying to drag him away. "Come on now! Come out of here!"

"But, Mary! We must do something!"

"Ye can do nothin', I tell ye! Ye'd ought to have sense enough to know it. I'll not let ye get yeself murdered! Come away now!" And half by force and half by cajoling, she got him farther down the street.

He was trying to think out the situation. Were the men in Number Two really in danger? Could it be possible that the bosses would take such a chance in cold blood? And right at this moment, with the disaster in the other mine before their eyes! He could not believe it; and meantime Mary, at his side, was declaring that the men were in no real danger — it was only Alec Stone's brutal words that had set her crazy.

"Don't ye remember the time when the air-course was blocked before, and ye helped to get up the mules yeself? Ye thought nothin' of it then, and 'tis the same now. They'll get everybody out in time!"

She was concealing her real feelings in order to keep him safe; he let her lead him on, while he tried to think of something else to do. He would think of the men in Number Two; they were his best friends, Jack David, Tim Rafferty, Wresmak, Androkulos, Klowoski. He would think of them, in their remote dungeons — breathing bad air, becoming sick and faint — in order that mules might be saved! He would stop in his tracks, and Mary would drag him on, repeating over and over, "Ye can do nothin'! Nothin'!" And then he would think, What could he do? He had put up his best bluff to Jeff Cotton a few hours earlier, and the answer had been the muzzle of the marshal's revolver in his face. All he could accomplish now would be to bring himself to Cotton's attention, and be thrust out of camp forthwith.

SECTION 28.

*T*hey came to Mary's home; and next door was the home of the Slav woman, Mrs. Zamboni, about whom in the past she had told him so many funny stories. Mrs. Zamboni had had a new baby every year for sixteen years, and eleven of these babies were still alive. Now her husband was trapped in Number One, and she was distracted, wandering about the streets with the greater part of her brood at her heels. At intervals she would emit a howl like a tortured animal, and her brood would take it up in various timbres. Hal stopped to listen to the sounds, but Mary put her fingers into her ears and fled into the house. Hal followed her, and saw her fling herself into a chair and burst into hysterical weeping. And suddenly Hal realized what a strain this terrible affair had been upon Mary. It had been bad enough to him — but he was a man, and more able to contemplate sights of horror. Men went to their deaths in industry and war, and other men saw them go and inured themselves to the spectacle. But women were the mothers of these men; it was women who bore them in pain, nursed them and reared them with endless patience — women could never become inured to the spectacle! Then too, the women's fate was worse. If the men were dead, that was the end of them; but the women must face the future, with its bitter memories, its lonely and desolate struggle for existence. The women must see the children suffering, dying by slow stages of deprivation.

Hal's pity for all suffering women became concentrated upon the girl beside him. He knew how tenderhearted she was. She had no man in the mine, but some day she would have, and she was suffering the pangs of that inexorable future. He looked at her, huddled in her chair, wiping away her tears with the hem of her old blue calico. She seemed unspeakably pathetic — like a child that has been hurt. She was sobbing out sentences now and then, as if to herself: "Oh, the poor women, the poor women! Did ye see the face of Mrs. Jonotch? She'd jumped into the smoking pit-mouth if they'd let her!"

"Don't suffer so, Mary!" pleaded Hal — as if he thought she could stop.

"Let me alone!" she cried. "Let me have it out!" And Hal, who had had no experience with hysteria, stood helplessly by.

"There's more misery than I ever knew there was!" she went on. "'Tis everywhere ye turn, a woman with her eyes burnin' with suffering wondering if she'll ever see her man again! Or some mother whose lad may be dying and she can do nothin' for him!"

"And neither can you do anything, Mary," Hal pleaded again. "You're only sorrowing yourself to death."

"Ye say that to me?" she cried. "And when ye were ready to let Jeff Cotton shoot ye, because you were so sorry for Mrs. David! No, the sights here nobody can stand."

He could think of nothing to answer. He drew up a chair and sat by her in silence, and after a while she began to grow calmer, and wiped away her tears, and sat gazing dully through the doorway into the dirty little street.

Hal's eyes followed hers. There were the ash-heaps and tomato-cans, there were two of Mrs. Zamboni's bedraggled brood, poking with sticks into a dump-heap — looking for something to eat, perhaps, or for something to play with. There was the dry, waste grass of the roadside, grimy with coal-dust, as was everything else in the village. What a scene! — And this girl's eyes had never a sight of anything more inspiring than this. Day in and day out, all her life long, she looked at this scene! Had he ever for a moment reproached her for her "black moods?" With such an environment could men or women be cheerful — could they dream of beauty, aspire to heights of nobility and courage, to happy service of their fellows? There was a miasma of despair over this place; it was not a real place — it was a dream-place — a horrible, distorted nightmare! It was like the black hole in the ground which haunted Hal's imagination, with men and boys at the bottom of it, dying of asphyxiation!

Suddenly it came to Hal — he wanted to get away from North Valley! To get away at all costs! The place had worn down his courage; slowly, day after day, the sight of misery and want, of dirt and disease, of hunger, oppression, despair, had eaten the soul out of him, had undermined his fine structure of altruistic theories. Yes, he wanted to escape — to a place where the sun shone, where the grass grew green, where human beings stood erect and laughed and were free. He wanted to shut from his eyes the dust and smoke of this nasty little village; to stop his ears to that tormenting sound of women wailing: "O, mein Mann! O, mein Mann!"

He looked at the girl, who sat staring before her, bent forward, her arms hanging limply over her knees.

"Mary," he said, "you must go away from here! It's no place for a tenderhearted girl to be. It's no place for anyone!"

She gazed at him dully for a moment. "It was me that was tellin' *you* to go away," she said, at last. "Ever since ye came here I been sayin' it! Now I guess ye know what I mean."

"Yes," he said, "I do, and I want to go. But I want you to go too."

"D'ye think 'twould do me any good, Joe?" she asked. "D'ye think 'twould do me any good to get away? Could I ever forget the sights I've seen this day? Could I ever have any real, honest happiness anywhere after this?"

He tried to reassure her, but he was far from reassured himself. How would it be with him? Would he ever feel that he had a right to happiness after this? Could he take any satisfaction in a pleasant and comfortable world, knowing that it was based upon such hideous misery? His thoughts went to that world, where careless, pleasure-loving people sought gratification of their desires. It came to him suddenly that what he wanted more than to get away was to bring those people here, if only for a day, for an hour, that they might hear this chorus of wailing women!

SECTION 29.

Mary made Hal swear that he would not get into a fight with Cotton; then they went to Number Two. They found the mules coming up, and the bosses promising that in a short while the men would be coming. Everything was all right — there was not a bit of danger! But Mary was afraid to trust Hal, in spite of his promise, so she lured him back to Number One.

They found that a rescue-car had just arrived from Pedro, bringing doctors and nurses, also several "helmets." These "helmets" were strange looking contrivances, fastened over the head and shoulders, air-tight, and provided with oxygen sufficient to last for an hour or more. The men who wore them sat in a big bucket which was let down the shaft with a windlass, and every now and then they pulled on a signal-cord to let those on the surface know they were alive. When the first of them came back, he reported that there were bodies near the foot of the shaft, but apparently all dead. There was heavy black smoke, indicating a fire somewhere in the mine; so nothing more could be done until the fan had been set up. By reversing the fan, they could draw out the smoke and gases and clear the shaft.

The state mine-inspector had been notified, but was ill at home, and was sending one of his deputies. Under the law this official would have charge of all the rescue work, but Hal found that the miners took no interest in his presence. It had been his duty to prevent the accident, and he had not done so. When he came, he would do what the company wanted.

Some time after dark the workers began to come out of Number Two, and their women, waiting at the pit-mouth, fell upon their necks with cries of thankfulness. Hal observed other women, whose men were in Number One, and would perhaps never come out again, standing and watching these greetings with wistful, tear-filled eyes. Among those who came out was Jack David, and Hal walked home with him and his wife, listening to the latter abuse Jeff Cotton and Alec Stone, which was an education in the vocabulary of class-consciousness. The little Welsh woman repeated the pit-boss's saying, "Damn the men, save the mules!" She said it again and again — it seemed to delight her like a work of art, it summed up so perfectly the attitude of the bosses to their men! There were many other people repeating that saying, Hal found; it went all over the village, in a few days it went all over the district. It summed up what the district believed to be the attitude of the coal-operators to the workers!

Having got over the first shock of the disaster, Hal wanted information, and he questioned Big Jack, a solid and well-read man who had given thought to every aspect of the industry. In his quiet, slow way, he explained to Hal that the frequency of accidents in this district was not due to any special difficulty in operating these mines, the explosiveness of the gases or the dryness of the atmosphere. It was merely the careless-ness of those in charge, their disregard of the laws for the protection of the men. There ought to be a law with "teeth" in it — for example, one providing that for every man killed in a coal-mine his heirs should receive a thousand dollars, regardless of who had been to blame for the accident. Then you would see how quickly the operators would get busy and find remedies for the "unusual" dangers!

As it was, they knew that no matter how great their culpability, they could get off with slight loss. Already, no doubt, their lawyers were on the spot, and by the time the first bodies were brought out, they would be fixing things up with the families. They would offer a widow a ticket back to the old country; they would offer a whole family of orphaned children, maybe fifty dollars, maybe a hundred dollars — and it would be a case of take it or leave it. You could get nothing from the courts; the case was so hopeless that you could not even find a lawyer to make the attempt. That was one reform in which the companies believed, said "Big Jack," with sarcasm; they had put the "shyster lawyer" out of business!

SECTION 30.

*T*here followed a night and then another day of torturing suspense. The fan came, but it had to be set up before anything could be done. As volumes of black smoke continued to pour from the shaft, the opening was made tight with a board and canvas cover; it was necessary, the bosses said, but to Hal it seemed the climax of horror. To seal up men and boys in a place of deadly gases!

There was something peculiarly torturing in the idea of men caught in a mine; they were directly under one's feet, yet it was impossible to get to them, to communicate with them in any way! The people on top yearned to them, and they, down below, yearned back. It was impossible to forget them for even a few minutes. People would become abstracted while they talked, and would stand staring into space; suddenly, in the midst of a crowd, a woman would bury her face in her hands and burst into tears, and then all the others would follow suit.

Few people slept in North Valley during those two nights. They held mourning parties in their homes or on the streets. Some house-work had to be done, of course, but no one did anything that could be left undone. The children would not play; they stood about, silent, pale, like wizened-up grown people, overmature in knowledge of trouble. The nerves of everyone were on edge, the self-control of everyone balanced upon a fine point.

It was a situation bound to be fruitful in imaginings and rumors, stimulated to those inclined to signs and omens — the seers of ghosts, or those who went into trances, or possessed second sight or other mysterious gifts. There were some living in a remote part of the village who declared they had heard explosions under the ground, several blasts in quick succession. The men underground were setting off dynamite by way of signaling!

In the course of the second day Hal sat with Mary Burke upon the steps of her home. Old Patrick lay within, having found the secret of oblivion at O'Callahan's. Now and then came the moaning of Mrs. Zamboni, who was in her cabin with her brood of children. Mary had been in to feed them, because the distracted mother let them starve and cry. Mary was worn out, herself; the wonderful Irish complexion had faded, and there were no curves to the vivid lips. They had been sitting in silence, for there was nothing to talk of but the disaster — and they

had said all there was to say about that. But Hal had been thinking while
he watched Mary.

"Listen, Mary," he said, at last; "when this thing is over, you must
really come away from here. I've thought it all out — I have friends in
Western City who will give you work, so you can take care of yourself,
and of your brother and sister too. Will you go?"

But she did not answer. She continued to gaze indifferently into the
dirty little street.

"Truly, Mary," he went on. "Life isn't so terrible everywhere as it is
here. Come away! Hard as it is to believe, you'll forget all this. People
suffer, but then they stop suffering; it's nature's way — to make them
forget."

"Nature's way has been to beat me dead," said she.

"Yes, Mary. Despair can become a disease, but it hasn't with you.
You're just tired out. If you'll try to rouse yourself —" And he reached
over and caught her hand with an attempt at playfulness. "Cheer up,
Mary! You're coming away from North Valley."

She turned and looked at him. "Am I?" she asked, impassively; and
she went on studying his face. "Who are ye, Joe Smith? What are ye
doin' here?"

"Working in a coal-mine," he laughed, still trying to divert her.

But she went on, as gravely as before. "Ye're no working man, that I
know. And ye're always offering me help! Ye're always sayin' what ye can
do for me!" She paused and there came some of the old defiance into
her face. "Joe, ye can have no idea of the feelin's that have got hold of
me just now. I'm ready to do something desperate; ye'd best be leavin'
me alone, Joe!"

"I think I understand, Mary. I would hardly blame you for anything
you did."

She took up his words eagerly. "Wouldn't ye, Joe? Ye're sure? Then
what I want is to get the truth from ye. I want ye to talk it out fair!"

"All right, Mary. What is it?"

But her defiance had vanished suddenly. Her eyes dropped, and he
saw her fingers picking nervously at a fold of her dress. "About us, Joe,"
she said. "I've thought sometimes ye cared for me. I've thought ye liked
to be with me — not just because ye were sorry for me, but because of
me. I've not been sure, but I can't help thinkin' it's so. Is it?"

"Yes, it is," he said, a little uncertainly. "I *do* care for you."

"Then is it that ye don't care for that other girl all the time?"

"No," he said, "it's not that."

"Ye can care for two girls at the same time?"

He did not know what to say. "It would seem that I can, Mary."

She raised her eyes again and studied his face. "Ye told me about that other girl, and I been wonderin', was it only to put me off? Maybe it's me own fault, but I can't make meself believe in that other girl, Joe!"

"You're mistaken, Mary," he answered, quickly. "What I told you was true."

"Well, maybe so," she said, but there was no conviction in her tone. "Ye come away from her, and ye never go where she is or see her — it's hard to believe ye'd do that way if ye were very close to her. I just don't think ye love her as much as ye might. And ye say you do care some for me. So I've thought — I've wondered —"

She stopped, forcing herself to meet his gaze: "I been tryin' to work it out! I know ye're too good a man for me, Joe. Ye come from a better place in life, ye've a right to expect more in a woman —"

"It's not that, Mary!"

But she cut him short. "I know that's true! Ye're only tryin' to save my feelin's. I know ye're better than me! I've tried hard to hold me head up, I've tried a long time not to let meself go to pieces. I've even tried to keep cheerful, telling meself I'd not want to be like Mrs. Zamboni, forever complainin'. But 'tis no use tellin' yourself lies! I been up to the church, and heard the Reverend Spragg tell the people that the rich and poor are the same in the sight of the Lord. And maybe 'tis so, but I'm not the Lord, and I'll never pretend I'm not ashamed to be livin' in a place like this."

"I'm sure the Lord has no interest in keeping you here —" he began.

But she broke in, "What makes it so hard to bear is knowin' there's so many wonderful things in the world, and ye can never have them! 'Tis as if ye had to see them through a pane of glass, like in the window of a store. Just think, Joe Smith — once, in a church in Sheridan, I heard a lady sing beautiful music; once in my whole lifetime! Can ye guess what it meant to me?"

"Yes, Mary, I can."

"But I had that all out with meself — years ago. I knew the price a workin' girl has to pay for such things, and I said, I'll not let meself think about them. I've hated this place, I've wanted to get away — but there's only one way to go, to let some man take ye! So I've stayed; I've kept straight, Joe. I want ye to believe that."

"Of course, Mary!"

"No! It's not been 'of course'! It means ye have to fight with temptations. It's many a time I've looked at Jeff Cotton, and thought about the things I need! And I've done without! But now comes the thing a woman wants more than all the other things in the world!"

She paused, but only for a moment. "They tell ye to love a man of your own class. Me old mother said that to me, before she died. But suppose ye didn't happen to? Suppose ye'd stopped and thought what it meant, havin' one baby after another, till ye're worn out and drop — like me old mother did? Suppose ye knew good manners when ye see them — ye knew interestin' talk when ye heard it!" She clasped her hands suddenly before her, exclaiming, "Ah, 'tis something different ye are, Joe — so different from anything around here! The way ye talk, the way ye move, the gay look in your eyes! No miner ever had that happy look, Joe; me heart stops beatin' almost when ye look at me!" She stopped with a sharp catching of her breath, and he saw that she was struggling for self-control. After a moment she exclaimed, defiantly: "But they'd tell ye, be careful, ye daren't love that kind of man; ye'd only have your heart broken!"

There was silence. For this problem the amateur sociologist had no solution at hand — whether for the abstract question, or for its concrete application!

SECTION 31.

Mary forced herself to go on. "This is how I've worked it out, Joe! I said to meself, 'Ye love this man; and it's his *love* ye want — nothin' else! If he's got a place in the world, ye'd only hold him back — and ye'd not want to do that. Ye don't want his name, or his friends, or any of those things — ye want *him!* Have ye ever heard of such a thing as that?"

Her cheeks were flaming, but she continued to meet his gaze. "Yes, I've heard of it," he answered, in a low voice.

"What would ye say to it? Is it honest? The Reverend Spragg would say 'twas the devil, no doubt; Father O'Gorman, down in Pedro, would call it mortal sin; and maybe they know — but I don't! I only know I can't stand it anymore!"

Tears sprang to her eyes, and she cried out suddenly, "Oh, take me away from here! Take me away and give me a chance, Joe! I'll ask nothing, I'll never stand in your way; I'll work for ye, I'll cook and wash and do everything for ye, I'll wear my fingers to the bone! Or I'll go out and work at some job, and earn my share. And I'll make ye this promise — if ever ye get tired and want to leave me, ye'll not hear a word of complaint!"

She made no conscious appeal to his senses; she sat gazing at him honestly through her tears, and that made it all the harder to answer her.

What could he say? He felt the old dangerous impulse — to take the girl in his arms and comfort her. When finally he spoke it was with an effort to keep his voice calm. "I'd say yes, Mary, if I thought it would work."

"It *would* work! It would, Joe! Ye can quit when ye want to. I mean it!"

"There's no woman lives who can be happy on such terms, Mary. She wants her man, and she wants him to herself, and she wants him always; she's only deluding herself if she believes anything else. You're over-wrought now, what you've seen in the last few days has made you wild —"

"No!" she exclaimed. "'Tis not only that! I been thinkin' about it for weeks."

"I know. You've been thinking, but you wouldn't have spoken if it hadn't been for this horror." He paused for a moment, to renew his own self-possession. "It won't do, Mary," he declared. "I've seen it tried more than once, and I'm not so old either. My own brother tried it once, and ruined himself."

"Ah, ye're afraid to trust me, Joe!"

"No, it's not that; what I mean is — he ruined his own heart, he made himself selfish. He took everything, and gave nothing. He's much older than I, so I've had a chance to see its effect on him. He's cold, he has no faith, even in his own nature; when you talk to him about making the world better he tells you you're a fool."

"It's another way of bein' afraid of me," she insisted. "Afraid you'd ought to marry me!"

"But, Mary — there's the other girl. I really love her, and I'm promised to her. What can I do?"

"'Tis that I've never believed you loved her," she said, in a whisper. Her eyes fell and she began picking nervously again at the faded blue dress, which was smutted and grease-stained, perhaps from her recent effort with Mrs. Zamboni's brood. Several times Hal thought she was going to speak, but she shut her lips tightly again; he watched her, his heart aching.

When finally she spoke, it was still in a whisper, and there was a note of humility he had never heard from her before. "Ye'll not be wantin' to speak to me, Joe, after what I've said."

"Oh, Mary!" he exclaimed, and caught her hand, "don't say I've made you more unhappy! I want to help you! Won't you let me be your friend — your real, true friend? Let me help you to get out of this trap; you'll have a chance to look about, you'll find a way to be happy – the whole world will seem different to you then, and you'll laugh at the idea that you ever wanted me!"

SECTION 32.

*T*he two of them went back to the pit-mouth. It had been two days since the disaster, and still the fan had not been started, and there was no sign of its being started. The hysteria of the women was growing, and there was a tension in the crowds. Jeff Cotton had brought in a force of men to assist him in keeping order. They had built a fence of barbed wire about the pit-mouth and its approaches, and behind this wire they walked – hard-looking citizens with policemen's "billies," and the bulge of revolvers plainly visible on their hips.

During this long period of waiting, Hal had talks with members of his check-weighman group. They told what had happened while he was in jail, and this reminded him of something which had been driven from his mind by the explosion. Poor old John Edstrom was down in Pedro, perhaps in dire need. Hal went to the old Swede's cabin that night, climbed through a window, and dug up the buried money. There were five five-dollar bills, and he put them in an envelope, addressed them in care of General Delivery, Pedro, and had Mary Burke take them to the post office and register them.

The hours dragged on, and still there was no sign of the pit-mouth being opened. There began to be secret gatherings of the miners and their wives to complain at the conduct of the company; and it was natural that Hal's friends who had started the check-weighman movement, should take the lead in these. They were among the most intelligent of the workers, and saw farther into the meaning of events. They thought, not merely of the men who were trapped underground at this moment, but of thousands of others who would be trapped through years to come. Hal, especially, was pondering how he could accomplish something definite before he left the camp; for of course he would have to leave soon – Jeff Cotton would remember him, and carry out his threat to get rid of him.

Newspapers had come in, with accounts of the disaster, and Hal and his friends read these. It was evident that the company had been at pains to have the accounts written from its own point of view. There existed some public sensitiveness on the subject of mine-disasters in this state. The death-rate from accidents was seen to be mounting steadily; the reports of the state mine inspector showed six per thousand in one year, eight and a half in the next, and twenty-one and a half in the next. When fifty or a hundred men were killed in a single accident, and when such accidents kept happening, one on the heels of another, even the most callous public could not help asking questions. So in this case the "G.F.C." had been careful to minimize the loss of life, and to make excuses. The accident had been owing to no fault of the company's; the mine had been regularly sprinkled, both with water and adobe dust, and so the cause of the explosion must have been the carelessness of the men in handling powder.

In Jack David's cabin one night there arose a discussion as to the number of men entombed in the mine. The company's estimate of the number was forty, but Minetti and Olson and David agreed that this was absurd. Any man who went about in the crowds could satisfy himself that there were two or three times as many unaccounted for. And this falsification was deliberate, for the company had a checking system, whereby it knew the name of every man in the mine. But most of these names were unpronounceable Slavish, and the owners of the names had no friends to mention them — at least not in any language understood by American newspaper editors.

It was all a part of the system, declared Jack David: its purpose and effect being to enable the company to go on killing men without paying for them, either in money or in prestige. It occurred to Hal that it might be worth while to contradict these false statements — almost as worth while as to save the men who were at this moment entombed. Anyone who came forward to make such a contradiction would of course be giving himself up to the black-list; but then, Hal regarded himself as a man already condemned to that penalty.

Tom Olson spoke up. "What would you do with your contradiction?"

"Give it to the papers," Hal answered.

"But what papers would print it?"

"There are two rival papers in Pedro, aren't there?"

"One owned by Alf Raymond, the sheriff-emperor, and the other by Vagleman, counsel for the 'G.F.C.' Which one would you try?"

"Well then, the outside papers — those in Western City. There are reporters here now, and some one of them would surely take it."

Olson answered, declaring that they would not get any but labor and Socialist papers to print such news. But even that was well worth doing. And Jack David, who was strong for unions and all their activities, put in, "The thing to do is to take a regular census, so as to know exactly how many are in the mine."

The suggestion struck fire, and they agreed to set to work that same evening. It would be a relief to do something, to have something in their minds but despair. They passed the word to Mary Burke, to Rovetta, Klowoski, and others; and at eleven o'clock the next morning they met again, and the lists were put together, and it was found that no less than a hundred and seven men and boys were positively known to be inside Number One.

SECTION 33.

*A*s it happened, however, discussion of this list and the method of giving it to the world was cut short by a more urgent matter. Jack David came in with news of fresh trouble at the pit-mouth. The new fan was being put in place; but they were slow about it, so slow that some people had become convinced that they did not mean to start the fan at all, but were keeping the mine sealed to prevent the fire from spreading. A group of such malcontents had presumed to go to Mr. Carmichael, the deputy state mine-inspector, to urge him to take some action; and the leader of these protestants, Huszar, the Austrian, who had been one of Hal's check-weighman group, had been taken into custody and marched at double-quick to the gate of the stockade!

Jack David declared furthermore that he knew a carpenter who was working in the fan-house, and who said that no haste whatever was being made. All the men at the fan-house shared that opinion; the mine was sealed, and would stay sealed until the company was sure the fire was out.

"But," argued Hal, "if they were to open it, the fire would spread; and wouldn't that prevent rescue work?"

"Not at all," declared "Big Jack." He explained that by reversing the fan they could draw the smoke up through the air-course, which would clear the main passages for a time. "But, you see, some coal might catch fire, and some timbers; there might be falls of rock so they couldn't work some of the rooms again."

"How long will they keep the mine sealed?" cried Hal, in consternation.

"Nobody can say. In a big mine like that, a fire might smolder for a week."

"Everybody be dead!" cried Rosa Minetti, wringing her hands in a sudden access of grief.

Hal turned to Olson. "Would they possibly do such a thing?"

"It's been done — more than once," was the organizer's reply.

"Did you never hear about Cherry, Illinois?" asked David. "They did it there, and more than three hundred people lost their lives." He went on to tell that dreadful story, known to every coal-miner. They had sealed the mine, while women fainted and men tore their clothes in frenzy — some going insane. They had kept it sealed for two weeks, and when they opened it, there were twenty-one men still alive!

"They did the same thing in Diamondville, Wyoming," added Olson. "They built up a barrier, and when they took it away they found a heap of dead men, who had crawled to it and torn their fingers to the bone trying to break through."

"My God!" cried Hal, springing to his feet. "And this man Carmichael — would he stand for that?"

"He'd tell you they were doing their best," said "Big Jack." "And maybe he thinks they are. But you'll see — something'll keep happening; they'll drag on from day to day, and they'll not start the fan till they're ready."

"Why, it's murder!" cried Hal.

"It's business," said Tom Olson, quietly.

Hal looked from one to another of the faces of these working people. Not one but had friends in that trap; not one but might be in the same trap tomorrow!

"You have to stand it!" he exclaimed, half to himself.

"Don't you see the guards at the pit-mouth?" answered David. "Don't you see the guns sticking out of their pockets?"

"They bring in more guards this morning," put in Jerry Minetti. "Rosa, she see them get off."

"They know what they doin'!" said Rosa. "They only fraid we find it out! They told Mrs. Zamboni she keep away or they send her out of camp. And old Mrs. Jonotch — her husband and three sons inside!"

"They're getting rougher and rougher," declared Mrs. David. "That big fellow they call Pete, that came up from Pedro — the way he's handling the women is a shame!"

"I know him," put in Olson; "Pete Hanun. They had him in Sheridan when the union first opened headquarters. He smashed one of our organizers in the mouth and broke four of his teeth. They say he has a jail-record."

All through the previous year at college Hal had listened to lectures upon political economy, filled with the praises of a thing called "Private Ownership." This Private Ownership developed initiative and economy; it kept the wheels of industry a-roll, it kept fat the pay-rolls of college faculties; it accorded itself with the sacred laws of supply and demand, it was the basis of the progress and prosperity wherewith America had been blessed. And here suddenly Hal found himself face to face with the reality of it; he saw its wolfish eyes glaring into his own, he felt its smoking hot breath in his face, he saw its gleaming fangs and clawlike fingers, dripping with the blood of men and women and children. Private Ownership of coal-mines! Private Ownership of sealed-up entrances and non-existent escape-ways! Private Ownership of fans which did not start, of sprinklers which did not sprinkle. Private Ownership of clubs and revolvers, and of thugs and ex-convicts to use them, driving away rescuers and shutting up agonized widows and orphans in their homes! Oh, the serene and well-fed priests of Private Ownership, chanting in academic halls the praises of the bloody Demon!

Suddenly Hal stopped still. Something had risen in him, the existence of which he had never suspected. There was a new look upon his face, his voice was deep as a strong man's when he spoke: "I am going to make them open that mine!"

They looked at him. They were all of them close to the border of hysteria, but they caught the strange note in his utterance. "I am going to make them open that mine!"

"How?" asked Olson.

"The public doesn't know about this thing. If the story got out, there'd be such a clamor, it couldn't go on!"

"But how will you get it out?"

"I'll give it to the newspapers! They can't suppress such a thing — I don't care how prejudiced they are!"

"But do you think they'd believe what a miner's buddy tells them?" asked Mrs. David.

"I'll find a way to make them believe me," said Hal. "I'm going to make them open that mine!"

SECTION 34.

*I*n the course of his wanderings about the camp, Hal had observed several wide-awake looking young men with notebooks in their hands. He could see that these young men were being made guests of the company, chatting with the bosses upon friendly terms; nevertheless, he believed that among them he might find one who had a conscience – or at any rate who would yield to the temptation of a "scoop." So, leaving the gathering at Mrs. David's, Hal went to the pit-mouth, watching out for one of these reporters; when he found him, he followed him for a while, desiring to get him where no company "spotter" might interfere. At the first chance, he stepped up, and politely asked the reporter to come into a side street, where they might converse undisturbed.

The reporter obeyed the request; and Hal, concealing the intensity of his feelings, so as not to repel the other, let it be known that he had worked in North Valley for some months, and could tell much about conditions in the camp. There was the matter of adobe-dust, for example. Explosions in dry mines could be prevented by spraying the walls with this material. Did the reporter happen to know that the company's claim to have used it was entirely false?

No, the reporter answered, he did not know this. He seemed interested, and asked Hal's name and occupation. Hal told him "Joe Smith," a "buddy," who had recently been chosen as check-weighman. The reporter, a lean and keen-faced young man, asked many questions – intelligent questions; incidentally he mentioned that he was the local correspondent of the great press association whose stories of the disaster were sent to every corner of the country. This seemed to Hal an extraordinary piece of good fortune, and he proceeded to tell this Mr. Graham about the census which some of the workers had taken; they were able to give the names of a hundred and seven men and boys who were inside the mine. The list was at Mr. Graham's disposal if he cared to see it. Mr. Graham seemed more interested than ever, and made notes in his book.

Another thing, more important yet, Hal continued; the matter of the delay in getting the fan started. It had been three days since the explosion, but there had been no attempt at entering the mine. Had Mr. Graham seen the disturbance at the pit-mouth that morning? Did he realize that a man had been thrown out of camp merely because he had appealed to the deputy state mine-inspector? Hal told what so many had come to believe — that the company was saving property at the expense of life. He went on to point out the human meaning of this — he told about old Mrs. Rafferty, with her failing health and her eight children; about Mrs. Zamboni, with eleven children; about Mrs. Jonotch, with a husband and three sons in the mine. Led on by the reporter's interest, Hal began to show some of his feeling. These were human beings, not animals; they loved and suffered, even though they were poor and humble!

"Most certainly!" said Mr. Graham. "You're right, and you may rest assured I'll look into this."

"There's one thing more," said Hal. "If my name is mentioned, I'll be fired, you know."

"I won't mention it," said the other.

"Of course, if you can't publish the story without giving its source —"

"I'm the source," said the reporter, with a smile. "Your name would not add anything."

He spoke with quiet assurance; he seemed to know so completely both the situation and his own duty in regard to it, that Hal felt a thrill of triumph. It was as if a strong wind had come blowing from the outside world, dispelling the miasma which hung over this coal-camp. Yes, this reporter *was* the outside world! He was the power of public opinion, making itself felt in this place of knavery and fear! He was the voice of truth, the courage and rectitude of a great organization of publicity, independent of secret influences, lifted above corruption!

"I'm indebted to you," said Mr. Graham, at the end, and Hal's sense of victory was complete. What an extraordinary chance — that he should have run into the agent of the great press association! The story would go out to the great world of industry, which depended upon coal as its life-blood. The men in the factories, the wheels of which were turned by coal — the travelers on trains which were moved by coal — they would hear at last of the sufferings of those who toiled in the bowels of the earth for them! Even the ladies, reclining upon the decks of palatial steamships in gleaming tropic seas — so marvelous was the power of modern news-spreading agencies, that these ladies too might hear the cry for help of these toilers, and of their wives and little ones! And from this great world would come an answer, a universal shout of horror, of execration, that would force even old Peter Harrigan to give way! So Hal mused — for he was young, and this was his first crusade.

He was so happy that he was able to think of himself again, and to realize that he had not eaten that day. It was noon-time, and he went into Reminitsky's, and was about half through with the first course of Reminitsky's two-course banquet, when his cruel disillusioning fell upon him!

He looked up and saw Jeff Cotton striding into the dining room, making straight for him. There was blood in the marshal's eye, and Hal saw it, and rose, instinctively.

"Come!" said Cotton, and took him by the coat-sleeve and marched him out, almost before the rest of the diners had time to catch their breath.

Hal had no opportunity now to display his "tea-party manners" to the camp-marshal. As they walked, Cotton expressed his opinion of him, that he was a skunk, a puppy, a person of undesirable ancestry; and when Hal endeavored to ask a question — which he did quite genuinely, not grasping at once the meaning of what was happening — the marshal bade him "shut his face," and emphasized the command by a twist at his coat-collar. At the same time two of the huskiest mine-guards, who had been waiting at the dining room door, took him, one by each arm, and assisted his progress.

They went down the street and past Jeff Cotton's office, not stopping this time. Their destination was the railroad-station, and when Hal got there, he saw a train standing. The three men marched him to it, not releasing him till they had jammed him down into a seat.

"Now, young fellow," said Cotton, "we'll see who's running this camp!"

By this time Hal had regained a part of his self-possession. "Do I need a ticket?" he asked.

"I'll see to that," said the marshal.

"And do I get my things?"

"You save some questions for your college professors," snapped the marshal.

So Hal waited; and a minute or two later a man arrived on the run with his scanty belongings, rolled into a bundle and tied with a piece of twine. Hal noted that this man was big and ugly, and was addressed by the camp-marshal as "Pete."

The conductor shouted, "All aboard!" And at the same time Jeff Cotton leaned over towards Hal and spoke in a menacing whisper: "Take this from me, young fellow; don't stop in Pedro, move on in a hurry, or something will happen to you on a dark night."

After which he strode down the aisle, and jumped off the moving train. But Hal noticed that Pete Hanun, the breaker of teeth, stayed on the car a few seats behind him.

BOOK THREE

THE HENCHMEN OF KING COAL

SECTION I.

*I*t was Hal's intention to get to Western City as quickly as possible to call upon the newspaper editors. But first he must have money to travel, and the best way he could think of to get it was to find John Edstrom. He left the train, followed by Pete Hanun; after some inquiry, he came upon the undertaker who had buried Edstrom's wife, and who told him where the old Swede was staying, in the home of a laboring-man nearby.

Edstrom greeted him with eager questions: Who had been killed? What was the situation? Hal told in brief sentences what had happened. When he mentioned his need of money, Edstrom answered that he had a little, and would lend it, but it was not enough for a ticket to Western City. Hal asked about the twenty-five dollars which Mary Burke had sent by registered mail; the old man had heard nothing about it, he had not been to the post office. "Let's go now!" said Hal, at once; but as they were starting downstairs, a fresh difficulty occurred to him. Pete Hanun was on the street outside, and it was likely that he had heard about this money from Jeff Cotton; he might hold Edstrom up and take it away.

"Let me suggest something," put in the old man. "Come and see my friend Ed MacKellar. He may be able to give us some advice — even to think of some way to get the mine open." Edstrom explained that MacKellar, an old Scotchman, had been a miner, but was now crippled, and held some petty office in Pedro. He was a persistent opponent of "Alf" Raymond's machine, and they had almost killed him on one occasion. His home was not far away, and it would take little time to consult him.

"All right," said Hal, and they set out at once. Pete Hanun followed them, not more than a dozen yards behind, but did not interfere, and they turned in at the gate of a little cottage. A woman opened the door for them, and asked them into the dining room where MacKellar was sitting — a grey-haired old man, twisted up with rheumatism and obliged to go about on crutches.

Hal told his story. As the Scotchman had been brought up in the mines, it was not necessary to go into details about the situation. When Hal told his idea of appealing to the newspapers, the other responded at once, "You won't have to go to Western City. There's a man right here who'll do the business for you; Keating, of the *Gazette.*"

"The Western City *Gazette?*" exclaimed Hal. He knew this paper; an evening journal selling for a cent, and read by working-men. Persons of culture who referred to it disposed of it with the adjective "yellow."

"I know," said MacKellar, noting Hal's tone. "But it's the only paper that will publish your story anyway."

"Where is this Keating?"

"He's been up at the mine. It's too bad you didn't meet him."

"Can we get hold of him now?"

"He might be in Pedro. Try the American Hotel."

Hal went to the telephone, and in a minute was hearing for the first time the cheery voice of his friend and lieutenant-to-be, "Billy" Keating. In a couple of minutes more the owner of the voice was at MacKellar's door, wiping the perspiration from his half-bald forehead. He was round-faced, like a full moon, and as jolly as Falstaff; when you got to know him better, you discovered that he was loyal as a Newfoundland dog. For all his bulk, Keating was a newspaper man, every inch of him "on the job."

He started to question the young miner as soon as he was introduced, and it quickly became clear to Hal that here was the man he was looking for. Keating knew exactly what questions to ask, and had the whole story in a few minutes. "By thunder!" he cried. "My last edition!" And he pulled out his watch, and sprang to the telephone. "Long distance," he called; then, "I want the city editor of the Western City *Gazette.* And, operator, please see if you can't rush it through. It's very urgent, and last time I had to wait nearly half an hour."

He turned back to Hal, and proceeded to ask more questions, at the same time pulling a bunch of copy-paper from his pocket and making notes. He got all Hal's statements about the lack of sprinkling, the absence of escape-ways, the delay in starting the fan, the concealing of the number of men in the mine. "I knew things were crooked up there!" he exclaimed. "But I couldn't get a lead! They kept a man with me every minute of the time. You know a fellow named Predovich?"

"I do," said Hal. "The company store-clerk; he once went through my pockets."

Keating made a face of disgust. "Well, he was my chaperon. Imagine trying to get the miners to talk to you with that sneak at your heels! I said to the superintendent, 'I don't need anybody to escort me around your place.' And he looked at me with a nasty little smile. 'We wouldn't want anything to happen to you while you're in this camp, Mr. Keating.' 'You don't consider it necessary to protect the lives of the other reporters,' I said. 'No,' said he; 'but the *Gazette* has made a great many enemies, you know.' 'Drop your fooling, Mr. Cartwright,' I said. 'You propose to have me shadowed while I'm working on this assignment?' 'You can put it that way,' he answered, 'if you think it'll please the readers of the *Gazette.*'"

"Too bad we didn't meet!" said Hal. "Or if you'd run into any of our check-weighman crowd!"

"Oh! You know about that check-weighman business!" exclaimed the reporter. "I got a hint of it — that's how I happened to be down here today. I heard there was a man named Edstrom, who'd been shut out for making trouble; and I thought if I could find him, I might get a lead."

Hal and MacKellar looked at the old Swede, and the three of them began to laugh. "Here's your man!" said MacKellar.

"And here's your check-weighman!" added Edstrom, pointing to Hal.

Instantly the reporter was on his job again; he began to fire another series of questions. He would use that check-weighman story as a "follow-up" for the next day, to keep the subject of North Valley alive. The story had a direct bearing on the disaster, because it showed what the North Valley bosses were doing when they should have been looking after the safety of their mine. "I'll write it out this afternoon and send it by mail," said Keating; he added, with a smile, "That's one advantage of handling news the other papers won't touch — you don't have to worry about losing your 'scoops'!"

SECTION 2.

*K*eating went to the telephone again, to worry "long distance"; then, grumbling about his last edition, he came back to ask more questions about Hal's experiences. Before long he drew out the story of the young man's first effort in the publicity game; at which he sank back in his chair, and laughed until he shook, as the nursery-rhyme describes it, "like a bowlful of jelly."

"Graham!" he exclaimed. "Fancy, MacKellar, he took that story to Graham!"

The Scotchman seemed to find it equally funny; together they explained that Graham was the political reporter of the *Eagle,* the paper in Pedro which was owned by the Sheriff-emperor. One might call him Alf Raymond's journalistic jackal; there was no job too dirty for him.

"But," cried Hal, "he told me he was correspondent for the Western press association!"

"He's that, too," replied Billy.

"But does the press association employ spies for the 'G.F.C.'?"

The reporter answered, dryly, "When you understand the news game better, you'll realize that the one thing the press association cares about in a correspondent is that he should have respect for property. If respect for property is the back-bone of his being, he can learn what news is, and the right way to handle it."

Keating turned to the Scotchman. "Do you happen to have a typewriter in the house, Mr. MacKellar?"

"An old one," said the other — "lame, like myself."

"I'll make out with it. I'd ask this young man over to my hotel, but I think he'd better keep off the streets as much as possible."

"You're right. If you take my advice, you'll take the typewriter upstairs, where there's no chance of a shot through the window."

"Great heavens!" exclaimed Hal. "Is this America, or mediaeval Italy?"

"It's the Empire of Raymond," replied MacKellar. "They shot my friend Tom Burton dead while he stood on the steps of his home. He was opposing the machine, and had evidence about ballot-frauds he was going to put before the Grand Jury."

While Keating continued to fret with "long distance," the old Scotchman went on trying to impress upon Hal the danger of his position. Quite recently an organizer of the miners' union had been beaten up in broad daylight and left insensible on the sidewalk; MacKellar had watched the trial and acquittal of the two thugs who had committed this crime — the foreman of the jury being a saloon-keeper one of Raymond's heelers, and the other jurymen being Mexicans, unable to comprehend a word of the court proceedings.

"Exactly such a jury as Jeff Cotton promised me!" remarked Hal, with a feeble attempt at a smile.

"Yes," answered the other; "and don't make any mistake about it, if they want to put you away, they can do it. They run the whole machine here. I know how it is, for I had a political job myself, until they found they couldn't use me."

The old Scotchman went on to explain that he had been elected justice of peace, and had tried to break up the business of policemen taking money from the women of the town; he had been forced to resign, and his enemies had made his life a torment. Recently he had been candidate for district judge on the Progressive ticket, and told of his efforts to carry on a campaign in the coal-camps — how his circulars had been confiscated, his posters torn down, his supporters "kangarooed." It was exactly as Alec Stone, the pit-boss, had explained to Hal. In some of the camps the meeting-halls belonged to the company; in others they belonged to saloon-keepers whose credit depended upon Alf Raymond. In the few places where there were halls that could be hired, the machine had gone to the extreme of sending in rival entertainments, furnishing free music and free beer in order to keep the crowds away from MacKellar.

All this time Billy Keating had been chafing and scolding at "long distance." Now at last he managed to get his call, and silence fell in the room. "Hello, Pringle, that you? This is Keating. Got a big story on the North Valley disaster. Last edition put to bed yet? Put Jim on the wire. Hello, Jim! Got your book?" And then Billy, evidently talking to a stenographer, began to tell the story he had got from Hal. Now and then he would stop to repeat or spell a word; once or twice Hal corrected him on details. So, in about a quarter of an hour, they put the job through; and Keating turned to Hal.

"There you are, son," said he. "Your story'll be on the street in Western City in a little over an hour; it'll be down here as soon thereafter as they can get telephone connections. And take my advice, if you want to keep a whole skin, you'll be out of Pedro when that happens!"

SECTION 3.

*W*hen Hal spoke, he did not answer Billy Keating's last remark. He had been listening to a retelling of the North Valley disaster over the telephone; so he was not thinking about his skin, but about a hundred and seven men and boys buried inside a mine.

"Mr. Keating," said he, "are you sure the *Gazette* will print that story?"

"Good Lord!" exclaimed the other. "What am I here for?"

"Well, I've been disappointed once, you know."

"Yes, but you got into the wrong camp. We're a poor man's paper, and this is what we live on."

"There's no chance of its being 'toned down'?"

"Not the slightest, I assure you."

"There's no chance of Peter Harrigan's suppressing it?"

"Peter Harrigan made his attempts on the *Gazette* long ago, my boy."

"Well," said Hal, "and now tell me this — will it do the work?"

"In what way?"

"I mean — in making them open the mine."

Keating considered for a moment. "I'm afraid it won't do much."

Hal looked at him blankly. He had taken it for granted the publication of the facts would force the company to move. But Keating explained that the *Gazette* read mainly by working-people, and so had comparatively little influence. "We're an afternoon paper," he said; "and when people have been reading lies all morning, it's not easy to make them believe the truth in the afternoon."

"But won't the story go to other papers — over the country, I mean?"

"Yes, we have a press service; but the papers are all like the *Gazette* — poor man's papers. If there's something very raw, and we keep pounding away for a long time, we can make an impression; at least we limit the amount of news the Western press association can suppress. But when it comes to a small matter like sealing up workingmen in a mine, all we can do is to worry the 'G.F.C.' a little."

So Hal was just where he had begun! "I must find some other plan," he exclaimed.

"I don't see what you can do," replied the other.

There was a pause, while the young miner pondered. "I had thought of going up to Western City and appealing to the editors," he said, a little uncertainly.

"Well, I can tell you about that — you might as well save your car-fare. They wouldn't touch your story."

"And if I appealed to the Governor?"

"In the first place, he probably wouldn't see you. And if he did, he wouldn't do anything. He's not really the Governor, you know; he's a puppet put up there to fool you. He only moves when Harrigan pulls a string."

"Of course I knew he was Old Peter's man," said Hal. "But then" — and he concluded, somewhat lamely, "What *can* I do?"

A smile of pity came upon the reporter's face. "I can see this is the first time you've been up against 'big business.'" And then he added, "You're young! When you've had more experience, you'll leave these problems to older heads!" But Hal failed to get the reporter's sarcasm. He had heard these exact words in such deadly seriousness from his brother! Besides, he had just come from scenes of horror.

"But don't you see, Mr. Keating?" he exclaimed. "It's impossible for me to sit still while those men die?"

"I don't know about your sitting still," said the other. "All I know is that all your moving about isn't going to do them any good."

Hal turned to Edstrom and MacKellar. "Gentlemen," he said, "listen to me for a minute." And there was a note of pleading in his voice — as if he thought they were deliberately refusing to help him! "We've got to do something about this. We've *got* to do something! I'm new at the game, as Mr. Keating says; but you aren't. Put your minds on it, gentlemen, and help me work out a plan!"

There was a long silence. "God knows," said Edstrom, at last. "I'd suggest something if I could."

"And I, too," said MacKellar. "You're up against a stone-wall, my boy. The government here is simply a department of the 'G.F.C.' The officials are crooks — company servants, all of them."

"Just a moment now," said Hal. "Let's consider. Suppose we had a real government — what steps would we take? We'd carry such a case to the District Attorney, wouldn't we?"

"Yes, no doubt of it," said MacKellar.

"You mentioned him before," said Hal. "He threatened to prosecute some mine-superintendents for ballot-frauds, you said."

"That was while he was running for election," said MacKellar.

"Oh! I remember what Jeff Cotton said — that he was friendly to the miners in his speeches, and to the companies in his acts."

"That's the man," said the other, dryly.

"Well," argued Hal, "oughtn't I go to him, to give him a chance, at least? You can't tell, he might have a heart inside him."

"It isn't a heart he needs," replied MacKellar; "it's a back-bone."

"But surely I ought to put it up to him! If he won't do anything, at least I'll put him on record, and it'll make another story for you, won't it, Mr. Keating?"

"Yes, that's true," admitted the reporter. "What would you ask him to do?"

"Why, to lay the matter before the Grand Jury; to bring indictments against the North Valley bosses."

"But that would take a long time; it wouldn't save the men in the mine."

"What might save them would be the threat of it." MacKellar put in. "I don't think any threat of Dick Barker's would count for that much. The bosses know they could stop him."

"Well, isn't there somebody else? Shouldn't I try the courts?"

"What courts?"

"I don't know. You tell me."

"Well," said the Scotchman, "to begin at the bottom, there's a justice of the peace."

"Who's he?"

"Jim Anderson, a horse-doctor. He's like any other J.P. you ever knew — he lives on petty graft."

"Is there a higher court?"

"Yes, the district court; Judge Denton. He's the law-partner of Vagleman, counsel for the 'G.F.C.' How far would you expect to get with him?"

"I suppose I'm clutching at straws," said Hal. "But they say that's what a drowning man does. Anyway, I'm going to see these people, and maybe out of the lot of them I can find one who'll act. It can't do any harm!"

The three men thought of some harm it might do; they tried to make Hal consider the danger of being slugged Or shot. "They'll do it!" exclaimed MacKellar. "And no trouble for them — they'll prove you were stabbed by a drunken Dago, quarreling over some woman."

But Hal had got his head set; he believed he could put this job through before his enemies had time to lay any plans. Nor would he let any of his friends accompany him; he had something more important for both Edstrom and Keating to do — and as for MacKellar, he could not get about rapidly enough. Hal bade Edstrom go to the post office and get the registered letter, and proceed at once to change the bills. It was his plan to make out affidavits, and if the officials here would not act, to take the affidavits to the Governor. And for this he would need money. Meantime, he said, let Billy Keating write out the check-weighman story, and in a couple of hours meet him at the American Hotel, to get copies of the affidavits for the *Gazette.*

Hal was still wearing the miner's clothes he had worn on the night of his arrest in Edstrom's cabin. But he declined MacKellar's offer to lend him a business-suit; the old Scotchman's clothes would not fit him, he knew, and it would be better to make his appeal as a real miner than as a misfit gentleman.

These matters being settled, Hal went out upon the street, where Pete Hanun, the breaker of teeth, fell in behind him. The young miner at once broke into a run, and the other followed suit, and so the two of them sped down the street, to the wonder of people on the way. As Hal had had practice as a sprinter, no doubt Pete was glad that the District Attorney's office was not far away!

SECTION 4.

Mr. Richard Parker was busy, said the clerk in toe outer office; for which Hal was not sorry, as it gave him a chance to get his breath. Seeing a young man flushed and panting, the clerk stared with curiosity; but Hal offered no explanation, and the breaker of teeth waited on the street outside.

Mr. Parker received his caller in a couple of minutes. He was a well-fed gentleman with generous neck and chin, freshly shaved and rubbed with talcum powder. His clothing was handsome, his linen immaculate; one got the impression of a person who "did himself well." There were papers on his desk, and he looked preoccupied.

"Well?" said he, with a swift glance at the young miner.

"I understand that I am speaking to the District Attorney of Pedro County?"

"That's right."

"Mr. Parker, have you given any attention to the circumstances of the North Valley disaster?"

"No," said Mr. Parker. "Why?"

"I have just come from North Valley, and I can give you information which may be of interest to you. There are a hundred and seven people entombed in the mine, and the company officials have sealed it, and are sacrificing those lives."

The other put down the correspondence, and made an examination of his caller from under his heavy eyelids. "How do you know this?"

"I left there only a few hours ago. The facts are known to all the workers in the camp."

"You are speaking from what you heard?"

"I am speaking from what I know at first hand. I saw the disaster, I saw the pit-mouth boarded over and covered with canvas. I know a man who was driven out of camp this morning for complaining about the delay in starting the fan. It has been over three days since the explosion, and still nothing has been done."

Mr. Parker proceeded to fire a series of questions, in the sharp, suspicious manner customary to prosecuting officials. But Hal did not mind that; it was the man's business to make sure.

Presently he demanded to know how he could get corroboration of Hal's statements.

"You'll have to go up there," was the reply.

"You say the facts are known to the men. Give me the names of some of them."

"I have no authority to give their names, Mr. Parker."

"What authority do you need? They will tell me, won't they?"

"They may, and they may not. One man has already lost his job; not every man cares to lose his job."

"You expect me to go up there on your bare say-so?"

"I offer you more than my say-so. I offer an affidavit."

"But what do I know about you?"

"You know that I worked in North Valley — or you can verify the fact by using the telephone. My name is Joe Smith, and I was a miner's helper in Number Two."

But that was not sufficient, said Mr. Parker; his time was valuable, and before he took a trip to North Valley he must have the names of witnesses who would corroborate these statements.

"I offer you an affidavit!" exclaimed Hal. "I say that I have knowledge that a crime is being committed — that a hundred and seven human lives are being sacrificed. You don't consider that a sufficient reason for even making inquiry?"

The District Attorney answered again that he desired to do his duty, he desired to protect the workers in their rights; but he could not afford to go off on a "wild goose chase," he must have the names of witnesses. And Hal found himself wondering. Was the man merely taking the first pretext for doing nothing? Or could it be that an official of the state would go as far as to help the company by listing the names of "trouble-makers?"

In spite of his distrust, Hal was resolved to give the man every chance he could. He went over the whole story of the disaster. He took Mr. Parker up to the camp, showed him the agonized women and terrified children crowding about the pit-mouth, driven back with clubs and revolvers. He named family after family, widows and mothers and orphans. He told of the miners clamoring for a chance to risk their lives to save their fellows. He let his own feelings sweep him along; he pleaded with fervor for his suffering friends.

"Young man," said the other, breaking in upon his eloquence, "how long have you been working in North Valley?"

"About ten weeks."

"How long have you been working in coal-mines?"

"That was my first experience."

"And you think that in ten weeks you have learned enough to entitle you to bring a charge of 'murder' against men who have spent their lives in learning the business of mining?"

"As I have told you," exclaimed Hal, "it's not merely my opinion; it's the opinion of the oldest and most experienced of the miners. I tell you no effort whatever is being made to save those men! The bosses care nothing about their men! One of them, Alec Stone, was heard by a crowd of people to say, 'Damn the men! Save the mules!'"

"Everybody up there is excited," declared the other. "Nobody can think straight at present — you can't think straight yourself. If the mine's on fire, and if the fire is spreading to such an extent that it can't be put out —"

"But, Mr. Parker, how can you say that it's spreading to such an extent?"

"Well, how can you say that it isn't?"

There was a pause. "I understand there's a deputy mine-inspector up there," said the District Attorney, suddenly. "What's his name?"

"Carmichael," said Hal.

"Well, and what does *he* say about it?"

"It was for appealing to him that the miner, Huszar, was turned out of camp."

"Well," said Mr. Parker — and there came a note into his voice by which Hal knew that he had found the excuse he sought — "Well, it's Carmichael's business, and I have no right to butt in on it. If he comes to me and asks for indictments, I'll act — but not otherwise. That's all I have to say about it."

And Hal rose. "Very well, Mr. Parker," said he. "I have put the facts before you. I was told you wouldn't do anything, but I wanted to give you a chance. Now I'm going to ask the Governor for your removal!"

And with these words the young miner strode out of the office.

SECTION 5.

*H*al went down the street to the American Hotel, where there was a public stenographer. When this young woman discovered the nature of the material he proposed to dictate, her fingers trembled visibly; but she did not refuse the task, and Hal proceeded to set forth the circumstances of the sealing of the pit-mouth of Number One Mine at North Valley, and to pray for warrants for the arrest of Enos Cartwright and Alec Stone. Then he gave an account of how he had been selected as check-weighman and been refused access to the scales; and with all the legal phraseology he could rake up, he prayed for the arrest of Enos Cartwright and James Peters, superintendent and tipple-boss at North Valley, for these offences. In another affidavit he narrated how Jeff Cotton, camp-marshal, had seized him at night, mistreated him, and shut him in prison for thirty-six hours without warrant or charge; also how Cotton, Pete Hanun, and two other parties by name unknown, had illegally driven him from the town of North Valley, threatening him with violence; for which he prayed the arrest of Jeff Cotton, Pete Hanun, and the two parties unknown.

Before this task was finished, Billy Keating came in, bringing the twenty-five dollars which Edstrom had got from the post office. They found a notary public, before whom Hal made oath to each document; and when these had been duly inscribed and stamped with the seal of the state, he gave carbon copies to Keating, who hurried off to catch a mail-train which was just due. Billy would not trust such things to the local post office; for Pedro was the hell of a town, he declared. As they went out on the street again they noticed that their body-guard had been increased by another husky-looking personage, who made no attempt to conceal what he was doing.

Hal went around the corner to an office bearing the legend, "J.W. Anderson, Justice of the Peace."

Jim Anderson, the horse-doctor, sat at his desk within. He had evidently chewed tobacco before he assumed the ermine, and his reddish-colored moustache still showed the stains. Hal observed such details, trying to weigh his chances of success. He presented the affidavit describing his treatment in North Valley, and sat waiting while His

Honor read it through with painful slowness.

"Well," said the man, at last, "what do you want?"

"I want a warrant for Jeff Cotton's arrest."

The other studied him for a minute. "No, young fellow," said he. "You can't get no such warrant here."

"Why not?"

"Because Cotton's a deputy-sheriff; he had a right to arrest you."

"To arrest me without a warrant?"

"How do you know he didn't have a warrant?"

"He admitted to me that he didn't."

"Well, whether he had a warrant or not, it was his business to keep order in the camp."

"You mean he can do anything he pleases in the camp?"

"What I mean is, it ain't my business to interfere. Why didn't you see Si Adams, up to the camp?"

"They didn't give me any chance to see him."

"Well," replied the other, "there's nothing I can do for you. You can see that for yourself. What kind of discipline could they keep in them camps if any fellow that had a kick could come down here and have the marshal arrested?"

"Then a camp-marshal can act without regard to the law?"

"I didn't say that."

"Suppose he had committed murder — would you give a warrant for that?"

"Yes, of course, if it was murder."

"And if you knew that he was in the act of committing murder in a coal-camp — would you try to stop him?"

"Yes, of course."

"Then here's another affidavit," said Hal; and he produced the one about the sealing of the mine. There was silence while Justice Anderson read it through.

But again he shook his head. "No, you can't get no such warrants here."

"Why not?"

"Because it ain't my business to run a coal-mine. I don't understand it, and I'd make a fool of myself if I tried to tell them people how to run their business."

Hal argued with him. Could company officials in charge of a coal-mine commit any sort of outrage upon their employees, and call it running their business? Their control of the mine in such an emergency as this meant the power of life and death over a hundred and seven men and boys; could it be that the law had nothing to say in such a situation?

But Mr. Anderson only shook his head; it was not his business to interfere. Hal might go up to the court-house and see Judge Denton about it. So Hal gathered up his affidavits and went out to the street again — where there were now three husky-looking personages waiting to escort him.

SECTION 6.

*T*he district court was in session and Hal sat for a while in the court-room, watching Judge Denton. Here was another prosperous and well-fed appearing gentleman, with a rubicund visage shining over the top of his black silk robe. The young miner found himself regarding both the robe and the visage with suspicion. Could it be that Hal was becoming cynical, and losing his faith in his fellow man? What he thought of, in connection with the Judge's appearance, was that there was a living to be made sitting on the bench, while one's partner appeared before the bench as coal-company counsel!

In an interval of the proceedings, Hal spoke to the clerk, and was told that he might see the judge at four-thirty; but a few minutes later Pete Hanun came in and whispered to this clerk. The clerk looked at Hal, then he went up and whispered to the Judge. At four-thirty, when the court was declared adjourned, the Judge rose and disappeared into his private office; and when Hal applied to the clerk, the latter brought out the message that Judge Denton was too busy to see him.

But Hal was not to be disposed of in that easy fashion. There was a side door to the court-room, with a corridor beyond it, and while he stood arguing with the clerk he saw the rubicund visage of the Judge flit past.

He darted in pursuit. He did not shout or make a disturbance; but when he was close behind his victim, he said, quietly, "Judge Denton, I appeal to you for justice!"

The Judge turned and looked at him, his countenance showing annoyance. "What do you want?"

It was a ticklish moment, for Pete Hanun was at Hal's heels, and it would have needed no more than a nod from the Judge to cause him to collar Hal. But the Judge, taken by surprise, permitted himself to parley with the young miner; and the detective hesitated, and finally fell back a step or two.

Hal repeated his appeal. "Your Honor, there are a hundred and seven men and boys now dying up at the North Valley mine. They are being murdered, and I am trying to save their lives!"

"Young man," said the Judge, "I have an urgent engagement down the street."

"Very well," replied Hal, "I will walk with you and tell you as you go." Nor did he give "His Honor" a chance to say whether this arrangement was pleasing to him; he set out by his side, with Pete Hanun and the other two men some ten yards in the rear.

Hal told the story as he had told it to Mr. Richard Parker; and he received the same response. Such matters were not easy to decide about; they were hardly a Judge's business. There was a state official on the ground, and it was for him to decide if there was violation of law.

Hal repeated his statement that a man who made a complaint to this official had been thrown out of camp. "And I was thrown out also, your Honor."

"What for?"

"Nobody told me what for."

"Tut, tut, young man! They don't throw men out without telling them the reason!"

"But they *do*, your Honor! Shortly before that they locked me up in jail, and held me for thirty-six hours without the slightest show of authority."

"You must have been doing something!"

"What I had done was to be chosen by a committee of miners to act as their check-weighman."

"Their check-weighman?"

"Yes, your Honor. I am informed there's a law providing that when the men demand a check-weighman, and offer to pay for him, the company must permit him to inspect the weights. Is that correct?"

"It is, I believe."

"And there's a penalty for refusing?"

"The law always carries a penalty, young man."

"They tell me that law has been on the statute-books for fifteen or sixteen years, and that the penalty is from twenty-five to five hundred dollars fine. It's a case about which there can be no dispute, your Honor — the miners notified the superintendent that they desired my services, and when I presented myself at the tipple, I was refused access to the scales; then I was seized and shut up in jail, and finally turned out of the camp. I have made affidavit to these facts, and I think I have the right to ask for warrants for the guilty men."

"Can you produce witnesses to your statements?"

"I can, your Honor. One of the committee of miners, John Edstrom, is now in Pedro, having been kept out of his home, which he had rented and paid for. The other, Mike Sikoria, was also thrown out of camp. There are many others at North Valley who know all about it."

There was a pause. Judge Denton for the first time took a good look at the young miner at his side; and then he drew his brows together in solemn thought, and his voice became deep and impressive. "I shall take this matter under advisement. What is your name, and where do you live?"

"Joe Smith, your Honor. I'm staying at Edward MacKellar's, but I don't know how long I'll be able to stay there. There are company thugs watching the place all the time."

"That's wild talk!" said the Judge, impatiently.

"As it happens," said Hal, "we are being followed by three of them at this moment — one of them the same Pete Hanun who helped to drive me out of North Valley. If you will turn your head you will see them behind us."

But the portly Judge did not turn his head.

"I have been informed," Hal continued, "that I am taking my life in my hands by my present course of action. I believe I'm entitled to ask for protection."

"What do you want me to do?"

"To begin with, I'd like you to cause the arrest of the men who are shadowing me."

"It's not my business to cause such arrests. You should apply to a policeman."

"I don't see any policeman. Will you tell me where to find one?"

His Honor was growing weary of such persistence. "Young man, what's the matter with you is that you've been reading dime novels, and they've got on your nerves!"

"But the men are right behind me, your Honor! Look at them!"

"I've told you it's not my business, young man!"

"But, your Honor, before I can find a policeman I may be dead!"

The other appeared to be untroubled by this possibility.

"And, your Honor, while you are taking these matters under advisement, the men in the mine will be dead!"

Again there was no reply.

"I have some affidavits here," said Hal. "Do you wish them?"

"You can give them to me if you want to," said the other.

"You don't ask me for them?"

"I haven't yet."

"Then just one more question — if you will pardon me, your Honor. Can you tell me where I can find an honest lawyer in this town — a man who might be willing to take a case against the interests of the General Fuel Company?"

There was a silence — a long, long silence. Judge Denton, of the firm of Denton and Vagleman, stared straight in front of him as he walked. Whatever complicated processes might have been going on inside his mind, his judicial features did not reveal them. "No, young man," he said at last, "it's not my business to give you information about lawyers." And with that the judge turned on his heel and went into the Elks' Club.

SECTION 7.

*H*al stood and watched the portly figure until it disappeared; then he turned back and passed the three detectives, who stopped. He stared at them, but made no sign, nor did they. Some twenty feet behind him, they fell in and followed as before.

Judge Denton had suggested consulting a policeman; and suddenly Hal noticed that he was passing the City Hall, and it occurred to him that this matter of his being shadowed might properly be brought to the attention of the mayor of Pedro. He wondered what the chief magistrate of such a "hell of a town" might be like; after due inquiry, he found himself in the office of Mr. Ezra Perkins, a mild-mannered little gentleman who had been in the undertaking-business, before he became a figure-head for the so-called "Democratic" machine.

He sat pulling nervously at a neatly trimmed brown beard, trying to wriggle out of the dilemma into which Hal put him. Yes, it might possibly be that a young miner was being followed on the streets of the town; but whether or not this was against the law depended on the circumstances. If he had made a disturbance in North Valley, and there was reason to believe that he might be intending trouble, doubtless the company was keeping track of him. But Pedro was a law-abiding place, and he would be protected in his rights so long as he behaved himself.

Hal replied by citing what MacKellar had told him about men being slugged on the streets in broad daylight. To this Mr. Perkins answered that there was uncertainty about the circumstances of these cases; anyhow, they had happened before he became mayor. His was a reform administration, and he had given strict orders to the Chief of Police that there were to be no more incidents of the sort.

"Will you go with me to the Chief of Police and give him orders now?" demanded Hal.

"I do not consider it necessary," said Mr. Perkins.

He was about to go home, it seemed. He was a pitiful little rodent, and it was a shame to torment him; but Hal stuck to him for ten or twenty minutes longer, arguing and insisting — until finally the little rodent bolted for the door, and made his escape in an automobile. "You can go to the Chief of Police yourself," were his last words, as he started the machine; and Hal decided to follow the suggestion. He had no hope left, but he was possessed by a kind of dogged rage. He *would* not let go!

Upon inquiry of a passer-by, he learned that police headquarters was in this same building, the entrance being just round the corner. He went in, and found a man in uniform writing at a desk, who stated that the Chief had "stepped down the street." Hal sat down to wait, by a window through which he could look out upon the three gunmen loitering across the way.

The man at the desk wrote on, but now and then he eyed the young miner with that hostility which American policemen cultivate toward the lower classes. To Hal this was a new phenomenon, and he found himself suddenly wishing that he had put on MacKellar's clothes. Perhaps a policeman would not have noticed the misfit!

The Chief came in. His blue uniform concealed a burly figure, and his moustache revealed the fact that his errand down the street had had to do with beer. "Well, young fellow?" said he, fixing his gaze upon Hal.

Hal explained his errand.

"What do you want me to do?" asked the Chief, in a decidedly hostile voice.

"I want you to make those men stop following me."

"How can I make them stop?"

"You can lock them up, if necessary. I can point them out to you, if you'll step to the window."

But the other made no move. "I reckon if they're follerin' you, they've got some reason for it. Have you been makin' trouble in the camps?" He asked this question with sudden force, as if it had occurred to him that it might be his duty to lock up Hal.

"No," said Hal, speaking as bravely as he could — "no indeed, I haven't been making trouble. I've only been demanding my rights."

"How do I know what you been doin'?"

The young miner was willing to explain, but the other cut him short. "You behave yourself while you're in this town, young feller, d'you see?

If you do, nobody'll bother you."

"But," said Hal, "they've already threatened to bother me."

"What did they say?"

"They said something might happen to me on a dark night."

"Well, so it might — you might fall down and hit your nose."

The Chief was pleased with this wit, but only for a moment. "Understand, young feller, we'll give you your rights in this town, but we got no love for agitators, and we don't pretend to have. See?"

"You call a man an agitator when he demands his legal rights?"

"I ain't got time to argue with you, young feller. It's no easy matter keepin' order in coal-camps, and I ain't going to meddle in the business. I reckon the company detectives has got as good a right in this town as you."

There was a pause. Hal saw that there was nothing to be gained by further discussion with the Chief. It was his first glimpse of the American policeman as he appears to the laboring man in revolt, and he found it an illuminating experience. There was dynamite in his heart as he turned and went out to the street; nor was the amount of the explosive diminished by the mocking grins which he noted upon the faces of Pete Hanun and the other two husky-looking personages.

SECTION 8.

*H*al judged that he had now exhausted his legal resources in Pedro; the Chief of Police had not suggested anyone else he might call upon, so there seemed nothing he could do but go back to MacKellar's and await the hour of the night train to Western City. He started to give his guardians another run, by way of working off at least a part of his own temper; but he found that they had anticipated this difficulty. An automobile came up and the three of them stepped in. Not to be outdone, Hal engaged a hack, and so the expedition returned in pomp to MacKellar's.

Hal found the old cripple in a state of perturbation. All that afternoon his telephone had been ringing; one person after another had warned him — some pleading with him, some abusing him. It was evident that among them were people who had a hold on the old man; but he was undaunted, and would not hear of Hal's going to stay at the hotel until train-time.

Then Keating returned, with an exciting tale to tell. Schulman, general manager of the "G.F.C.," had been sending out messengers to hunt for him, and finally had got him in his office, arguing and pleading, cajoling and denouncing him by turns. He had got Cartwright on the telephone, and the North Valley superintendent had labored to convince Keating that he had done the company a wrong. Cartwright had told a story about Hal's efforts to hold up the company for money. "Incidentally," said Keating, "he added the charge that you had seduced a girl in his camp."

Hal stared at his friend. "Seduced a girl!" he exclaimed.

"That's what he said; a red-headed Irish girl."

"Well, damn his soul!"

There followed a silence, broken by a laugh from Billy. "Don't glare at me like that. *I* didn't say it!"

But Hal continued to glare, nevertheless. "The dirty little skunk!"

"Take it easy, sonny," said the fat man, soothingly. "It's quite the usual thing, to drag in a woman. It's so easy — for of course there always *is* a woman. There's one in this case, I suppose?"

"There's a perfectly decent girl."

"But you've been friendly with her? You've been walking around where people can see you?"

"Yes."

"So you see, they've got you. There's nothing you can do about a thing of that sort."

"You wait and see!" Hal burst out.

The other gazed curiously at the angry young miner. "What'll you do? Beat him up some night?"

But the young miner did not answer. "You say he described the girl?"

"He was kind enough to say she was a red-headed beauty, and with no one to protect her but a drunken father. I could understand that must have made it pretty hard for her, in one of these coal-camps." There was a pause. "But see here," said the reporter, "you'll only do the girl harm by making a row. Nobody believes that women in coal-camps have any virtue. God knows, I don't see how they do have, considering the sort of men who run the camps, and the power they have."

"Mr. Keating," said Hal, "did *you* believe what Cartwright told you?"

Keating had started to light a cigar. He stopped in the middle, and his eyes met Hal's. "My dear boy," said he, "I didn't consider it my business to have an opinion."

"But what did you say to Cartwright?"

"Ah! That's another matter. I said that I'd been a newspaper man for a good many years, and I knew his game."

"Thank you for that," said Hal. "You may be interested to know there isn't any truth in the story."

"Glad to hear it," said the other. "I believe you."

"Also you may be interested to know that I shan't drop the matter until I've made Cartwright take it back."

"Well, you're an enterprising cuss!" laughed the reporter. "Haven't you got enough on your hands, with all the men you're going to get out of the mine?"

SECTION 9.

*B*illy Keating went out again, saying that he knew a man who might be willing to talk to him on the quiet, and give him some idea what was going to happen to Hal. Meantime Hal and Edstrom sat down to dinner with MacKellar. The family were afraid to use the dining room of their home, but spread a little table in the upstairs hall. The distress of mind of MacKellar's wife and daughter was apparent, and this brought home to Hal the terror of life in this coal-country. Here were American women, in an American home, a home with evidences of refinement and culture; yet they felt and acted as if they were Russian conspirators, in terror of Siberia and the knout!

The reporter was gone a couple of hours; when he came back, he brought news. "You can prepare for trouble, young fellow."

"Why so?"

"Jeff Cotton's in town."

"How do you know?"

"I saw him in an automobile. If he left North Valley at this time, it was for something serious, you may be sure."

"What does he mean to do?"

"There's no telling. He may have you slugged; he may have you run out of town and dumped out in the desert; he may just have you arrested."

Hal considered for a moment. "For slander?"

"Or for vagrancy; or on suspicion of having robbed a bank in Texas, or murdered your great-grandmother in Tasmania. The point is, he'll keep you locked up till this trouble has blown over."

"Well," said Hal, "I don't want to be locked up. I want to go up to Western City. I'm waiting for the train."

"You may have to wait till morning," replied Keating. "There's been trouble on the railroad — a freight-car broke down and ripped up the track; it'll be some time before it's clear."

They discussed this new problem back and forth. MacKellar wanted to get in half a dozen friends and keep guard over Hal during the night; and Hal had about agreed to this idea, when the discussion was given a new turn by a chance remark of Keating's. "Somebody else is tied up by the railroad accident. The Coal King's son!"

"The Coal King's son?" echoed Hal.

"Young Percy Harrigan. He's got a private car here — or rather a whole train. Think of it — dining-car, drawing room car, two whole cars with sleeping apartments! Wouldn't you like to be a son of the Coal King?"

"Has he come on account of the mine-disaster?"

"Mine-disaster?" echoed Keating. "I doubt if he's heard of it. They've been on a trip to the Grand Canyon, I was told; there's a baggage-car with four automobiles."

"Is Old Peter with them?"

"No, he's in New York. Percy's the host. He's got one of his automobiles out, and was up in town — two other fellows and some girls."

"Who's in his party?"

"I couldn't find out. You can see, it might be a story for the *Gazette* — the Coal King's son, coming by chance at the moment when a hundred and seven of his serfs are perishing in the mine! If I could only have got him to say a word about the disaster! If I could even have got him to say he didn't know about it!"

"Did you try?"

"What am I a reporter for?"

"What happened?"

"Nothing happened; except that he froze me stiff."

"Where was this?"

"On the street. They stopped at a drug-store, and I stepped up. 'Is this Mr. Percy Harrigan?' He was looking into the store, over my head. 'I'm a reporter,' I said, 'and I'd like to ask you about the accident up at North Valley.' 'Excuse me,' he said, in a tone — gee, it makes your blood cold to think of it! 'Just a word,' I pleaded. 'I don't give interviews,' he answered; and that was all — he continued looking over my head, and everybody else staring in front of them. They had turned to ice at my first word. If ever I felt like a frozen worm!"

There was a pause.

"Ain't it wonderful," reflected Billy, "how quick you can build up an aristocracy! When you looked at that car, the crowd in it and the airs they wore, you'd think they'd been running the world since the time of William the Conqueror. And Old Peter came into this country with a peddler's pack on his shoulders!"

"We're hustlers here," put in MacKellar.

"We'll hustle all the way to hell in a generation more," said the reporter. Then, after a minute, "Say, but there's one girl in that bunch that was the real thing! She sure did get me! You know all those fluffy things they do themselves up in — soft and fuzzy, makes you think of spring-time orchards. This one was exactly the color of apple-blossoms."

"You're susceptible to the charms of the ladies?" inquired Hal, mildly.

"I am," said the other. "I know it's all fake, but just the same, it makes my little heart go pit-a-pat. I always want to think they're as lovely as they look."

Hal's smile became reminiscent, and he quoted:

"Oh Liza-Ann, come out with me,
    The moon is a-shinin' in the monkey-puzzle tree!"

Then he stopped, with a laugh. "Don't wear your heart on your sleeve, Mr. Keating. She wouldn't be above taking a peck at it as she passed."

"At me? A worm of a newspaper reporter?"

"At you, a man!" laughed Hal. "I wouldn't want to accuse the lady of posing; but a lady has her role in life, and has to keep her hand in."

There was a pause. The reporter was looking at the young miner with sudden curiosity. "See here," he remarked, "I've been wondering about you. How do you come to know so much about the psychology of the leisure class?"

"I used to have money once," said Hal. "My family's gone down as quickly as the Harrigans have come up."

SECTION 10.

*H*al went on to question Keating about the apple-blossom girl. "Maybe I could guess who she is. What color was her hair?"

"The color of molasses taffy when you've pulled it," said Billy; "but all fluffy and wonderful, with star-dust in it. Her eyes were brown, and her cheeks pink and cream."

"She had two rows of pearly white teeth, that flashed at you when she smiled?"

"She didn't smile, unfortunately."

"Then her brown eyes gazed at you, wide open, full of wonder?"

"Yes, they did — only it was into the drug-store window."

"Did she wear a white hat of soft straw, with a green and white flower garden on it, and an olive green veil, and maybe cream white ribbons?"

"By George, I believe you've seen her!" exclaimed the reporter.

"Maybe," said Hal. "Or maybe I'm describing the girl on the cover of one of the current magazines!" He smiled; but then, seeing the other's curiosity, "Seriously, I think I do know your young lady. If you announce that Miss Jessie Arthur is a member of the Harrigan party, you won't be taking a long chance."

"I can't afford to take any chance at all," said the reporter. "You mean Robert Arthur's daughter?"

"Heiress-apparent of the banking business of Arthur and Sons," said Hal. "It happens I know her by sight."

"How's that?"

"I worked in a grocery-store where she used to come."

"Whereabouts?"

"Peterson and Company, in Western City."

"Oho! And you used to sell her candy."

"Stuffed dates."

"And your little heart used to go pit-a-pat, so that you could hardly count the change?"

"Gave her too much, several times!"

"And you wondered if she was as good as she was beautiful! One day you were thrilled with hope, the next you were cynical and bitter — till at last you gave up in despair, and ran away to work in a coal-mine!"

They laughed, and MacKellar and Edstrom joined in. But suddenly Keating became serious again. "I ought to be away on that story!" he exclaimed. "I've got to get something out of that crowd about the disaster. Think what copy it would make!"

"But how can you do it?"

"I don't know; I only know I ought to be trying. I'll hang round the train, and maybe I can get one of the porters to talk."

"Interview with the Coal King's porter!" chuckled Hal. "How it feels to make up a multi-millionaire's bed!"

"How it feels to sell stuffed dates to a banker's daughter!" countered the other.

But suddenly it was Hal's turn to become serious. "Listen, Mr.

Keating," said he, "why not let *me* interview young Harrigan?"

"*You?*"

"Yes! I'm the proper person — one of his miners! I help to make his money for him, don't I? I'm the one to tell him about North Valley."

Hal saw the reporter staring at him in sudden excitement; he continued: "I've been to the District Attorney, the Justice of the Peace, the District Judge, the Mayor and the Chief of Police. Now, why shouldn't I go to the Owner?"

"By thunder!" cried Billy. "I believe you'd have the nerve!"

"I believe I would," replied Hal, quietly.

The other scrambled out of his chair, wild with delight. "I dare you!" he exclaimed.

"I'm ready," said Hal.

"You mean it?"

"Of course I mean it."

"In that costume?"

"Certainly. I'm one of his miners."

"But it won't go," cried the reporter. "You'll stand no chance to get near him unless you're well dressed."

"Are you sure of that? What I've got on might be the garb of a railroad-hand. Suppose there was something out of order in one of the cars — the plumbing, for example?"

"But you couldn't fool the conductor or the porter."

"I might be able to. Let's try it."

There was a pause, while Keating thought. "The truth is," he said, "it doesn't matter whether you succeed or not — it's a story if you even make the attempt. The Coal King's son appealed to by one of his serfs! The hard heart of Plutocracy rejects the cry of Labor!"

"Yes," said Hal, "but I really mean to get to him. Do you suppose he's got back to the train yet?"

"They were starting to it when I left."

"And where *is* the train?"

"Two or three hundred yards east of the station, I was told."

MacKellar and Edstrom had been listening enthralled to this exciting conversation. "That ought to be just back of my house," said the former.

"It's a short train — four parlor-cars and a baggage-car," added Keating. "It ought to be easy to recognize."

The old Scotchman put in an objection. "The difficulty may be to get out of this house. I don't believe they mean to let you get away tonight."

"By Jove, that's so!" exclaimed Keating. "We're talking too much — let's get busy. Are they watching the back door, do you suppose?"

"They've been watching it all day," said MacKellar.

"Listen," broke in Hal — "I've an idea. They haven't tried to interfere with your going out, have they, Mr. Keating?"

"No, not yet."

"Nor with you, Mr. MacKellar?"

"No, not yet," said the Scotchman.

"Well," Hal suggested, "suppose you lend me your crutches?"

Whereat Keating gave an exclamation of delight. "The very thing!"

"I'll take your overcoat and hat," Hal added. "I've watched you get about, and I think I can give an imitation. As for Mr. Keating, he's not easy to mistake."

"Billy, the fat boy!" laughed the other. "Come, let's get on the job!"

"I'll go out by the front door at the same time," put in Edstrom, his old voice trembling with excitement. "Maybe that'll help to throw them off the track."

SECTION 11.

*T*hey had been sitting upstairs in MacKellar's room. Now they rose, and were starting for the stairs, when suddenly there came a ring at the front door bell. They stopped and stared at one another. "There they are!" whispered Keating.

And MacKellar sat down suddenly, and held out his crutches to Hal. "The hat and coat are in the front hall," he exclaimed. "Make a try for it!" His words were full of vigor, but like Edstrom, his voice was trembling. He was no longer young, and could not take adventure gaily.

Hal and Keating ran downstairs, followed by Edstrom. Hal put on the coat and hat, and they went to the back door, while at the same time Edstrom answered the bell in front.

The back door opened into a yard, and this gave, through a side gate, into an alley. Hal's heart was pounding furiously as he began to hobble along with the crutches. He had to go at MacKellar's slow pace — while Keating, at his side, started talking. He informed "Mr. MacKellar," in a casual voice, that the *Gazette* was a newspaper which believed in the people's cause, and was pledged to publish the people's side of all public questions. Discoursing thus, they went out of the gate and into the alley.

A man emerged from the shadows and walked by them. He passed within three feet of Hal, and peered at him, narrowly. Fortunately there was no moon; Hal could not see the man's face, and hoped the man could not see his.

Meantime Keating was proceeding with his discourse. "You understand, Mr. MacKellar," he was saying, "sometimes it's difficult to find out the truth in a situation like this. When the interests are filling their newspapers with falsehoods and exaggerations, it's a temptation for us to publish falsehoods and exaggerations on the other side. But we find in the long run that it pays best to publish the truth, Mr. MacKellar — we can stand by it, and there's no come-back."

Hal, it must be admitted, was not paying much attention to this edifying sermon. He was looking ahead, to where the alley debouched onto the street. It was the street behind MacKellar's house, and only a block from the railroad-track.

He dared not look behind, but he was straining his ears. Suddenly he heard a shout, in John Edstrom's voice. "Run! Run!"

In a flash, Hal dropped the two crutches, and started down the alley, Keating at his heels. They heard cries behind them, and a voice, sounding quite near, commanded, "Halt!" They had reached the end of the alley, and were in the act of swerving, when a shot rang out and there was a crash of glass in a house beyond them on the far side of the street.

Farther on was a vacant lot with a path running across it. Following this, they dodged behind some shanties, and came to another street — and so to the railroad tracks. There was a long line of freight-cars before them, and they ran between two of these, and climbing over the couplings, saw a great engine standing, its headlight gleaming full in their eyes. They sprang in front of it, and alongside the train, passing a tender, then a baggage-car, then a parlor-car.

"Here we are!" exclaimed Keating, who was puffing like a bellows.

Hal saw that there were only three more cars to the train; also, he saw a man in a blue uniform standing at the steps. He dashed towards him. "Your car's on fire!" he cried.

"What?" exclaimed the man. "Where?"

"Here!" cried Hal; and in a flash he had sprung past the other, up the steps and into the car.

There was a long, narrow corridor, to be recognized as the kitchen portion of a dining-car; at the other end of this corridor was a swinging door, and to this Hal leaped. He heard the conductor shouting to him to stop, but he paid no heed. He slipped off his overcoat and hat; and then, pushing open the door, he entered a brightly lighted apartment — and the presence of the Coal King's son.

SECTION 12.

*W*hite linen and cut glass of the dining-saloon shone brilliantly under electric lights, softened to the eye by pink shades. Seated at the tables were half a dozen young men and as many young ladies, all in evening costume; also two or three older ladies. They had begun the first course of their meal, and were laughing and chatting, when suddenly came this unexpected visitor, clad in coal-stained miner's jumpers. He was not disturbing in the manner of his entry; but immediately behind him came a fat man, perspiring, wild of aspect, and wheezing like an old fashioned steam-engine; behind him came the conductor of the train, in a no less evident state of agitation. So, of course, conversation ceased. The young ladies turned in their chairs, while several of the young men sprang to their feet.

There followed a silence: until finally one of the young men took a step forward. "What's this?" he demanded, as one who had a right to demand.

Hal advanced towards the speaker, a slender youth, correct in appearance, but not distinguished looking. "Hello, Percy!" said Hal.

A look of amazement came upon the other's face. He stared, but seemed unable to believe what he saw. And then suddenly came a cry from one of the young ladies; the one having hair the color of molasses taffy when you've pulled it — but all fluffy and wonderful, with stardust in it. Her cheeks were pink and cream, and her brown eyes gazed, wide open, full of wonder. She wore a dinner gown of soft olive green, with a cream white scarf of some filmy material thrown about her bare shoulders.

She had started to her feet. "It's Hal!" she cried.

"Hal Warner!" echoed young Harrigan. "Why, what in the world — ?"

He was interrupted by a clamor outside. "Wait a moment," said Hal, quietly. "I think someone else is coming in."

The door was pushed violently open. It was pushed so violently that Billy Keating and the conductor were thrust to one side; and Jeff Cotton appeared in the entrance.

The camp-marshal was breathless, his face full of the passion of the hunt. In his right hand he carried a revolver. He glared about him, and saw the two men he was chasing; also he saw the Coal King's son, and the rest of the astonished company. He stood, stricken dumb.

The door was pushed again, forcing him aside, and two more men crowded in, both of them carrying revolvers in their hands. The foremost was Pete Hanun, and he also stood staring. The "breaker of teeth" had two teeth of his own missing, and when his prize-fighter's jaw dropped down, the deficiency became conspicuous. It was probably his first entrance into society, and he was like an overgrown boy caught in the jam-closet.

Percy Harrigan's manner became distinctly imperious. "What does this mean?" he demanded.

It was Hal who answered. "I am seeking a criminal, Percy."

"What?" There were little cries of alarm from the women.

"Yes, a criminal; the man who sealed up the mine."

"Sealed up the mine?" echoed the other. "What do you mean?"

"Let me explain. First, I will introduce my friends. Harrigan, this is my friend Keating."

Billy suddenly realized that he had a hat on his head. He jerked it off; but for the rest, his social instincts failed him. He could only stare. He had not yet got all his breath.

"Billy's a reporter," said Hal. "But you needn't worry — he's a gentleman, and won't betray a confidence. You understand, Billy."

"Y — yes," said Billy, faintly.

"And this," said Hal, "is Jeff Cotton, camp-marshal at North Valley. I suppose you know, Percy, that the North Valley mines belong to the 'G.F.C.' Cotton, this is Mr. Harrigan."

Then Cotton remembered his hat; also his revolver, which he tried to get out of sight behind his back.

"And this," continued Hal, "is Mr. Pete Hanun, by profession a breaker of teeth. This other gentleman, whose name I don't know, is presumably an assistant-breaker." So Hal went on, observing the forms of social intercourse, his purpose being to give his mind a chance to work. So much depended upon the tactics he chose in this emergency! Should he take Percy to one side and tell him the story quietly, leaving it to his sense of justice and humanity? No, that was not the way one dealt with the Harrigans! They had bullied their way to the front; if anything were done with them, it would be by force! If anything were done with Percy, it would be by laying hold of him before these guests, exposing the situation, and using their feelings to coerce him!

The Coal King's son was asking questions again. What was all this about? So Hal began to describe the condition of the men inside the mine. "They have no food or water, except what they had in their dinner-pails; and it's been three days and a half since the explosion! They are breathing bad air; their heads are aching, the veins swelling in their foreheads; their tongues are cracking, they are lying on the ground, gasping. But they are waiting — kept alive by the faith they have in their friends on the surface, who will try to get to them. They dare not take down the barriers, because the gases would kill them at once. But they know the rescuers will come, so they listen for the sounds of axes and picks. That is the situation."

Hal stopped and waited for some sign of concern from young Harrigan. But no such sign was given. Hal went on:

"Think of it, Percy! There is one old man in that mine, an Irishman who has a wife and eight children waiting to learn about his fate. I know one woman who has a husband and three sons in the mine. For three days and a half the women and children have been standing at the pit-mouth; I have seen them sitting with their heads sunk upon their knees, or shaking their fists, screaming curses at the criminal who is to blame."

There was a pause. "The criminal?" inquired young Harrigan. "I don't understand!"

"You'll hardly be able to believe it; but nothing has been done to rescue these men. The criminal has nailed a cover of boards over the pit-mouth, and put tarpaulin over it — sealing up men and boys to die!"

There was a murmur of horror from the diners.

"I know, you can't conceive such a thing. The reason is, there's a fire in the mine; if the fan is set to working, the coal will burn. But at the same time, some of the passages could be got clear of smoke, and some of the men could be rescued. So it's a question of property against lives; and the criminal has decided for the property. He proposes to wait a week, two weeks, until the fire has been smothered; *then* of course the men and boys will be dead."

There was a silence. It was broken by young Harrigan. "Who has done this?"

"His name is Enos Cartwright."

"But who *is* he?"

"Just now when I said that I was seeking the criminal, I misled you a little, Percy. I did it because I wanted to collect my thoughts." Hal paused: when he continued, his voice was sharper, his sentences falling like blows. "The criminal I've been telling you about is the superintendent of the mine — a man employed and put in authority by the General Fuel Company. The one who is being chased is not the one who sealed up the mine, but the one who proposed to have it opened. He is being treated as a malefactor, because the laws of the state, as well as the laws of humanity, have been suppressed by the General Fuel Company; he was forced to seek refuge in your car, in order to save his life from thugs and gunmen in the company's employ!"

SECTION 13.

*K*nowing these people well, Hal could measure the effect of the thunderbolt he had hurled among them. They were people to whom good taste was the first of all the virtues; he knew how he was offending them. If he was to win them to the least extent, he must explain his presence here — a trespasser upon the property of the Harrigans.

"Percy," he continued, "you remember how you used to jump on me last year at college, because I listened to 'muckrakers.' You saw fit to take personal offence at it. You knew that their tales couldn't be true. But I wanted to see for myself, so I went to work in a coal-mine. I saw the explosion; I saw this man, Jeff Cotton, driving women and children away from the pit-mouth with blows and curses. I set out to help the men in the mine, and the marshal rushed me out of camp. He told me that if I didn't go about my business, something would happen to me on a dark night. And you see — this is a dark night!"

Hal waited, to give young Harrigan a chance to grasp this situation and to take command. But apparently young Harrigan was not aware of the presence of the camp-marshal and his revolver. Hal tried again:

"Evidently these men wouldn't have minded killing me; they fired at me just now. The marshal still has the revolver and you can smell the powder-smoke. So I took the liberty of entering your car, Percy. It was to save my life, and you'll have to excuse me."

The Coal King's son had here a sudden opportunity to be magnanimous. He made haste to avail himself of it. "Of course, Hal," he said. "It was quite all right to come here. If our employees were behaving in such fashion, it was without authority, and they will surely pay for it." He spoke with quiet certainty; it was the Harrigan manner, and before it Jeff Cotton and the two mine-guards seemed to wither and shrink.

"Thank you, Percy," said Hal. "It's what I knew you'd say. I'm sorry to have disturbed your dinner-party —"

"Not at all, Hal; it was nothing of a party."

"You see, Percy, it was not only to save myself, but the people in the mine! They are dying, and every moment is precious. It will take a day at least to get to them, so they'll be at their last gasp. Whatever's to be done must be done at once."

Again Hal waited — until the pause became awkward. The diners had so far been looking at him; but now they were looking at young Harrigan, and young Harrigan felt the change.

"I don't know just what you expect of me, Hal. My father employs competent men to manage his business, and I certainly don't feel that I know enough to give them any suggestions." This again in the Harrigan manner; but it weakened before Hal's firm gaze. "What can I do?"

"You can give the order to open the mine, to reverse the fan and start it. That will draw out the smoke and gases, and the rescuers can go down."

"But Hal, I assure you I have no authority to give such an order."

"You must *take* the authority. Your father's in the East, the officers of the company are in their beds at home; you are here!"

"But I don't understand such things, Hal! I don't know anything of the situation — except what you tell me. And while I don't doubt your word, any man may make a mistake in such a situation."

"Come and see for yourself, Percy! That's all I ask, and it's easy enough. Here is your train, your engine with steam up; have us switched onto the North Valley branch, and we can be at the mine in half an hour. Then — let me take you to the men who know! Men who've been working all their lives in mines, who've seen accidents like this many times, and who will tell you the truth — that there's a chance of saving many lives, and that the chance is being thrown away to save some thousands of dollars' worth of coal and timbers and track."

"But even if that's true, Hal, I have no *power!*"

"If you come there, you can cut the red-tape in one minute. What those bosses are doing is a thing that can only be done in darkness!"

Under the pressure of Hal's vehemence, the Harrigan manner was failing; the Coal King's son was becoming a bewildered and quite ordinary youth. But there was a power greater than Hal behind him. He shook his head. "It's the old man's business, Hal. I've no right to butt in!"

The other, in his desperate need, turned to the rest of the party. His gaze, moving from one face to another, rested upon the magazine-cover countenance, with the brown eyes wide open, full of wonder.

"Jessie! What do you think about it?"

The girl started, and distress leaped into her face. "How do you mean, Hal?"

"Tell him he ought to save those lives!"

The moments seemed ages as Hal waited. It was a test, he realized. The brown eyes dropped. "I don't understand such things, Hal!"

"But, Jessie, I am explaining them! Here are men and boys being suffocated to death, in order to save a little money. Isn't that plain?"

"But how can I *know*, Hal?"

"I'm giving you my word, Jessie. Surely I wouldn't appeal to you unless I knew."

Still she hesitated. And there came a swift note of feeling into his voice: "Jessie, dear!"

As if under a spell, the girl's eyes were raised to his; he saw a scarlet flame of embarrassment spreading over her throat and cheeks. "Jessie, I know — it seems an intolerable thing to ask! You've never been rude to a friend. But I remember once you forgot your good manners, when you saw a rough fellow on the street beating an old drudge-horse. Don't you remember how you rushed at him — like a wild thing! And now — think of it, dear, here are old drudge-creatures being tortured to death; but not horses — working-men!"

Still the girl gazed at him. He could read grief, dismay in her eyes; he saw tears steal from them, and stream down her cheeks. "Oh, I don't know, I don't *know!*" she cried; and hid her face in her hands, and began to sob aloud.

SECTION 14.

*T*here was a painful pause. Hal's gaze traveled on, and came to a grey-haired lady in a black dinner-gown, with a rope of pearls about her neck. "Mrs. Curtis! Surely *you* will advise him!"

The grey-haired lady started — was there no limit to his impudence? She had witnessed the torturing of Jessie. But Jessie was his fiancée; he had no such claim upon Mrs. Curtis. She answered, with iciness in her tone: "I could not undertake to dictate to my host in such a matter."

"Mrs. Curtis! You have founded a charity for the helping of stray cats and dogs!" These words rose to Hal's lips; but he did not say them. His eyes moved on. Who else might help to bully a Harrigan?

Next to Mrs. Curtis sat Reggie Porter, with a rose in the buttonhole of his dinner-jacket. Hal knew the rôle in which Reggie was there — a kind of male chaperon, an assistant host, an admirer to the wealthy, a solace to the bored. Poor Reggie lived other people's lives, his soul perpetually a-quiver with other people's excitements, with gossip, preparations for tea-parties, praise of tea-parties past. And always the soul was pushing; calculating, measuring opportunities, making up in tact and elegance for distressing lack of money. Hal got one swift glimpse of the face; the sharp little black moustaches seemed standing up with excitement, and in a flash of horrible intuition Hal read the situation — Reggie was expecting to be questioned, and had got ready an answer that would increase his social capital in the Harrigan family bank!

Across the aisle sat Genevieve Halsey: tall, erect, built on the scale of a statue. You thought of the ox-eyed Juno, and imagined stately emotions; but when you came to know Genevieve, you discovered that her mind was slow, and entirely occupied with herself. Next to her was Bob Creston, smooth-shaven, rosy-cheeked, exuding well-being — what is called a "good fellow," with a wholesome ambition to win cups for his athletic club, and to keep up the score of his rifle-team of the state militia. Jolly Bob might have spoken, out of his good heart; but he was in love with a cousin of Percy's, Betty Gunnison, who sat across the table from him — and Hal saw her black eyes shining, her little fists clenched tightly, her lips pressed white. Hal understood Betty — she was one of the Harrigans, working at the Harrigan family task of making the children of a pack-peddler into leaders in the "younger set!"

Next sat "Vivie" Cass, whose talk was of horses and dogs and such ungirlish matters; Hal had discussed social questions in her presence, and heard her view expressed in one flashing sentence — "If a man eats with his knife, I consider him my personal enemy!" Over her shoulder peered the face of a man with pale eyes and yellow moustaches — Bert Atkins, cynical and world-weary, whom the papers referred to as a "club-man," and whom Hal's brother had called a "tame cat." There was "Dicky" Everson, like Hal, a favorite of the ladies, but nothing more; "Billy" Harris, son of another "coal man"; Daisy, his sister; and Blanche Vagleman, whose father was Old Peter's head lawyer, whose brother was the local counsel, and publisher of the Pedro *Star.*

So Hal's eyes moved from face to face, and his mind from personality to personality. It was like the unrolling of a scroll; a panorama of a world he had half forgotten. He had no time for reflection, but one impression came to him, swift and overwhelming. Once he had lived in this world and taken it as a matter of course. He had known these people, gone about with them; they had seemed friendly, obliging, a good sort of people on the whole. And now, what a change! They seemed no longer friendly! Was the change in them? Or was it Hal who had become cynical — so that he saw them in this terrifying new light, cold, and unconcerned as the stars about men who were dying a few miles away!

Hal's eyes came back to the Coal King's son, and he discovered that Percy was white with anger. "I assure you, Hal, there's no use going on with this. I have no intention of letting myself be bulldozed."

Percy's gaze shifted with sudden purpose to the camp-marshal. "Cotton, what do you say about this? Is Mr. Warner correct in his idea of the situation?"

"You know what such a man would say, Percy!" broke in Hal.

"I don't," was the reply. "I wish to know. What is it, Cotton?"

"He's mistaken, Mr. Harrigan." The marshal's voice was sharp and defiant.

"In what way?"

"The company's doing everything to get the mine open, and has been from the beginning."

"Oh!" And there was triumph in Percy's voice. "What is the cause of the delay?"

"The fan was broken, and we had to send for a new one. It's a job to set it up — such things can't be done in an hour."

Percy turned to Hal. "You see! There are two opinions, at least!"

"Of course!" cried Betty Gunnison, her black eyes snapping at Hal. She would have said more, but Hal interrupted, stepping closer to his host. "Percy," he said, in a low voice, "come back here, please. I have a word to say to you alone."

There was just a hint of menace in Hal's voice; his gaze went to the far end of the car, a space occupied only by two Negro waiters. These retired in haste as the young men moved towards them; and so, having the Coal King's son to himself, Hal went in to finish this fight.

SECTION 15.

*P*ercy Harrigan was known to Hal, as a college-boy is known to his class-mates. He was not brutal, like his grim old father; he was merely self-indulgent, as one who had always had everything; he was weak, as one who had never had to take a bold resolve. He had been brought up by the women of the family, to be a part of what they called "society"; in which process he had been given high notions of his own importance. The life of the Harrigans was dominated by one painful memory — that of a peddler's pack; and Hal knew that Percy's most urgent purpose was to be regarded as a real and true and freehanded aristocrat. It was this knowledge Hal was using in his attack.

He began with apologies, attempting to soothe the other's anger. He had not meant to make a scene like this; it was the gunmen who had forced it, putting his life in danger. It was the very devil, being chased about at night and shot at! He had lost his nerve, really; he had forgot what little manners he had been able to keep as a miner's buddy. He had made a spectacle of himself; good Lord yes, he realized how he must seem!

— And Hal looked at his dirty miner's jumpers, and then at Percy. He could see that Percy was in hearty agreement thus far — he had indeed made a spectacle of himself, and of Percy too! Hal was sorry about this latter, but here they were, in a pickle, and it was certainly too late now. This story was out — there could be no suppressing it! Hal might sit down on his reporter-friend, Percy might sit down on the waiters and the conductor and the camp-marshal and the gunmen — but he could not possibly sit down on all his friends! They would talk about nothing else for weeks! The story would be all over Western City in a day — this amazing, melodramatic, ten-twenty-thirty story of a miner's buddy in the private car of the Coal King's son!

"And you must see, Percy," Hal went on, "it's the sort of thing that sticks to a man. It's the thing by which everybody will form their idea of you as long as you live!"

"I'll take my chances with my friends' criticism," said the other, with some attempt at the Harrigan manner.

"You can make it whichever kind of story you choose," continued Hal, implacably. "The world will say, He decided for the dollars; or it will say, He decided for the lives. Surely, Percy, your family doesn't need those particular dollars so badly! Why, you've spent more on this one train-trip!"

And Hal waited, to give his victim time to calculate.

The result of the thinking was a question worthy of Old Peter. "What are *you* getting out of this?"

"Percy," said Hal, "you must *know* I'm getting nothing! If you can't understand it otherwise, say to yourself that you are dealing with a man who's irresponsible. I've seen so many terrible things — I've been chased around so much by camp-marshals — why, Percy, that man Cotton has six notches on his gun! I'm simply crazy!" And into the brown eyes of this miner's buddy came a look wild enough to convince a stronger man than Percy Harrigan. "I've got just one idea left in the world, Percy — to save those miners! You make a mistake unless you realize how desperate I am. So far I've done this thing incog! I've been Joe Smith, a miner's buddy. If I'd come out and told my real name — well, maybe I wouldn't have made them open the mine, but at least I'd have made a lot of trouble for the G.F.C.! But I didn't do it; I knew what a scandal it would make, and there was something I owed my father. But if I see there's no other way, if it's a question of letting those people perish, I'll throw everything else to the winds. Tell your father that; tell him I threatened to turn this man Keating loose and blow the thing wide open — denounce the company, appeal to the Governor, raise a disturbance and get arrested on the street, if necessary, in order to force the facts before the public. You see, I've got the facts, Percy! I've been there and seen with my own eyes. Can't you realize that?"

The other did not answer, but it was evident that he realized.

"On the other hand, see how you can fix it, if you choose. You were on a pleasure trip when you heard of this disaster; you rushed up and took command, you opened the mine, you saved the lives of your employees. That is the way the papers will handle it."

Hal, watching his victim intently, and groping for the path to his mind, perceived that he had gone wrong. Crude as the Harrigans were, they had learned that it is not aristocratic to be picturesque.

"All right then!" said Hal, quickly. "If you prefer, you needn't be mentioned. The bosses up at the camp have the reporters under their thumbs, they'll handle the story any way you want it. The one thing I care about is that you run your car up and see the mine opened. Won't you do it, Percy?"

Hal was gazing into the other's eyes, knowing that life and death for the miners hung upon his nod. "Well? What is the answer?"

"Hal," exclaimed Percy, "my old man will give me hell!"

"All right; but on the other hand, *I'll* give you hell; and which will be worse?"

Again there was a silence. "Come along, Percy! For God's sake!" And Hal's tone was desperate, alarming.

And suddenly the other gave way. "All right!"

Hal drew a breath. "But mind you!" he added. "You're not going up there to let them fool you! They'll try to bluff you out — they may go as far as to refuse to obey you. But you must stand by your guns — for, you see, I'm going along, I'm going to see that mine open. I'll never quit till the rescuers have gone down!"

"Will they go, Hal?"

"Will they go? Good God, man, they're clamoring for the chance to go! They've almost been rioting for it. I'll go with them — and you, too, Percy — the whole crowd of us idlers will go! When we come out, we'll know something about the business of coal-mining!"

"All right, I'm with you," said the Coal King's son.

SECTION 16.

*H*al never knew what Percy said to Cartwright that night; he only knew that when they arrived at the mine the superintendent was summoned to a consultation, and half an hour later Percy emerged smiling, with the announcement that Hal Warner had been mistaken all along; the mine authorities had been making all possible haste to get the fan ready, with the intention of opening the mine at the earliest moment. The work was now completed, and in an hour or two the fan was to be started, and by morning there would be a chance of rescuers getting in. Percy said this so innocently that for a moment Hal wondered if Percy himself might not believe it. Hal's position as guest of course required that he should graciously pretend to believe it, consenting to appear as a fool before the rest of the company.

Percy invited Hal and Billy Keating to spend the night in the train; but this Hal declined. He was too dirty, he said; besides, he wanted to be up at daylight, to be one of the first to go down the shaft. Percy answered that the superintendent had vetoed this proposition – he did not want anyone to go down but experienced men, who could take care of themselves. When there were so many on hand ready and eager to go, there was no need to imperil the lives of amateurs.

At the risk of seeming ungracious, Hal declared that he would "hang around" and see them take the cover off the pit-mouth. There were mourning parties in some of the cabins, where women were gathered together who could not sleep, and it would be an act of charity to take them the good news.

Hal and Keating set out; they went first to the Raffertys', and saw Mrs. Rafferty spring up and stare at them, and then scream aloud to the Holy Virgin, waking all the little Raffertys to frightened clamor. When the woman had made sure that they really knew what they were talking about, she rushed out to spread the news, and so pretty soon the streets were alive with hurrying figures, and a crowd gathered once more at the pit-mouth.

Hal and Keating went on to Jerry Minetti's. Out of a sense of loyalty to Percy, Hal did no more than repeat Percy's own announcement, that it had been Cartwright's intention all along to have the mine opened. It was funny to see the effect of this statement — the face with which Jerry looked at Hal! But they wasted no time in discussion; Jerry slipped into his clothes and hurried with them to the pit-mouth.

Sure enough, a gang was already tearing off the boards and canvas. Never since Hal had been in North Valley had he seen men working with such a will! Soon the great fan began to stir, and then to roar, and then to sing; and there was a crowd of a hundred people, roaring and singing also.

It would be some hours before anything more could be done; and suddenly Hal realized that he was exhausted. He and Billy Keating went back to the Minetti cabin, and spreading themselves a blanket on the floor, lay down with sighs of relief. As for Billy, he was soon snoring; but to Hal there came sudden reaction from all the excitement, and sleep was far from him.

An ocean of thoughts came flooding into his mind: the world outside, *his* world, which he had banished deliberately for several months, and which he had so suddenly been compelled to remember! It had seemed so simple, what he had set out to do that summer: to take another name, to become a member of another class, to live its life and think its thoughts, and then come back to his own world with a new and fascinating adventure to tell about! The possibility that his own world, the world of Hal Warner, might find him out as Joe Smith, the miner's buddy — that was a possibility which had never come to his mind. He was like a burglar, working away at a job in darkness, and suddenly finding the room flooded with light.

He had gone into the adventure, prepared to find things that would shock him; he had known that somehow, somewhere, he would have to fight the "system." But he had never expected to find himself in the thick of the class-war, leading a charge upon the trenches of his own associates. Nor was this the end, he knew; this war would not be settled by the winning of a trench! Lying here in the darkness and silence, Hal was realizing what he had got himself in for. To employ another simile, he was a man who begins a flirtation on the street, and wakes up next morning to find himself married.

It was not that he had regrets for the course he had taken with Percy. No other course had been thinkable. But while Hal had known these North Valley people for ten weeks, he had known the occupants of Percy's car for as many years. So these latter personalities loomed large in his consciousness, and here in the darkness their thoughts about him, whether actively hostile or passively astonished, laid siege to the defenses of his mind.

Particularly he found himself wrestling with Jessie Arthur. Her face rose up before him, appealing, yearning. She had one of those perfect faces, which irresistibly compel the soul of a man. Her brown eyes, soft and shining, full of tenderness; her lips, quick to tremble with emotion; her skin like apple-blossoms, her hair with star-dust in it! Hal was cynical enough about coal-operators and mine-guards, but it never occurred to him that Jessie's soul might be anything but what these bodily charms implied. He was in love with her; and he was too young, too inexperienced in love to realize that underneath the sweetness of girlhood, so genuine and so lovable, might lie deep, unconscious cruelty, inherited and instinctive — the cruelty of caste, the hardness of worldly prejudice. A man has to come to middle age, and to suffer much, before he understands that the charms of women, those rare and magical perfections of eyes and teeth and hair, that softness of skin and delicacy of feature, have cost labor and care of many generations, and imply inevitably that life has been feral, that customs and conventions have been murderous and inhuman.

Jessie had failed Hal in his desperate emergency. But now he went over the scene, and told himself that the test had been an unfair one. He had known her since childhood, and loved her, and never before had he seen an act or heard a word that was not gracious and kind. But — so he told himself — she gave her sympathy to those she knew; and what chance had she ever had to know working-people? He must give her the chance; he must compel her, even against her will, to broaden her understanding of life! The process might hurt her, it might mar the unlined softness of her face, but nevertheless, it would be good for her — it would be a "growing pain!"

So, lying there in the darkness and silence, Hal found himself absorbed in long conversation with his sweetheart. He escorted her about the camp, explaining things to her, introducing her to this one and that. He took others of his private-car friends and introduced them to his North Valley friends. There were individuals who had qualities in common, and would surely hit it off! Bob Creston, for example, who was good at a "song and dance" — he would surely be interested in "Blinky," the vaudeville specialist of the camp! Mrs. Curtis, who liked cats, would find a bond of sisterhood with old Mrs. Nagle, who lived next door to the Minettis, and kept five! And even Vivie Cass, who hated men who ate with their knives — she would be driven to murder by the table-manners of Reminitsky's boarders, but she would take delight in "Dago Charlie," the tobacco-chewing mule which had once been Hal's pet! Hal could hardly wait for daylight to come, so that he might begin these efforts at social amalgamation!

SECTION 17.

*T*owards dawn Hal fell asleep; he was awakened by Billy Keating, who sat up yawning, at the same time grumbling and bewailing. Hal realized that Billy also had discovered troubles during the night. Never in all his career as a journalist had he had such a story; never had any man had such a story – and it must be killed!

Cartwright had got the reporters together late the night before and told them the news – that the company had at last succeeded in getting the mine ready to be opened; also that young Mr. Harrigan was there in his private train, prompted by his concern for the entombed miners. The reporters would mention his coming, of course, but were requested not to "play it up," nor to mention the names of Mr. Harrigan's guests. Needless to say they were not told that the "buddy" who had been thrown out of camp for insubordination had turned out to be the son of Edward S. Warner, the "coal magnate."

A fine, cold rain was falling, and Hal borrowed an old coat of Jerry's and slipped it on. Little Jerry clamored to go with him, and after some controversy Hal wrapped him in a shawl and slung him onto his shoulder. It was barely daylight, but already the whole population of the village was on hand at the pit-mouth. The helmet-men had gone down to make tests, so the hour of final revelation was at hand. Women stood with wet shawls about their hunched shoulders, their faces white and strained, their suspense too great for any sort of utterance. A ghastly thought it was, that while they were shuddering in the wet, their men below might be expiring for lack of a few drops of water!

The helmet-men, coming up, reported that lights would burn at the bottom of the shaft; so it was safe for men to go down without helmets, and the volunteers of the first rescue party made ready. All night there had been a clattering of hammers, where the carpenters were working on a new cage. Now it was swung from the hoist, and the men took their places in it. When at last the hoist began to move, and the group disappeared below the surface of the ground, you could hear a sigh from a thousand throats, like the moaning of wind in a pine tree. They were leaving women and children above, yet not one of these women would have asked them to stay – such was the deep unconscious bond of solidarity which made these toilers of twenty nations one!

It was a slow process, letting down the cage; on account of the danger of gas, and the newness of the cage, it was necessary to proceed a few feet at a time, waiting for a pull upon the signal-cord to tell that the men were all right. After they had reached the bottom, there would be more time, no one could say how long, before they came upon survivors with signs of life in them. There were bodies near the foot of the shaft, according to the reports of the helmet-men, but there was no use delaying to bring these up, for they must have been dead for days. Hal saw a crowd of women clamoring about the helmet-men, trying to find out if these bodies had been recognized. Also he saw Jeff Cotton and Bud Adams at their old duty of driving the women back.

The cage returned for a second load of men. There was less need of caution now; the hoist worked quickly, and group after group of men with silent, set faces, and pickaxes and crow-bars and shovels in their hands, went down into the pit of terror. They would scatter through the workings, testing everywhere ahead of them with safety-lamps, and looking for barriers erected by the imprisoned men for defense against the gases. As they hammered on these barriers, perhaps they would hear the signals of living men on the other side; or they would break through in silence, and find men too far gone to make a sound, yet possibly with the spark of life still in them.

One by one, Hal's friends went down — "Big Jack" David, and Wresmak, the Bohemian, Klowoski, the Pole, and finally Jerry Minetti. Little Jerry waved his hand from his perch on Hal's shoulder; while Rosa, who had come out and joined them, was clinging to Hal's arm, silent, as if her soul were going down in the cage. There went blue-eyed Tim Rafferty to look for his father, and black-eyed "Andy," the Greek boy, whose father had perished in a similar disaster years ago; there went Rovetta, and Carmino, the pit-boss, Jerry's cousin. One by one their names ran through the crowd, as of heroes marching out to battle.

SECTION 18.

*L*ooking about, Hal saw some of the guests of the Harrigan party. There was Vivie Cass, standing under an umbrella with Bert Atkins; and there was Bob Creston with Dicky Everson. These two had on mackintoshes and waterproof hats, and were talking to Cartwright; tall, immaculate men, who seemed like creatures of another world beside the stunted and coal-smutted miners.

Seeing Hal, they moved over to him. "Where did you get the kid?" inquired Bob, his rosy, smooth-shaven face breaking into a smile.

"I picked him up," said Hal, giving Little Jerry a toss and sliding him off his shoulder.

"Hello, kid!" said Bob.

And the answer came promptly, "Hello, yourself!" Little Jerry knew how to talk American; he was a match for any society man! "My father's went down in that cage," said he, looking up at the tall stranger, his bright black eyes sparkling.

"Is that so!" replied the other. "Why don't you go?"

"My father'll get 'em out. He ain't afraid o' nothin', my father!"

"What's your father's name?"

"Big Jerry."

"Oho! And what'll you be when you grow up?"

"I'm goin' to be a shot-firer."

"In this mine?"

"You bet not!"

"Why not?"

Little Jerry looked mysterious. "I ain't tellin' all I know," said he.

The two young fellows laughed. Here was education for them! "Maybe you'll go back to the old country?" put in Dicky Everson.

"No, sir-ee!" said Little Jerry. "I'm American."

"Maybe you'll be president some day."

"That's what my father says," replied the little chap — "president of a miners' union."

Again they laughed; but Rosa gave a nervous whisper and caught at the child's sleeve. That was not the sort of thing to say to mysterious and rich-looking strangers! "This is Little Jerry's mother, Mrs. Minetti," put in Hal, by way of reassuring her.

"Glad to meet you, Mrs. Minetti," said the two young men, taking off their hats with elaborate bows; they stared, for Rosa was a pretty object as she blushed and made her shy response. She was much embarrassed, having never before in her life been bowed to by men like these.

And here they were greeting Joe Smith as an old friend, and calling him by a strange name! She turned her black Italian eyes upon Hal in inquiry, and he felt a flush creeping over him. It was almost as uncomfortable to be found out by North Valley as to be found out by Western City!

The men talked about the rescue-work, and what Cartwright had been telling of its progress. The fire was in one of the main passages, and was burning out the timbering, spreading rapidly under the draft from the reversed fan. There could be little hope of rescue in this part of the mine, but the helmet-men would defy the heat and smoke in the burned out passages. They knew how likely was the collapse of such portions of the mine; but also they knew that men had been working here before the explosion. "I must say they're a game lot!" remarked Dicky.

A group of women and children were gathered about to listen, their shyness overcome by their torturing anxiety for news. They made one think of women in war-time, listening to the roar of distant guns and waiting for the bringing in of the wounded. Hal saw Bob and Dicky glance now and then at the ring of faces about them; they were getting something of this mood, and that was a part of what he had desired for them.

"Are the others coming out?" he asked.

"I don't know," said Bob. "I suppose they're having breakfast. It's time we went in."

"Won't you come with us?" added Dicky.

"No, thanks," replied Hal, "I've an engagement with the kid here." And he gave Little Jerry's hand a squeeze. "But tell some of the other fellows to come. They'll be interested in these things."

"All right," said the two, as they moved away.

SECTION 19.

*A*fter allowing a sufficient time for the party in the dining-car to finish breakfast, Hal went down to the tracks, and induced the porter to take in his name to Percy Harrigan. He was hoping to persuade Percy to see the village under other than company chaperonage; he heard with dismay the announcement that the party had arranged to depart in the course of a couple of hours.

"But you haven't seen anything at all!" Hal protested.

"They won't let us into the mine," replied the other. "What else is there we can do?"

"I wanted you to talk to the people and learn something about conditions here. You ought not to lose this chance, Percy!"

"That's all right, Hal, but you might understand this isn't a convenient time. I've got a lot of people with me, and I've no right to ask them to wait."

"But can't they learn something also, Percy?"

"It's raining," was the reply; "and ladies would hardly care to stand round in a crowd and see dead bodies brought out of a mine."

Hal got the rebuke. Yes, he had grown callous since coming to North Valley; he had lost that delicacy of feeling, that intuitive understanding of the sentiments of ladies, which he would surely have exhibited a short time earlier in his life. He was excited about this disaster; it was a personal thing to him, and he lost sight of the fact that to the ladies of the Harrigan party it was, in its details, merely sordid and repelling. If they went out in the mud and rain of a mining-village and stood about staring, they would feel that they were exhibiting, not human compassion, but idle curiosity. The sights they would see would harrow them to no purpose; and incidentally they would be exposing themselves to distressing publicity. As for offering sympathy to widows and orphans — well, these were foreigners mostly, who could not understand what was said to them, and who might be more embarrassed than helped by the intrusion into their grief of persons from an alien world.

The business of offering sympathy had been reduced to a system by the civilization which these ladies helped to maintain; and, as it happened, there was one present who was familiar with this system. Mrs. Curtis had already acted, so Percy informed Hal; she had passed about a subscription-paper, and in a couple of minutes over a thousand dollars had been pledged. This would be paid by check to the "Red Cross," whose agents would understand how to distribute relief among such sufferers. So the members of Percy's party felt that they had done the proper and delicate thing, and might go their ways with a quiet conscience.

"The world can't stop moving just because there's been a mine-disaster," said the Coal King's son. "People have engagements they must keep."

And he went on to explain what these engagements were. He himself had to go to a dinner that evening, and would barely be able to make it. Bert Atkins was to play a challenge match at billiards, and Mrs. Curtis was to attend a committee meeting of a woman's club. Also it was the last Friday of the month; had Hal forgotten what that meant?

After a moment Hal remembered — the "Young People's Night" at the country club! He had a sudden vision of the white colonial mansion on the mountainside, with its doors and windows thrown wide, and the strains of an orchestra floating out. In the ballroom the young ladies of Percy's party would appear — Jessie, his sweetheart, among them — gowned in filmy chiffons and laces, floating in a mist of perfume and color and music. They would laugh and chatter, they would flirt and scheme against one another for the sovereignty of the ballroom – while here in North Valley the sobbing widows would be clutching their mangled dead in their arms! How strange, how ghastly it seemed! How like the scenes one read of on the eve of the French Revolution!

SECTION 20.

*P*ercy wanted Hal to come away with the party. He suggested this tactfully at first, and then, as Hal did not take the hint, he began to press the matter, showing signs of irritation. The mine was open now – what more did Hal want? When Hal suggested that Cartwright might order it closed again, Percy revealed the fact that the matter was in his father's hands. The superintendent had sent a long telegram the night before, and an answer was due at any moment. Whatever the answer ordered would have to be done.

There was a grim look upon Hal's face, but he forced himself to speak politely. "If your father orders anything that interferes with the rescuing of the men – don't you see, Percy, that I have to fight him?"

"But how *can* you fight him?"

"With the one weapon I have – publicity."

"You mean –" Percy stopped, and stared.

"I mean what I said before – I'd turn Billy Keating loose and blow this whole story wide open."

"Well, by God!" cried young Harrigan. "I must say I'd call it damned dirty of you! You said you'd not do it, if I'd come here and open the mine!"

"But what good does it do to open it, if you close it again before the men are out?" Hal paused, and when he went on it was in a sincere attempt at apology. "Percy, don't imagine I fail to appreciate the embarrassments of this situation. I know I must seem a cad to you – more than you've cared to tell me. I called you my friend in spite of all our quarrels. All I can do is to assure you that I never intended to get into such a position as this."

"Well, what the hell did you want to come here for? You knew it was the property of a friend –"

"That's the question at issue between us, Percy. Have you forgotten our arguments? I tried to convince you what it meant that you and I should own the things by which other people have to live. I said we were ignorant of the conditions under which our properties were worked, we were a bunch of parasites and idlers. But you laughed at me, called me a crank, an anarchist, said I swallowed what any muckraker fed me. So I said: 'I'll go to one of Percy's mines! Then, when he tries to argue with me, I'll have him!' That was the way the thing started — as a joke. But then I got drawn into things. I don't want to be nasty, but no man with a drop of red blood in his veins could stay in this place a week without wanting to fight! That's why I want you to stay — you ought to stay, to meet some of the people and see for yourself."

"Well, I can't stay," said the other, coldly. "And all I can tell you is that I wish you'd go somewhere else to do your sociology."

"But where could I go, Percy? Somebody owns everything. If it's a big thing, it's almost certain to be somebody we know."

Said Percy, "If I might make a suggestion, you could have begun with the coal-mines of the Warner Company."

Hal laughed. "You may be sure I thought of that, Percy. But see the situation! If I was to accomplish my purpose, it was essential that I shouldn't be known. And I had met some of my father's superintendents in his office, and I knew they'd recognize me. So I *had* to go to some other mines."

"Most fortunate for the Warner Company," replied Percy, in an ugly tone.

Hal answered, gravely, "Let me tell you, I don't intend to leave the Warner Company permanently out of my sociology."

"Well," replied the other, "all I can say is that we pass one of their properties on our way back, and nothing would please me better than to stop the train and let you off!"

SECTION 21.

*H*al went into the drawing room car. There were Mrs. Curtis and Reggie Porter, playing bridge with Genevieve Halsey and young Everson. Bob Creston was chatting with Betty Gunnison, telling her what he had seen outside, no doubt. Bert Atkins was looking over the morning paper, yawning. Hal went on, seeking Jessie Arthur, and found her in one of the compartments of the car, looking out of the rain-drenched window — learning about a mining-camp in the manner permitted to young ladies of her class.

He expected to find her in a disturbed state of mind, and was prepared to apologize. But when he met the look of distress she turned upon him, he did not know just where to begin. He tried to speak casually — he had heard she was going away. But she caught him by the hand, exclaiming: "Hal, you are coming with us!"

He did not answer for a moment, but sat down by her. "Have I made you suffer so much, Jessie?"

He saw tears start into her eyes. "Haven't you *known* you were making me suffer? Here I was as Percy's guest; and to have you put such questions to me! What could I say? What do I know about the way Mr. Harrigan should run his business?"

"Yes, dear," he said, humbly. "Perhaps I shouldn't have drawn you into it. But the matter was so complicated and so sudden. Can't you understand that, and forgive me? Everything has turned out so well!"

But she did not think that everything had turned out well. "In the first place, for you to be here, in such a plight! And when I thought you were hunting mountain-goats in Mexico!"

He could not help laughing; but Jessie had not even a smile. "And then — to have you drag our love into the thing, there before everyone!"

"Was that really so terrible, Jessie?"

She looked at him with amazement. That he, Hal Warner, could have done such a thing, and not realize how terrible it was! To put her in a position where she had to break either the laws of love or the laws of good-breeding! Why, it had amounted to a public quarrel. It would be the talk of the town — there was no end to the embarrassment of it!

"But, sweetheart!" argued Hal. "Try to see the reality of this thing — think about those people in the mine. You really *must* do that!"

She looked at him, and noticed the new, grim lines that had come upon his youthful face. Also, she caught the note of suppressed passion in his voice. He was pale and weary looking, in dirty clothes, his hair unkempt and his face only half washed. It was terrifying — as if he had gone to war.

"Listen to me, Jessie," he insisted. "I want you to know about these things. If you and I are ever to make each other happy, you must try to grow up with me. That was why I was glad to have you here — you would have a chance to see for yourself. Now I ask you not to go without seeing."

"But I have to go, Hal. I can't ask Percy Harrigan to stay and inconvenience everybody!"

"You can stay without him. You can ask one of the ladies to chaperon you."

She gazed at him in dismay. "Why, Hal! What a thing to suggest!"

"Why so?"

"Think how it would look!"

"I can't think so much about looks, dear —"

She broke in: "Think what Mamma would say!"

"She wouldn't like it, I know —"

"She would be wild! She would never forgive either of us. She would never forgive anyone who stayed with me. And what would Percy say, if I came here as his guest, and stayed to spy on him and his father? Don't you see how preposterous it would be?"

Yes, he saw. He was defying all the conventions of her world, and it seemed to her a course of madness. She clutched his hands in hers, and the tears ran down her cheeks.

"Hal," she cried, "I can't leave you in this dreadful place! You look like a ghost, and a scarecrow, too! I want you to go and get some decent clothes and come home on this train."

But he shook his head. "It's not possible, Jessie."

"Why not?"

"Because I have a duty to do here. Can't you understand, dear? All my life, I've been living on the labor of coal-miners, and I've never taken the trouble to go near them, to see how my money was got!"

"But, Hal! These aren't your people! They are Mr. Harrigan's people!"

"Yes," he said, "but it's all the same. They toil, and we live on their toil, and take it as a matter of course."

"But what can one *do* about it, Hal?"

"One can understand it, if nothing else. And you see what I was able to do in this case — to get the mine open."

"Hal," she exclaimed, "I can't understand you! You've become so cynical, you don't believe in anyone! You're quite convinced that these officials meant to murder their working people! As if Mr. Harrigan would let his mines be run that way!"

"Mr. Harrigan, Jessie? He passes the collection plate at St. George's! That's the only place you've ever seen him, and that's all you know about him."

"I know what everybody says, Hal! Papa knows him, and my brothers — yes, your own brother, too! Isn't it true that Edward would disapprove what you're doing?"

"Yes, dear, I fear so."

"And you set yourself up against them — against everybody you know! Is it reasonable to think the older people are all wrong, and only you are right? Isn't it at least possible you're making a mistake? Think about it — honestly, Hal, for my sake!"

She was looking at him pleadingly; and he leaned forward and took her hand. "Jessie," he said, his voice trembling, "I *know* that these working people are oppressed; I know it, because I have been one of them! And I know that such men as Peter Harrigan, and even my own brother, are to blame! And they've got to be faced by someone — they've got to be made to see! I've come to see it clearly this summer — that's the job I have to do!"

She was gazing at him with her wide-open, beautiful eyes; underneath her protests and her terror, she was thrilling with awe at this amazing madman she loved. "They will *kill* you!" she cried.

"No, dearest — you don't need to worry about that — I don't think they'll kill me."

"But they shot at you!"

"No, they shot at Joe Smith, a miner's buddy. They won't shoot at the son of a millionaire — not in America, Jessie."

"But some dark night —"

"Set your mind at rest," he said, "I've got Percy tied up in this, and everybody knows it. There's no way they could kill me without the whole story's coming out — and so I'm as safe as I would be in my bed at home!"

SECTION 22.

*H*al was still possessed by his idea that Jessie must be taught — she must have knowledge forced upon her, whether she would or no. The train would not start for a couple of hours, and he tried to think of some use he could make of that precious interval. He recalled that Rosa Minetti had returned to her cabin to attend to her baby. A sudden vision came to him of Jessie in that little home. Rosa was sweet and good, and assuredly Little Jerry was a "winner."

"Sweetheart," he said, "I wish you'd come for a walk with me."

"But it's raining, Hal!"

"It won't hurt you to spoil one dress; you have plenty."

"I'm not thinking of that —"

"I *wish* you'd come."

"I don't feel comfortable about it, Hal. I'm here as Percy's guest, and he mightn't like —"

"I'll ask him if he objects to your taking a stroll," he suggested, with pretended gravity.

"No, no! That would make it worse!" Jessie had no humor whatever about these matters.

"Well, Vivie Cass was out, and some of the others are going. He hasn't objected to that."

"I know, Hal. But he knows they're all right."

Hal laughed. "Come on, Jessie. Percy won't hold you for my sins! You have a long train journey before you, and some fresh air will be good for you."

She saw that she must make some concession to him, if she was to keep any of her influence over him.

"All right," she said, with resignation, and disappeared and returned with a heavy veil over her face, to conceal her from prying reportorial eyes; also an equipment of mackintosh, umbrella and overshoes, against the rain. The two stole out of the car, feeling like a couple of criminals.

Skirting the edge of the throng about the pit-mouth, they came to the muddy, unpaved quarter in which the Italians had their homes; he held her arm, steering her through the miniature sloughs and creeks. It was thrilling to him to have her with him thus, to see her sweet face and hear her voice full of love. Many a time he had thought of her here, and told her in his imagination of his experiences!

He told her now — about the Minetti family, and how he had met Big and Little Jerry on the street, and how they had taken him in, and then been driven by fear to let him go again. He told his check-weighman story, and was telling how Jeff Cotton had arrested him; but they came to the Minetti cabin, and the terrifying narrative was cut short.

It was Little Jerry who came to the door, with the remains of breakfast distributed upon his cheeks; he stared in wonder at the mysteriously veiled figure. Entering, they saw Rosa sitting in a chair nursing her baby. She rose in confusion; but she did not quite like to turn her back upon her guests, so she stood trying to hide her breast as best she could, blushing and looking very girlish and pretty.

Hal introduced Jessie, as an old friend who was interested to meet his new friends, and Jessie threw back her veil and sat down. Little Jerry wiped off his face at his mother's command, and then came where he could stare at this incredibly lovely vision.

"I've been telling Miss Arthur what good care you took of me," said Hal to Rosa. "She wanted to come and thank you for it."

"Yes," added Jessie, graciously. "Anybody who is good to Hal earns my gratitude."

Rosa started to murmur something; but Little Jerry broke in, with his cheerful voice, "Why you call him Hal? His name's Joe!"

"Ssh!" cried Rosa. But Hal and Jessie laughed — and so the process of Americanizing Little Jerry was continued.

"I've got lots of names," said Hal. "They called me Hal when I was a kid like you."

"Did *she* know you then?" inquired Little Jerry.

"Yes, indeed."

"Is she your girl?"

Rosa laughed shyly, and Jessie blushed, and looked charming. She realized vaguely a difference in manners. These people accepted the existence of "girls," not concealing their interest in the phenomenon.

"It's a secret," warned Hal. "Don't you tell on us!"

"I can keep a secret," said Little Jerry. After a moment's pause he added, dropping his voice, "You gotta keep secrets if you work in North Valley."

"You bet your life," said Hal.

"My father's a Socialist," continued the other, addressing Jessie; then, since one thing leads on to another, "My father's a shot-firer."

"What's a shot-firer?" asked Jessie, by way of being sociable.

"Jesus!" exclaimed Little Jerry. "Don't you know nothin' about minin'?"

"No," said Jessie. "You tell me."

"You couldn't get no coal without a shot-firer," declared Little Jerry. "You gotta get a good one, too, or maybe you bust up the mine. My father's the best they got."

"What does he do?"

"Well, they got a drill — long, long, like this, all the way across the room; and they turn it and bore holes in the coal. Sometimes they got machines to drill, only we don't like them machines, 'cause it takes the men's jobs. When they got the holes, then the shot-firer comes and sets off the powder. You gotta have —" and here Little Jerry slowed up, pronouncing each syllable very carefully — "per-miss-i-ble powder — what don't make no flame. And you gotta know just how much to put in. If you put in too much, you smash the coal, and the miner raises hell; if you don't put in enough, you make too much work for him, an' he raises hell again. So you gotta get a good shot-firer."

Jessie looked at Hal, and he saw that her dismay was mingled with genuine amusement. He judged this a good way for her to get her education, so he proceeded to draw out Little Jerry on other aspects of coal-mining: on short weights and long hours, grafting bosses and camp-marshals, company-stores and boarding-houses, Socialist agitators and union organizers. Little Jerry talked freely of the secrets of the camp. "It's all right for you to know," he remarked gravely. "You're Joe's girl!"

"You little cherub!" exclaimed Jessie.

"What's a cherub?" was Little Jerry's reply.

SECTION 23.

So the time passed in a way that was pleasant. Jessie was completely won by this little Dago mine-urchin, in spite of all his frightful curse-words; and Hal saw that she was won, and was delighted by the success of this experiment in social amalgamation. He could not read Jessie's mind, and realize that underneath her genuine delight were reservations born of her prejudices, the instinctive cruelty of caste. Yes, this little mine chap was a cherub, now; but how about when he grew big? He would grow ugly and coarse-looking, in ten years one would not know him from any other of the rough and dirty men of the village. Jessie took the fact that common people grow ugly as they mature as a proof that they are, in some deep and permanent way, the inferiors of those above them. Hal was throwing away his time and strength, trying to make them into something which Nature had obviously not intended them to be! She decided to make that point to Hal on their way back to the train. She realized that he had brought her here to educate her; like all the rest of the world, she resented forcible education, and she was not without hope that she might turn the tables and educate Hal.

Pretty soon Rosa finished nursing the baby, and Jessie remarked the little one's black eyes. This topic broke down the mother's shyness, and they were chatting pleasantly, when suddenly they heard sounds outside which caused them to start up. It was a clamor of women's voices; and Hal and Rosa sprang to the door. Just now was a critical time, when everyone was on edge for news.

Hal threw open the door and called to those outside "What is it?" There came a response, in a woman's voice, "They've found Rafferty!"

"Alive?"

"Nobody knows yet."

"Where?"

"In Room Seventeen. Eleven of them — Rafferty, and young Flanagan, and Johannson, the Swede. They're near dead — can't speak, they say.

They won't let anybody near them."

Other voices broke in; but the one which answered Hal had a different quality; it was a warm, rich voice, unmistakably Irish, and it held Jessie's attention. "They've got them in the tipple-room, and the women want to know about their men, and they won't tell them. They're beatin' them back like dogs!"

There was a tumult of weeping, and Hal stepped out of the cabin, and in a minute or so he entered again, supporting on his arm a girl, clad in a faded blue calico dress, and having a head of very conspicuous red hair. She seemed half fainting, and kept moaning that it was horrible, horrible. Hal led her to a chair, and she sank into it and hid her face in her hands, sobbing, talking incoherently between her sobs.

Jessie stood looking at this girl. She felt the intensity of her excitement, and shared it; yet at the same time there was something in Jessie that resented it. She did not wish to be upset about things like this, which she could not help. Of course these unfortunate people were suffering; but — what a shocking lot of noise the poor thing was making! A part of the poor thing's excitement was rage, and Jessie realized that, and resented it still more. It was as if it were a personal challenge to her; the same as Hal's fierce social passions, which so bewildered and shocked her.

"They're beatin' the women back like dogs!" the girl repeated.

"Mary," said Hal, trying to soothe her, "the doctors will be doing their best. The women couldn't expect to crowd about them!"

"Maybe they couldn't; but that's not it, Joe, and ye know it! They been bringin' up dead bodies, some they found where the explosion was — blown all to pieces. And they won't let anybody see them. Is that because of the doctors? No, it ain't! It's because they want to tell lies about the number killed! They want to count four or five legs to a man! And that's what's drivin' the women crazy! I saw Mrs. Zamboni, tryin' to get into the shed, and Pete Hanun caught her by the breasts and shoved her back. 'I want my man!' she screamed. 'Well, what do you want him for? He's all in pieces!' 'I want the pieces!' 'What good'll they do you? Are you goin' to eat him?'"

There were cries of horror now, even from Jessie; and the strange girl hid her face in her hands and began to sob again. Hal put his hand gently on her arm.

"Mary," he pleaded, "it's not so bad — at least they're getting the people out."

"How do ye know what they're doin'? They might be sealin' up parts of the mine down below! That's what makes it so horrible — nobody knows what's happenin'! Ye should have heard poor Mrs. Rafferty screamin'. Joe, it went through me like a knife. Just think, it's been half an hour since they brought him up, and the poor lady can't be told if her man is alive."

SECTION 24.

*H*al stood for a few moments in thought. He was surprised that such things should be happening while Percy Harrigan's train was in the village. He was considering whether he should go to Percy, or whether a hint to Cotton or Cartwright would not be sufficient.

"Mary," he said, in a quiet voice, "you needn't distress yourself so. We can get better treatment for the women, I'm sure."

But her sobbing went on. "What can ye do? They're bound to have their way!"

"No," said Hal. "There's a difference now. Believe me — something can be done. I'll step over and have a word with Jeff Cotton."

He started towards the door; but there came a cry: "Hal!" It was Jessie, whom he had almost forgotten in his sudden anger at the bosses.

At her protest he turned and looked at her; then he looked at Mary. He saw the latter's hands fall from her tear-stained face, and her expression of grief give way to one of wonder. "Hal!"

"Excuse me," he said, quickly. "Miss Burke, this is my friend, Miss Arthur." Then, not quite sure if this was a satisfactory introduction, he added, "Jessie, this is my friend, Mary."

Jessie's training could not fail in any emergency. "Miss Burke," she said, and smiled with perfect politeness. But Mary said nothing, and the strained look did not leave her face.

In the first excitement she had almost failed to notice this stranger; but now she stared, and realization grew upon her. Here was a girl, beautiful with a kind of beauty hardly to be conceived of in a mining-camp; reserved, yet obviously expensive — even in a mackintosh and rubber-shoes. Mary was used to the expensiveness of Mrs. O'Callahan, but here was a new kind of expensiveness, subtle and compelling, strangely unconscious. And she laid claim to Joe Smith, the miner's buddy! She called him by a name hitherto unknown to his North Valley associates! It needed no word from Little Jerry to guide Mary's instinct; she knew in a flash that here was the "other girl."

Mary was seized with sudden acute consciousness of the blue calico dress, patched at the shoulder and stained with grease-spots; of her hands, big and rough with hard labor; of her feet, clad in shoes worn sideways at the heel, and threatening to break out at the toes. And as for Jessie, she too had the woman's instinct; she too saw a girl who was beautiful, with a kind of beauty of which she did not approve, but which she could not deny — the beauty of robust health, of abounding animal energy. Jessie was not unaware of the nature of her own charms, having been carefully educated to conserve them; nor did she fail to make note of the other girl's handicaps — the patched and greasy dress, the big rough hands, the shoes worn sideways. But even so, she realized that "Red Mary" had a quality which she lacked — that beside this wild rose of a mining-camp, she, Jessie Arthur, might possibly seem a garden flower, fragile and insipid.

She had seen Hal lay his hand upon Mary's arm, and heard her speak to him. She called him Joe! And a sudden fear had leaped into Jessie's heart.

Like many girls who have been delicately reared, Jessie Arthur knew more than she admitted, even to herself. She knew enough to realize that young men with ample means and leisure are not always saints and ascetics. Also, she had heard the remark many times made that these women of the lower orders had "no morals." Just what did such a remark mean? What would be the attitude of such a girl as Mary Burke — full-blooded and intense, dissatisfied with her lot in life — to a man of culture and charm like Hal? She would covet him, of course; no woman who knew him could fail to covet him. And she would try to steal him away from his friends, from the world to which he belonged, the future of happiness and ease to which he was entitled. She would have powers — dark and terrible powers, all the more appalling to Jessie because they were mysterious. Might they possibly be able to overcome even the handicap of a dirty calico dress, of big rough hands and shoes worn sideways?

These reflections, which have taken many words to explain, came to Jessie in one flash of intuition. She understood now, all at once, the incomprehensible phenomenon — that Hal should leave friends and home and career, to come and live amid this squalor and suffering! She saw the old drama of the soul of man, heaven and hell contending for mastery of it; and she knew that she was heaven, and that this "Red Mary" was hell.

She looked at Hal. He seemed to her so fine and true; his face was frank, he was the soul of honorableness. No, it was impossible to believe that he had yielded to such a lure! If that had been the case, he would never have brought her to this cabin, he would never have taken a chance of her meeting the girl. No; but he might be struggling against temptation, he might be in the toils of it, and only half aware of it. He was a man, and therefore blind; he was a dreamer, and it would be like him to idealize this girl, calling her naïve and primitive, thinking that she had no wiles! Jessie had come just in time to save him! And she would fight to save him — using wiles more subtle than those at the command of any mining-camp hussy!

SECTION 25.

*I*t was the surging up in Jessie Arthur of that instinctive self, the creature of hereditary cruelty, of the existence of which Hal had no idea. She drew back, and there was a quiet *hauteur* in her tone as she spoke. "Hal, come here, please."

He came; and she waited until he was close enough for intimacy, and then said, "Have you forgotten you have to take me back to the train?"

"Can't you come with me for a few minutes?" he pleaded. "It would have such a good effect if you did."

"I can't go into that crowd," she answered; and suddenly her voice trembled, and the tears came into her sweet brown eyes. "Don't you know, Hal, that I couldn't stand such terrible sights? This poor girl — she is used to them — she is hardened! But I — I — oh, take me away, take me away, dear Hal!" This cry of a woman for protection came with a familiar echo to Hal's mind. He did not stop to think — he was moved by it instinctively. Yes, he had exposed the girl he loved to suffering! He had meant it for her own good, but even so, it was cruel!

He stood close to her, and saw the love-light in her eyes; he saw the tears, the trembling of her sensitive chin. She swayed to him, and he caught her in his arms — and there, before these witnesses, she let him press her to him, while she sobbed and whispered her distress. She had been shy of caresses hitherto, watched and admonished by an experienced mother; certainly she had never before made what could by the remotest stretch of the imagination be considered an advance towards him. But now she made it, and there was a cry of triumph in her soul as she saw that he responded to it. He was still hers — and these low people should know it, this "other girl" should know it!

Yet, in the midst of this very exultation, Jessie Arthur really felt the grief she expressed for the women of North Valley; she really felt horror at the story of Mrs. Zamboni's "man": so intricate is the soul of woman, so puzzling that faculty, older than the ages, which enables her to be hysterical, and at the same time to be guided in the use of that hysteria by deep and infallible calculation.

But she made Hal realize that it was necessary for him to take her away. He turned to Mary Burke and said, "Miss Arthur's train is leaving in a short time. I'll have to take her back, and then I'll go to the pit-mouth with you and see what I can do."

"Very well," Mary answered; and her voice was hard and cold. But Hal did not notice this. He was a man, and not able to keep up with the emotions of one woman — to say nothing of two women at the same time.

He took Jessie out, and all the way back to the train she fought a desperate fight to get him away from here. She no longer even suggested that he get decent clothing; she was willing for him to come as he was, in his coal-stained mining-jumpers, in the private train of the Coal King's son. She besought him in the name of their affection. She threatened him that if he did not come, this might be the last time they would meet. She even broke down in the middle of the street, and let him stand there in plain sight of miners' wives and children, and of possible newspaper reporters, holding her in his arms and comforting her.

Hal was much puzzled; but he would not give way. The idea of going off in Percy Harrigan's train had come to seem morally repulsive to him; he hated Percy Harrigan's train, and Percy Harrigan also, he declared. And Jessie saw that she was only making him unreasonable — that before long he might be hating her. With her instinctive *savoir faire,* she brought up his suggestion that she might find someone to chaperon her, and stay with him at North Valley until he was ready to come away.

Hal's heart leaped at that; he had no idea what was in her mind — the certainty that no one of the ladies of the Harrigan party would run the risk of offending her host by staying under such circumstances.

"You mean it, sweetheart?" he cried, happily.

She answered, "I mean that I love you, Hal."

"All right, dear!" he said. "We'll see if we can arrange it."

But as they walked on, she managed, without his realizing it, to cause him to reflect upon the effect of her staying. She was willing to do it, if it was what he wanted; but it would injure, perhaps irrevocably, his standing with her parents. They would telegraph her to come at once; and if she did not obey, they would come by the next train. So on, until at last Hal was moved to withdraw his own suggestion. After all, what was the use of her staying, if her mind was on the people at home, if she would simply keep him in hot water? Before the conversation was over Hal had become clear in his mind that North Valley was no place for Jessie Arthur, and that he had been a fool to think he could bring the two together.

She tried to get him to promise to leave as soon as the last man had been brought out of the mine. He answered that he intended to leave then, unless some new emergency should arise. She tried to get an unqualified promise; and failing in that, when they had nearly got to the train she suddenly made a complete surrender. Let him do what he pleased — but let him remember that she loved him, that she needed him, that she could not do without him. No matter what he might do, no matter what people might say about him, she believed in him, she would stand by him. Hal was deeply touched, and took her in his arms again and kissed her tenderly under the umbrella, in the presence of the wondering stares of several urchins with coal-smutted faces. He pledged anew his love for her, assuring her that no amount of interest in mining-camps should ever steal him from her.

Then he put her on the train, and shook hands with the departing guests. He was so very somber and harassed-looking that the young men forbore to "kid" him as they would otherwise have done. He stood on the station-platform and saw the train roll away — and felt, to his own desperate bewilderment, that he hated these friends of his boyhood and youth. His reason protested against it; he told himself there was nothing they could do, no reason on earth for them to stay — and yet he hated them. They were hurrying off to dance and flirt at the country club — while he was going back to the pit-mouth, to try to get Mrs. Zamboni the right to inspect the pieces of her "man!"

BOOK FOUR
THE WILL OF KING COAL
SECTION I.

*T*he pit of death was giving up its secrets. The hoist was busy, and cage-load after cage-load came up, with bodies dead and bodies living and bodies only to be classified after machines had pumped air into them for a while. Hal stood in the rain and watched the crowd and thought that he had never witnessed a scene so compelling to pity and terror. The silence that would fall when anyone appeared who might have news to tell! The sudden shriek of anguish from some woman whose hopes were struck dead! The moans of sympathy that ran through the crowd, alternating with cheers at some good tidings, shaking the souls of the multitude as a storm of wind shakes a reed-field!

And the stories that ran through the camp — brought up from the underground world — stories of incredible sufferings, and of still more incredible heroisms! Men who had been four days without food or water, yet had resisted being carried out of the mine, proposing to stay and help rescue others! Men who had lain together in the darkness and silence, keeping themselves alive by the water which seeped from the rocks overhead, taking turns lying face upwards where the drops fell, or wetting pieces of their clothing and sucking out the moisture! Members of the rescue parties would tell how they knocked upon the barriers, and heard the faint answering signals of the imprisoned men; how madly they toiled to cut through, and how, when at last a little hole appeared, they heard the cries of joy, and saw the eyes of men shining from the darkness, while they waited, gasping, for the hole to grow bigger, so that water and food might be passed in!

In some places they were fighting the fire. Long lines of hose had been sent down, and men were moving forward foot by foot, as the smoke and steam were sucked out ahead of them by the fan. Those who did this work were taking their lives in their hands, yet they went without hesitation. There was always hope of finding men in barricaded rooms beyond.

Hal sought out Jeff Cotton at the entrance to the tipple-room, which had been turned into a temporary hospital. It was the first time the two had met since the revelation in Percy's car, and the camp-marshal's face took on a rather sheepish grin. "Well, Mr. Warner, you win," he remarked; and after a little arguing he agreed to permit a couple of women to go into the tipple-room and make a list of the injured, and go out and give the news to the crowd. Hal went to the Minettis to ask Mary Burke to attend to this; but Rosa said that Mary had gone out after he and Miss Arthur had left, and no one knew where she was. So Hal went to Mrs. David, who consented to get a couple of friends, and do the work without being called a "committee." "I won't have any damned committees!" the camp-marshal had declared.

So the night passed, and part of another day. A clerk from the office came to Hal with a sealed envelope, containing a telegram, addressed in care of Cartwright. "I most urgently beg of you to come home at once. It will be distressing to Dad if he hears what has happened, and it will not be possible to keep the matter from him for long."

As Hal read, he frowned; evidently the Harrigans had got busy without delay! He went to the office and telephoned his answer. "Am planning to leave in a day or two. Trust you will make an effort to spare Dad until you have heard my story."

This message troubled Hal. It started in his mind long arguments with his brother, and explanations and apologies to his father. He loved the old man tenderly. What a shame if some emissary of the Harrigans were to get to him to upset him with misrepresentations!

Also these ideas had a tendency to make Hal homesick; they brought more vividly to his thoughts the outside world, with its physical allurements — there being a limit to the amount of unwholesome meals and dirty beds and repulsive sights a man of refinement can force himself to endure. Hal found himself obsessed by a vision of a club dining room, with odors of grilled steaks and hot rolls, and the colors of salads and fresh fruits and cream. The conviction grew suddenly strong in him that his work in North Valley was nearly done!

Another night passed, and another day. The last of the bodies had been brought out, and the corpses shipped down to Pedro for one of those big wholesale funerals which are a feature of mine-life. The fire was out, and the rescue-crews had given place to a swarm of carpenters and timbermen, repairing the damage and making the mine safe. The reporters had gone; Billy Keating having clasped Hal's hand, and promised to meet him for luncheon at the club. An agent of the "Red Cross" was on hand, and was feeding the hungry out of Mrs. Curtis's subscription-list. What more was there for Hal to do — except to bid good-bye to his friends, and assure them of his help in the future?

First among these friends was Mary Burke, whom he had had no chance to talk to since the meeting with Jessie. He realized that Mary had been deliberately avoiding him. She was not in her home, and he went to inquire at the Raffertys', and stopped for a good-bye chat with the old woman whose husband he had saved.

Rafferty was going to pull through. His wife had been allowed in to see him, and tears rolled down her shrunken cheeks as she told about it. He had been four days and nights blocked up in a little tunnel, with no food or water, save for a few drops of coffee which he had shared with other men. He could still not speak, he could hardly move a hand; but there was life in his eyes, and his look had been a greeting from the soul she had loved and served these thirty years and more. Mrs. Rafferty sang praises to the Rafferty God, who had brought him safely through these perils; it seemed obvious that He must be more efficient than the Protestant God of Johannson, the giant Swede, who had lain by Rafferty's side and given up the ghost.

But the doctor had stated that the old Irishman would never be good to work again; and Hal saw a shadow of terror cross the sunshine of Mrs. Rafferty's rejoicing. How could a doctor say a thing like that? Rafferty was old, to be sure; but he was tough — and could any doctor imagine how hard a man would try who had a family looking to him? Sure, he was not the one to give up for a bit of pain now and then! Besides him, there was only Tim who was earning; and though Tim was a good lad, and worked steady, any doctor ought to know that a big family could not be kept going on the wages of one eighteen-year-old pit-boy. As for the other lads, there was a law that said they were too young to work. Mrs. Rafferty thought there should be someone to put a little sense into the heads of them that made the laws — for if they wanted to forbid children to work in coal-mines, they should surely provide some other way to feed the children.

Hal listened, agreeing sympathetically, and meantime watching her, and learning more from her actions than from her words. She had been obedient to the teachings of her religion, to be fruitful and multiply; she had fed three grown sons into the maw of industry, and had still eight children and a man to care for. Hal wondered if she had ever rested a single minute of daylight in all her fifty-four years. Certainly not while he had been in her house! Even now, while praising the Rafferty God and blaming the capitalist law-makers, she was getting a supper, moving swiftly, silently, like a machine. She was lean as an old horse that has toiled across a desert; the skin over her cheekbones was tight as stretched rubber, and cords stood out in her wrists like piano-wires.

And now she was cringing before the specter of destitution. He asked what she would do about it, and saw the shadow of terror cross her face again. There was one recourse from starvation, it seemed — to have her children taken from her, and put in some institution! At the mention of this, one of the special nightmares of the poor, the old woman began to sob and cry again that the doctor was wrong; he would see, and Hal would see — Old Rafferty would be back at his job in a week or two!

SECTION 2.

*H*al went out on the street again. It was the hour which would have been sunset in a level region; the tops of the mountains were touched with a purple light, and the air was fresh and chill with early fall. Down the darkening streets he saw a gathering of men; there was shouting, and people running towards the place, so he hurried up, with the thought in his mind, "What's the matter now?" There were perhaps a hundred men crying out, their voices mingling like the sound of waves on the sea. He could make out words: "Go on! Go on! We've had enough of it! Hurrah!"

"What's happened?" he asked, of someone on the outskirts; and the man, recognizing him, raised a cry which ran through the throng: "Joe Smith! He's the boy for us! Come in here, Joe! Give us a speech!"

But even while Hal was asking questions, trying to get the situation clear, other shouts had drowned out his name. "We've had enough of them walking over us!" And somebody cried, more loudly, "Tell us about it! Tell it again! Go on!"

A man was standing upon the steps of a building at one side. Hal stared in amazement; it was Tim Rafferty. Of all people in the world — Tim, the light-hearted and simple, Tim of the laughing face and the merry Irish blue eyes! Now his sandy hair was tousled and his features distorted with rage. "Him near dead!" he yelled. "Him with his voice gone, and couldn't move his hand! Eleven years he's slaved for them, and near killed in an accident that's their own fault — every man in this crowd knows it's their own fault, by God!"

"Sure thing! You're right!" cried a chorus of voices "Tell it all!"

"They give him twenty-five dollars and his hospital expenses — and what'll his hospital expenses be? They'll have him out on the street again before he's able to stand. You know that — they done it to Pete Cullen!"

"You bet they did!"

"Them damned lawyers in there — gettin' 'em to sign papers when they don't know what they're doin'. An' me that might help him can't get near! By Christ, I say it's too much! Are we slaves, or are we dogs, that we have to stand such things?"

"We'll stand no more of it!" shouted one. "We'll go in there and see to it ourselves!"

"Come on!" shouted another. "To hell with their gunmen!"

Hal pushed his way into the crowd. "Tim!" he cried. "How do you know this?"

"There's a fellow in there seen it."

"Who?"

"I can't tell you — they'd fire him; but it's somebody you know as well as me. He come and told me. They're beatin' me old father out of damages!"

"They do it all the time!" shouted Wauchope, an English miner at Hal's side. "That's why they won't let us in there."

"They done the same thing to my father!" put in another voice. Hal recognized Andy, the Greek boy.

"And they want to start Number Two in the mornin'!" yelled Tim. "Who'll go down there again? And with Alec Stone, him that damns the men and saves the mules!"

"We'll not go back in them mines till they're safe!" shouted Wauchope. "Let them sprinkle them — or I'm done with the whole business."

"And let 'em give us our weights!" cried another. "We'll have a check-weighman, and we'll get what we earn!"

So again came the cry, "Joe Smith! Give us a speech, Joe! Soak it to 'em! You're the boy!"

Hal stood helpless, dismayed. He had counted his fight won — and here was another beginning! The men were looking to him, calling upon him as the boldest of the rebels. Only a few of them knew about the sudden change in his fortunes.

Even while he hesitated, the line of battle had swept past him; the Englishman, Wauchope, sprang upon the steps and began to address the throng. He was one of the bowed and stunted men, but in this emergency he developed sudden lung-power. Hal listened in astonishment; this silent and dull-looking fellow was the last he would have picked for a fighter. Tom Olson had sounded him out, and reported that he would hear nothing, so they had dismissed him from mind. And here he was, shouting terrible defiance!

"They're a set of robbers and murderers! They rob us everywhere we turn! For my part, I've had enough of it! Have you?"

There was a roar from everyone within reach of his voice. They had all had enough.

"All right, then — we'll fight them!"

"Hurrah! Hurrah! We'll have our rights!"

Jeff Cotton came up on the run, with "Bud" Adams and two or three of the gunmen at his heels. The crowd turned upon them, the men on the outskirts clenching their fists, showing their teeth like angry dogs. Cotton's face was red with rage, but he saw that he had a serious matter in hand; he turned and went for more help — and the mob roared with delight. Already they had begun their fight! Already they had won their first victory!

SECTION 3.

*T*he crowd moved down the street, shouting and cursing as it went. Someone started to sing the Marseillaise, and others took it up, and the words mounted to a frenzy:

> "To arms! To arms, ye brave!
> March on, march on, all hearts resolved
> On victory or death!"

There were the oppressed of many nations in this crowd; they sang in a score of languages, but it was the same song. They would sing a few bars, and the yells of others would drown them out. "March on! March on! All hearts resolved!" Some rushed away in different directions to spread the news, and very soon the whole population of the village was on the spot; the men waving their caps, the women lifting up their hands and shrieking — or standing terrified, realizing that babies could not be fed upon revolutionary singing.

Tim Rafferty was raised up on the shoulders of the crowd and made to tell his story once more. While he was telling it, his old mother came running, and her shrieks rang above the clamor: "Tim! Tim! Come down from there! What's the matter wid ye?" She was twisting her hands together in an agony of fright; seeing Hal, she rushed up to him. "Get him out of there, Joe! Sure, the lad's gone crazy! They'll turn us out of the camp, they'll give us nothin' at all — and what'll become of us? Mother of God, what's the matter with the b'y?" She called to Tim again; but Tim paid no attention, if he heard her. Tim was on the march to Versailles!

Someone shouted that they would go to the hospital to protect the injured men from the "damned lawyers." Here was something definite, and the crowd moved in that direction, Hal following with the stragglers, the women and children, and the less bold among the men. He noticed some of the clerks and salaried employees of the company; presently he saw Jeff Cotton again, and heard him ordering these men to the office to get revolvers.

"Big Jack" David came along with Jerry Minetti, and Hal drew back to consult with them. Jerry was on fire. It had come — the revolt he had been looking forward to for years! Why were they not making speeches, getting control of the men and organizing them?

Jack David voiced uncertainty. They had to consider if this outburst could mean anything permanent.

Jerry answered that it would mean what they chose to make it mean. If they took charge, they could guide the men and hold them together. Wasn't that what Tom Olson had wanted?

No, said the big Welshman, Olson had been trying to organize the men secretly, as preliminary to a revolt in all the camps. That was quite another thing from an open movement, limited to one camp. Was there any hope of success for such a movement? If not, they would be foolish to start, they would only be making sure of their own expulsion.

Jerry turned to Hal. What did he think?

And so at last Hal had to speak. It was hard for him to judge, he said. He knew so little about labor matters. It was to learn about them that he had come to North Valley. It was a hard thing to advise men to submit to such treatment as they had been getting; but on the other hand, anyone could see that a futile outbreak would discourage everybody, and make it harder than ever to organize them.

So much Hal spoke; but there was more in his mind, which he could not speak. He could not say to these men, "I am a friend of yours, but I am also a friend of your enemy, and in this crisis I cannot make up my mind to which side I owe allegiance. I'm bound by a duty of politeness to the masters of your lives; also, I'm anxious not to distress the girl I am to marry!" No, he could not say such things. He felt himself a traitor for having them in his mind, and he could hardly bring himself to look these men in the eye. Jerry knew that he was in some way connected with the Harrigans; probably he had told the rest of Hal's friends, and they had been discussing it and speculating about the meaning of it. Suppose they should think he was a spy?

So Hal was relieved when Jack David spoke firmly. They would only be playing the game of the enemy if they let themselves be drawn in prematurely. They ought to have the advice of Tom Olson.

Where was Olson? Hal asked; and David explained that on the day when Hal had been thrown out of camp, Olson had got his "time" and set out for Sheridan, the local headquarters of the union, to report the situation. He would probably not come back; he had got his little group together, he had planted the seed of revolt in North Valley.

They discussed back and forth the problem of getting advice. It was impossible to telephone from North Valley without everything they said being listened to; but the evening train for Pedro left in a few minutes, and "Big Jack" declared that someone ought to take it. The town of Sheridan was only fifteen or twenty miles from Pedro, and there would be a union official there to advise them; or they might use the long distance telephone, and persuade one of the union leaders in Western City to take the midnight train, and be in Pedro next morning.

Hal, still hoping to withdraw himself, put this task off on Jack David. They emptied out the contents of their pockets, so that he might have funds enough, and the big Welshman darted off to catch the train. In the meantime Jerry and Hal agreed to keep in the background, and to seek out the other members of their group and warn them to do the same.

SECTION 4.

*T*his program was a convenient one for Hal; but as he was to find almost at once, it had been adopted too late. He and Jerry started after the crowd, which had stopped in front of one of the company buildings; and as they came nearer they heard someone making a speech. It was the voice of a woman, the tones rising clear and compelling. They could not see the speaker, because of the throng, but Hal recognized her voice, and caught his companion by the arm. "It's Mary Burke!"

Mary Burke it was, for a fact; and she seemed to have the crowd in a kind of frenzy. She would speak one sentence, and there would come a roar from the throng; she would speak another sentence, and there would come another roar. Hal and Jerry pushed their way in, to where they could make out the words of this litany of rage.

"Would they go down into the pit themselves, do ye think?"

"They would not!"

"Would they be dressed in silks and laces, do ye think?"

"They would not!"

"Would they have such fine soft hands, do ye think?"

"They would not!"

"Would they hold themselves too good to look at ye?"

"They would not! They would not!"

And Mary swept on: "If only ye'd stand together, they'd come to ye on their knees to ask for terms! But ye're cowards, and they play on your fears! Ye're traitors, and they buy ye out! They break ye into pieces, they do what they please with ye — and then ride off in their private cars, and leave gunmen to beat ye down and trample on your faces! How long will ye stand it? How long?"

The roar of the mob rolled down the street and back again. "We'll not stand it! We'll not stand it!" Men shook their clenched fists, women shrieked, even children shouted curses. "We'll fight them! We'll slave no more for them!"

And Mary found a magic word. "We'll have a union!" she shouted. "We'll get together and stay together! If they refuse us our rights, we'll know what to answer — we'll have a *strike!*"

There was a roar like the crashing of thunder in the mountains. Yes, Mary had found the word! For many years it had not been spoken aloud in North Valley, but now it ran like a flash of gunpowder through the throng. "Strike! Strike! Strike! Strike!" It seemed as if they would never have enough of it. Not all of them had understood Mary's speech, but they knew this word, "Strike!" They translated and proclaimed it in Polish and Bohemian and Italian and Greek. Men waved their caps, women waved their aprons — in the semi-darkness it was like some strange kind of vegetation tossed by a storm. Men clasped one another's hands, the more demonstrative of the foreigners fell upon one another's necks. "Strike! Strike! Strike!"

"We're no longer slaves!" cried the speaker. "We're men — and we'll live as men! We'll work as men — or we'll not work at all! We'll no longer be a herd of cattle, that they can drive about as they please! We'll organize, we'll stand together — shoulder to shoulder! Either we'll win together, or we'll starve and die together! And not a man of us will yield, not a man of us will turn traitor! Is there anybody here who'll scab on his fellows?"

There was a howl, which might have come from a pack of wolves. Let the man who would scab on his fellows show his dirty face in that crowd!

"Ye'll stand by the union?"

"We'll stand by it!"

"Ye'll swear?"

"We'll swear!"

She flung her arms to heaven with a gesture of passionate adjuration. "Swear it on your lives! To stick to the rest of us, and never a man of ye give way till ye've won! Swear! *Swear!*"

Men stood, imitating her gesture, their hands stretched up to the sky. "We swear! We swear!"

"Ye'll not let them break ye! Ye'll not let them frighten ye!"

"No! No!"

"Stand by your word, men! Stand by it! 'Tis the one chance for your wives and childer!" The girl rushed on — exhorting with leaping words and passionate out-flung arms — a tall, swaying figure of furious rebellion. Hal listened to the speech and watched the speaker, marveling. Here was a miracle of the human soul, here was hope born of despair! And the crowd around her — they were sharing the wonderful rebirth; their waving arms, their swaying forms responded to Mary as an orchestra to the baton of a leader.

A thrill shook Hal — a thrill of triumph! He had been beaten down himself, he had wanted to run from this place of torment; but now there was hope in North Valley — now there would be victory, freedom!

Ever since he had come to the coal-country, the knowledge had been growing in Hal that the real tragedy of these people's lives was not their physical suffering, but their mental depression — the dull, hopeless misery in their minds. This had been driven into his consciousness day by day, both by what he saw and by what others told him. Tom Olson had first put it into words: "Your worst troubles are inside the heads of the fellows you're trying to help!" How could hope be given to men in this environment of terrorism? Even Hal himself, young and free as he was, had been brought to despair. He came from a class which is accustomed to say, "Do this," or "Do that," and it will be done. But these mine-slaves had never known that sense of power, of certainty; on the contrary, they were accustomed to having their efforts balked at every turn, their every impulse to happiness or achievement crushed by another's will.

But here was this miracle of the human soul! Here was hope in North Valley! Here were the people rising — and Mary Burke at their head! It was his vision come true — Mary Burke with a glory in her face, and her hair shining like a crown of gold! Mary Burke mounted upon a snow-white horse, wearing a robe of white, soft and lustrous — like Joan of Arc, or a leader in a suffrage parade! Yes, and she was at the head of a host, he had the music of its marching in his ears!

Underneath Hal's jesting words had been a real vision, a real faith in this girl. Since that day when he had first discovered her, a wild rose of the mining-camp taking in the family wash, he had realized that she was no pretty young working-girl, but a woman with a mind and a personality. She saw farther, she felt more deeply than the average of these wage-slaves. Her problem was the same as theirs, yet more complex. When he had wanted to help her and had offered to get her a job, she had made clear that what she craved was not merely relief from drudgery, but a life with intellectual interest. So then the idea had come to him that Mary should become a teacher, a leader of her people. She loved them, she suffered for them and with them, and at the same time she had a mind that was capable of seeking out the causes of their misery. But when he had gone to her with plans of leadership, he had been met by her corroding despair; her pessimism had seemed to mock his dreams, her contempt for these mine-slaves had belittled his efforts in their behalf and in hers.

And now, here she was taking up the role he had planned for her! Her very soul was in this shouting throng, he thought. She had lived the lives of these people, shared their every wrong, been driven to rebellion with them. Being a mere man, Hal missed one important point about this startling development; he did not realize that Mary's eloquence was addressed, not merely to the Rafferties and the Wauchopes, and the rest of the North Valley mine-slaves, but to a certain magazine-cover girl, clad in a mackintosh and a pale green hat and a soft and filmy and horribly expensive motoring veil!

SECTION 5.

Mary's speech was brought to a sudden end. A group of the men had moved down the street, and there arose a disturbance there. The noise of it swelled louder, and more people began to move in that direction. Mary turned to look, and all at once the whole throng surged down the street.

The trouble was at the hospital. In front of this building was a porch, and on it Cartwright and Alec Stone were standing, with a group of the clerks and office-employees, among whom Hal saw Predovich, Johnson, the postmaster, and Si Adams. At the foot of the steps stood Tim Rafferty, with a swarm of determined men at his back. He was shouting, "We want them lawyers out of there!"

The superintendent himself had undertaken to parley with him. "There are no lawyers in here, Rafferty."

"We don't trust you!" And the crowd took up the cry: "We'll see for ourselves!"

"You can't go into this building," declared Cartwright.

"I'm goin' to see my father!" shouted Tim. "I've got a right to see my father, ain't I?"

"You can see him in the morning. You can take him away, if you want to. We've no desire to keep him. But he's asleep now, and you can't disturb the others."

"You weren't afraid to disturb them with your damned lawyers!" And there was a roar of approval — so loud that Cartwright's denial could hardly be heard.

"There have been no lawyers near him, I tell you."

"It's a lie!" shouted Wauchope. "They been in there all day, and you know it. We mean to have them out."

"Go on, Tim!" cried Andy, the Greek boy, pushing his way to the front. "Go on!" cried the others; and thus encouraged, Rafferty started up the steps.

"I mean to see my father!" As Cartwright caught him by the shoulder, he yelled, "Let me go, I say!"

It was evident that the superintendent was trying his best not to use violence; he was ordering his own followers back at the same time that he was holding the boy. But Tim's blood was up; he shoved forward, and the superintendent, either striking him or trying to ward off a blow, threw him backwards down the steps. There was an uproar of rage from the throng; they surged forward, and at the same time some of the men on the porch drew revolvers.

The meaning of that situation was plain enough. In a moment more the mob would be up the steps, and there would be shooting. And if once that happened, who could guess the end? Wrought up as the crowd was, it might not stop till it had fired every company building, perhaps not until it had murdered every company representative.

Hal had resolved to keep in the back-ground, but he saw that to keep in the back-ground at that moment would be an act of cowardice, almost a crime. He sprang forward, his cry rising above the clamor. "Stop, men! Stop!"

There was probably no other man in North Valley who could have got himself heeded at that moment. But Hal had their confidence, he had earned the right to be heard. Had he not been to prison for them, had they not seen him behind the bars? "Joe Smith!" The cry ran from one end of the excited throng to the other.

Hal was fighting his way forward, shoving men to one side, imploring, commanding silence. "Tim Rafferty! Wait!" And Tim, recognizing the voice, obeyed.

Once clear of the press, Hal sprang upon the porch, where Cartwright did not attempt to interfere with him.

"Men!" he cried. "Hold on a moment! This isn't what you want! You don't want a fight!" He paused for an instant; but he knew that no mere negative would hold them at that moment. They must be told what they did want. Just now he had learned the particular words that would carry, and he proclaimed them at the top of his voice: "What you want is a union! A *strike!*"

He was answered by a roar from the crowd, the loudest yet. Yes, that was what they wanted! A strike! And they wanted Joe Smith to organize it, to lead it. He had been their leader once, he had been thrown out of camp for it. How he had got back they were not quite clear — but here he was, and he was their darling. Hurrah for him! They would follow him to hell and back!

And wasn't he the boy with the nerve! Standing there on the porch of the hospital, right under the very noses of the bosses, making a union speech to them, and the bosses never daring to touch him! The crowd, realizing this situation, went wild with delight. The English-speaking men shouted assent to his words; and those who could not understand, shouted because the others did.

They did not want fighting — of course not! Fighting would not help them! What would help them was to get together, and stand a solid body of free men. There would be a union committee, able to speak for all of them, to say that no man would go to work anymore until justice was secured! They would have an end to the business of discharging men because they asked for their rights, of blacklisting men and driving them out of the district because they presumed to want what the laws of the state awarded them!

SECTION 6.

*H*ow long could a man expect to stand on the steps of a company building, with a super and a pit-boss at his back, and organize a union of mine-workers? Hal realized that he must move the crowd from that perilous place.

"You'll do what I say, now?" he demanded; and when they agreed in chorus, he added the warning: "There'll be no fighting! And no drinking! If you see any man drunk tonight, sit on him and hold him down!"

They laughed and cheered. Yes, they would keep straight. Here was a job for sober men, you bet!

"And now," Hal continued, "the people in the hospital. We'll have a committee go in and see about them. No noise — we don't want to disturb the sick men. We only want to make sure nobody else is disturbing them. Someone will go in and stay with them. Does that suit you?"

Yes, that suited them.

"All right," said Hal. "Keep quiet for a moment."

And he turned to the superintendent. "Cartwright," said he, "we want a committee to go in and stay with our people." Then, as the superintendent started to expostulate, he added, in a low voice, "Don't be a fool, man! Don't you see I'm trying to save your life?"

The superintendent knew how bad it would be for discipline to let Hal carry his point with the crowd; but also he saw the immediate danger — and he was not sure of the courage and shooting ability of book-keepers and stenographers.

"Be quick, man!" exclaimed Hal. "I can't hold these people long. If you don't want hell breaking loose, come to your senses."

"All right," said Cartwright, swallowing his dignity.

And Hal turned to the men and announced the concession. There was a shout of triumph.

"Now, who's to go?" said Hal, when he could he heard again; and he looked about at the upturned faces. There Were Tim and Wauchope, the most obvious ones; but Hal decided to keep them under his eye. He thought of Jerry Minetti and of Mrs. David — but remembered his agreement with "Big Jack," to keep their own little group in the background. Then he thought of Mary Burke; she had already done herself all the harm she could do, and she was a person the crowd would trust.

He called her, and called Mrs. Ferris, an American woman in the crowd. The two came up the steps, and Hal turned to Cartwright.

"Now, let's have an understanding," he said. "These people are going in to stay with the sick men, and to talk to them if they want to, and nobody's going to give them any orders but the doctors and nurses. Is that right?"

"All right," said the superintendent, sullenly.

"Good!" said Hal. "And for God's sake have a little sense and stand by your word; this crowd has had all it can endure, and if you do anymore to provoke it, the consequences will be on you. And while you're about it, see that the saloons are closed and kept closed until this trouble is settled. And keep your people out of the way — don't let them go about showing their guns and making faces."

Without waiting to hear the superintendent's reply, Hal turned to the throng, and held up his hand for silence. "Men," he said, "we have a big job to do — we're going to organize a union. And we can't do it here in front of the hospital. We've made too much noise already. Let's go off quietly, and have our meeting on the dump in back of the power-house. Does that suit you?"

They answered that it suited them; and Hal, having seen the two women passed safely into the hospital, sprang down from the porch to lead the way. Jerry Minetti came to his side, trembling with delight; and Hal clutched him by the arm and whispered, excitedly, "Sing, Jerry! Sing them some Dago song!"

SECTION 7.

*T*hey got to the place appointed without any fighting. And meantime Hal had worked out in his mind a plan for communicating with this polyglot horde. He knew that half the men could not understand a word of English, and that half the remainder understood very little. Obviously, if he was to make matters clear to them, they must be sorted out according to nationality, and a reliable interpreter found for each group.

The process of sorting proved a slow one, involving no end of shouting and good-natured jostling — Polish here, Bohemian here, Greek here, Italian here! When this job had been done, and a man found from each nationality who understood enough English to translate to his fellows, Hal started in to make a speech. But before he had spoken many sentences, pandemonium broke loose. All the interpreters started interpreting at the same time — and at the top of their lungs; it was like a parade with the bands close together! Hal was struck dumb; then he began to laugh, and the various audiences began to laugh; the orators stopped, perplexed — then they too began to laugh. So wave after wave of merriment rolled over the throng; the mood of the assembly was changed all at once, from rage and determination to the wildest hilarity. Hal learned his first lesson in the handling of these hordes of childlike people, whose moods were quick, whose tempers were balanced upon a fine point.

It was necessary for him to make his speech through to the end, and then move the various audiences apart, to be addressed by the various interpreters. But then arose a new difficulty. How could anyone control these floods of eloquence? How be sure that the message was not being distorted? Hal had been warned by Olson of company detectives who posed as workers, gaining the confidence of men in order to incite them to violence. And certainly some of these interpreters were violent-looking, and one's remarks sounded strange in their translations!

There was the Greek orator, for example; a wild man, with wild hair and eyes, who tore all his passions to tatters. He stood upon a barrel-head, with the light of two pit-lamps upon him, and some two score of his compatriots at his feet; he waved his arms, he shook his fists, he shrieked, he bellowed. But when Hal, becoming uneasy, went over and asked another English-speaking Greek what the orator was saying, the answer was that he was promising that the law should be enforced in North Valley!

Hal stood watching this perfervid little man, a study in the possibilities of gesture. He drew back his shoulders and puffed out his chest, almost throwing himself backwards off the barrel-head; he was saying that the miners would be able to live like men. He crouched down and bowed his head, moaning; he was telling them what would happen if they gave up. He fastened his fingers in his long black hair and began tugging desperately; he pulled, and then stretched out his empty hands; he pulled again, so hard that it almost made one cry out with pain to watch him. Hal asked what that was for; and the answer was, "He say, 'Stand by union! Pull one hair, he come out; pull all hairs, no come out'!" It carried one back to the days of Aesop and his fables!

Tom Olson had told Hal something about the technique of an organizer, who wished to drill these ignorant hordes. He had to repeat and repeat, until the dullest in his audience had grasped his meaning, had got into his head the all-saving idea of solidarity. When the various orators had talked themselves out, and the audiences had come back to the cinder-heap, Hal made his speech all over again, in words of one syllable, in the kind of pidgin-English which does duty in the camps. Sometimes he would stop to reinforce it with Greek or Italian or Slavish words he had picked up. Or perhaps his eloquence would inflame some one of the interpreters afresh, and he would wait while the man shouted a few sentences to his compatriots. It was not necessary to consider the possibility of boring anyone, for these were patient and long-suffering men, and now desperately in earnest.

They were going to have a union; they were going to do the thing in regular form, with membership cards and officials chosen by ballot. So Hal explained to them, step by step. There was no use organizing unless they meant to stay organized. They would choose leaders, one from each of the principal language groups; and these leaders would meet and draw up a set of demands, which would be submitted in mass-meeting, and ratified, and then presented to the bosses with the announcement that until these terms were granted, not a single North Valley worker would go back into the pits.

Jerry Minetti, who knew all about unions, advised Hal to enroll the men at once; he counted on the psychological effect of having each man come forward and give in his name. But here at once they met a difficulty encountered by all would-be organizers — lack of funds. There must be pencils and paper for the enrollment; and Hal had emptied his pockets for Jack David! He was forced to borrow a quarter, and send a messenger off to the store. It was voted by the delegates that each member as he joined the union should be assessed a dime. There would have to be some telegraphing and telephoning if they were going to get help from the outside world.

A temporary committee was named, consisting of Tim Rafferty, Wauchope and Hal, to keep the lists and the funds, and to run things until another meeting could be held on the morrow; also a body-guard of a dozen of the sturdiest and most reliable men were named to stay by the committee. The messenger came back with pads and pencils, and sitting on the ground by the light of pit-lamps, the interpreters wrote down the names of the men who wished to join the union, each man in turn pledging his word for solidarity and discipline. Then the meeting was declared adjourned till daylight of the morrow, and the workers scattered to their homes to sleep, with a joy and sense of power such as few of them had ever known in their lives before.

SECTION 8.

*T*he committee and its body-guard repaired to the dining room of Reminitsky's, where they stretched themselves out on the floor; no one attempted to interfere with them, and while the majority snored peacefully, Hal and a small group sat writing out the list of demands which were to be submitted to the bosses in the morning. It was arranged that Jerry should go down to Pedro by the early morning train, to get into touch with Jack David and the union officials, and report to them the latest developments. Because the officials were sure to have detectives following them, Hal warned Jerry to go to MacKellar's house, and have MacKellar bring "Big Jack" to meet him there. Also Jerry must have MacKellar get the *Gazette* on the long distance phone, and tell Billy Keating about the strike.

A hundred things like this Hal had to think of; his head was a-buzz with them, so that when he lay down to sleep he could not. He thought about the bosses, and what they might be doing. The bosses would not be sleeping, he felt sure!

And then came thoughts about his private-car friends; about the strangeness of this plight into which he had got himself! He laughed aloud in a kind of desperation as he recalled Percy's efforts to get him away from here. And poor Jessie! What could he say to her now?

The bosses made no move that night; and when morning came, the strikers hurried to the meeting place, some of them without even stopping for breakfast. They came tousled and unkempt, looking anxiously at their fellows, as if unable to credit the memory of the bold thing they had done on the night before. But finding the committee and its body-guard on hand and ready for business, their courage revived, they felt again the wonderful sentiment of solidarity which had made men of them. Pretty soon speech-making began, and cheering and singing, which brought out the laggards and the cowards. So in a short while the movement was in full swing, with practically every man, woman and child among the workers present.

Mary Burke came from the hospital, where she had spent the night. She looked weary and bedraggled, but her spirit of battle had not slumped. She reported that she had talked with some of the injured men, and that many of them had signed "releases," whereby the company protected itself against even the threat of a lawsuit. Others had refused to sign, and Mary had been vehement in warning them to stand out. Two other women volunteered to go to the hospital, in order that she might have a chance to rest; but Mary did not wish to rest, she did not feel as if she could ever rest again.

The members of the newly-organized union proceeded to elect officers. They sought to make Hal president, but he was shy of binding himself in that irrevocable way, and succeeded in putting the honor off on Wauchope. Tim Rafferty was made treasurer and secretary. Then a committee was chosen to go to Cartwright with the demands of the men. It included Hal, Wauchope, and Tim; an Italian named Marcelli, whom Jerry had vouched for; a representative of the Slavs and one of the Greeks — Rusick and Zammakis, both of them solid and faithful men. Finally, with a good deal of laughter and cheering, the meeting voted to add Mary Burke to this committee. It was a new thing to have a woman in such a role, but Mary was the daughter of a miner and the sister of a breaker-boy, and had as good a right to speak as anyone in North Valley.

SECTION 9.

*H*al read the document which had been prepared the night before. They demanded the right to have a union without being discharged for it. They demanded a check-weighman, to be elected by the men themselves. They demanded that the mines should be sprinkled to prevent explosions, and properly timbered to prevent falls. They demanded the right to trade at any store they pleased. Hal called attention to the fact that every one of these demands was for a right guaranteed by the laws of the state; this was a significant fact, and he urged the men not to include other demands. After some argument they voted down the proposition of the radicals, who wanted a ten percent increase in wages. Also they voted down the proposition of a syndicalist-anarchist, who explained to them in a jumble of English and Italian that the mines belonged to them, and that they should refuse all compromise and turn the bosses out forthwith.

While this speech was being delivered, young Rovetta pushed his way through the crowd and drew Hal to one side. He had been down by the railroad-station and seen the morning train come in. From it had descended a crowd of thirty or forty men, of that "hard citizen" type which every miner in the district could recognize at the first glance. Evidently the company officials had been keeping the telephone-wires busy that night; they were bringing in, not merely this train-load of guards, but automobile loads from other camps — from the Northeastern down the canyon, and from Barela, in a side canyon over the mountain.

Hal told this news to the meeting, which received it with howls of rage. So that was the bosses' plan! Hot-heads sprang upon the cinder-heap, half a dozen of them trying to make speeches at once. The leaders had to suppress these too impetuous ones by main force; once more Hal gave the warning of "No fighting!" They were going to have faith in their union; they were going to present a solid front to the company, and the company would learn the lesson that intimidation would not win a strike.

So it was agreed, and the committee set out for the company's office, Wauchope carrying in his hand the written demands of the meeting. Behind the committee marched the crowd in a solid mass; they packed the street in front of the office, while the heroic seven went up the steps and passed into the building. Wauchope made inquiry for Mr. Cartwright, and a clerk took in the message.

They stood waiting; and meanwhile, one of the office-people, coming in from the street, beckoned to Hal. He had an envelope in his hand, and gave it over without a word. It was addressed, "Joe Smith," and Hal opened it, and found within a small visiting card, at which he stared. "Edward S. Warner, Jr.!"

For a moment Hal could hardly believe the evidence of his eyesight. Edward in North Valley! Then, turning the card over, he read, in his brother's familiar handwriting, "I am at Cartwright's house. I must see you. The matter concerns Dad. Come instantly."

Fear leaped into Hal's heart. What could such a message mean?

He turned quickly to the committee and explained. "My father's an old man, and had a stroke of apoplexy three years ago. I'm afraid he may be dead, or very ill. I must go."

"It's a trick!" cried Wauchope excitedly.

"No, not possibly," answered Hal. "I know my brother's handwriting. I must see him."

"Well," declared the other, "we'll wait. We'll not see Cartwright until you get back."

Hal considered this. "I don't think that's wise," he said. "You can do what you have to do just as well without me."

"But I wanted you to do the talking!"

"No," replied Hal, "that's your business, Wauchope. You are the president of the union. You know what the men want, as well as I do; you know what they complain of. And besides, there's not going to be any need of talking with Cartwright. Either he's going to grant our demands or he isn't."

They discussed the matter back and forth. Mary Burke insisted that they were pulling Hal away just at the critical moment! He laughed as he answered. She was as good as any man when it came to an argument. If Wauchope showed signs of weakening, let her speak up!

SECTION 10.

So Hal hurried off, and climbed the street which led to the superintendent's house, a concrete bungalow set upon a little elevation overlooking the camp. He rang the bell, and the door opened, and in the entrance stood his brother.

Edward Warner was eight years older than Hal; the perfect type of the young American business man. His figure was erect and athletic, his features were regular and strong, his voice, his manner, everything about him spoke of quiet decision, of energy precisely directed. As a rule, he was a model of what the tailor's art could do, but just now there was something abnormal about his attire as well as his manner.

Hal's anxiety had been increasing all the way up the street. "What's the matter with Dad?" he cried.

"Dad's all right," was the answer — "that is, for the moment."

"Then what — ?"

"Peter Harrigan's on his way back from the East. He's due in Western City tomorrow. You can see that something will be the matter with Dad unless you quit this business at once."

Hal had a sudden reaction from his fear. "So that's all!" he exclaimed.

His brother was gazing at the young miner, dressed in sooty blue overalls, his face streaked with black, his wavy hair all mussed. "You wired me you were going to leave here, Hal!"

"So I was; but things happened that I couldn't foresee. There's a strike."

"Yes; but what's that got to do with it?" Then, with exasperation in his voice, "For God's sake, Hal, how much farther do you expect to go?"

Hal stood for a few moments, looking at his brother. Even in a tension as he was, he could not help laughing. "I know how all this must seem to you, Edward. It's a long story; I hardly know how to begin."

"No, I suppose not," said Edward, dryly.

And Hal laughed again. "Well, we agree that far, at any rate. What I was hoping was that we could talk it all over quietly, after the excitement was past. When I explain to you about conditions in this place —"

But Edward interrupted. "Really, Hal, there's no use of such an argument. I have nothing to do with conditions in Peter Harrigan's camps."

The smile left Hal's face. "Would you have preferred to have me investigate conditions in the Warner camps?" Hal had tried to suppress his irritation, but there was simply no way these two could get along. "We've had our arguments about these things, Edward, and you've always had the best of me — you could tell me I was a child, it was presumptuous of me to dispute your assertions. But now — well, I'm a child no longer, and we'll have to meet on a new basis."

Hal's tone, more than his words, made an impression. Edward thought before he spoke. "Well, what's your new basis?"

"Just now I'm in the midst of a strike, and I can hardly stop to explain."

"You don't think of Dad in all this madness?"

"I think of Dad, and of you too, Edward; but this is hardly the time —"

"If ever in the world there was a time, this is it!"

Hal groaned inwardly. "All right," he said, "sit down. I'll try to give you some idea how I got swept into this."

He began to tell about the conditions he had found in this stronghold of the "G.F.C." As usual, when he talked about it, he became absorbed in its human aspects; a fervor came into his tone, he was carried on, as he had been when he tried to argue with the officials in Pedro. But his eloquence was interrupted, even as it had been then; he discovered that his brother was in such a state of exasperation that he could not listen to a consecutive argument.

It was the old, old story; it had been thus as far back as Hal could remember. It seemed one of the mysteries of nature, how she could have brought two such different temperaments out of the same parentage. Edward was practical and positive; he knew what he wanted in the world, and he knew how to get it; he was never troubled with doubts, nor with self-questioning, nor with any other superfluous emotions; he could not understand people who allowed that sort of waste in their mental processes. He could not understand people who got "swept into things."

In the beginning, he had had with Hal the prestige of the elder brother. He was handsome as a young Greek god, he was strong and masterful; whether he was flying over the ice with sure, strong strokes, or cutting the water with his glistening shoulders, or bringing down a partridge with the certainty and swiftness of a lightning stroke, Edward was the incarnation of Success. When he said that one's ideas were "rot," when he spoke with contempt of "mollycoddles" — then indeed one suffered in soul, and had to go back to Shelley and Ruskin to renew one's courage.

The questioning of life had begun very early with Hal; there seemed to be something in his nature which forced him to go to the roots of things; and much as he looked up to his wonderful brother, he had been made to realize that there were sides of life to which this brother was blind. To begin with, there were religious doubts; the distresses of mind which plague a young man when first it dawns upon him that the faith he has been brought up in is a higher kind of fairy-tale. Edward had never asked such questions, apparently. He went to church, because it was the thing to do; more especially because it was pleasing to the young lady he wished to marry to have him put on stately clothes, and escort her to a beautiful place of music and flowers and perfumes, where she would meet her friends, also in stately clothes. How abnormal it seemed to Edward that a young man should give up this pleasant custom, merely because he could not be sure that Jonah had swallowed a whale!

But it was when Hal's doubts attacked his brother's week-day religion — the religion of the profit-system — that the controversy between them had become deadly. At first Hal had known nothing about practical affairs, and it had been Edward's duty to answer his questions. The prosperity of the country had been built up by strong men; and these men had enemies — evil-minded persons, animated by jealousy and other base passions, seeking to tear down the mighty structure. At first this devil-theory had satisfied the boy; but later on, as he had come to read and observe, he had been plagued by doubts. In the end, listening to his brother's conversation, and reading the writings of so-called "muckrakers," the realization was forced upon him that there were two types of mind in the controversy — those who thought of profits, and those who thought of human beings.

Edward was alarmed at the books Hal was reading; he was still more alarmed when he saw the ideas Hal was bringing home from college. There must have been some strange change in Harrigan in a few years; no one had dreamed of such ideas when Edward was there! No one had written satiric songs about the faculty, or the endowments of eminent philanthropists!

In the meantime Edward Warner Senior had had a paralytic stroke, and Edward Junior had taken charge of the company. Three years of this had given him the point of view of a coal-operator, hard and set for a life-time. The business of a coal-operator was to buy his labor cheap, to turn out the maximum product in the shortest time, and to sell the product at the market price to parties whose credit was satisfactory. If a concern was doing that, it was a successful concern; for anyone to mention that it was making wrecks of the people who dug the coal, was to be guilty of sentimentality and impertinence.

Edward had heard with dismay his brother's announcement that he meant to study industry by spending his vacation as a common laborer. However, when he considered it, he was inclined to think that the idea might not be such a bad one. Perhaps Hal would not find what he was looking for; perhaps, working with his hands, he might get some of the nonsense knocked out of his head!

But now the experiment had been made, and the revelation had burst upon Edward that it had been a ghastly failure. Hal had not come to realize that labor was turbulent and lazy and incompetent, needing a strong hand to rule it; on the contrary, he had become one of these turbulent ones himself! A champion of the lazy and incompetent, an agitator, a fomenter of class-prejudice, an enemy of his own friends, and of his brother's business associates!

Never had Hal seen Edward in such a state of excitement. There was something really abnormal about him, Hal realized; it puzzled him vaguely while he talked, but he did not understand it until his brother told how he had come to be here. He had been attending a dinner-dance at the home of a friend, and Percy Harrigan had got him on the telephone at half past eleven o'clock at night. Percy had had a message from Cartwright, to the effect that Hal was leading a riot in North Valley; Percy had painted the situation in such lurid colors that Edward had made a dash and caught the midnight train, wearing his evening clothes, and without so much as a tooth-brush with him!

Hal could hardly keep from bursting out laughing. His brother, his punctilious and dignified brother, alighting from a sleeping-car at seven o'clock in the morning, wearing a dress suit and a silk hat! And here he was, Edward Warner Junior, the fastidious, who never paid less than a hundred and fifty dollars for a suit of clothes, clad in a "hand-me-down" for which he had expended twelve dollars and forty-eight cents in a "Jew-store" in a coal-town!

SECTION 11.

*B*ut Edward would not stop for a single smile; his every faculty was absorbed in the task he had before him, to get his brother out of this predicament, so dangerous and so humiliating. Hal had come to a town owned by Edward's business friends, and had proceeded to meddle in their affairs, to stir up their laboring people and imperil their property. That North Valley was the property of the General Fuel Company — not merely the mines and the houses, but likewise the people who lived in them — Edward seemed to have no doubt whatever; Hal got only exclamations of annoyance when he suggested any other point of view. Would there have been any town of North Valley, if it had not been for the capital and energy of the General Fuel Company? If the people of North Valley did not like the conditions which the General Fuel Company offered them, they had one simple and obvious remedy — to go somewhere else to work. But they stayed; they got out the General Fuel Company's coal, they took the General Fuel Company's wages —

"Well, they've stopped taking them now," put in Hal.

All right, that was their affair, replied Edward. But let them stop because they wanted to — not because outside agitators put them up to it. At any rate, let the agitators not include a member of the Warner family!

The elder brother pictured old Peter Harrigan on his way back from the East; the state of unutterable fury in which he would arrive, the storm he would raise in the business world of Western City. Why, it was unimaginable, such a thing had never been heard of! "And right when we're opening up a new mine — when we need every dollar of credit we can get!"

"Aren't we big enough to stand off Peter Harrigan?" inquired Hal.

"We have plenty of other people to stand off," was the answer. "We don't have to go out of our way to make enemies."

Edward spoke, not merely as the elder brother, but also as the money-man of the family. When the father had broken down from overwork, and had been changed in one terrible hour from a driving man of affairs into a childish and pathetic invalid, Hal had been glad enough that there was one member of the family who was practical; he had been perfectly willing to see his brother shoulder these burdens, while he went off to college, to amuse himself with satiric songs. Hal had no responsibilities, no one asked anything of him — except that he would not throw sticks into the wheels of the machine his brother was running. "You are living by the coal industry! Every dollar you spend comes from it —"

"I know it! I know it!" cried Hal. "That's the thing that torments me! The fact that I'm living upon the bounty of such wage-slaves —"

"Oh, cut it out!" cried Edward. "That's not what I mean!"

"I know — but it's what *I* mean! From now on I mean to know about the people who work for me, and what sort of treatment they get. I'm no longer your kid-brother, to be put off with platitudes."

"You know ours are union mines, Hal —"

"Yes, but what does that mean? How do we work it? Do we give the men their weights?"

"Of course! They have their check-weighmen."

"But then, how do we compete with the operators in this district, who pay for a ton of three thousand pounds?"

"We manage it — by economy."

"Economy? I don't see Peter Harrigan wasting anything here!" Hal paused for an answer, but none came. "Do we buy the check-weighmen? Do we bribe the labor leaders?"

Edward colored slightly. "What's the use of being nasty, Hal? You know I don't do dirty work."

"I don't mean to be nasty, Edward; but you must know that many a business-man can say he doesn't do dirty work, because he has others do it for him. What about politics, for instance? Do we run a machine, and put our clerks and bosses into the local offices?"

Edward did not answer, and Hal persisted, "I mean to know these things! I'm not going to be blind anymore!"

"All right, Hal — you can know anything you want; but for God's sake, not now! If you want to be taken for a man, show a man's common sense! Here's Old Peter getting back to Western City tomorrow night! Don't you know that he'll be after me, raging like a mad bull? Don't you know that if I tell him I can do nothing — that I've been down here and tried to pull you away — don't you know he'll go after Dad?"

Edward had tried all the arguments, and this was the only one that counted. "You must keep him away from Dad!" exclaimed Hal.

"You tell me that!" retorted the other. "And when you know Old Peter! Don't you know he'll get at him, if he has to break down the door of the house? He'll throw the burden of his rage on that poor old man! You've been warned about it clearly; you know it may be a matter of life and death to keep Dad from getting excited. I don't know what he'd do; maybe he'd fly into a rage with you, maybe he'd defend you. He's old and weak, he's lost his grip on things. Anyhow, he'd not let Peter abuse you — and like as not he'd drop dead in the midst of the dispute! Do you want to have that on your conscience, along with the troubles of your workingmen friends?"

SECTION 12.

*H*al sat staring in front of him, silent. Was it a fact that every man had something in his life which palsied his arm, and struck him helpless in the battle for social justice?

When he spoke again, it was in a low voice. "Edward, I'm thinking about a young Irish boy who works in these mines. He, too, has a father; and this father was caught in the explosion. He's an old man, with a wife and seven other children. He's a good man, the boy's a good boy. Let me tell you what Peter Harrigan has done to them!"

"Well," said Edward, "whatever it is, it's all right, you can help them. They won't need to starve."

"I know," said Hal, "but there are so many others; I can't help them all. And besides, can't you see, Edward — what I'm thinking about is not charity, but *justice*. I'm sure this boy, Tim Rafferty, loves his father just exactly as much as I love my father; and there are other old men here, with sons who love them —"

"Oh, Hal, for Christ's sake!" exclaimed Edward, in a sort of explosion. He had no other words to express his impatience. "Do you expect to take all the troubles in the world on your shoulders?" And he sprang up and caught the other by the arm. "Boy, you've got to come away from here!"

Hal got up, without answering. He seemed irresolute, and his brother started to draw him towards the door. "I've got a car here. We can get a train in an hour —"

Hal saw that he had to speak firmly. "No, Edward," he said. "I can't come just yet."

"I tell you you *must* come!"

"I can't. I made these men a promise!"

"In God's name — what are these men to you? Compared with your own father!"

"I can't explain it, Edward. I've talked for half an hour, and I don't think you've even heard me. Suffice it to say that I see these people caught in a trap — and one that my whole life has helped to make. I can't leave them in it. What's more, I don't believe Dad would want me to do it, if he understood."

The other made a last effort at self-control. "I'm not going to call you a sentimental fool. Only, let me ask you one plain question. What do you think you can *do* for these people?"

"I think I can help to win decent conditions for them."

"Good God!" cried Edward; he sighed, in his agony of exasperation. "In Peter Harrigan's mines! Don't you realize that he'll pick them up and throw them out of here, neck and crop — the whole crew, every man in the town, if necessary?"

"Perhaps," answered Hal; "but if the men in the other mines should join them — if the big union outside should stand by them —"

"You're dreaming, Hal! You're talking like a child! I talked to the superintendent here; he had telegraphed the situation to Old Peter, and had just got an answer. Already he's acted, no doubt."

"Acted?" echoed Hal. "How do you mean?" He was staring at his brother in sudden anxiety.

"They were going to turn the agitators out, of course."

"*What?* And while I'm here talking!"

Hal turned toward the door. "You knew it all the time!" he exclaimed. "You kept me here deliberately!"

He was starting away, but Edward sprang and caught him. "What could you have done?"

"Turn me loose!" cried Hal, angrily.

"Don't be a fool, Hal! I've been trying to keep you out of the trouble. There may be fighting."

Edward threw himself between Hal and the door, and there was a sharp struggle. But the elder man was no longer the athlete, the young bronzed god; he had been sitting at a desk in an office, while Hal had been doing hard labor. Hal threw him to one side, and in a moment more had sprung out of the door, and was running down the slope.

SECTION 13.

*C*oming to the main street of the village, Hal saw the crowd in front of the office. One glance told him that something had happened. Men were running this way and that, gesticulating, shouting. Some were coming in his direction, and when they saw him they began to yell to him. The first to reach him was Klowoski, the little Pole, breathless; gasping with excitement. "They fire our committee!"

"Fire them?"

"Fire 'em out! Down canyon!" The little man was waving his arms in wild gestures; his eyes seemed about to start out of his head. "Take 'em off! Whole bunch fellers — gunmen! People see them — come out back door. Got ever'body's arm tied. Gunmen fellers hold 'em, don't let 'em holler, can't do nothin'! Got them cars waitin' — what you call? —"

"Automobiles?"

"Sure, got three! Put ever'body in, quick like that — they go down road like wind! Go down canyon, all gone! They bust our strike!" And the little Pole's voice ended in a howl of despair.

"No, they won't bust our strike!" exclaimed Hal. "Not yet!"

Suddenly he was reminded of the fact that his brother had followed him — puffing hard, for the run had been strenuous. He caught Hal by the arm, exclaiming, "Keep out of this, I tell you!"

Thus while Hal was questioning Klowoski, he was struggling half-unconsciously, to free himself from his brother's grasp. Suddenly the matter was forced to an issue, for the little Polack emitted a cry like an angry cat, and went at Edward with fingers outstretched like claws. Hal's dignified brother would have had to part with his dignity, if Hal had not caught Klowoski's onrush with his other arm. "Let him alone!" he said. "It's my brother!" Whereupon the little man fell back and stood watching in bewilderment.

Hal saw Androkulos running to him. The Greek boy had been in the street back of the office, and had seen the committee carried off; nine people had been taken — Wauchope, Tim Rafferty, and Mary Burke, Marcelli, Zammakis and Rusick, and three others who had served as interpreters on the night before. It had all been done so quickly that the crowd had scarcely realized what was happening.

Now, having grasped the meaning of it, the men were beside themselves with rage. They shook their fists, shouting defiance to a group of officials and guards who were visible upon the porch of the office-building. There was a clamor of shouts for revenge.

Hal could see instantly the dangers of the situation; he was like a man watching the burning fuse of a bomb. Now, if ever, this polyglot horde must have leadership — wise and cool and resourceful leadership.

The crowd, discovering his presence, surged down upon him like a wave. They gathered round him, howling. They had lost the rest of their committee, but they still had Joe Smith. Joe Smith! Hurrah for Joe! Let the gunmen take him, if they could! They waved their caps, they tried to lift him upon their shoulders, so that all could see him.

There was clamor for a speech, and Hal started to make his way to the steps of the nearest building, with Edward holding on to his coat. Edward was jostled; he had to part with his dignity — but he did not part with his brother. And when Hal was about to mount the steps, Edward made a last desperate effort, shouting into his ear, "Wait a minute! Wait! Are you going to try to talk to this mob?"

"Of course. Don't you see there'll be trouble if I don't?"

"You'll get yourself killed! You'll start a fight, and get a lot of these poor devils shot! Use your common sense, Hal; the company has brought in guards, and they are armed, and your people aren't."

"That's exactly why I have to speak!"

The discussion was carried on under difficulties, the elder brother clinging to the younger's arm, while the younger sought to pull free, and the mob shouted with a single voice, "Speech! Speech!" There were some near by who, like Klowoski, did not relish having this stranger interfering with their champion, and showed signs of a disposition to "mix in"; so at last Edward gave up the struggle, and the orator mounted the steps and faced the throng.

SECTION 14.

*H*al raised his arms as a signal for silence.

"Boys," he cried, "they've kidnapped our committee. They think they'll break our strike that way — but they'll find they've made a mistake!"

"They will! Right you are!" roared a score of voices.

"They forget that we've got a union. Hurrah for our North Valley union!"

"Hurrah! Hurrah!" The cry echoed to the canyon-walls.

"And hurrah for the big union that will back us — the United Mine-Workers of America!"

Again the yell rang out; again and again. "Hurrah for the union! Hurrah for the United Mine-Workers!" A big American miner, Ferris, was in the front of the throng, and his voice beat in Hal's ears like a steam-siren.

"Boys," Hal resumed, when at last he could be heard, "use your brains a moment. I warned you they would try to provoke you! They would like nothing better than to start a scrap here, and get a chance to smash our union! Don't forget that, boys, if they can make you fight, they'll smash the union, and the union is our only hope!"

Again came the cry: "Hurrah for the union!" Hal let them shout it in twenty languages, until they were satisfied.

"Now, boys," he went on, at last, "they've shipped out our committee. They may ship me out in the same way —"

"No, they won't!" shouted voices in the crowd. And there was a bellow of rage from Ferris. "Let them try it! We'll burn them in their beds!"

"But they *can* ship me out!" argued Hal. "You *know* they can beat us at that game! They can call on the sheriff, they can get the soldiers, if necessary! We can't oppose them by force — they can turn out every man, woman and child in the village, if they choose. What we have to get clear is that even that won't crush our union! Nor the big union outside, that will be backing us! We can hold out, and make them take us back in the end!"

Some of Hal's friends, seeing what he was trying to do, came to his support. "No fighting! No violence! Stand by the union!" And he went on to drive the lesson home; even though the company might evict them, the big union of the four hundred and fifty thousand mine-workers of the country would feed them, it would call out the rest of the workers in the district in sympathy. So the bosses, who thought to starve and cow them into submission, would find their mines lying permanently idle. They would be forced to give way, and the tactics of solidarity would triumph.

So Hal went on, recalling the things Olson had told him, and putting them into practice. He saw hope in their faces again, dispelling the mood of resentment and rage.

"Now, boys," said he, "I'm going in to see the superintendent for you. I'll be your committee, since they've shipped out the rest."

The steam-siren of Ferris bellowed again: "You're the boy! Joe Smith!"

"All right, men — now mind what I say! I'll see the super, and then I'll go down to Pedro, where there'll be some officers of the United Mine-workers this morning. I'll tell them the situation, and ask them to back you. That's what you want, is it?"

That was what they wanted. "Big union!"

"All right. I'll do the best I can for you, and I'll find some way to get word to you. And meantime you stand firm. The bosses will tell you lies, they'll try to deceive you, they'll send spies and trouble-makers among you — but you hold fast, and wait for the big union."

Hal stood looking at the cheering crowd. He had time to note some of the faces upturned to him. Pitiful, toil-worn faces they were, each making its separate appeal, telling its individual story of deprivation and defeat. Once more they were transfigured, shining with that wonderful new light which he had seen for the first time the previous evening. It had been crushed for a moment, but it flamed up again; it would never die in the hearts of men — once they had learned the power it gave. Nothing Hal had yet seen moved him so much as this new birth of enthusiasm. A beautiful, a terrible thing it was!

Hal looked at his brother, to see how he had been moved. What he saw on his brother's face was satisfaction, boundless relief. The matter had turned out all right! Hal was coming away!

Hal turned again to the men; somehow, after his glance at Edward, they seemed more pitiful than ever. For Edward typified the power they were facing — the unseeing, uncomprehending power that meant to crush them. The possibility of failure was revealed to Hal in a flash of emotion, overwhelming him. He saw them as they would be, when no leader was at hand to make speeches to them. He saw them waiting, their life-long habit of obedience striving to reassert itself; a thousand fears besetting them, a thousand rumors preying upon them — wild beasts set on them by their cunning enemies. They would suffer, not merely for themselves, but for their wives and children — the very same pangs of dread that Hal suffered when he thought of one old man up in Western City, whose doctors had warned him to avoid excitement.

If they stood firm, if they kept their bargain with their leader, they would be evicted from their homes, they would face the cold of the coming winter, they would face hunger and the black-list. And he, meantime — what would he be doing? What was his part of the bargain? He would interview the superintendent for them, he would turn them over to the "big union" — and then he would go off to his own life of ease and pleasure. To eat grilled steaks and hot rolls in a perfectly appointed club, with suave and softly-moving servitors at his beck! To dance at the country club with exquisite creatures of chiffon and satin, of perfume and sweet smiles and careless, happy charms! No, it was too easy! He might call that his duty to his father and brother, but he would know in his heart that it was treason to life; it was the devil, taking him onto a high mountain and showing him all the kingdoms of the earth!

Moved by a sudden impulse, Hal raised his hands once more. "Boys," he said, "we understand each other now. You'll not go back to work till the big union tells you. And I, for my part, will stand by you. Your cause is my cause, I'll go on fighting for you till you have your rights, till you can live and work as men! Is that right?"

"That's right! That's right!"

"Very good, then — we'll swear to it!" And Hal raised his hands, and the men raised theirs, and amid a storm of shouts, and a frantic waving of caps, he made them the pledge which he knew would bind his own conscience. He made it deliberately, there in his brother's presence. This was no mere charge on a trench, it was enlisting for a war! But even in that moment of fervor, Hal would have been frightened had he realized the period of that enlistment, the years of weary and desperate conflict to which he was pledging his life.

SECTION 15.

*H*al descended from his rostrum, and the crowds made way for him, and with his brother at his side he went down the street to the office building, upon the porch of which the guards were standing. His progress was a triumphal one; rough voices shouted words of encouragement in his ears, men jostled and fought to shake his hand or to pat him on the back; they even patted Edward and tried to shake his hand, because he was with Hal, and seemed to have his confidence. Afterwards Hal thought it over and was merry. Such an adventure for Edward!

The younger man went up the steps of the building and spoke to the guards. "I want to see Mr. Cartwright."

"He's inside," answered one, not cordially. With Edward following, Hal entered, and was ushered into the private office of the superintendent.

Having been a working-man, and class-conscious, Hal was observant of the manners of mine-superintendents; he noted that Cartwright bowed politely to Edward, but did not include Edward's brother. "Mr. Cartwright," he said, "I have come to you as a deputation from the workers of this camp."

The superintendent did not appear impressed by the announcement.

"I am instructed to say that the men demand the redress of four grievances before they return to work. First —"

Here Cartwright spoke, in his quick, sharp way. "There's no use going on, sir. This company will deal only with its men as individuals. It will recognize no deputations."

Hal's answer was equally quick. "Very well, Mr. Cartwright. In that case, I come to you as an individual."

For a moment the superintendent seemed nonplussed.

"I wish to ask four rights which are granted to me by the laws of this state. First, the right to belong to a union, without being discharged for it."

The other had recovered his manner of quiet mastery. "You have that right, sir; you have always had it. You know perfectly well that the company has never discharged anyone for belonging to a union."

The man was looking at Hal, and there was a duel of the eyes between them. A cold anger moved Hal. His ability to endure this sort of thing was at an end. "Mr. Cartwright," he said, "you are the servant of one of the world's greatest actors; and you support him ably."

The other flushed and drew back; Edward put in quickly: "Hal, there's nothing to be gained by such talk!"

"He has all the world for an audience," persisted Hal. "He plays the most stupendous farce — and he and all his actors wearing such solemn faces!"

"Mr. Cartwright," said Edward, with dignity, "I trust you understand that I have done everything I can to restrain my brother."

"Of course, Mr. Warner," replied the superintendent. "And you must know that I, for my part, have done everything to show your brother consideration."

"Again!" exclaimed Hal. "This actor is a genius!"

"Hal, if you have business with Mr. Cartwright —"

"He showed me consideration by sending his gunmen to seize me at night, drag me out of a cabin, and nearly twist the arm off me! Such humor never was!"

Cartwright attempted to speak — but looking at Edward, not at Hal. "At that time —"

"He showed me consideration by having me locked up in jail and fed on bread and water for two nights and a day! Can you beat that humor?"

"At that time I did not know —"

"By forging my name to a letter and having it circulated in the camp! Finally — most considerate of all — by telling a newspaper man that I had seduced a girl here!"

The superintendent flushed still redder. *"No!"* he declared.

"What?" cried Hal. "You didn't tell Billy Keating of the *Gazette* that I had seduced a girl in North Valley? You didn't describe the girl to him — a red-haired Irish girl?"

"I merely said, Mr. Warner, that I had heard certain rumors —"

"*Certain* rumors, Mr. Cartwright? The certainty was all of your making! You made a definite and explicit statement to Mr. Keating —"

"I did not!" declared the other.

"I'll soon prove it!" And Hal started towards the telephone on Cartwright's desk.

"What are you going to do, Hal?"

"I am going to get Billy Keating on the wire, and let you hear his statement."

"Oh, rot, Hal!" cried Edward. "I don't care anything about Keating's statement. You know that at that time Mr. Cartwright had no means of knowing who you were."

Cartwright was quick to grasp this support. "Of course not, Mr. Warner! Your brother came here, pretending to be a working boy —"

"Oh!" cried Hal. "So that's it! You think it proper to circulate slanders about working boys in your camp?"

"You have been here long enough to know what the morals of such boys are."

"I have been here long enough, Mr. Cartwright, to know that if you want to go into the question of morals in North Valley, the place for you to begin is with the bosses and guards you put in authority, and allow to prey upon women."

Edward broke in: "Hal, there's nothing to be gained by pursuing this conversation. If you have any business here, get it over with, for God's sake!"

Hal made an effort to recover his self-possession. He came back to the demands of the strike — but only to find that he had used up the superintendent's self-possession. "I have given you my answer," declared Cartwright, "I absolutely decline any further discussion."

"Well," said Hal, "since you decline to permit a deputation of your men to deal with you in plain, businesslike fashion, I have to inform you as an individual that every other individual in your camp refuses to work for you."

The superintendent did not let himself be impressed by this elaborate sarcasm. "All I have to tell you, sir, is that Number Two mine will resume work in the morning, and that anyone who refuses to work will be sent down the canyon before night."

"So quickly, Mr. Cartwright? They have rented their homes from the company, and you know that according to the company's own lease they are entitled to three days' notice before being evicted!"

Cartwright was so unwise as to argue. He knew that Edward was hearing, and he wished to clear himself. "They will not be evicted by the company. They will be dealt with by the town authorities."

"Of which you yourself are the head?"

"I happen to have been elected mayor of North Valley."

"As mayor of North Valley, you gave my brother to understand that you would put me out, did you not?"

"I asked your brother to persuade you to leave."

"But you made clear that if he could not do this, you would put me out?"

"Yes, that is true."

"And the reason you gave was that you had had instructions by telegraph from Mr. Peter Harrigan. May I ask to what office Mr. Harrigan has been elected in your town?"

Cartwright saw his difficulty. "Your brother misunderstood me," he said, crossly.

"Did you misunderstand him, Edward?"

Edward had walked to the window in disgust; he was looking at tomato-cans and cinder-heaps, and did not see fit to turn around. But the superintendent knew that he was hearing, and considered it necessary to cover the flaw in his argument. "Young man," said he, "you have violated several of the ordinances of this town."

"Is there an ordinance against organizing a union of the miners?"

"No; but there is one against speaking on the streets."

"Who passed that ordinance, if I may ask?"

"The town council."

"Consisting of Johnson, postmaster and company-store clerk; Ellison, company bookkeeper; Strauss, company pit-boss; O'Callahan, company saloon-keeper. Have I the list correct?"

Cartwright did not answer.

"And the fifth member of the town council is yourself, ex-officio — Mr. Enos Cartwright, mayor and company-superintendent."

Again there was no answer.

"You have an ordinance against street-speaking; and at the same time your company owns the saloon-buildings, the boarding-houses, the church and the school. Where do you expect the citizens to do their speaking?"

"You would make a good lawyer, young man. But we who have charge here know perfectly well what you mean by 'speaking'!"

"You don't approve, then, of the citizens holding meetings?"

"I mean that we don't consider it necessary to provide agitators with opportunity to incite our employees."

"May I ask, Mr. Cartwright, are you speaking as mayor of an American community, or as superintendent of a coal-mine?"

Cartwright's face had been growing continually redder. Addressing

Edward's back, he said, "I don't see any reason why this should continue."

And Edward was of the same opinion. He turned. "Really, Hal —"

"But, Edward! A man accuses your brother of being a law-breaker! Have you hitherto known of any criminal tendencies in our family?"

Edward turned to the window again and resumed his study of the cinder-heaps and tomato-cans. It was a vulgar and stupid quarrel, but he had seen enough of Hal's mood to realize that he would go on and on, so long as anyone was indiscreet enough to answer him.

"You say, Mr. Cartwright, that I have violated the ordinance against speaking on the street. May I ask what penalty this ordinance carries?"

"You will find out when the penalty is exacted of you."

Hal laughed. "From what you said just now, I gather that the penalty is expulsion from the town! If I understand legal procedure, I should have been brought before the justice of the peace — who happens to be another company store-clerk. Instead of that, I am sentenced by the mayor — or is it the company superintendent? May I ask how that comes to be?"

"It is because of my consideration —"

"When did I ask consideration?"

"Consideration for your brother, I mean."

"Oh! Then your ordinance provides that the mayor — or is it the superintendent? — may show consideration for the brother of a law-breaker, by changing his penalty to expulsion from the town. Was it consideration for Tommie Burke that caused you to have his sister sent down the canyon?"

Cartwright clenched his hands. "I've had all I'll stand of this!"

He was again addressing Edward's back; and Edward turned and answered, "I don't blame you, sir." Then to Hal, "I really think you've said enough!"

"I hope I've said enough," replied Hal — "to convince you that the pretence of American law in this coal-camp is a silly farce, an insult and a humiliation to any man who respects the institutions of his country."

"You, Mr. Warner," said the superintendent, to Edward, "have had experience in managing coal-mines. You know what it means to deal with ignorant foreigners, who have no understanding of American law —"

Hal burst out laughing. "So you're teaching them American law! You're teaching them by setting at naught every law of your town and state, every constitutional guarantee — and substituting the instructions you get by telegraph from Peter Harrigan!"

Cartwright turned and walked to the door. "Young man," said he, over his shoulder, "it will be necessary for you to leave North Valley this morning. I only hope your brother will be able to persuade you to leave without trouble." And the bang of the door behind him was the superintendent's only farewell.

SECTION 17.

*E*dward turned upon his brother. "Now what the devil did you want to put me through a scene like that for? So undignified! So utterly uncalled for! A quarrel with a man so far beneath you!"

Hal stood where the superintendent had left him. He was looking at his brother's angry face. "Was that all you got out of it, Edward?"

"All that stuff about your private character! What do you care what a fellow like Cartwright thinks about you?"

"I care nothing at all what he thinks, but I care about having him use such a slander. That's one of their regular procedures, so Billy Keating says."

Edward answered, coldly, "Take my advice, and realize that when you deny a scandal, you only give it circulation."

"Of course," answered Hal. "That's what makes me so angry. Think of the girl, the harm done to her!"

"It's not up to you to worry about the girl."

"Suppose that Cartwright had slandered some woman friend of yours. Would you have felt the same indifference?"

"He'd not have slandered any friend of mine; I choose my friends more carefully."

"Yes, of course. What that means is that you choose them among the rich. But I happen to be more democratic in my tastes —"

"Oh, for heaven's sake!" cried Edward. "You reformers are all alike — you talk and talk and talk!"

"I can tell you the reason for that, Edward — a man like you can shut his eyes, but he can't shut his ears!"

"Well, can't you let up on me for awhile — long enough to get out of this place? I feel as if I were sitting on the top of a volcano, and I've no idea when it may break out again."

Hal began to laugh. "All right," he said; "I guess I haven't shown much appreciation of your visit. I'll be more sociable now. My next business is in Pedro, so I'll go that far with you. There's one thing more —"

"What is it?"

"The company owes me money —"

"What money?"

"Some I've earned."

It was Edward's turn to laugh. "Enough to buy you a shave and a bath?"

He took out his wallet, and pulled off several bills; and Hal, watching him, realized suddenly a change which had taken place in his own psychology. Not merely had he acquired the class-consciousness of the working-man, he had acquired the money-consciousness as well. He was actually concerned about the dollars the company owed him! He had earned those dollars by back- and heart-breaking toil, lifting lumps of coal into cars; the sum was enough to keep the whole Rafferty family alive for a week or two. And here was Edward, with a smooth brown leather wallet full of ten- and twenty-dollar bills, which he peeled off without counting, exactly as if money grew on trees, or as if coal came out of the earth and walked into furnaces to the sound of a fiddle and a flute!

Edward had of course no idea of these abnormal processes going on in his brother's mind. He was holding out the bills. "Get yourself some decent things," he said. "I hope you don't have to stay dirty in order to feel democratic?"

"No," answered Hal; and then, "How are we going?"

"I've a car waiting, back of the office."

"So you had everything ready!" But Edward made no answer; afraid of setting off the volcano again.

SECTION 18.

*T*hey went out by the rear door of the office, entered the car, and sped out of the village, unseen by the crowd. And all the way down the canyon Edward pleaded with Hal to drop the controversy and come home at once. He brought up the tragic question of Dad again; when that did not avail, he began to threaten. Suppose Hal's money-resources were to be cut off, suppose he were to find himself left out of his father's will — what would he do then? Hal answered, without a smile, "I can always get a job as organizer for the United Mine-Workers."

So Edward gave up that line of attack. "If you won't come," he declared, "I'm going to stay by you till you do!"

"All right," said Hal. He could not help smiling at this dire threat. "But if I take you about and introduce you to my friends, you must agree that what you hear shall be confidential."

The other made a face of disgust. "What the devil would I want to talk about your friends for?"

"I don't know what might happen," said Hal. "You're going to meet Peter Harrigan and take his side, and I can't tell what you might conceive it your duty to do."

The other exclaimed, with sudden passion, "I'll tell you right now! If you try to go back to that coal-camp, I swear to God I'll apply to the courts and have you shut up in a sanitarium. I don't think I'd have much trouble in persuading a judge that you're insane."

"No," said Hal, with a laugh — "not a judge in this part of the world!"

Then, after studying his brother's face for a moment, it occurred to him that it might be well not to let such an idea rest unimpeached in Edward's mind. "Wait," said he, "till you meet my friend Billy Keating, of the *Gazette,* and hear what he would do with such a story! Billy is crazy to have me turn him loose to 'play up' my fight with Old Peter!" The conversation went no farther — but Hal was sure that Edward would "put that in his pipe and smoke it."

They came to the MacKellar home in Pedro, and Edward waited in the automobile while Hal went inside. The old Scotchman welcomed him warmly, and told him what news he had. Jerry Minetti had been there that morning, and MacKellar at his request had telephoned to the office of the union in Sheridan, and ascertained that Jack David had brought word about the strike on the previous evening. All parties had been careful not to mention names, for "leaks" in the telephone were notorious, but it was clear who the messenger had been. As a result of the message, Johann Hartman, president of the local union of the miners, was now at the American Hotel in Pedro, together with James Moylan, secretary of the district organization — the latter having come down from Western City on the same train as Edward.

This was all satisfactory; but MacKellar added a bit of information of desperate import — the officers of the union declared that they could not support a strike at the present time! It was premature, it could lead to nothing but failure and discouragement to the larger movement they were planning.

Such a possibility Hal had himself realized at the outset. But he had witnessed the new birth of freedom at North Valley, he had seen the hungry, toil-worn faces of men looking up to him for support; he had been moved by it, and had come to feel that the union officials must be moved in the same way. "They've simply got to back it!" he exclaimed. "Those men must not be disappointed! They'll lose all hope, they'll sink into utter despair! The labor men must realize that – I must make them!"

The old Scotchman answered that Minetti had felt the same way. He had flung caution to the winds, and rushed over to the hotel to see Hartman and Moylan. Hal decided to follow, and went out to the automobile.

He explained matters to his brother, whose comment was, Of course! It was what he had foretold. The poor, misguided miners would go back to their work, and their would-be leader would have to admit the folly of his course. There was a train for Western City in a couple of hours; it would be a great favor if Hal would arrange to take it.

Hal answered shortly that he was going to the American Hotel. His brother might take him there, if he chose. So Edward gave the order to the driver of the car. Incidentally, Edward began asking about clothing-stores in Pedro. While Hal was in the hotel, pleading for the life of his newly-born labor union, Edward would seek a costume in which he could "feel like a human being."

SECTION 19.

*H*al found Jerry Minetti with the two officials in their hotel-room: Jim Moylan, district secretary, a long, towering Irish boy, black-eyed and black-haired, quick and sensitive, the sort of person one trusted and liked at the first moment; and Johann Hartman, local president, a grey-haired miner of German birth, reserved and slow-spoken, evidently a man of much strength, both physical and moral. He had need of it, anyone could realize, having charge of a union headquarters in the heart of this "Empire of Raymond!"

Hal first told of the kidnapping of the committee. This did not surprise the officials, he found; it was the thing the companies regularly did when there was threat of rebellion in the camps. That was why efforts to organize openly were so utterly hopeless. There was no chance for anything but a secret propaganda, maintained until every camp had the nucleus of an organization.

"So you can't back this strike!" exclaimed Hal.

Not possibly, was Moylan's reply. It would be lost as soon as it was begun. There was no slightest hope of success until a lot of organization work had been done.

"But meantime," argued Hal, "the union at North Valley will go to pieces!"

"Perhaps," was the reply. "We'll only have to start another. That's what the labor movement is like."

Jim Moylan was young, and saw Hal's mood. "Don't misunderstand us!" he cried. "It's heartbreaking — but it's not in our power to help. We are charged with building up the union, and we know that if we supported everything that looked like a strike, we'd be bankrupt the first year. You can't imagine how often this same thing happens — hardly a month we're not called on to handle such a situation."

"I can see what you mean," said Hal. "But I thought that in this case, right after the disaster, with the men so stirred —"

The young Irishman smiled, rather sadly. "You're new at this game," he said. "If a mine-disaster was enough to win a strike, God knows our job would be easy. In Barela, just down the canyon from you, they've had three big explosions — they've killed over five hundred men in the past year!"

Hal began to see how, in his inexperience, he had lost his sense of proportion.

He looked at the two labor leaders, and recalled the picture of such a person which he had brought with him to North Valley — a hotheaded and fiery agitator, luring honest workingmen from their jobs. But here was the situation exactly reversed! Here was he in a blaze of excitement — and two labor leaders turning the fire-hose on him! They sat quiet and businesslike, pronouncing a doom upon the slaves of North Valley. Back to their black dungeons with them!

"What can we tell the men?" he asked, making an effort to repress his chagrin.

"We can only tell them what I'm telling you — that we're helpless, till we've got the whole district organized. Meantime, they have to stand the gaff; they must do what they can to keep an organization."

"But all the active men will be fired!"

"No, not quite all — they seldom get them all."

Here the stolid old German put in. In the last year the company had turned out more than six thousand men because of union activity or suspicion of it.

"*Six thousand!*" echoed Hal. "You mean from this one district?"

"That's what I mean."

"But there aren't more than twelve or fifteen thousand men in the district!"

"I know that."

"Then how can you ever keep an organization?"

The other answered, quietly, "They treat the new men the same as they treated the old."

Hal thought suddenly of John Edstrom's ants! Here they were — building their bridge, building it again and again, as often as floods might destroy it! They had not the swift impatience of a youth of the leisure-class, accustomed to having his own way, accustomed to thinking of freedom and decency and justice as necessities of life. Much as Hal learned from the conversation of these men, he learned more from their silences — the quiet, matter-of-fact way they took things which had driven him beside himself with indignation. He began to realize what it would mean to stand by his pledge to those poor devils in North Valley. He would need more than one blaze of excitement; he would need brains and patience and discipline, he would need years of study and hard work!

SECTION 20.

*H*al found himself forced to accept the decision of the labor-leaders. They had had experience, they could judge the situation. The miners would have to go back to work, and Cartwright and Alec Stone and Jeff Cotton would drive them as before! All that the rebels could do was to try to keep a secret organization in the camp.

Jerry Minetti mentioned Jack David. He had gone back this morning, without having seen the labor-leaders. So he might escape suspicion, and keep his job, and help the union work.

"How about you?" asked Hal. "I suppose you've cooked your goose."

Jerry had never heard this phrase, but he got its meaning. "Sure thing!" said he. "Cooked him plenty!"

"Didn't you see the 'dicks' down stairs in the lobby?" inquired Hartman.

"I haven't learned to recognize them yet."

"Well, you will, if you stay at this business. There hasn't been a minute since our office was opened that we haven't had half a dozen on the other side of the street. Every man that comes to see us is followed back to his camp and fired that same day. They've broken into my desk at night and stolen my letters and papers; they've threatened us with death a hundred times."

"I don't see how you make any headway at all!"

"They can never stop us. They thought when they broke into my desk, they'd get a list of our organizers. But you see, I carry the lists in my head!"

"No small task, either," put in Moylan. "Would you like to know how many organizers we have at work? Ninety-seven. And they haven't caught a single one of them!"

Hal heard him, amazed. Here was a new aspect of the labor movement! This quiet, resolute old "Dutchy," whom you might have taken for a delicatessen-proprietor; this merry-eyed Irish boy, whom you would have expected to be escorting a lady to a firemen's ball — they were captains of an army of sappers who were undermining the towers of Peter Harrigan's fortress of greed!

Hartman suggested that Jerry might take a chance at this sort of work. He would surely be fired from North Valley, so he might as well send word to his family to come to Pedro. In this way he might save himself to work as an organizer; because it was the custom of these company "spotters" to follow a man back to his camp and there identify him. If Jerry took a train for Western City, they would be thrown off the track, and he might get into some new camp and do organizing among the Italians. Jerry accepted this proposition with alacrity; it would put off the evil day when Rosa and her little ones would be left to the mercy of chance.

They were still talking when the telephone rang. It was Hartman's secretary in Sheridan, reporting that he had just heard from the kidnapped committee. The entire party, eight men and Mary Burke, had been taken to Horton, a station not far up the line, and put on the train with many dire threats. But they had left the train at the next stop, and declared their intention of coming to Pedro. They were due at the hotel very soon.

Hal desired to be present at this meeting, and went downstairs to tell his brother. There was another dispute, of course. Edward reminded Hal that the scenery of Pedro had a tendency to monotony; to which Hal could only answer by offering to introduce his brother to his friends. They were men who could teach Edward much, if he would consent to learn. He might attend the session with the committee — eight men and a woman who had ventured an act of heroism and been made the victims of a crime. Nor were they bores, as Edward might be thinking! There was blue-eyed Tim Rafferty, for example, a silent, smutty-faced gnome who had broken out of his black cavern and spread unexpected golden wings of oratory; and Mary Burke, of whom Edward might read in that afternoon's edition of the Western City *Gazette* — a "Joan of Arc of the coal-camps," or something equally picturesque. But Edward's mood was not to be enlivened. He had a vision of his brother's appearance in the paper as the companion of this Hibernian Joan!

Hal went off with Jerry Minetti to what his brother described as a "hash-house," while Edward proceeded in solitary state to the dining room of the American Hotel. But he was not left in solitary state; pretty soon a sharp-faced young man was ushered to a seat beside him, and started up a conversation. He was a "drummer," he said; his "line" was hardware, what was Edward's? Edward answered coldly that he had no "line," but the young man was not rebuffed — apparently his "line" had hardened his sensibilities. Perhaps Edward was interested in coal-mines? Had he been visiting the camps? He questioned so persistently, and came back so often to the subject, that at last it dawned over Edward what this meant — he was receiving the attention of a "spotter!" Strange to say, the circumstance caused Edward more irritation against Peter Harrigan's regime than all his brother's eloquence about oppression at North Valley.

SECTION 21.

*S*oon after dinner the kidnapped committee arrived, bedraggled in body and weary in soul. They inquired for Johann Hartman, and were sent up to the room, where there followed a painful scene. Eight men and a woman who had ventured an act of heroism and been made the victims of a crime could not easily be persuaded to see their efforts and sacrifices thrown on the dump-heap, nor were they timid in expressing their opinions of those who were betraying them.

"You been tryin' to get us out!" cried Tim Rafferty. "Ever since I can remember you been at my old man to help you — an' here, when we do what you ask, you throw us down!"

"We never asked you to go on strike," said Moylan.

"No, that's true. You only asked us to pay dues, so you fellows could have fat salaries."

"Our salaries aren't very fat," replied the young leader, patiently. "You'd find that out if you investigated."

"Well, whatever they are, they go on, while ours stop. We're on the streets, we're done for. Look at us — and most of us has got families, too! I got an old mother an' a lot of brothers and sisters, an' my old man done up an' can't work. What do you think's to become of us?"

"We'll help you out a little, Rafferty —"

"To hell with you!" cried Tim. "I don't want your help! When I need charity, I'll go to the county. They're another bunch of grafters, but they don't pretend to be friends to the workin' man."

Here was the thing Tom Olson had told Hal at the outset — the workingmen bedeviled, not knowing whom to trust, suspecting the very people who most desired to help them. "Tim," he put in, "there's no use talking like that. We have to learn patience —"

And the boy turned upon Hal. "What do you know about it? It's all a joke to you. You can go off and forget it when you get ready. You've got money, they tell me!"

Hal felt no resentment at this; it was what he heard from his own conscience. "It isn't so easy for me as you think, Tim. There are other ways of suffering besides not having money —"

"Much sufferin' you'll do — with your rich folks!" sneered Tim.

There was a murmur of protest from others of the committee.

"Good God, Rafferty!" broke in Moylan. "We can't help it, man — we're just as helpless as you!"

"You say you're helpless — but you don't even try!"

"*Try?* Do you want us to back a strike that we know hasn't a chance? You might as well ask us to lie down and let a load of coal run over us. We can't win, man! I tell you we can't *win!* We'd only be throwing away our organization!"

Moylan became suddenly impassioned. He had seen a dozen sporadic strikes in this district, and many a dozen young strikers, homeless, desolate, embittered, turning their disappointment on him. "We might support you with our funds, you say — we might go on doing it, even while the company ran the mine with scabs. But where would that land us, Rafferty? I seen many a union on the rocks — and I ain't so old either! If we had a bank, we'd support all the miners of the country, they'd never need to work again till they got their rights. But this money we spend is the money that other miners are earnin' — right now, down in the pits, Rafferty, the same as you and your old man. They give us this money, and they say, 'Use it to build up the union. Use it to help the men that aren't organized — take them in, so they won't beat down our wages and scab on us. But don't waste it, for God's sake; we have to work hard to make it, and if we don't see results, you'll get no more out of us.' Don't you see how that is, man? And how it weighs on us, worse even then the fear that maybe we'll lose our poor salaries — though you might refuse to believe anything so good of us? You don't need to talk to me like I was Peter Harrigan's son. I was a spragger when I was ten years old, and I ain't been out of the pits so long that I've forgot the feeling. I assure you, the thing that keeps me awake at night ain't the fear of not gettin' a living, for I give myself a bit of education, working nights, and I know I could always turn out and earn what I need; but it's wondering whether I'm spending the miners' money the best way, whether maybe I mightn't save them a little misery if I hadn't 'a' done this or had 'a' done that. When I come down on that sleeper last night, here's what I was thinking, Tim Rafferty — all the time I listened to the train bumping — 'Now I got to see some more of the suffering, I got to let some good men turn against us, because they can't see why we should get salaries while they get the sack. How am I going to show them that I'm working for them — working as hard as I know how — and that I'm not to blame for their trouble?'"

Here Wauchope broke in. "There's no use talking anymore. I see we're up against it. We'll not trouble you, Moylan."

"You trouble me," cried Moylan, "unless you stand by the movement!"

The other laughed bitterly. "You'll never know what I do. It's the road for me — and you know it!"

"Well, wherever you go, it'll be the same; either you'll be fighting for the union, or you'll be a weight that we have to carry."

The young leader turned from one to another of the committee, pleading with them not to be embittered by this failure, but to turn it to their profit, going on with the work of building up the solidarity of the miners. Every man had to make his sacrifices, to pay his part of the price. The thing of importance was that every man who was discharged should be a spark of unionism, carrying the flame of revolt to a new part of the country. Let each one do his part, and there would soon be no place to which the masters could send for "scabs."

SECTION 22.

*T*here was one member of this committee whom Hal watched with especial anxiety — Mary Burke. She had not yet said a word; while the others argued and protested, she sat with her lips set and her hands clenched. Hal knew what rage this failure must bring to her. She had risen and struggled and hoped, and the result was what she had always said it would be — nothing! Now he saw her, with eyes large and dark with fatigue, fixed on this fiery young labor-leader. He knew that a war must be going on within her. Would she drop out entirely now? It was the test of her character — as it was the test of the characters of all of them.

"If only we're strong enough and brave enough," Jim Moylan was saying, "we can use our defeats to educate our people and bring them together. Right now, if we can make the men at North Valley see what we're doing, they won't go back beaten, they won't be bitter against the union, they'll only go back to wait. And ain't that a way to beat the bosses — to hold our jobs, and keep the union alive, till we've got into all the camps, and can strike and win?"

There was a pause; then Mary spoke. "How're you meanin' to tell the men?" Her voice was without emotion, but nevertheless, Hal's heart leaped. Whether Mary had any hope or not, she was going to stay in line with the rest of the ants!

Johann Hartman explained his idea. He would have circulars printed in several languages and distributed secretly in the camp, ordering the men back to work. But Jerry met this suggestion with a prompt no. The people would not believe the circulars, they would suspect the bosses of having them printed. Hadn't the bosses done worse than that, "framing up" a letter from Joe Smith to balk the check-weighman movement? The only thing that would help would be for some of the committee to get into the camp and see the men face to face.

"And it got to be quick!" Jerry insisted. "They get notice to work in morning, and them that don't be fired. They be the best men, too — men we want to save."

Other members of the committee spoke up, agreeing with this. Said Rusick, the Slav, slow-witted and slow-spoken, "Them fellers get mighty damn sore if they lose their job and don't got no strike." And Zammakis, the Greek, quick and nervous, "We say strike; we got to say no strike."

What could they do? There was, in the first place, the difficulty of getting away from the hotel, which was being watched by the "spotters." Hartman suggested that if they went out all together and scattered, the detectives could not follow all of them. Those who escaped might get into North Valley by hiding in the "empties" which went up to the mine.

But Moylan pointed out that the company would be anticipating this; and Rusick, who had once been a hobo, put in: "They sure search them cars. They give us plenty hell, too, when they catch us."

Yes, it would be a dangerous mission. Mary spoke again. "Maybe a lady could do it better."

"They'd beat a lady," said Minetti.

"I know, but maybe a lady might fool them. There's some widows that came to Pedro for the funerals, and they're wearin' veils that hide their faces. I might pretend to be one of them and get into the camp."

The men looked at one another. There was an idea! The scowl which had stayed upon the face of Tim Rafferty ever since his quarrel with Moylan, gave place suddenly to a broad grin.

"I seen Mrs. Zamboni on the street," said he. "She had on black veils enough to hide the lot of us."

And here Hal spoke, for the first time since Tim Rafferty had silenced him. "Does anybody know where to find Mrs. Zamboni?"

"She stay with my friend, Mrs. Swajka," said Rusick.

"Well," said Hal, "there's something you people don't know about this situation. After they had fired you, I made another speech to the men, and made them swear they'd stay on strike. So now I've got to go back and eat my words. If we're relying on veils and things, a man can be fixed up as well as a woman."

They were staring at him. "They'll beat you to death if they catch you!" said Wauchope.

"No," said Hal, "I don't think so. Anyhow, it's up to me" — he glanced at Tim Rafferty — "because I'm the only one who doesn't have to suffer for the failure of our strike."

There was a pause.

"I'm sorry I said that!" cried Tim, impulsively.

"That's all right, old man," replied Hal. "What you said is true, and I'd like to do something to ease my conscience." He rose to his feet, laughing. "I'll make a peach of a widow!" he said. "I'm going up and have a tea-party with my friend Jeff Cotton!"

SECTION 23.

*H*al proposed going to find Mrs. Zamboni at the place where she was staying; but Moylan interposed, objecting that the detectives would surely follow him. Even though they should all go out of the hotel at once, the one person the detective would surely stick to was the arch-rebel and trouble-maker, Joe Smith. Finally they decided to bring Mrs. Zamboni to the room. Let her come with Mrs. Swajka or some other woman who spoke English, and go to the desk and ask for Mary Burke, explaining that Mary had borrowed money from her, and that she had to have it to pay the undertaker for the burial of her man. The hotel-clerk might not know who Mary Burke was; but the watchful "spotters" would gather about and listen, and if it was mentioned that Mary was from North Valley, someone would connect her with the kidnapped committee.

This was made clear to Rusick, who hurried off, and in the course of half an hour returned with the announcement that the women were on the way. A few minutes later came a tap on the door, and there stood the black-garbed old widow with her friend. She came in; and then came looks of dismay and horrified exclamations. Rusick was requesting her to give up her weeds to Joe Smith!

"She say she don't got nothing else," explained the Slav.

"Tell her I give her plenty money buy more," said Hal.

"Ai! Jesu!" cried Mrs. Zamboni, pouring out a sputtering torrent.

"She say she don't got nothing to put on. She say it ain't good to go no clothes!"

"Hasn't she got on a petticoat?"

"She say petticoat got holes!"

There was a burst of laughter from the company, and the old woman turned scarlet from her forehead to her ample throat. "Tell her she wrap up in blankets," said Hal. "Mary Burke buy her new things."

It proved surprisingly difficult to separate Mrs. Zamboni from her widow's weeds, which she had purchased with so great an expenditure of time and tears. Never had a respectable lady who had borne sixteen children received such a proposition; to sell the insignia of her grief — and here in a hotel room, crowded with a dozen men! Nor was the task made easier by the unseemly merriment of the men. "Ai! Jesu!" cried Mrs. Zamboni again.

"Tell her it's very, very important," said Hal. "Tell her I must have them." And then, seeing that Rusick was making poor headway, he joined in, in the compromise-English one learns in the camps. "Got to have! Sure thing! Got to hide! Quick! Get away from boss! See? Get killed if no go!"

So at last the frightened old woman gave way. "She say all turn backs," said Rusick. And everybody turned, laughing in hilarious whispers, while, with Mary Burke and Mrs. Swajka for a shield, Mrs. Zamboni got out of her waist and skirt, putting a blanket round her red shoulders for modesty's sake. When Hal put the garments on, there was a foot to spare all round; but after they had stuffed two bed pillows down in the front of him, and drawn them tight at the waist-line, the disguise was judged more satisfactory. He put on the old lady's ample if ragged shoes, and Mary Burke set the widow's bonnet on his head and adjusted the many veils; after that Mrs. Zamboni's own brood of children would not have suspected the disguise.

It was a merry party for a few minutes; worn and hopeless as Mary had seemed, she was possessed now by the spirit of fun. But then quickly the laughter died. The time for action had come. Mary Burke said that she would stay with what was left of Mrs. Zamboni, to answer the door in case any of the hotel people or the detectives should come. Hal asked Jim Moylan to see Edward, and say that Hal was writing a manifesto to the North Valley workers, and would not be ready to leave until the midnight train.

These things agreed upon, Hal shook hands all round, and the eleven men left the room at once, going down stairs and through the lobby, scattering in every direction on the streets. Mrs. Swajka and the pseudo-Mrs. Zamboni followed a minute later — and, as they anticipated, found the lobby swept clear of detectives.

SECTION 24.

*B*idding Mrs. Swajka farewell, Hal set out for the railroad station. But before he had gone a block from the hotel, he ran into his brother, coming straight towards him.

Edward's face wore a bored look; his very manner of carrying the magazine under his arm said that he had selected it in a last hopeless effort against the monotony of Pedro. Such a trick of fate, to take a man of important affairs, and immure him at the mercy of a maniac in a God-forsaken coal-town! What did people do in such a hole? Pay a nickel to look at moving pictures of cow-boys and counterfeiters?

Edward's aspect was too much for Hal's sense of humor. Besides, he had a good excuse; was it not proper to make a test of his disguise, before facing the real danger in North Valley?

He placed himself in the path of his brother's progress, and in Mrs. Zamboni's high, complaining tones, began, "Mister!"

Edward stared at the interrupting black figure. "Mister, you Joe Smith's brother, hey?"

The question had to be repeated before Edward gave his grudging answer. He was not proud of the relationship.

"Mister," continued the whining voice, "my old man got blow up in mine. I get five pieces from my man what I got to bury yesterday in grave-yard. I got to pay thirty dollar for bury them pieces and I don't got no more money left. I don't got no money from them company fellers. They come lawyer feller and he say maybe I get money for bury my man, if I don't jay too much. But, Mister, I got eleven children I got to feed, and I don't got no more man, and I don't find no new man for old woman like me. When I go home I hear them children crying and I don't got no food, and them company-stores don't give me no food. I think maybe you Joe Smith's brother you good man, maybe you sorry for poor widow-woman, you maybe give me some money, Mister, so I buy some food for them children."

"All right," said Edward. He pulled out his wallet and extracted a bill, which happened to be for ten dollars. His manner seemed to say, "For heaven's sake, here!"

Mrs. Zamboni clutched the bill with greedy fingers, but was not appeased. "You got plenty money, Mister! You rich man, hey! You maybe give me all them moneys, so I got plenty feed them children? You don't know them company-stores, Mister, them prices is way up high like mountains; them children is hungry, they cry all day and night, and one piece money don't last so long. You give me some more piece moneys, Mister — hey?"

"I'll give you one more," said Edward. "I need some for myself." He pulled off another bill.

"What you need so much, Mister? You don't got so many children, hey? And you got plenty more money home, maybe!"

"That's all I can give you," said the man. He took a step to one side, to get round the obstruction in his path.

But the obstruction took a step also — and with surprising agility.

"Mister, I thank you for them moneys. I tell them children I get moneys from good man. I like you, Mister Smith, you give money for poor widow-woman — you nice man."

And the dreadful creature actually stuck out one of her paws, as if expecting to pat Edward on the cheek, or to chuck him under the chin. He recoiled, as from a contagion; but she followed him, determined to do something to him, he could not be sure what. He had heard that these foreigners had strange customs!

"It's all right! It's nothing!" he insisted, and fell back — at the same time glancing nervously about, to see if there were spectators of this scene.

"Nice man, Mister! Nice man!" cried the old woman, with increasing cordiality. "Maybe some day I find man like you, Mr. Edward Smith — so I don't stay widow-woman no more. You think maybe you like to marry nice Slavish woman, got plenty nice children?"

Edward, perceiving that the matter was getting desperate, sprang to one side. It was a spring which should have carried him to safety; but to his dismay the Slavish widow sprang also — her claws caught him under the armpit, and fastening in his ribs, gave him a ferocious pinch. After which the owner of the claws went down the street, not looking back, but making strange gobbling noises, which might have been the weeping of a bereaved widow in Slavish, or might have been almost anything else.

SECTION 25.

*T*he train up to North Valley left very soon, and Hal figured that there would be just time to accomplish his errand and catch the last train back. He took his seat in the car without attracting attention, and sat in his place until they were approaching their destination, the last stop up the canyon. There were several of the miners' women in the car, and Hal picked out one who belonged to Mrs. Zamboni's nationality, and moved over beside her. She made place, with some remark; but Hal merely sobbed softly, and the woman felt for his hand to comfort him. As his hands were clasped together under the veils, she patted him reassuringly on the knee.

At the boundary of the stockaded village the train stopped, and Bud

Adams came through the car, scrutinizing every passenger. Seeing this, Hal began to sob again, and murmured something indistinct to his companion — which caused her to lean towards him, speaking volubly in her native language. "Bud" passed by.

When Hal came to leave the train, he took his companion's arm; he sobbed some more, and she talked some more, and so they went down the platform, under the very eyes of Pete Hanun, the "breaker of teeth." Another woman joined them, and they walked down the street, the women conversing in Slavish, apparently without a suspicion of Hal.

He had worked out his plan of action. He would not try to talk with the men secretly — it would take too long, and he might be betrayed before he had talked with a sufficient number. One bold stroke was the thing. In half an hour it would be supper-time, and the feeders would gather in Reminitsky's dining room. He would give his message there!

Hal's two companions were puzzled that he passed the Zamboni cabin, where presumably the Zamboni brood were being cared for by neighbors. But he let them make what they could of this, and went on to the Minetti home. To the astonished Rosa he revealed himself, and gave her husband's message — that she should take herself and the children down to Pedro, and wait quietly until she heard from him. She hurried out and brought in Jack David, to whom Hal explained matters. "Big Jack's" part in the recent disturbance had apparently not been suspected; he and his wife, with Rovetta, Wresmak, and Klowoski, would remain as a nucleus through which the union could work upon the men.

The supper-hour was at hand, and the pseudo-Mrs. Zamboni emerged and toddled down the street. As she passed into the dining room of the boarding-house, men looked at her, but no one spoke. It was the stage of the meal where everybody was grabbing and devouring, in the effort to get the best of his grabbing and devouring neighbors. The black-clad figure went to the far end of the room; there was a vacant chair, and the figure pulled it back from the table and climbed upon it. Then a shout rang through the room: "Boys! Boys!"

The feeders looked up, and saw the widow's weeds thrown back, and their leader, Joe Smith, gazing out at them. "Boys! I've come with a message from the union!"

There was a yell; men leaped to their feet, chairs were flung back, falling with a crash to the floor. Then, almost instantly, came silence; you could have heard the movement of any man's jaws, had any man continued to move them.

"Boys! I've been down to Pedro and seen the union people. I knew the bosses wouldn't let me come back, so I dressed up, and here I am!"

It dawned upon them, the meaning of this fantastic costume; there were cheers, laughter, yells of delight.

But Hal stretched out his hands, and silence fell again. "Listen to me! The bosses won't let me talk long, and I've something important to say. The union leaders say we can't win a strike now."

Consternation came into the faces before him. There were cries of dismay. He went on:

"We are only one camp, and the bosses would turn us out, they'd get in scabs and run the mines without us. What we must have is a strike of all the camps at once. One big union and one big strike! If we walked out now, it would please the bosses; but we'll fool them — we'll keep our jobs, and keep our union too! You are members of the union, you'll go on working for the union! Hooray for the North Valley union!"

For a moment there was no response. It was hard for men to cheer over such a prospect! Hal saw that he must touch a different chord.

"We mustn't be cowards, boys! We've got to keep our nerve! I'm doing my part — it took nerve to get in here! In Mrs. Zamboni's clothes, and with two pillows stuffed in front of me!"

He thumped the pillows, and there was a burst of laughter. Many in the crowd knew Mrs. Zamboni — it was what comedians call a "local gag." The laughter spread, and became a gale of merriment. Men began to cheer: "Hurrah for Joe! You're the girl! Will you marry me, Joe?" And so, of course, it was easy for Hal to get a response when he shouted, "Hurrah for the North Valley union!"

Again he raised his hands for silence, and went on again. "Listen, men. They'll turn me out, and you're not going to resist them. You're going to work and keep your jobs, and get ready for the big strike. And you'll tell the other men what I say. I can't talk to them all, but you tell them about the union. Remember, there are people outside planning and fighting for you. We're going to stand by the union, all of us, till we've brought these coal-camps back into America!" There was a cheer that shook the walls of the room. Yes, that was what they wanted — to live in America!

A crowd of men had gathered in the doorway, attracted by the uproar; Hal noticed confusion and pushing, and saw the head and burly shoulders of his enemy, Pete Hanun, come into sight.

"Here come the gunmen, boys!" he cried; and there was a roar of anger from the crowd. Men turned, clenching their fists, glaring at the guard. But Hal rushed on, quickly:

"Boys, hear what I say! Keep your heads! I can't stay in North Valley, and you know it! But I've done the thing I came to do, I've brought you the message from the union. And you'll tell the other men — tell them to stand by the union!"

Hal went on, repeating his message over and over. Looking from one to another of these toil-worn faces, he remembered the pledge he had made them, and he made it anew: "I'm going to stand by you! I'm going on with the fight, boys!"

There came more disturbance at the door, and suddenly Jeff Cotton appeared, with a couple of additional guards, shoving their way into the room, breathless and red in the face from running.

"Ah, there's the marshal!" cried Hal. "You needn't push, Cotton, there's not going to be any trouble. We are union men here, we know how to control ourselves. Now, boys, we're not giving up, we're not beaten, we're only waiting for the men in the other camps! We have a union, and we mean to keep it! Three cheers for the union!"

The cheers rang out with a will: cheers for the union, cheers for Joe Smith, cheers for the widow and her weeds!

"You belong to the union! You stand by it, no matter what happens! If they fire you, you take it on to the next place! You teach it to the new men, you never let it die in your hearts! In union there is strength, in union there is hope! Never forget it, men — *Union!*"

The voice of the camp-marshal rang out. "If you're coming, young woman, come now!"

Hal dropped a shy curtsey. "Oh, Mr. Cotton! This is so sudden!" The crowd howled; and Hal descended from his platform. With coquettish gesturing he replaced the widow's veils about his face, and tripped mincingly across the dining room. When he reached the camp-marshal, he daintily took that worthy's arm, and with the "breaker of teeth" on the other side, and Bud Adams bringing up the rear, he toddled out of the dining room and down the street.

Hungry men gave up their suppers to behold that sight. They poured out of the building, they followed, laughing, shouting, jeering. Others came from every direction — by the time the party had reached the depot, a good part of the population of the village was on hand; and everywhere went the word, "It's Joe Smith! Come back with a message from the union!" Big, coal-grimed miners laughed till the tears made streaks on their faces; they fell on one another's necks for delight at this trick which had been played upon their oppressors.

Even Jeff Cotton could not withhold his tribute. "By God, you're the limit!" he muttered. He accepted the "tea-party" aspect of the affair, as the easiest way to get rid of his recurrent guest, and avert the possibilities of danger. He escorted the widow to the train and helped her up the steps, posting escorts at the doors of her car; nor did the attentions of these gallants cease until the train had moved down the canyon and passed the limits of the North Valley stockade!

SECTION 26.

*H*al took off his widow's weeds; and with them he shed the merriment he had worn for the benefit of the men. There came a sudden reaction; he realized that he was tired.

For ten days he had lived in a whirl of excitement, scarcely stopping to sleep. Now he lay back in the car-seat, pale, exhausted; his head ached, and he realized that the sum-total of his North Valley experience was failure. There was left in him no trace of that spirit of adventure with which he had set out upon his "summer course in practical sociology." He had studied his lessons, tried to recite them, and been "flunked." He smiled a bitter smile, recollecting the careless jesting that had been on his lips as he came up that same canyon:

"He keeps them a-roll, that merry old soul —
    The wheels of industree;
  A-roll and a-roll, for his pipe and his bowl
    And his college facultee!"

The train arrived in Pedro, and Hal took a hack at the station and drove to the hotel. He still carried the widow's weeds rolled into a bundle. He might have left them in the train, but the impulse to economy which he had acquired during the last ten weeks had become a habit. He would return them to Mrs. Zamboni. The money he had promised her might better be used to feed her young ones. The two pillows he would leave in the car; the hotel might endure the loss!

Entering the lobby, the first person Hal saw was his brother, and the sight of that patrician face made human by disgust relieved Hal's headache in part. Life was harsh, life was cruel; but here was weary, waiting Edward, that boon of comic relief!

Edward demanded to know where the devil he had been; and Hal answered, "I've been visiting the widows and orphans."

"Oh!" said Edward. "And while I sit in this hole and stew! What's that you've got under your arm?"

Hal looked at the bundle. "It's a souvenir of one of the widows," he said, and unrolled the garments and spread them out before his brother's puzzled eyes. "A lady named Mrs. Swajka gave them to me. They belonged to another lady, Mrs. Zamboni, but she doesn't need them anymore."

"What have *you* got to do with them?"

"It seems that Mrs. Zamboni is going to get married again." Hal lowered his voice, confidentially. "It's a romance, Edward — it may interest you as an illustration of the manners of these foreign races. She met a man on the street, a fine, fine man, she says — and he gave her a lot of money. So she went and bought herself some new clothes, and she wants to give these widow's weeds to the new man. That's the custom in her country, it seems — her sign that she accepts him as a suitor."

Seeing the look of wonderment growing on his brother's face, Hal had to stop for a moment to keep his own face straight. "If that man wasn't serious in his intention, Edward, he'll have trouble, for I know Mrs. Zamboni's emotional nature. She'll follow him about everywhere —"

"Hal, that creature is insane!" And Edward looked about him nervously, as if he thought the Slavish widow might appear suddenly in the hotel lobby to demonstrate her emotional nature.

"No," replied Hal, "it's just one of those differences in national customs." And suddenly Hal's face gave way. He began to laugh; he laughed, perhaps more loudly than good form permitted.

Edward was much annoyed. There were people in the lobby, and they were staring at him. "Cut it out, Hal!" he exclaimed. "Your fool jokes bore me!" But nevertheless, Hal could see uncertainty in his brother's face. Edward recognized those widow's weeds. And how could he be sure about the "national customs" of that grotesque creature who had pinched him in the ribs on the street?

"Cut it out!" he cried again.

Hal, changing his voice suddenly to the Zamboni key, exclaimed: "Mister, I got eight children I got to feed, and I don't got no more man, and I don't find no new man for old woman like me!"

So at last the truth in its full enormity began to dawn upon Edward. His consternation and disgust poured themselves out; and Hal listened, his laughter dying. "Edward," he said, "you don't take me seriously even yet!"

"Good God!" cried the other. "I believe you're really insane!"

"You were up there, Edward! You heard what I said to those poor devils! And you actually thought I'd go off with you and forget about them!"

Edward ignored this. "You're really insane!" he repeated. "You'll get yourself killed, in spite of all I can do!"

But Hal only laughed. "Not a chance of it! You should have seen the tea-party manners of the camp-marshal!"

SECTION 27.

*E*dward would have endeavored to carry his brother away forthwith, but there was no train until late at night; so Hal went upstairs, where he found Moylan and Hartman with Mary Burke and Mrs. Zamboni, all eager to hear his story. As the members of the committee, who had been out to supper, came straggling in, the story was told again, and yet again. They were almost as much delighted as the men in Reminitsky's. If only all strikes that had to be called off could be called off as neatly as that!

Between these outbursts of satisfaction, they discussed their future. Moylan was going back to Western City, Hartman to his office in Sheridan, from which he would arrange to send new organizers into North Valley. No doubt Cartwright would turn off many men — those who had made themselves conspicuous during the strike, those who continued to talk union out loud. But such men would have to be replaced, and the union knew through what agencies the company got its hands. The North Valley miners would find themselves mysteriously provided with union literature in their various languages; it would be slipped under their pillows, or into their dinner-pails, or the pockets of their coats while they were at work.

Also there was propaganda to be carried on among those who were turned away; so that, wherever they went, they would take the message of unionism. There had been a sympathetic outburst in Barela, Hal learned — starting quite spontaneously that morning, when the men heard what had happened at North Valley. A score of workers had been fired, and more would probably follow in the morning. Here was a job for the members of the kidnapped committee; Tim Rafferty, for example — would he care to stay in Pedro for a week or two, to meet such men, and give them literature and arguments?

This offer was welcome; for life looked desolate to the Irish boy at this moment. He was out of a job, his father was a wreck, his family destitute and helpless. They would have to leave their home, of course;

there would be no place for any Rafferty in North Valley. Where they would go, God only knew; Tim would become a wanderer, living away from his people, starving himself and sending home his pitiful savings.

Hal was watching the boy, and reading these thoughts. He, Hal Warner, would play the god out of a machine in this case, and in several others equally pitiful. He had the right to sign his father's name to checks, a privilege which he believed he could retain, even while undertaking the role of Haroun al Raschid in a mine-disaster. But what about the mine-disasters and abortive strikes where there did not happen to be any Haroun al Raschid at hand? What about those people, right in North Valley, who did not happen to have told Hal of their affairs? He perceived that it was only by turning his back and running that he would escape from his adventure with any portion of his self-possession. Truly, this fair-seeming and wonderful civilization was like the floor of a charnel-house or a field of battle; anywhere one drove a spade beneath its surface, he uncovered horrors, sights for the eyes and stenches for the nostrils that caused him to turn sick!

There was Rusick, for example; he had a wife and two children, and not a dollar in the world. In the year and more that he had worked, faithfully and persistently, to get out coal for Peter Harrigan, he had never once been able to get ahead of his bill for the necessities of life at Old Peter's store. All his belongings in the world could be carried in a bundle on his back, and whether he ever saw these again would depend upon the whim of old Peter's camp-marshal and guards. Rusick would take to the road, with a ticket purchased by the union. Perhaps he would find a job and perhaps not; in any case, the best he could hope for in life was to work for some other Harrigan, and run into debt at some other company-store.

There was Hobianish, a Serbian, and Hernandez, a Mexican, of whom the same things were true, except that one had four children and the other six. Bill Wauchope had only a wife — their babies had died, thank heaven, he said. He did not seem to have been much moved by Jim Moylan's pleadings; he was down and out; he would take to the road, and beat his way to the East and back to England. They called this a free country! By God, if he were to tell what had happened to him, he could not get an English miner to believe it!

Hal gave these men his real name and address, and made them promise to let him know how they got along. He would help a little, he said; in his mind he was figuring how much he ought to do. How far shall a man go in relieving the starvation about him, before he can enjoy his meals in a well-appointed club? What casuist will work out this problem — telling him the percentage he shall relieve of the starvation

he happens personally to know about, the percentage of that which he
sees on the streets, the percentage of that about which he reads in
government reports on the rise in the cost of living. To what extent is
he permitted to close his eyes, as he walks along the streets on his way
to the club? To what extent is he permitted to avoid reading government
reports before going out to dinner-dances with his fiancée? Problems
such as these the masters of the higher mathematics have neglected to
solve; the wise men of the academies and the holy men of the churches
have likewise failed to work out the formulas; and Hal, trying to obtain
them by his crude mental arithmetic, found no satisfaction in the
results.

SECTION 28.

*H*al wanted a chance to talk to Mary Burke; they had had no
intimate talk since the meeting with Jessie Arthur, and now he was going
away, for a long time. He wanted to find out what plans Mary had for
the future, and — more important yet — what was her state of mind. If
he had been able to lift this girl from despair, his summer course in
practical sociology had not been all a failure!

He asked her to go with him to say good-bye to John Edstrom, whom
he had not seen since their unceremonious parting at MacKellar's, when
Hal had fled to Percy Harrigan's train. Downstairs in the lobby Hal
explained his errand to his waiting brother, who made no comment,
but merely remarked that he would follow, if Hal had no objection. He
did not care to make the acquaintance of the Hibernian Joan of Arc,
and would not come close enough to interfere with Hal's conversation
with the lady; but he wished to do what he could for his brother's
protection. So there set out a moonlight procession — first Hal and
Mary, then Edward, and then Edward's dinner-table companion, the
"hardware-drummer!"

Hal was embarrassed in beginning his farewell talk with Mary. He
had no idea how she felt towards him, and he admitted with a guilty
pang that he was a little afraid to find out! He thought it best to be
cheerful, so he started to tell her how fine he thought her conduct during
the strike. But she did not respond to his remarks, and at last he realized
that she was laboring with some thoughts of her own.

"There's somethin' I got to say to ye!" she began, suddenly. "A couple of days ago I knew how I meant to say it, but now I don't."

"Well," he laughed, "say it as you meant to."

"No; 'twas bitter — and now I'm on my knees before ye."

"Not that I want you to be bitter," said Hal, still laughing, "but it's I that ought to be on my knees before you. I didn't accomplish anything, you know."

"Ye did all ye could — and more than the rest of us. I want ye to know I'll never forget it. But I want ye to hear the other thing, too!"

She walked on, staring before her, doubling up her hands in agitation. "Well?" said he, still trying to keep a cheerful tone.

"Ye remember that day just after the explosion? Ye remember what I said about — about goin' away with ye? I take it back."

"Oh, of course!" said he, quickly. "You were distracted, Mary — you didn't know what you were saying."

"No, no! That's not it! But I've changed my mind; I don't mean to throw meself away."

"I told you you'd see it that way," he said. "No man is worth it."

"Ah, lad!" said she. "'Tis the fine soothin' tongue ye have — but I'd rather ye knew the truth. 'Tis that I've seen the other girl; and I hate her!"

They walked for a bit in silence. Hal had sense enough to realize that here was a difficult subject. "I don't want to be a prig, Mary," he said gently; "but you'll change your mind about that, too. You'll not hate her; you'll be sorry for her."

She laughed — a raw, harsh laugh. "What kind of a joke is that?"

"I know — it may seem like one. But it'll come to you some day. You have a wonderful thing to live and fight for; while she" — he hesitated a moment, for he was not sure of his own ideas on this subject — "she has so many things to learn; and she may never learn them. She'll miss some fine things."

"I know one of the fine things she does not mean to miss," said Mary, grimly; "that's Mr. Hal Warner." Then, after they had walked again in silence: "I want ye to understand me, Mr. Warner —"

"Ah, Mary!" he pleaded. "Don't treat me that way! I'm Joe."

"All right," she said, "Joe ye shall be. 'Twill remind ye of a pretty adventure — bein' a workin' man for a few weeks. Well, that's a part of what I have to tell ye. I've got my pride, even if I'm only a poor miner's daughter; and the other day I found out me place."

"How do you mean?" he asked.

"Ye don't understand? Honest?"

"No, honest," he said.

"Ye're stupid with women, Joe. Ye didn't see what the girl did to me! 'Twas some kind of a bug I was to her. She was not sure if I was the kind that bites, but she took no chances — she threw me off, like that." And Mary snapped her hand, as one does when troubled with a bug.

"Ah, now!" pleaded Hal. "You're not being fair!"

"I'm bein' just as fair as I've got it in me to be, Joe. I been off and had it all out. I can see this much — 'tis not her fault, maybe — 'tis her class; 'tis all of ye — the very best of ye, even yeself, Joe Smith!"

"Yea," he replied, "Tim Rafferty said that."

"Tim said too much — but a part of it was true. Ye think ye've come here and been one of us workin' people. But don't your own sense tell you the difference, as if it was a canyon a million miles across — between a poor ignorant creature in a minin' camp, and a rich man's daughter, a lady? Ye'd tell me not to be ashamed of poverty; but would ye ever put me by the side of her — for all your fine feelin's of friendship for them that's beneath ye? Didn't ye show that at the Minettis'?"

"But don't you see, Mary —" He made an effort to laugh. "I got used to obeying Jessie! I knew her a long time before I knew you."

"Ah, Joe! Ye've a kind heart, and a pleasant way of speakin'. But wouldn't it interest ye to know the real truth? Ye said ye'd come out here to learn the truth!"

And Hal answered, in a low voice, "Yes," and did not interrupt again.

SECTION 29.

Mary's voice had dropped low, and Hal thought how rich and warm it was when she was deeply moved. She went on:

"I lived all me life in minin' camps, Joe Smith, and I seen men robbed and beaten, and women cryin' and childer hungry. I seen the company, like some great wicked beast that eat them up. But I never knew why, or what it meant — till that day, there at the Minettis'. I'd read about fine ladies in books, ye see; but I'd never been spoke to by one, I'd never had to swallow one, as ye might say. But there I did — and all at once I seemed to know where the money goes that's wrung out of the miners. I saw why people were robbin' us, grindin' the life out of us — for fine ladies like that, to keep them so shinin' and soft! 'Twould not have been so bad, if she'd not come just then, with all the men and boys dyin' down in the pits — dyin' for that soft, white skin, and those soft, white hands, and all those silky things she swished round in. My God, Joe — d'ye know what she seemed to me like? Like a smooth, sleek cat that has just eat up a whole nest full of baby mice, and has the blood of them all over her cheeks!"

Mary paused, breathing hard. Hal kept silence, and she went on again: "I had it out with meself, Joe! I don't want ye to think I'm any better than I am, and I asked meself this question — Is it for the men in the pits that ye hate her with such black murder? Or is it for the one man ye want, and that she's got? And I knew the answer to that! But then I asked meself another question, too — Would ye be like her if ye could? Would ye do what she's doin' right now — would ye have it on your soul? And as God hears me, Joe, 'tis the truth I speak — I'd not do it! No, not for the love of any man that ever walked on this earth!"

She had lifted her clenched fist as she spoke. She let it fall again, and strode on, not even glancing at him. "Ye might try a thousand years, Joe, and ye'd not realize the feelin's that come to me there at the Minettis'. The shame of it — not what she done to me, but what she made me in me own eyes! Me, the daughter of a drunken old miner, and her — I don't know what her father is, but she's some sort of princess, and she knows it. And that's the thing that counts, Joe! 'Tis not that she has so much money, and so many fine things; that she knows how to talk, and I don't, and that her voice is sweet, and mine is ugly, when I'm ragin' as I am now. No — 'tis that she's so *sure!* That's the word I found to say it; she's sure — sure — *sure!* She has the fine things, she's always had them, she has a right to have them! And I have a right to nothin' but trouble, I'm hunted all day by misery and fear, I've lost even the roof over me head! Joe, ye know I've got some temper — I'm not easy to beat down; but when I'd got through bein' taught me place, I went off and hid meself, I ground me face in the dirt, for the black rage of it! I said to meself, 'Tis true! There's somethin' in her better than me! She's some kind of finer creature. — Look at these hands!" She held them out in the moonlight, with a swift, passionate gesture. "So she's a right to her man, and I'm a fool to have ever raised me eyes to him! I have to see him go away, and crawl back into me leaky old shack! Yes, that's the truth! And when I point it out to the man, what d'ye think he says? Why, he tells me gently and kindly that I ought to be sorry for her! Christ! did ye ever hear the like of that?"

There was a long silence. Hal could not have said anything now, if he had wished to. He knew that this was what he had come to seek! This was the naked soul of the class-war!

"Now," concluded Mary, with clenched hands, and a voice that corresponded, "now, I've had it out. I'm no slave; I've just as good a right to life as any lady. I know I'll never have it, of course; I'll never wear good clothes, nor live in a decent home, nor have the man I want; but I'll know that I've done somethin' to help free the workin' people from the shame that's put on them. That's what the strike done for me, Joe! The strike showed me the way. We're beat this time, but somehow it hasn't made the difference ye might think. I'm goin' to make more strikes before I quit, and they won't all of them be beat!"

She stopped speaking; and Hal walked beside her, stirred by a conflict of emotions. His vision of her was indeed true; she would make more strikes! He was glad and proud of that; but then came the thought that while she, a girl, was going on with the bitter war, he, a man, would be eating grilled beefsteaks at the club!

"Mary," he said, "I'm ashamed of myself —"

"That's not it, Joe! Ye've no call to be ashamed. Ye can't help it where ye were born —"

"Perhaps not, Mary. But when a man knows he's never paid for any of the things he's enjoyed all his life, surely the least he can do is to be ashamed. I hope you'll try not to hate me as you do the others."

"I never hated ye, Joe! Not for one moment! I tell ye fair and true, I love ye as much as ever. I can say it, because I'd not have ye now; I've seen the other girl, and I know ye'd never be satisfied with me. I don't know if I ought to say it, but I'm thinkin' ye'll not be altogether satisfied with her, either. Ye'll be unhappy either way — God help ye!"

The girl had read deeply into his soul in this last speech; so deeply that Hal could not trust himself to answer. They were passing a street-lamp, and she looked at him, for the first time since they had started on their walk, and saw harassment in his face. A sudden tenderness came into her voice. "Joe," she said; "ye're lookin' bad. 'Tis good ye're goin' away from this place!"

He tried to smile, but the effort was feeble.

"Joe," she went on, "ye asked me to be your friend. Well, I'll be that!" And she held out the big, rough hand.

He took it. "We'll not forget each other, Mary," he said. There was a catch in his voice.

"Sure, lad!" she exclaimed. "We'll make another strike some day, just like we did at North Valley!"

Hal pressed the big hand; but then suddenly, remembering his brother stalking solemnly in the rear, he relinquished the clasp, and failed to say all the fine things he had in his mind. He called himself a rebel, but not enough to be sentimental before Edward!

SECTION 30.

*T*hey came to the house where John Edstrom was staying. The laboring man's wife opened the door. In answer to Hal's question, she said, "The old gentleman's pretty bad."

"What's the matter with him?"

"Didn't you know he was hurt?"

"No. How?"

"They beat him up, sir. Broke his arm, and nearly broke his head."

Hal and Mary exclaimed in chorus, "Who did it? When?"

"We don't know who did it. It was four nights ago."

Hal realized it must have happened while he was escaping from MacKellar's. "Have you had a doctor for him?"

"Yes, sir; but we can't do much, because my man is out of work, and I have the children and the boarders to look after."

Hal and Mary ran upstairs. Their old friend lay in darkness, but he recognized their voices and greeted them with a feeble cry. The woman brought a lamp, and they saw him lying on his back, his head done up in bandages, and one arm bound in splints. He looked really desperately bad, his kindly old eyes deep-sunken and haggard, and his face — Hal remembered what Jeff Cotton had called him, "that dough-faced old preacher!"

They got the story of what had happened at the time of Hal's flight to Percy's train. Edstrom had shouted a warning to the fugitives, and set out to run after them; when one of the mine-guards, running past him, had fetched him a blow over the eye, knocking him down. He had struck his head upon the pavement, and lain there unconscious for many hours. When finally someone had come upon him, and summoned a policeman, they had gone through his pockets, and found the address of this place where he was staying written on a scrap of paper. That was all there was to the story — except that Edstrom had refrained from sending to MacKellar for help, because he had felt sure they were all working to get the mine open, and he did not feel he had the right to put his troubles upon them.

Hal listened to the old man's feeble statements, and there came back to him a surge of that fury which his North Valley experience had generated in him. It was foolish, perhaps; for to knock down an old man who had been making trouble was a comparatively slight exercise of the functions of a mine-guard. But to Hal it seemed the most characteristic of all the outrages he had seen; it was an expression of the company's utter blindness to all that was best in life. This old man, who was so gentle, so patient, who had suffered so much, and not learned to hate, who had kept his faith so true! What did his faith mean to the thugs of the General Fuel Company? What had his philosophy availed him, his saintliness, his hopes for mankind? They had fetched him one swipe as they passed him, and left him lying — alive or dead, it was all the same.

Hal had got some satisfaction out of his little adventure in widow-hood, and some out of Mary's self-victory; but there, listening to the old man's whispered story, his satisfaction died. He realized again the grim truth about his summer's experience — that the issue of it had been defeat. Utter, unqualified defeat! He had caused the bosses a momentary chagrin; but it would not take them many hours to realize that he had really done them a service in calling off the strike for them. They would start the wheels of industry again, and the workers would be just where they had been before Joe Smith came to be stableman and buddy among them. What was all the talk about solidarity, about hope for the future; what would it amount to in the long run, the daily rolling of the wheels of industry? The workers of North Valley would have exactly the right they had always had — the right to be slaves, and if they did not care for that, the right to be martyrs!

Mary sat holding the old man's hand and whispering words of passionate sympathy, while Hal got up and paced the tiny attic, all ablaze with anger. He resolved suddenly that he would not go back to Western City; he would stay here, and get an honest lawyer to come, and set out to punish the men who were guilty of this outrage. He would test out the law to the limit; if necessary, he would begin a political fight, to put an end to coal-company rule in this community. He would find some-one to write up these conditions, he would raise the money and publish a paper to make them known! Before his surging wrath had spent itself, Hal Warner had actually come out as a candidate for governor, and was overturning the Republican machine — all because an unidentified coal-company detective had knocked a dough-faced old miner into the gutter and broken his arm!

SECTION 31.

*I*n the end, of course, Hal had to come down to practical matters. He sat by the bed and told the old man tactfully that his brother had come to see him and had given him some money. This brother had plenty of money, so Edstrom could be taken to the hospital; or, if he preferred, Mary could stay near here and take care of him. They turned to the landlady, who had been standing in the doorway; she had three boarders in her little home, it seemed, but if Mary could share a bed with the landlady's two children, they might make out. In spite of Hal's protest, Mary accepted this offer; he saw what was in her mind — she would take some of his money, because of old Edstrom's need, but she would take just as little as she possibly could.

John Edstrom of course knew nothing of events since his injury, so Hal told him the story briefly — though without mentioning the transformation which had taken place in the miner's buddy. He told about the part Mary had played in the strike; trying to entertain the poor old man, he told how he had seen her mounted upon a snow-white horse, and wearing a robe of white, soft and lustrous, like Joan of Arc, or the leader of a suffrage parade.

"Sure," said Mary, "he's forever callin' attention to this old dress!"

Hal looked; she was wearing the same blue calico. "There's something mysterious about that dress," said he. "It's one of those that you read about in fairy-stories, that forever patch themselves, and keep themselves new and starchy. A body only needs one dress like that!"

"Sure, lad," she answered. "There's no fairies in coal-camps — unless 'tis meself, that washes it at night, and dries it over the stove, and irons it next mornin'."

She said this with unwavering cheerfulness; but even the old miner lying in pain on the cot could realize the tragedy of a young girl's having only one old dress in her love-hunting season. He looked at the young couple, and saw their evident interest in each other; after the fashion of the old, he was disposed to help along the romance. "She may need some orange blossoms," he ventured, feebly.

"Go along with ye!" laughed Mary, still unwavering.

"Sure," put in Hal, with hasty gallantry, "'tis a blossom she is herself! A rose in a mining-camp — and there's a dispute about her in the poetry-books. One tells you to leave her on her stalk, and another says to gather ye rosebuds while ye may, old time is still a-flying!"

"Ye're mixin' me up," said Mary. "A while back I was ridin' on a white horse."

"I remember," said Old Edstrom, "not so far back, you were an ant, Mary."

Her face became grave. To jest about her personal tragedy was one thing, to jest about the strike was another. "Yes, I remember. Ye said I'd stay in the line! Ye were wiser than me, Mr. Edstrom."

"That's one of the things that come with being old, Mary." He moved his gnarled old hand toward hers. "You're going on, now?" he asked. "You're a unionist now, Mary?"

"I am that!" she answered, promptly, her grey eyes shining.

"There's a saying," said he — "once a striker, always a striker. Find a way to get some education for yourself, Mary, and when the big strike comes you'll be one of those the miners look to. I'll not be here, I know — the young people must take my place."

"I'll do my part," she answered. Her voice was low; it was a kind of benediction the old man was giving her.

The woman had gone downstairs to attend to her children; she came back now to say that there was a gentleman at the door, who wanted to know when his brother was coming. Hal remembered suddenly — Edward had been pacing up and down all this while, with no company but a "hardware drummer!" The younger brother's resolve to stay in Pedro had already begun to weaken somewhat, and now it weakened still further; he realized that life is complex, that duties conflict! He assured the old miner again of his ability to see that he did not suffer from want, and then he bade him farewell for a while.

He started out, and Mary went as far as the head of the stairway with him. He took the girl's big, rough hand in his — this time with no one to see. "Mary," he said, "I want you to know that nothing will make me forget you; and nothing will make me forget the miners."

"Ah, Joe!" she cried. "Don't let them win ye away from us! We need ye so bad!"

"I'm going back home for a while," he answered, "but you can be sure that no matter what happens in my life, I'm going to fight for the working people. When the big strike comes, as we know it's coming in this coal-country, I'll be here to do my share."

"Sure lad," she said, looking him bravely in the eye, "and good-bye to ye, Joe Smith." Her eyes did not waver; but Hal noted a catch in her voice, and he found himself with an impulse to take her in his arms. It was very puzzling. He knew he loved Jessie Arthur; he remembered the question Mary had once asked him — could he be in love with two girls at the same time? It was not in accord with any moral code that had been impressed upon him, but apparently he could!

SECTION 32.

*H*e went out to the street, where his brother was pacing up and down in a ferment. The "hardware drummer" had made another effort to start a conversation, and had been told to go to hell — no less!

"Well, are you through now?" Edward demanded, taking out his irritation on Hal.

"Yes," replied the other. "I suppose so." He realized that Edward would not be concerned about Edstrom's broken arm.

"Then, for God's sake, get some clothes on and let's have some food."

"All right," said Hal. But his answer was listless, and the other looked at him sharply. Even by the moonlight Edward could see the lines in the face of his younger brother, and the hollows around his eyes. For the first time he realized how deeply these experiences were cutting into the boy's soul. "You poor kid!" he exclaimed, with sudden feeling. But Hal did not answer; he did not want sympathy, he did not want anything!

Edward made a gesture of despair. "God knows, I don't know what to do for you!"

They started back to the hotel, and on the way Edward cast about in his mind for a harmless subject of conversation. He mentioned that he had foreseen the shutting up of the stores, and had purchased an outfit for his brother. There was no need to thank him, he added grimly; he had no intention of traveling to Western City in company with a hobo.

So the young miner had a bath, the first real one in a long time. (Never again would it be possible for ladies to say in Hal Warner's presence that the poor might at least keep clean!) He had a shave; he trimmed his fingernails, and brushed his hair, and dressed himself as a gentleman. In spite of himself he found his cheerfulness partly restored. A strange and wonderful sensation — to be dressed once more as a gentleman. He thought of the saying of the old Negro, who liked to stub his toe, because it felt so good when it stopped hurting!

They went out to find a restaurant, and on the way one last misadventure befell Edward. Hal saw an old miner walking past, and stopped with a cry: "Mike!" He forgot all at once that he was a gentleman; the old miner forgot it also. He stared for one bewildered moment, then he rushed at Hal and seized him in the hug of a mountain grizzly.

"My buddy! My buddy!" he cried, and gave Hal a prodigious thump on the back. "By Judas!" And he gave him a thump with the other hand. "Hey! you old son-of-a-gun!" And he gave him a hairy kiss!

But in the very midst of these raptures it dawned over him that there was something wrong about his buddy. He drew back, staring. "You got good clothes! You got rich, hey?"

Evidently the old fellow had heard no rumor concerning Hal's secret. "I've been doing pretty well," Hal said.

"What you work at, hey?"

"I been working at a strike in North Valley."

"What's that? You make money working at strike?"

Hal laughed, but did not explain. "What you working at?"

"I work at strike too — all alone strike."

"No job?"

"I work two days on railroad. Got busted track up there. Pay me two-twenty-five a day. Then no more job."

"Have you tried the mines?"

"What? Me? They got me all right! I go up to San José. Pit-boss say, 'Get the hell out of here, you old groucher! You don't get no more jobs in this district!'"

Hal looked Mike over, and saw that his dirty old face was drawn and white, belying the feeble cheerfulness of his words. "We're going to have something to eat," he said. "Won't you come with us?"

"Sure thing!" said Mike, with alacrity. "I go easy on grub now."

Hal introduced "Mr. Edward Warner," who said "How do you do?" He accepted gingerly the calloused paw which the old Slovak held out to him, but he could not keep the look of irritation from his face. His patience was utterly exhausted. He had hoped to find a decent restaurant and have some real food; but now, of course, he could not enjoy anything, with this old gobbler in front of him.

They entered an all-night lunch-room, where Hal and Mike ordered cheese-sandwiches and milk, and Edward sat and wondered at his brother's ability to eat such food. Meantime the two cronies told each other their stories, and Old Mike slapped his knee and cried out with delight over Hal's exploits. "Oh, you buddy!" he exclaimed; then, to Edward, "Ain't he a daisy, hey?" And he gave Edward a thump on the shoulder. "By Judas, they don't beat my buddy!"

Mike Sikoria had last been seen by Hal from the window of the North Valley jail, when he had been distributing the copies of Hal's signature, and Bud Adams had taken him in charge. The mine-guard had marched him into a shed in back of the power-house, where he had found Kauser and Kalovac, two other fellows who had been arrested while helping in the distribution.

Mike detailed the experience with his usual animation. "'Hey, Mister Bud,' I say, 'if you going to send me down canyon, I want to get my things.' 'You go to hell for your things,' says he. And then I say, 'Mister Bud, I want to get my time.' And he says, 'I give you plenty time right here!' And he punch me and throw me over. Then he grab me up' again and pull me outside, and I see big automobile waiting, and I say, 'Holy Judas! I get ride in automobile! Here I am, old fellow fifty-seven years old, never been in automobile ride all my days. I think always I die and never get in automobile ride!' We go down canyon, and I look round and see them mountains, and feel nice cool wind in my face, and I say, 'Bully for you, Mister Bud, I don't never forget this automobile. I don't have such good time any day all my life.' And he say, 'Shut your face, you old wop!' Then we come out on prairie, we go up in Black Hills, and they stop, and say, 'Get out here, you sons o' guns.' And they leave us there all alone. They say, 'You come back again, we catch you and we rip the guts out of you!' They go away fast, and we got to walk seven hours, us fellers, before we come to a house! But I don't mind that, I begged some grub, and then I got job mending track; only I don't find out if you get out of jail, and I think maybe I lose my buddy and never see him no more."

Here the old man stopped, gazing affectionately at Hal. "I write you letter to North Valley, but I don't hear nothing, and I got to walk all the way on railroad track to look for you."

How was it? Hal wondered. He had encountered naked horror in this coal-country — yet here he was, not entirely glad at the thought of leaving it! He would miss Old Mike Sikoria, his hairy kiss and his grizzly-bear hug!

He struck the old man dumb by pressing a twenty-dollar bill into his hand. Also he gave him the address of Edstrom and Mary, and a note to Johann Hartman, who might use him to work among the Slovaks who came down into the town. Hal explained that he had to go back to Western City that night, but that he would never forget his old friend, and would see that he had a good job. He was trying to figure out some occupation for the old man on his father's country-place. A pet grizzly!

Train-time came, and the long line of dark sleepers rolled in by the depot-platform. It was late — after midnight; but, nevertheless, there was Old Mike. He was in awe of Hal now, with his fine clothes and his twenty-dollar bills; but, nevertheless, under stress of his emotion, he gave him one more hug, and one more hairy kiss. "Good-bye, my buddy!" he cried. "You come back, my buddy! I don't forget my buddy!" And when the train began to move, he waved his ragged cap, and ran along the platform to get a last glimpse, to call a last farewell. When Hal turned into the car, it was with more than a trace of moisture in his eyes.

Postscript

From previous experiences the writer has learned that many people, reading a novel such as *King Coal*, desire to be informed as to whether it is true to fact. They write to ask if the book is meant to be so taken; they ask for evidence to convince themselves and others. Having answered thousands of such letters in the course of his life, it seems to the author the part of common-sense to answer some of them in advance.

King Coal is a picture of the life of the workers in unorganized labor-camps in many parts of America, The writer has avoided naming a definite place, for the reason that such conditions are to be found as far apart as West Virginia, Alabama, Michigan, Minnesota, and Colorado. Most of the details of his picture were gathered in the last-named state, which the writer visited on three occasions during and just after the great coal-strike of 1913-14. The book gives a true picture of conditions and events observed by him at this time. Practically all the characters are real persons, and every incident which has social significance is not merely a true incident, but a typical one. The life portrayed in *King Coal* is the life that is lived today by hundreds of thousands of men, women and children in this "land of the free."

The reader who wishes evidence may be accommodated. There was never a strike more investigated than the Colorado coal-strike. The material about it in the writer's possession cannot be less than eight million words, the greater part of it sworn testimony taken under government supervision. There is, first, the report of the Congressional Committee, a government document of three thousand closely printed pages, about two million words; an equal amount of testimony given before the U.S. Commission on Industrial Relations, also a government document; a special report on the Colorado strike, prepared for the same commission, a book of 189 pages, supporting every contention of this story; about four hundred thousand words of testimony given before a committee appointed at the suggestion of the Governor of Colorado; a report made by the Rev. Henry A. Atkinson, who investigated the strike as representative of the Federal Council of the Churches of Christ in America, and of the Social Service Commission of the Congregational Churches; the report of an elaborate investigation by the Colorado state militia; the bulletins issued by both sides during the controversy; the testimony given at various coroners' inquests; and, finally, articles by different writers to be found in the files of *Everybody's Magazine*, the *Metropolitan Magazine*, the *Survey*, *Harper's Weekly*, and *Collier's Weekly*, all during the year 1914.

The writer prepared a collection of extracts from these various sources, meaning to publish them in this place; but while the manuscript was in the hands of the publishers, there appeared one document, which, in the weight of its authority, seemed to discount all others. A decision was rendered by the Supreme Court of the State of Colorado, in a case which included the most fundamental of the many issues raised in *King Coal*. It is not often that the writer of a novel of contemporary life is so fortunate as to have the truth of his work passed upon and established by the highest judicial tribunal of the community!

In the elections of November, 1914, in Huerfano County, Colorado, J.B. Farr, Republican candidate for re-election as sheriff, a person known throughout the coal-country as "the King of Huerfano County," was returned as elected by a majority of 329 votes. His rival, the Democratic candidate, contested the election, alleging "malconduct, fraud and corruption." The district court found in Farr's favor, and the case was appealed on error to the Supreme Court of the State. On June 21st, 1916, after Farr had served nearly the whole of his term of office, the Supreme Court handed down a decision which unseated him and the entire ticket elected with him, finding in favor of the opposition ticket in all cases and upon all grounds charged.

The decision is long — about ten thousand words, and its legal technicalities would not interest the reader. It will suffice to reprint the essential paragraphs. The reader is asked to give these paragraphs careful study, considering, not merely the specific offence denounced by the court, but its wider implications. The offence was one so unprecedented that the justices of the court, men chosen for their learning in the history of offences, were moved to say: "We find no such example of fraud within the books, and must seek the letter and spirit of the law in a free government, as a scale in which to weigh such conduct." And let it be noted, this "crime without a name" was not a crime of passion, but of policy; it was a crime deliberately planned and carried out by profit-seeking corporations of enormous power. Let the reader imagine the psychology of the men of great wealth who ordered this crime, as a means of keeping and increasing their wealth; let him realize what must be the attitude of such men to their helpless workers; and then let him ask himself whether there is any act portrayed in *King Coal* which men of such character would shrink from ordering.

The Court decision first gives an outline of the case, using for the most part the statements of the counsel for the defendant, Farr; so that for practical purposes the following may be taken as the coal companies' own account of their domain: "Round the shaft of each mine are clustered the tipple, the mine office, the shops, sheds and outbuildings; and huddled close by, within a stone's throw, cottages of the miners built on the land of, and owned by, the mining company. All the dwellers in the camp are employees of the mine. There is no other industry. This is 'the camp.' Of the eight 'closed camps' it appears that practically the same conditions existed in all of them, and those conditions were in general that members of the United Mine Workers of America, their organizers or agitators, were prevented from coming into the camps, so far as it was possible to keep them out, and to this end guards were stationed about them. Of the eight 'closed camps' one of them, 'Walsen,' was, and at the time of the trial still was, enclosed by a fence erected at the beginning of the strike in October, 1913: Rouse and Cameron were partly, but never entirely, enclosed by fences. It is admitted that all persons entering these camps and precincts were required by the companies to have passes, and it is contended that this was an 'industrial necessity.'"

The Court then goes on as follows:

"The Federal troops entered the district in May of 1914, and the testimony is in agreement that no serious acts of violence occurred thereafter, and that order was preserved up to and subsequent to the election, and to the time of this trial.

"It was under this condition that in July, 1914, the Board of County Commissioners changed certain of the election precincts so as to constitute each of such camps an election precinct, and with but one exception where a few ranches were included, these precincts were made to conform to the fences and lines around each camp, protected by fences in some instances and with armed guards in all cases. Thus each election precinct by this unparalleled act of the commissioners was placed exclusively within and upon the private grounds and under the private control of a coal corporation, which autocratically declared who should and who should not enter upon the territory of this political entity of the state, so purposely bounded by the county commissioners.

"With but one exception all the lands and buildings within each of these election precincts as so created, were owned or controlled by the coal corporations; every person resident within such precincts was an employee of these private corporations or their allied companies, with the single exception: every judge, clerk or officer of election with the exception of a saloon keeper, and partner of Farr, was an employee of the coal-companies.

"The polling places were upon the grounds, and in the buildings of these companies; the registration lists were kept within the private offices or buildings of such companies, and used and treated as their private property.

"Thus were the public election districts and the public election machinery turned over to the absolute domination and imperial control of private coal corporations, and used by them as absolutely and privately as were their mines, to and for their own private purposes, and upon which public territory no man might enter for either public or private purpose, save and except by the express permission of these private corporations.

"This right to determine who should enter such so called election precincts, appears from the record to have been exercised as against all classes; merchants, tradesmen or what not, and whether the business of such person was public or private. Indeed, it appears that in one instance the governor and adjutant general of the state while on official business, were denied admission to one of these closed camps. And that on the day of election, the Democratic watchers and challengers for Walsen Mine precinct, one of which was Neelley, the Democratic candidate for sheriff, were forced to seek and secure a detail of Federal soldiers to escort them into the precinct and to the polls, and that such soldiers remained as such guard during the day and a part of the night. . . .

"But if there was any doubt concerning the condition of the closed camps and precincts, and the exclusion of representatives of the Democratic party from discussing the issues of the campaign within the precincts comprising the closed camps, it is entirely removed by the testimony of the witness Weitzel, for contestee (Farr). He testified that he was a resident of Pueblo, and was manager of the Colorado Fuel and Iron Company; that Rouse, Lester, Ideal, Cameron, Walsen, Pictou and McNally are camps under his jurisdiction. That he had general charge of the camps and that there was no company official in Colorado superior to him in this respect except the president; that the superintendent and other employees are under his supervision; that the Federal troops came about the 1st of May, 1914, and continued until January, 1915. That in all those camps he tried to keep out the people who were antagonistic to the company's interests; that it was private property and so treated by his company; that through him the company and its officials assumed to exercise authority as to who might or who might

not enter; that if persons could assure or satisfy the man at the gate, or
the superintendent that they were not connected with the United Mine
Workers, or in their employ as agitators, they were let into the camp.
That 'no one we were fighting against got in for social intercourse or
any other'; that he and officials under him assumed to pass upon the
question of whether or not any person coming there came for the
purpose of agitation. That Mr. Mitchell, the chairman of the Democratic committee, as he recalled it, was identified with the agitators, ran
a newspaper and was connected either directly or indirectly with the
United Mine Workers; that Mr. Neelley, Democratic candidate for
sheriff, was identified with the strikers, and that he would be considered
as an objectionable character. That when the Federal troops came, they
restored peace and normal conditions; there was no rioting after that,
there was no fear on the part of the company when the Federal soldiers
were here, except fear of agitation. Asked if he guarded the camp against
discussion, against the espousal of the cause of the company, he replied,
'We didn't encourage it.' The company would not encourage organizers
to come into the camp, no matter how peacefully they conducted
themselves; that the company did not permit men to come into the
camp to discuss with the employees certain principles, or to carry on
arguments with them or to appeal to their reason, or to discuss with
them things along reasonable lines, because it was known from experience that if they were allowed to come in they would resort to threats
of violence. They might not resort to any violence at the time, but it
might result in the people becoming frightened and leaving, and they
were anxious to hold their employees. He was asked whether or not one
had business there depended upon the decision of the official in charge;
he replied that the superintendent probably would inquire of him what
his business was. That anyone that Farr asked for a permit to enter the
camp would likely get it. . . .

"There was but one attempt to hold a political meeting in the closed
precincts. Joseph Patterson, who attempted to hold this meeting, testi-
fies concerning it as follows:

"Was at a political meeting at Oakview. Had been a warm, personal
friend of Mr. Jones, the assistant superintendent of the Oakview mine,
and had written him a letter asking the courtesy of holding a political
meeting. On Saturday evening received a letter that he could hold such
meeting. On the day previous to the meeting witness received a 'phone
message from the assistant superintendent, in which the latter inquired
whether witness was coming up there to cause any trouble, and witness
replied, certainly not, and if the superintendent felt that way they would
not come. Had advised the superintendent that he and others were going

to hold a political meeting for the Democratic party. Jones, the super-intendent, stated that witness should come to the office that night before he went to the school house for the purpose of the meeting; when witness arrived at the meeting there were about six or eight English speaking people and a dozen to fourteen Mexicans. The superintendent, Mr. Morgan, and Mr. Price, were outside of the door most of the time. Witness noticed that the first few fellows that came toward the school house, the superintendent stopped and talked with them and they turned back to the camp. This happened several times: as soon as they talked with Morgan they turned back. After he saw that, witness went into the school house and said that it was no use to hold any meeting; that it seemed that nobody was allowed to come. This meeting was supposed to be in a public school house on the company property. Had to get permission from the superintendent of the Oakview mining Company to hold said political meeting." . . .

"It appears that the number of registered voters in the closed precincts was very largely in excess of the number of votes cast, and this of itself was sufficient to demand an open and fair investigation as to the qualifications of the alleged voters.

"It appears from the testimony that in these closed precincts many of those who voted were unable to speak or read the English language, and that in numerous instances, the election judges assisted such, by marking the ballots for them in violation of the law. Again, it appears that the ballots were printed so that. . . . (The decision here goes on to explain in detail a device whereby the ballot was so printed that voting could be controlled with the help of a card device.) Thus such voters were not choosing candidates, but, under the direction of the compa-nies, were simply placing the cross where they found the particular letter R on the ballot, so that the ballot was not an expression of opinion or judgment, not an intelligent exercise of suffrage, but plainly a dictated coal company vote, as much so as if the agents of these companies had marked the ballots without the intervention of the voter. No more fraudulent and infamous prostitution of the ballot is conceivable. . . .

"Counsel contend that the closed precincts were an 'industrial neces-sity,' and for such reason the conduct of the coal companies during the campaign was justified. However such conduct may be viewed when confined to the private property of such corporations in their private operation, the fact remains that there is no justification when they were dealing with such territory after it had been dedicated to a public use, and particularly involving the right of the people to exercise their duties and powers as electors in a popular government.

"The fact appears that the members of the board of county commissioners and all other county officers were Republicans, and as stated by counsel for the contestees, the success of the Republican candidates was considered by the coal companies, vital to their interests. The close relationship of the coal companies and the Republican officials and candidates appears to have been so marked both before and during the campaign, as to justify the conclusion that such officers regarded their duty to the coal companies as paramount to their duty to the public service. To say that the closed precincts were not so created to suit the convenience and interests of these corporations, or that they were not so formed with the advice and consent of these corporations, is to discredit human intelligence, and to deny human experience. The plain purpose of the formation of the new precincts was that the coal companies might have opportunity to conduct and control the elections therein, just as such elections were conducted. The irresistible conclusion is that these close precincts were so formed by the county commissioners with the connivance of the representatives of the coal companies, if not by their express command.

"There can be no free, open and fair election as contemplated by the constitution, where private industrial corporations so throttle public opinion, deny the free exercise of choice by sovereign electors, dictate and control all election officers, prohibit public discussion of public questions, and imperially command what citizens may and what citizens may not, peacefully and for lawful purposes, enter upon election or public territory. . . .

"We find no such example of fraud within the books, and must seek the letter and spirit of the law in a free government, as a scale in which to weigh such conduct. . . .

"The denial of the right of peaceful assemblage, can have been for no other purpose than to influence the election. There was no disturbance in any of these precincts after they were created, up to the time of the election, and up to the time of this trial. The Federal troops were present at all times to preserve the peace and to protect life and property. There was no reason to anticipate any disturbance. Therefore this bold denial was an inexcusable and corrupt violation of the natural and inalienable rights of the citizens.

"The defense relies not upon conflicting evidence, but upon the contention that the conduct of the election was justified as an 'industrial necessity.'

"We have heard much in this state in recent years as to the denial of inherent and constitutional rights of citizens being justified by 'military necessity,' but this we believe is the first time in our experience when the violation of the fundamental rights of freemen has been attempted to be justified by the plea of 'industrial necessity.'

"Even if we were to concede that there may be some palliation in the plea of military necessity on the theory that such acts purport to be acts of the government itself, through its military arm and with the purpose of preserving the public peace and safety: yet that a private corporation, with its privately armed forces, may violate the most sacred right of the citizenship of the state and find lawful excuse in the plea of private 'industrial necessity' savors too much of anarchy to find approval by courts of justice.

"This case clearly comes within another exception to the rule, in that it is plain that the findings were influenced by the bias and prejudice of the trial judge.

"A careful reading of the record discloses the rejection by the court of so much palpably pertinent and competent testimony offered by the contestors, as to force the conclusion that the trial judge was influenced by bias and prejudice, to the extent at least, charged in the application for a change of venue, and sufficient in itself to justify a reversal of judgment. . . .

"For the foregoing reasons the judgment of the court in each case before us, is reversed, and the entire poll in the said precincts of Niggerhead, Ravenwood, Walsen Mine, Oakview, Pryor, Rouse and Cameron is annulled, and held for naught, and the election in each of said precincts is hereby set aside. This leaves a substantial and unquestioned majority for each of the contestors in the county, and which entitles each contestor to be declared elected to the office for which he was a candidate.

"We find further, that J.B. Farr, the defendant in error, was not and is not the duly elected sheriff of Huerfano county, and that E.L. Neelley, the plaintiff in error, was and is the duly elected sheriff of said county. It is therefore ordered that the said county, and that the said E.L. Neelley, immediately and upon qualification as required by law, enter and discharge the duties of the said office of sheriff of Huerfano county. . . ."

So much for the court opinion upon coal-camp politics. In relation thereto, the writer has only one comment to offer. Let the reader not drop the matter with the idea that because one set of corrupt officials have been turned out of office in one American county, therefore justice has been vindicated, and there is no longer need to be concerned about the conditions portrayed in *King Coal*. The defeat of the "King of Huerfano County" is but one step in a long road which the miners of Colorado have to travel if ever they are to be free men. The industrial power of the great corporations remains untouched by this decision; and this power is greater than any political power ever wielded by the government of Huerfano County, or even of the state of Colorado. This industrial power is a deep, far-spreading root; and so long as it is allowed to thrive, it will send up again and again the poisonous plant of political "malconduct, fraud and corruption." The citizens and workers of such industrial communities, whether in Colorado, in West Virginia, Alabama, Michigan or Minnesota, in the Chicago stockyards, the steel-mills of Pittsburgh, the woolen-mills of Lawrence or the silk-mills of Paterson, will find that they have neither peace nor freedom, until they have abolished the system of production for profit, and established in the field of industry what they are supposed to have already in the field of politics – a government of the people, by the people, for the people.

*N*OTE: On the day that the author finished the reading of the proofs of *King Coal,* the following item appeared in his daily newspaper:

COLORADO MINE WORKERS
ASK LEAVE TO STRIKE
[BY A.P. NIGHT WIRE]

DENVER (Colo.), June 14. — Officers of the United Mine Workers representing members of that organization employed by the Colorado Fuel and Iron Company, have telegraphed their national officers asking permission to strike.

At the morning session a resolution was adopted expressing disapprobation of the action of J.F. Welborn, president of the fuel company, for failure to attend the meeting, which was a part of the "peace program" to prevent industrial differences in the State during the war.

The grievances of the men, according to John McLennan, spokesman for them, center about the operation of the so-called "Rockefeller plan" at the mines. McLennan said the failure of Mr. Welborn to attend the meeting and discuss these grievances with the men precipitated the strike agitation.

THE END